I0762011

BOOKS BY PATRICK SAMPHIRE

The Mennik Thorn Novels

Shadow of a Dead God

Nectar for the God

Strange Cargo

Legacy of a Hated God

The Casebook of Harriet George Series

The Dinosaur Hunters

A Spy in the Deep

The Secrets of the Dragon Tomb Series

(for children)

Secrets of the Dragon Tomb

The Emperor of Mars

Short Story Collection

At the Gates and Other Stories

LEGACY OF A HATED GOD

A MENNIK THORN NOVEL (BOOK 4)

PATRICK SAMPHIRE

FIVE FATHOMS PRESS

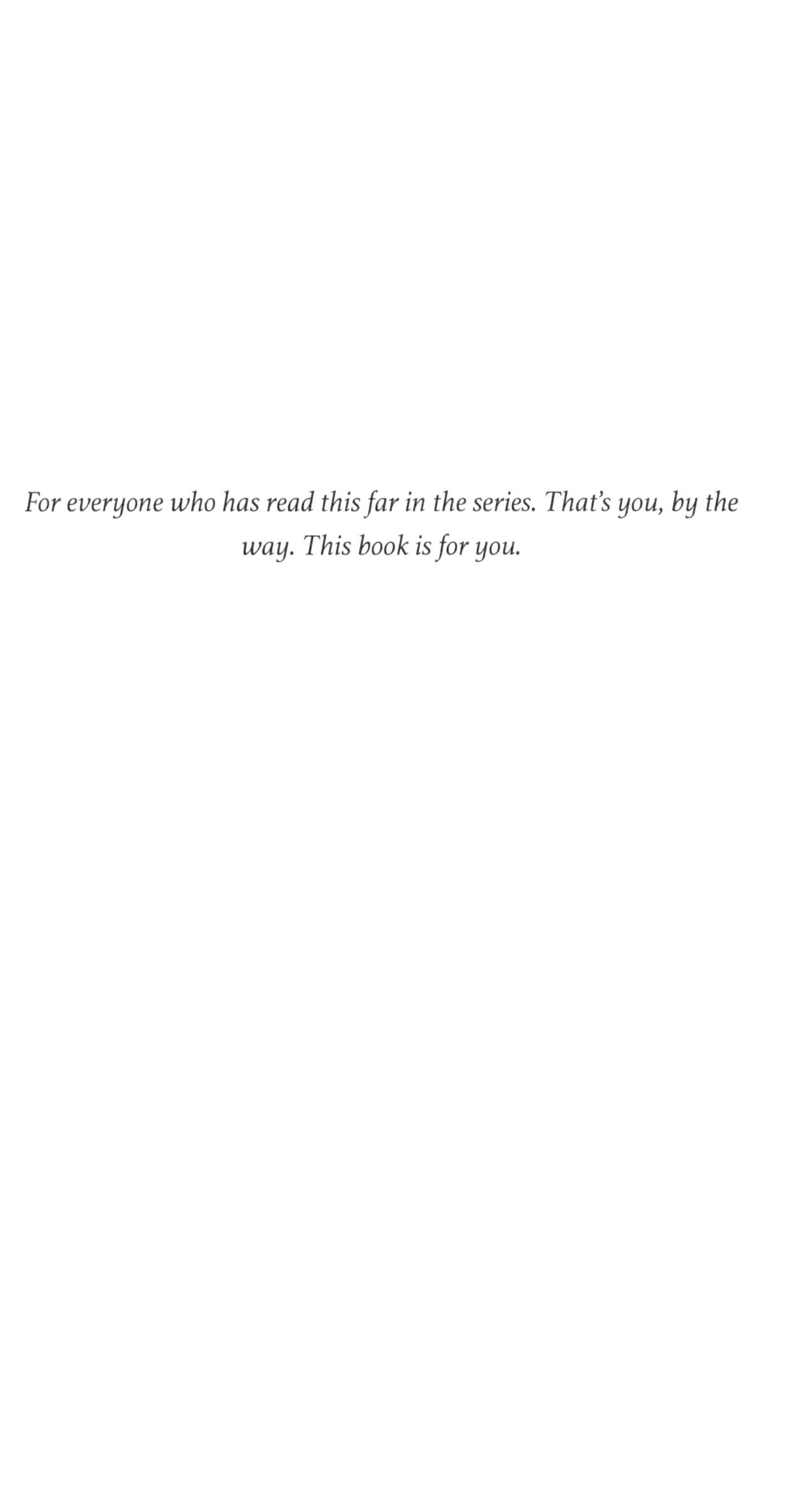

For everyone who has read this far in the series. That's you, by the way. This book is for you.

The City of Agatos

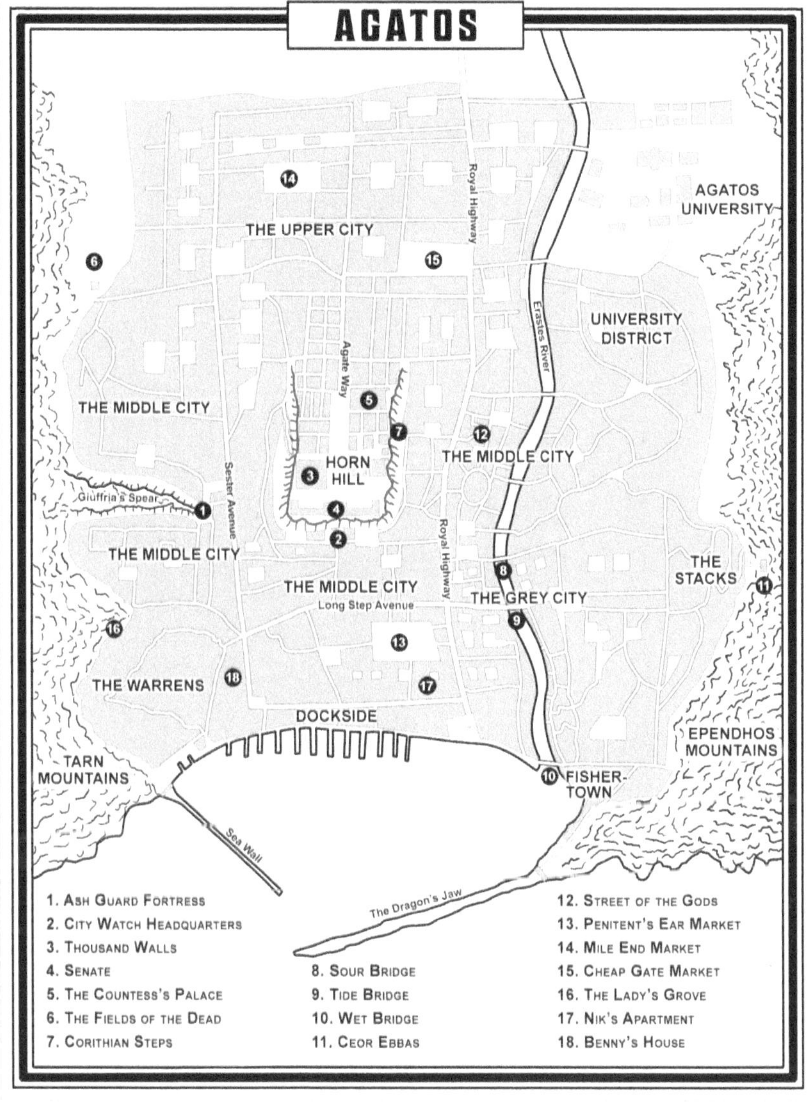

To see a full-size map, visit:
patricksamphire.com/agatos-map-4

THE STORY SO FAR

KEY CONCEPTS

Agatos – A large city at the mouth of the Erastes River, looking out onto the Erastes Bay and the Yttradian Sea beyond. Agatos is a trading city situated at the beginning of the Lidharan Highway, which carries most trade to the cities of the north. The city is theoretically ruled by the Senate, but the city's high mages and the Ash Guard also hold significant power and influence.

The Gods – Many gods, alive, dead, and of indeterminate status, are worshipped in Agatos, although they rarely bother lending their power to their worshippers. You can find a list of the gods mentioned in the Mennik Thorn books in Appendix 2.

Magic – When gods die, their mortal remains begin to rot. The effluent from this permeates the air, the water, and the earth anywhere they were worshipped, being particularly intense where their remains are found. This effluent is the raw magic that mages draw on to shape into spells. They try not to talk about the origin of their power too often.

The Ash Guard – A martial order who use the ashes of the dead sun god, Sharshak, to neutralise all forms of magic and even the power of most gods. They rigorously police the actions of mages, supernatural entities, and gods that step out of line.

MAIN CHARACTERS

Mennik (Nik) Thorn, our protagonist – A minor mage who has set himself up as a freelance operator in the poorer parts of Agatos, having walked away from the machinations and corruption of the high mages, particularly those of the Countess, his estranged mother.

Benyon (Benny) Field – Nik's best friend since childhood, although they have recently fallen out over Nik putting Benny's daughter, Sereh, in danger. Benny is an unapologetic thief governed by a complicated and unbreakable code of favours and debts.

Sereh Field – Benny's daughter. A terrifying 11-year-old far too competent and dangerous with a knife and with the apparent ability to move undetected through shadows. Nik thinks she is probably one of the most dangerous people in the city, although Benny sees her as vulnerable and in need of protection.

Mica Coldrock, formerly **Mica Thorn** – Nik's younger

half-sister, a powerful mage who has maintained a relationship with their mother.

Jettuk Kehsereen – A scholar from the city of Khorasan now living in Agatos. He and Nik worked together to rescue Kehsereen's nephew from the god of nightmares, Enabgal. Now Kehsereen's nephew is in the protective care of the Ash Guard, whose Ash suppresses the boy's out-of-control natural magical abilities.

Captain Meroi Gale – A captain of the Ash Guard. Nik has an unrequited crush on Captain Gale and works casually for her as an informant. He has yet to gather the courage to ask her out on a date.

Elosyn and Holera Brook – Two of Nik's most tolerant friends. A married couple. Elosyn works as a baker at Nuil's Coffee House, and Holera is a chef at her own restaurant. Both have been known to feed Nik when his business is doing particularly badly and patch him up when he's been injured. Which happens far more often than it should.

The Countess, Senator Anatase Coldrock formerly **Solone Thorn** – Nik's estranged mother. A high mage controlling much of the Senate.

The Wren – A high mage controlling crime in the lower parts of Agatos.

Melecho Kael – The Wren's bodyguard / enforcer / assistant / gardener.

Squint – An information broker working for the Wren out of Dumonoc's bar.

Dumonoc – The world's must unwelcoming barman.

Scholar Longstream – a scholar at Agatos University to

whom Nik turned for help in SHADOW OF A DEAD GOD, but who refused all assistance unless Nik would raise the body of the founder of Agatos, **Agate Blackspear**, known as the **Godkiller**, the city's first high mage. Nik refused, as a point of principle.

RECENT EVENTS

In SHADOW OF A DEAD GOD, Nik Thorn is a second-rate mage, just about getting by, keeping his head down, drinking at Dumonoc's bar, and taking on small jobs that require magic, such as breaking curses, spying on cheating spouses, finding lost pets, and hunting ghosts. That all changes when he agrees to help Benny steal a ledger from the high mage, Carnelian Silkstar, and they find themselves framed for a brutal, magical murder they didn't commit.

As Nik desperately tries to prove their innocence, more murders seem to follow him around, each of them apparently committed by an impossible ghost-beast.

Eventually, Nik tracks the origin of these attacks to a powerful mage, Enne Lowriver, who supposedly works for the Countess, but who is in fact the secret leader of a cult of the dead beast god, Ah'té. Nik, Benny, and Sereh manage to disrupt Lowriver's attempted resurrection of the beast god and injure Lowriver, who is eventually killed by Captain Gale. In the process, Benny swallows the relic that summoned the ghost of the beast god, a claw. Nik, meanwhile, has incurred a debt to the criminal high mage, the Wren.

In NECTAR FOR THE GOD, Nik's attempts to dodge the debt he owes to the Wren finally fail and he is forced to infiltrate his mother's court to obtain information the Wren can use against the Countess in their ongoing feud. At the same time, he is employed by a widower, Mr. Mirian, whose wife murdered a stranger in public and then killed herself. Mr. Mirian wants Nik to prove that his wife was under magical influence.

As Nik follows the clues, he finds the murder victim's closest friends all being killed, too, by a force that seems to have command of astonishing magical power and the ability to take over bystanders. During his investigation, he encounters a scholar, Jettuk Kehsereen, who is searching for his nephew who went missing weeks earlier and who appears to have a link to the murder victims.

Nik and Kehsereen discover that the victims have been feeding natural mages to the until-now lost god of nightmares in exchange for success. But those victims made a mistake by trying to feed the god a natural high mage whose power is too great to contain and who, in his madness, has been lashing out and killing them. Nik rescues the boy – Kehsereen's nephew – from the god and turns the god over to the Ash Guard.

The other half of his quest hasn't gone so well, though. Nik was traumatised by his experience growing up with his mother's impossibly high standards and her obvious contempt for him. When he puts off his job for the Wren too long, Benny and Sereh's lives are put at risk, leading to a rift between them. Benny has been Nik's best friend since child, but now he wants nothing to do with him. The loss hits Nik hard, and he knows it's his fault.

Nik finally hands over the information the Wren wanted, only to discover that, without his knowledge, he has been used by his mother, once again, as no more than a tool in her own schemes.

In STRANGE CARGO, Nik finds himself confronted and captured by a gang of smugglers he came up against in Nectar for the God. Under threat, he agrees to help them smuggle an illegal magical cargo into the city, while plotting with Captain Gale to intercept them.

He also takes on a job for his barman nemesis, Dumonoc. Someone or something has been souring the drinks in Dumonoc's bar, making them even more undrinkable than usual. Nik diagnoses a kind of magical infection, although he can't find the origin. He attempts to track down the perpetrator without much luck. However, he does notice that levels of raw magic in one of the city's nearby temples have grown enormously. This leads him to discover that the disruption is being caused by a parasitical magical creature called a Jaunt's Ghost that feeds on high levels of raw magic and consumes everything around it. To trap the creature, Nik needs a valuable gem, which he steals from the temple of Gwillan-Whose-Light-Falls-on-the-Few-Not-the-Many, accidentally burning down the temple in the process.

At the last moment, the smugglers change plans, leaving Nik without his expected back-up from the Ash Guard. He discovers they are smuggling in a powerful magical relic, the foot of a dead god, which is feeding the levels of raw magic in the city. Escaping the smugglers, he captures the Jaunt's Ghost – half destroying Dumonoc's bar in the process and getting himself banned – and brings it to the smugglers' ship, where he releases it. Its voracious magical appetite in the presence of the power of the relic destroys not only the smugglers' ship and crew, but also a large portion of the docks, and it leaves him finally free of the gang's influence.

Now read on...

CHAPTER ONE

I HAD OPINIONS ON RELIGION.

Depths, given the chance, I had opinions on most things. It was one of my most endearing qualities. But when it came to religion, I had plenty, and they could be summed up fairly neatly:

Gods were complete bastards, and only an idiot would get involved with them.

The priest sitting opposite me would probably have been the first to agree. Ironically, his people had built an entire religion on how much they hated their god. I could empathise, but if I'd had any sense at all, I would have told him to fuck right off out the door and keep fucking off out of my city, into the ocean.

Unfortunately, he'd caught me off guard. I'd just taken a long lunch at a coffee house close to where my former best friend, Benny, lived. It had become a bit of a habit recently. I could tell myself it was because the coffee was good, the food was cheap, and the waitress seemed to like me, against all logic. But that was only part of it.

I'd started coming here in the hope of running into Benny. But either he'd known I was here, or I had bad luck. Now, I just liked it. And if Benny wandered by, well, that was hardly my fault.

I'd chatted for a while with the waitress, Ileoni Silver, about her brother's latest doomed attempt to make his fortune. Being able to talk to someone who wasn't a client, a crook, or a mage was a nice change, and sometimes, I forgot that I'd missed Benny again. Today, I'd returned home feeling more satisfied and content than I had for a while, and that feeling had lasted all the way until I reached my small office and apartment on Corrastar Street and saw the Brythanii priest waiting patiently for me.

It was almost enough to send me running in the opposite direction. But I was in a good mood, and so I only had myself to blame.

The Brythanii people had arrived in Agatos and several other cities around the Yttradian Sea a few centuries back, refugees from some disaster far to the south. They were easy to spot with their near-white skin, hair the colour of old paper, and eyes a pale, washed-out blue.

Agatos was a city where people mixed, arriving by ship or caravan, some settling, others moving through. My own father, I had always assumed, had come on a ship from Tor or Secellia, although I had never met the man, and my mother, the blessed Countess, refused to speak of him. The Brythanii mixed less than others. I had known a few kids with Brythanii blood growing up in the Warrens, but they had been as much of Agatos as I was, and our ancestry mattered far less than being Warrens kids. Nonetheless, there was a tight-knit and closed Brythanii community in the Middle City, the Grey City, and the Stacks. They kept to themselves, and my position was that if people didn't bother me, I wouldn't bother them.

This guy had decided to bother me.

I didn't have anything against the Brythanii, but I did have something against priests, and the long robes, religious symbols, and the scars where his little fingers had been severed were a dead giveaway.

I should never have let him in the door. What can I say? I was terrible at saying no. I ushered him in and took my own seat behind my desk. "What can I do for you, Mr....?"

"Cursed Ethemattian."

Don't ask. "Cursed? Is that a name or a title?"

"My title. Cursed Ard Ethemattian."

I was already regretting this. "So, what can I do for you, er, Cursed Ethemattian?" There was no way I was calling him that every time.

He straightened, pale hands crossing on my desk. "Someone is trying to kill me."

Never let it be said that I was culturally insensitive or intolerant of other people's customs, but I had to ask. "Um. Isn't that kind of the point?"

The pale eyes didn't blink. "What do you know about our religion, Mr. Thorn?"

"I know you like beating your priests to death." Each year, in the last week of the month of Enetha, the Brythanii gathered in the temple and kicked and punched one of their priests until he or she was no more than a bloody stain on the flagstones. It had been going on for as long as there had been Brythanii in Agatos, and probably for a lot longer. Every now and then, the Senate, the City Watch, or some other self-appointed busybodies attempted to stop the practice, but it happened anyway, and in the end, it was apparently consensual. Trying to get in the way of people's religious practices lifted too many rocks that other religions didn't want anyone to look under. "I know they call your god the Hated God."

"You are right. But we have our reasons."

I held up my hands. "None of my business. Some religions it's all incense and gold, others it's weird sex, and some it's goats' blood all over the place. If you guys want to kill your priests, that's up to you. I'm just not sure why you're telling me."

"The priests who die are volunteers."

It looked like we were going to talk about it anyway. I settled back in my chair. "Yeah. That's the bit I have trouble with. You want me to believe people actually volunteer to die? That they're not forced into it? Because I've seen the way some people get volunteered, and there's not a whole lot of volunteering in it." I knew people did crazy shit for their religion, but this was extreme.

Ethemattian wasn't a big man. His shoulders were narrow, his body slight under his robes, but his pale eyes held the intensity I usually only saw in fanatics, lunatics, and the terminally ambitious. With a priest, it could be any of those, or all three. His gaze seemed to pursue me across the desk. "Only one priest must die each year, the one vessel for the god, but many put their names forward. It is the only way to progress from Cursed to Most Cursed."

Aha! I reckoned I had a handle on this now. Religion wasn't so different to politics or business or magic. It was about power.

"So, let me get this straight. No one is actually trying to murder you. You wanted a promotion. You took a gamble against becoming the vessel for your god. You lost, and now you're regretting it." What a waste of my time. "That's between you and your religion. I have a rule about not getting involved in religion."

"You misunderstand me. I was chosen, it is true, but I did not put my name forward. I did not volunteer. Someone *is* trying to have me killed. I want you to find out who, and I want you to stop them."

I bet he did. "Tell whoever's in charge. Tell them there's been a mistake."

He was shaking his head before I finished speaking. "I already have. It is too late. The choosing is our most sacred rite." From the first time since I had let him in, his features twisted into a bitter expression. It looked at home on his face. "In five days, a couple of hours before midnight, I will be beaten to death in my own temple by our own congregation. Help me."

And there it was. The sob story. It was always the sob story that got me. This man had been set up for a brutal death. The same thing had happened to me and Benny not so long ago, and I'd only just got us cleared of a murder we hadn't committed. So, how could I say no? How could I let a man be killed when I might be able to save him, even if he was a priest?

Me and religion didn't mix. Not if I could help it. It looked like I was about to break that rule.

I knew I was going to regret it.

One thing you could say about priests was that they were never short of money.

People would blow a fortune if they thought it would get them on the right side of their god. Not that the gods would lift a metaphorical finger, claw, or tentacle to help.

I named an outrageous price, and the priest didn't even blink.

"So." I leant back and eyed him. "Who have you pissed off?"

Outrage crossed his face before he mastered it. "I beg your pardon?"

"If someone goes to all that effort to kill you, you've pissed someone off, even if you didn't mean to." Or you were just an unfortunate patsy, a convenient scapegoat, in the wrong place at the wrong time. But I couldn't do anything with that. "Who did you piss off?"

His eyes went distant for a moment, then he nodded. "My brother, Retha, I suppose. He was ... jealous when I became a priest. He had wanted to dedicate his life to the temple. Unfortunately, I was accepted instead of him. But he would have no access to the choosing. Only a priest could reach the Sanctum." I wouldn't be so sure of that, but I didn't interrupt. "Anyway, it's been years. He has a life, a family, and the family business. There are some other priests I've had disagreements with. None would take it this far."

"Anyone stand out?"

"Menatha Keffen, most recently. A week ago." He spread his hands. "It was merely a theological difference, but we argued furiously for a while."

Did priests take that kind of thing to heart? How personal were those disagreements? I knew mages who hated each other over minor differences in magical theory, and here there was a god involved, which made everything more exciting.

"Did this Menatha Keffen put her name forward for your, um," – *getting beaten to death* – "ritual?"

"The Choosing. She did."

The Choosing. "I bet you spell that with a capital C, don't you?"

"What?"

"Nothing."

A double motive. Fixing the selection so that she wouldn't be the bloody sacrifice and getting back at a rival. Of course, that 'avoiding death' motive would fit everyone who had volunteered, and perhaps people just didn't like this guy.

In any case, in my experience, if you thought someone was pissed off at you, there was always someone else holding a bigger grudge. Often that person was me. But I had to start somewhere.

"All right." I pushed back my chair. "I'll look into it. I need you to leave your brother's address and the details of everyone else who entered this Choosing of yours."

I pushed over a sheet of paper and pencil and waited for him to make his list. When he was done, Cursed Ethemattian stood. "You have five days, Mr. Thorn. Then I will be dead. I am relying on you."

I WAITED UNTIL HE'D CLOSED THE DOOR BEHIND HIM, THEN I buried my head in my arms on the desk. "What in all the cursed Depths are you doing, Nik Thorn?"

Religion and gods were bad news. Inserting myself into the middle of the Brythanii's most sacred rite was like reaching down a shark's throat to grab its balls. If sharks even had balls, which I had no intention of finding out.

And that was exactly the point here. I had no idea what kind of teeth this religion had, nor what kind of balls it was hiding in its dark belly. (Yeah, the analogy was getting away from me.) But everyone was hiding something. The bigger and more established the religion, the bigger and darker their secrets. These guys were happy to see their own priests ritualistically murdered. I doubted they would take kindly to a stray mage poking around their business.

The obvious move would be to ask Ethemattian for the dirt on his religion. But I didn't trust a priest to tell me – or even know – the truth, even if his life depended on it. Maybe even more so when his life depended on it. The greater the stakes, the more people retrenched. It didn't make any sense, but people rarely did.

That left me in a dilemma. Charging in without knowing the Brythanii's secrets could be a good way to get myself fucked over, but I couldn't trust my client to tell me the truth.

So, where else could I find out what I needed?

The University and its library, as well as the city's museum and various private collections, would have material. But how accurate would their sources really be? If I'd been a head priest with secrets to hide, I would have dribbled out a lot of misinformation and goat shit over the years. I doubted the city's scholars had done the work to separate the truth from the sewage.

I did know one scholar I'd learned to rely on. I wouldn't find him at Agatos University, though. Jettuk Kehsereen had stayed in Agatos after I'd helped rescue his nephew from Enabgal, the god of dark dreams. That kind of thing bought you a lot of credit. His nephew, an untrained high mage, was recovering in the care of the Ash Guard, and I doubted he would ever leave. Kehsereen had made it his job to look out for the boy.

If anyone knew the unfiltered truth about the Brythanii religion, it would be Kehsereen, or at least he would know how to discover it. By this point, he probably didn't owe me any favours, but he always seemed willing. I pulled on my heavy, black mage's cloak – still too warm for the late summer – and headed out.

The worst of summer had broken a couple of weeks back, at the beginning of the month of Enetha. The cool wind had cleared the last of the brutal heat from the stone of the city, and heavy, broken clouds ran fast across the sky. The smell of rain haunted the air. Winter wouldn't come for months yet, but I always thought there was something ominous about this time of year, like a shadow where one shouldn't be.

Kehsereen had found himself a small apartment further up in the Middle City, just to the south and west of Horn Hill. It was a better part of town than I lived in, and his apartment was nicer, too. I still didn't know how a scholar could afford it, but even if I had been rich enough, I wouldn't have lived here. My business worked best when my clients thought I wasn't part of the same privileged, uncaring society as the city's other mages. Oddly, this worked both for my poorer clients, who felt I understood them, and my occasional richer clients, who thought they must be getting one over on me.

I turned left out of my door, but I hadn't gone more than a few steps before a frantic barking and a rush of knee-high, mottled fur sent me stumbling.

I recognised the dog immediately. He belonged to one of

my regular clients, Mr. Inles. I had spent much of the summer returning this dog when Mr. Inles managed to lose him. I hadn't seen either of them in the last month, and I'd thought Mr. Inles had finally figured out how to keep his dog safe. Or he had run out of money to pay me. Not that I'd charged him the last few times. Maybe that had been what had stopped him coming. The poorer people were, the less comfortable they were with receiving charity, and Mr. Inles had been very poor.

I knelt beside the dog and scratched behind his ears. "Let's get you back home." Unusually, he didn't try to escape from me. For some reason, that disturbed me more than the many times I had chased him up and down the streets, trying to get a hand on his collar. Instead, he wagged enthusiastically.

I grabbed a length of string from my office, looped it through his collar, and headed for Mr. Inles's little house near the edge of the Warrens. The blustering wind whipped my cloak around my legs as I walked, bringing the stench of the harbour in sudden, unexpected gusts. Sweat prickled on my skin under my cloak.

Mr Inles's home was out of my way, but only a little, and as it was still the afternoon, Kehsereen would probably be out. The houses were tighter here, smaller, their whitewash thin and faded, the streets narrower. Pass through an alley, over another street, and I would find myself in the maze of shacks and half-decayed homes that made up the Warrens. The gravity of the place seemed to tug on these liminal streets, as though it would let its people stray this far and no further, a steepening slope down which the unfortunate would tumble, too slippery and sheer to clamber back up.

"You're being overdramatic," I muttered. The dog looked up at me. "Not you."

Even so, I could feel the pull of the place I had grown up in.

I knocked on Mr. Inles's door.

No answer. It looked like Kehsereen wasn't the only one out. A fair number of people hurried along the street – now the summer had broken, most business had shifted to the daytime again – but no sign of Mr. Inles.

I looked down at the dog. He wagged hopefully up at me.

"You can wait inside. I'm sure he won't be long."

I released the lock with a quick spell then pushed the old door open. I hadn't been inside before. There were only two rooms, the living room with a kitchen and wash area at the back, bucket sitting half empty, and narrow, steep stairs leading up to what must be a bedroom. The air smelled slightly stale and dusty. Old, like the house.

"Hello?" I shouted. "Mr. Inles?"

Still no reply.

The living room was simple but tidy. The walls were bare, plastered, and whitewashed not too long back. A single small portrait hung in the centre of the left wall. I recognised the man in the portrait as a younger Mr. Inles. The woman must have been Mrs. Inles. She looked young, fashionable. Not wealthy, but not poor. A shop worker in a Middle City business, perhaps. All I knew of her was that she had died a long time ago.

A couple of chairs and a rug occupied this end of the room, a couple more and a table the kitchen area. That was it. Little enough for a long life, but more than I could boast.

I let the dog off his makeshift leash. He bounded up the stairs in a clatter of claws.

“What are you up to?” I demanded. Did Mr. Inles even let his dog upstairs? If it pissed on the bed, I wasn’t going to be popular. Did dogs do that? I had no idea.

Sighing, I followed.

The smell grew worse as I climbed, changing from musty and old to something fouler. A waste bucket that hadn’t been emptied for too long. It couldn’t be easy for Mr. Inles to haul it up and down these stairs. Maybe I could empty it in the street drain before I left.

Fuck it, Nik, he’s not your responsibility. But he was, in a way. He didn’t have anyone else, and I was sure that most of the time he’d paid me to find his dog was just because he wanted human contact. That he had been reduced to talking to me was a fucking tragedy. The way my life was going, if I survived, his life was my future, but without the loved one as a memory on my wall.

I stuck my head through the opening. “Hello?”

The dog answered with a burst of barking.

I climbed through.

Mr. Inles hadn’t gone out. In fact, I didn’t think he’d gone anywhere for a while. He was lying motionless on his bed, empty eyes staring at the ceiling.

“Lady of the Grove,” I muttered.

The dog wagged at me.

There were no wounds or injuries on Mr. Inles that I could see, no blood on the sheets or contusions on his skin. His face looked peaceful.

He had just died, that was all. He had been old, frail, alone. Perhaps he had gone to sleep and not woken. A couple of days ago, I reckoned. If it had been longer, this room would have smelled worse than the unemptied bucket.

Poor old bastard.

The dog barked at me again.

"I'm sorry," I said. "There's nothing I can do about it."

That wasn't wholly true. A well-trained mage could raise the dead, and while I lacked power, I didn't lack training. But the dead came back wrong, and things only got worse from there. It never ended well. I didn't have many lines I refused to cross in this job. That was one of them.

What a fucking day.

"Come on, boy."

I headed down and to the front door. The street was still busy, but no one was looking this way. *Keep out of other people's business,* that was the Agatos motto, particularly in the lower city.

I flagged down a passing messenger girl. "Go to the City Watch. Tell them the man who lives here has died." Mr. Inles had no family. The city would take care of his burial, and no doubt claim his property in payment.

The girl gave me a cynical look and held out her hand. With a sigh, I passed her a round – a copper coin. "You can claim the reporting reward, too. That'll bring you another shield."

I watched her dart off into the crowd. I hadn't known Mr. Inles well, but I still felt a heavy loss. This city wasn't kind, and he had been alone. I knew what that was like.

I looked down at Mr. Inles's dog. "I guess you're coming with me." I looped the string back around his collar. I had absolutely no idea what to do with a dog.

CHAPTER TWO

KEHSEREEN'S APARTMENT WAS SITUATED IN A GENEROUS building halfway up Sester Avenue. A high, iron gate opened to a small front courtyard shaded by fig, lemon, and orange trees and featuring a small, cheerful fountain. A guard sat in a small hut just inside the gate, but he recognized me and waved me through, only sparing a brief glance for my new dog.

I was going to have to come up with a name for this dog if I was keeping it, and I didn't know anyone who would be happy to have a dog dumped on them. Kehsereen wasn't the type. Benny wasn't talking to me. Elosyn and Holera were far too busy, what with Elosyn being a chef at Nuil's coffee house and Holera running her own restaurant. Captain Gale ... well, I didn't need the withering sarcasm that would result if I tried to offer her a dog.

"Looks like you're stuck with me," I told the dog. "So,

what did Mr. Inles call you?" He had told me at some point, but I had quickly realised that the damned creature wasn't going to come just because I shouted its name, and I had forgotten. Something starting with a B, perhaps. Or an S. The dog panted. "Yeah, no point asking you, is there?" At least when people caught me talking to myself, they would think I was talking to this mutt. Score one for having a dog.

I pushed through the polished wooden door into the marble lobby of the building. Just being there made me feel ragged and filthy, even though I was wearing my newest, cleanest outfit and it had been months since I had been attacked, dropped in a sewer, or blown up in a ship. The poor dog didn't look any better. His head hung, as though he knew he shouldn't be here.

"We're a right pair, aren't we?"

The dog didn't answer. I sighed. "Come on."

The apartment was up two flights of pristine stairs, past walls elaborately painted in murals showing scenes of Agatos – well, an Agatos that was distinctly cleaner and more elegant than the views out the windows. The fashion for murals on walls had fallen out of favour a few decades back, and although these were well-maintained, it was the only sign that this house was in the Middle City, not the Upper City.

We had just reached the bottom of the second flight of stairs when a figure appeared at the top and descended towards us. She was tall, with a long blue robe and hood, which she had pulled up. Beneath it, I caught a glimpse of dark, loosely-curled hair and the olive-brown skin of an

Agatos native, but I couldn't get a full view of her features. As she passed us, she turned her head away and pulled her hood tighter.

At that moment, I was bit by an absolute certainty that something had happened to Kehsereen. Call it intuition, instinct, call it the run of bad luck that hit anyone who knew me, but I was sure that this woman had done something to him. Why else hide her face and turn away?

I pulled in raw magic, shaped it, and tossed a thread onto her. If I was right, if she had done something, I would be able to find her now. Then I was up the stairs, taking three steps at a time. The dog chased up after me.

You're paranoid, Nik.

Yeah? Better to be paranoid than caught out.

I hammered on the door, then without waiting, shaped a spell to pop the lock.

I didn't have time to use it. The door opened immediately to reveal a short Khorasani man with light brown skin and straight black hair cut unevenly above his eyes.

"Fuck." Kehsereen. I slumped.

Idiot. Why in all the dark Depths would anything have happened to him?

If he was surprised by my greeting, he didn't show it. "Nik. Good." He stepped back and ushered me in.

Since settling here, Kehsereen had adopted the typical Agatos dress of shirt, loose trousers, and light jacket, but underneath the sleeves I saw the bandages he wore tightly wrapped around his limbs. I had seen the skin under the bandages once, and it was red and raw, as though partly eaten away by a corrosive liquid. He'd never volunteered an explanation, and I had never asked. *None of my business.*

"Did you pass a woman on the stairs?" he asked.

"Yeah. What's going on?"

"She's a priest of the cult of Sharshak. We need to follow her."

Great. Another Cepra-damned god. I was cursed by them. "There's a cult of Sharshak?"

Sharshak had been a sun god, until he'd died thousands of years ago. The story went that Sharshak's presence had neutralised the powers of other gods, leading undoubtedly to a lot of muttering and cold shoulders at god parties. That was how I interpreted it, anyway. But, popular or unpopular, Sharshak had died, so make of that what you will.

The story continued that Sharshak's burning body had crashed to earth somewhere in the region of Agatos, where it continued to smoulder in a deep pit. The ashes of his body were then used as Ash by the Ash Guard, and those ashes could themselves neutralise magic. With raw magic being the rotting remains of other dead gods, there was a certain logic to that, which immediately made me suspicious. A story that was too neat was almost certainly at least part bollocks.

"There are cults and religions of all gods if you look hard enough," Kehsereen said.

"I thought the Ash Guard had the whole Sharshak thing sewed up." But then I couldn't imagine Captain Gale and her people worshipping any god. Fucking them up if they stepped out of line, yes. Worshipping, no.

"The cult considers the Guard profane in their use of Sharshak's body. They're dedicated to ending the Ash Guard."

"How's that working out for them?"

As always, Kehsereen seemed jittery and unable to settle, but I had known him long enough to realise that, unless he was engrossed in research, he was always like this.

"I really don't want to lose track of her," he said.

I waved a hand. "Don't worry. I tagged her." As long as she didn't get too far ahead, I would be able to follow. She was out on the street now, heading south, not hurrying exactly, but not hanging around. Far enough away that if she looked back, she wouldn't see us trailing her. "Let's get going." I started down the stairs. "And while we're at it, you can tell me why we're following a cultist of a dead god."

Kehsereen waited until we were on the street and following the cultist's trail before he dropped his voice. "I have been undertaking a study of Ash."

I almost tripped over a cobble. "Are you crazy? If you're bored of life, there are easier means of suicide." The Ash Guard were notoriously protective of Ash, and understandably. In a city in the shadow of high mages, Ash was the only true guarantee of peace. Even possessing Ash without being a member of the Guard was an immediate death sentence.

Kehsereen shook his head. "We know very little about Ash. We don't know if it truly comes from dead Sharshak. We don't know if instead the Guard manufacture it nor, if so, how. We don't even know the range or its effect nor how that is related to the concentration of Ash."

I couldn't deny I had been curious, but despite evidence to the contrary, I did have some sense of self-preservation. "Is this about your nephew?"

"Asarian."

"Yeah. Him." Kehsereen had told me before, but I was bad with names, as my new dog could attest. My sister, Mica, said it was because I didn't really pay attention to other people, and I didn't know the kid. When we had rescued him from Enabgal, he had been unconscious and half dead, and since then he had been kept deep in the Ash Guard fortress. His powers as a natural, untrained high mage would have been a threat in the best of circumstances, but Asarian had been tormented for months by the madness of the god of nightmares. The Ash baked into the walls of the fortress prevented his powers from breaking loose.

"It is likely that Asarian will need Ash for the rest of his life. I must consider his future. I cannot think that the Guard are the best people to help him recover, and I cannot feed him *ulu-aru* forever." Kehsereen had used *ulu-aru* on me, once. It was a drug, and it had confused my mind so I couldn't access my magic. Maybe it would keep Asarian's powers suppressed, too, but I wouldn't have wanted to live in that state forever. "The Guard's focus is ever the safety of Agatos. I do not doubt they would sacrifice one child to that aim."

I wanted to argue. I wanted to say that Captain Gale was a better person than that. But I knew he was right. I couldn't even say the Guard were wrong.

"You think this cult might have Ash? That they might sell you some?"

"No. As I said, they consider Ash profane. Like all cults and religions of dead gods, they long for the return of their god."

Some hope of that. Dead was dead, even for a god. At least, I hoped so. "So, what do you want from them?"

"Information about Sharshak. The god's powers and aspects. Maybe even how he died and where his body fell."

"You think they have that?"

"Maybe. Religions often have secret archives – cults, too. Separating the truth from faith, myth, and dogma is the hard part."

"And so we're following her because...?"

"Because cults are secretive. I wish to find their place of worship and observe their reaction to my proposal of exchanging information."

We were deep in the Middle City, now, not far from Long Step Avenue, which cut east to west, all the way from the Grey City to the Warrens. The cultist took a left before she could reach it, down a street that was lined with well-appointed shops, restaurants, and coffee houses. The smell of frying spices and roasting coffee made my stomach rumble. Trees, their leaves dark green with end-of-summer age, stirred and ruffled in the wind. The awnings jutting from coffee houses flapped and snapped like poorly trimmed sails. A few more weeks, and those awnings would be furled for the autumn and winter.

We kept our distance, well out of sight, as we followed the

cultist, relying on the thread of magic I had attached to her to guide us. It was a reliable method provided I didn't let my quarry get too far ahead, I wasn't trying to follow a mage, and I didn't have the bad luck to run into a Guard patrol carrying Ash and have my spell fucked up. But now I got the feeling she was approaching her destination – she sped up, her movements becoming more nervous and erratic – and I wanted to see what exactly she was up to.

I caught a glimpse of the blue robe stepping out of the way of an ox cart and hurried to close the gap.

With one last look around – where she entirely failed to spot Kehsereen or me, the amateur – she ducked into a shoemaker's halfway down Tarragon Street. Of course, cultists were as likely to need new shoes as anyone. More so with the mess of entrails, blood, and other bodily fluids that accompanied some of the more enthusiastic acts of worship. But the trail of magic showed that she kept going through to the back of the shop and then headed down, into some cellar, I supposed, or, worse, to the sewers or ruins and collapsed tunnels beneath the modern city.

"Why does it always have to be down?" I muttered. Sharshak had been a sun god. Surely the cult should head for the highest spot, to open ground, where they could bask in the glory of what their god used to be. But no. They went into the dark. If that wasn't an admission they were up to no good, I didn't know what was.

"I beg your pardon?"

"Just talking to the dog."

He glanced down. "I was going to ask about the dog..."

I perked up. "You don't want a dog, do you?"

"No."

"Never mind." The dog was giving me a resentful look, I thought. "Just you and me, eh?" I glanced at Kehsereen. "What do you want to do now?"

"Can you tell what she's doing?"

"She's gone down into a cellar. That's all I know."

"Can you listen in?"

"Not from this far, and I'm not going to be able to hold my spell for much longer." I could feel it weakening. Either something was interfering with it, or my grip was starting to slip. Interference wasn't impossible. When I unfocused my eyes, I could see the flow of magic beneath the street leading to the morgue-lamps that would illuminate this street at night. A couple of weak natural mages strolled through the crowd, drawing in raw power and shedding half-formed magic around them, almost certainly unawares. At the back of the shoemaker's, and in several other shops, were what I guessed to be warded safes. Magic could get pretty crowded sometimes, and I was using a delicate spell. I looked down at my feet. "Maybe it's time to get some new shoes."

The shoemaker's shop was clean and well-lit, with shelves displaying the latest styles. Heels appeared to be in this season, a fashion I would definitely not be following as I was already taller than most people and running for my life had become a regular part of my day recently. I couldn't see a single pair of good, solid boots suitable for kicking someone in the nuts. A counter blocked passage to the back of the shop, and a curtain cut off the view. A couple of comfortable chairs flanked a small table in the centre of the room.

I leant close to Kehsereen. "Don't say anything. Just listen."

I used raw magic to shape a spell. It consisted – in my way of seeing it – of a net of magic that I let sink into and through the floor. When I saw it tremble in response to the vibrations of spoken words, I directed the vibrations into Kehsereen's ear. He started at the sudden noise.

This spell was easy enough to cast and maintain, and equally easy to deflect or avoid for a mage. From Kehsereen's expression of concentration, the people below hadn't noticed the intrusion.

The curtain pulled aside, and the proprietor emerged. He looked about as impressed by the sight of me and Kehsereen as I had been by his selection of shoes. A scholar and a second-rate mage probably weren't his first choice of customers. Neither of us were dressed as though we were wealthy, and a black cloak put off other customers as often as not. But it took a brave man to argue with a mage. I saw his face fall further as he stepped up to the counter and saw my dog-on-a-string.

I didn't let him make the wrong decision. I drew myself up. "I require new shoes."

His gaze dropped to my boots, and he shuddered. Fucking snob. I would put my boots against his shoes in any contest he chose.

"Do you have a style in mind, sir?"

I settled myself into one of the chairs, crossed my legs,

and smiled up at him. "Nope. Why don't you show me what you've got?" I tapped the table next to me. "Maybe some tea while we're waiting? And some water for my dog."

If he'd had the balls, he would have told me to fuck off. But everyone knew mages were rich – ha! – and connected, and maybe the potential outweighed my shabby appearance. Either that, or he thought I might pull his spleen out through his eyeball if he refused. He headed back behind the curtain. I pulled Kehsereen down into the chair beside me.

"I'll try to drag this out as long as possible."

While the shoemaker was out of the room, I unfocused my eyes and followed the thread of magic down through the floor. No one quite knew what magic was. We knew where it *came* from. We knew that when dead gods rotted, the effluent left behind was what we called raw magic. But that didn't mean that we really understood what it actually was. Every mage sensed magic, both shaped and raw, differently. Me, I saw it as coloured patterns and shapes when I unfocused my eyes, but others might interpret it as a melody, or broken glass scraping across skin, or, as had been the case with one mage I had heard of, sexual arousal. It was as though our brains lacked the facility to process whatever sense it was that mages possessed and instead flailed about to choose some alternate interpretation. A kind of magical synaesthesia. I couldn't 'see' through the floor, but I could sense the magic beneath. I could see the web of my spell vibrating gently in response to the words being spoken, but there was something else down there, too. Not a god's power. Sharshak was dead, and in any case, there were distinct differences between the power of a living god, the decay of a dead god, and the magic formed by mages from that decay. But there was magic down there, or an attempt at it.

This lot wouldn't be the first cult or religion to use magic to convince their followers of the puissance of their god and the need to leave generous donations. But whatever they were up to, they weren't having much success. They appeared to be trying something similar to a technique I had used to concentrate raw magic into an opal, but they were getting it all wrong, and I could have scraped up more magic with a teaspoon than they were managing. In fact, they were using more raw magic in forming the spell than they were managing to gather. They just weren't grabbing for the right stuff. *That's why you go through mage training, boys and girls.* This wasn't for amateurs.

"Your tea. Sir." A cup slammed down on the table next to me. I jumped.

"Good." I focused my eyes again and tried to ignore the headache that keeping my eyes unfocussed for so long always gave me. "So, what have you got for me?"

I dragged it out for as long as I could, as I'd promised, pretending to examine each pair carefully before rejecting them and asking for something new. "Maybe something simpler." "Maybe something more elaborate." "Darker." "Lighter." "With less of a heel." "More of a heel." "Perhaps the first pair again."

Eventually, the shoemaker mutinied. "That is all I have, sir."

I took a last sip of my tea, then set the cup back down.

"You know what? I think I'll stick with my boots." I tapped Kehsereen on the shoulder. "Come on."

The shoemaker shot daggers at me. I smiled sweetly in response. "I think you might have brewed your tea too hot. You might want to see about that."

I waited until we were out of sight of the shop, cast around both magically and non-magically to see if we were being followed, then said, "Did you get what you needed?"

Kehsereen looked thoughtful. "Perhaps. I do not think they will be able to tell me much about Ash, but from what I heard, they do have old records of their god. Whether those contain truth or just hints of it in myth, I won't be able to tell until I examine them. I may be able to work with the cult. There was also a lot of praying and chanting, but it did not seem relevant."

"They were trying to cast a spell. They were making a mess of it."

"Strange. Sharshak is always taken to embody the antithesis of magic. It will be interesting to see how their beliefs skirt around this."

"Yeah. Sure. Interesting." I would find watching seaweed rot more enthralling, but each to their own.

We stopped for a minute while the dog sniffed around the gutter. I was coming to conclusion that going anywhere fast with this dog was a non-starter.

"I had some questions for you, too, while we're talking about religion."

Kehsereen tilted his head.

"I've got a case involving a Brythanii priest. What can you tell me about their religion?"

"The betrayer god. They are an insular religion, something of a death cult, it might be fair to say."

"The Hated God, they call it here." The dog cocked his leg and proceeded to piss on the same spot he had been sniffing. I pretended not to notice.

"Yes. The Brythanii arrived in the Yttradian Sea about three hundred years ago, fleeing a disaster in their homeland. No one knows exactly where their homeland is, other than it is far south of Melaru. I believe they had been fleeing for generations before they reached the Yttradian Sea. Do you know their prayer?"

I shook my head and managed to tug the dog a few yards further down the street.

"They say, 'You did not help us when we needed you.' They consider their god to have betrayed them, and that is why they hate it. They won't even say its name. The ritual murder of a priest is designed, I believe, as an insult to the god who is out of reach."

I sympathised. I had met a couple of gods, and I wasn't a fan. One had tried to rip my heart out with its arm-long claws, and the other had tried to drive me insane. Why anyone would choose to worship these manifestations of ego, greed, and brutality was beyond me. I had to say I admired a people who could hold a grudge for hundreds of years. That was proper dedication.

"Correct me if I'm wrong, but I'm guessing they're not terribly welcoming to outsiders."

"They hold their resentments tight."

Again, fair enough, even if it didn't make things easier for me. "I need to find a way into their temple to question people, and I need to know about this ritual murder. How does the priest get chosen? Who's involved in it at all stages? That kind of thing. My client has been selected as the sacrifice, but he didn't volunteer for their selection. He was set up."

"I know some independent scholars whose knowledge of religion is greater than mine. I may be able to find out more."

That wasn't quite what I'd hoped for. Maybe I'd come to rely too heavily on Kehsereen's expertise, because when he answered, my head drooped in disappointment. My client only had five days left. I didn't have time to wait for Kehsereen to search out contacts, do research...

What else are you going to do?

Why the fuck had I even taken the job?

Because someone had to.

I could barge into the temple and start throwing around accusations, which would get me laughed out of the place or arrested, I could ask Cursed Ethemattian, which I'd already ruled out, or I could trust Kehsereen. He'd never let me down before, and a lot could happen in five days.

I could handle this.

I still should never have taken the job. *No gods or mages, remember?* That was supposed to be my rule.

Except I wouldn't have to get anywhere near their god, right? The one advantage of working with the Brythanii was that they didn't want to get any closer to their god than I did.

Ah, but fuck it, this afternoon had reminded me why I hated religion.

Was I really going to let him die?

He's not your problem.

That might have been true before. But I had taken his money. I had agreed to help.

The dog let out a little bark.

"You're probably hungry, aren't you?" I said. The day was drawing in, although it was still a few hours before dark. "Or thirsty." Pity! I had a hard enough time keeping myself alive and healthy. This dog had attached itself to the wrong idiot.

"Thanks," I told Kehsereen. I glanced back in the direction of the shoemaker's. "And be careful. Cults are bad news."

We parted, and the dog and I headed for my usual restaurant, where I paid double to feed us both. There had to be a better way of doing this.

That night, I felt the dog leap onto my bed.

"Fuck off," I muttered.

He tucked himself in close to me. At least it was warm, and he didn't smell as bad as some people who had shared my bed.

For once, I slept well.

CHAPTER THREE

When I woke, there was a cold depression beside me in the bed and a vague memory of warmth.

I flapped a hand behind me, trying to bring back that feeling, before I remembered Mr. Inles's dog.

No. My dog now.

I rolled over, forcing my eyes open and closed repeatedly to clear them. My mouth was dry and my brain tired in that way that I only experienced after an unexpectedly good night's sleep.

Where in the Depths had my dog got to?

Rubbing my eyes, I lurched through the apartment, only to hear barking from my small backyard.

I pushed open the door and saw the dog waiting.

"How did you get out here?" My bedroom window was ajar, but only just, and surely too high up. No wonder Mr. Inles had struggled not to lose this creature. "I'm not coming to find you if you fuck off," I told the dog. He wagged back up at me, as though I was encouraging him. I shook my head. Breakfast for both of us, then I could figure out my day. I had no idea how long it would take Kehsereen to discover what I needed, but I didn't have to wait for him. Barging into the temple would be a bad idea, but Cursed Ethemattian had mentioned a jealous brother. In my experience, no one could be as pissed off at you nor as vengeful as family. My mother was living proof. But breakfast first, definitely.

When I stepped into my office, Benny's daughter, Sereh, was waiting for me, propped up against a wall.

It was so unexpected that it took me several seconds to react. Emotions tumbled through me like stones churned under a wave on a beach. Fear, yes, but also hope and a suppressed misery.

Sereh could kill me if she chose. She wouldn't hesitate, and I wouldn't be able to stop her. But if she wanted me dead, I would already be dead, and no one would have seen her arrive or leave.

As the fear leeched away, the other emotions emerged. I had missed her and Benny. When they'd cut me off – fairly, after I had put Sereh's life at risk in the course of one of my jobs – it had torn away a great chunk of my life. I didn't often get lonely. But I had been, then. I had squeezed those feelings tight down into a chunk of rock and tried to hide them away.

"Fuck it! Sereh, I..." I just wanted to... What? Throw my arms around her? Hug her? That really would get me knifed.

"Dad says you have to come." The hope that leapt up

inside me must have shown, even though I tried not to let it, because she added, "He hasn't forgiven you. But you have to come anyway. There's something you need to see."

"All right," I said carefully. I would take it. It was more than I'd had these last couple of months. I wondered for a moment if she was leading me somewhere to kill me. But that wasn't Sereh's style.

It was early as we headed out through the streets of Agatos. The air was warmer than yesterday, cloudy but still, free of blustering winds, the kind of weather that said summer wasn't quite done with us yet, that autumn needed to wait its turn yet. The smell of the ocean, the trash and sewage in the harbour, and baked goods from the Penitent's Ear market hung in the air. Waiting, that was what all of this felt like, a city holding its breath, suspended between seasons, paths, choices.

I left my mage's cloak behind and brought my light, blue jacket in case the city finally came to a decision and decided to piss down on me.

Sereh led me through the backstreets and alleys of the Middle City towards the Warrens. I didn't think she was particularly trying to hide or avoid being noticed. It was just habit. At first, I thought she was taking me to her and Benny's house, but we passed it and kept going into the tumbledown maze of the Warrens proper.

Benny and I had grown up here, street kids who had known every alley, courtyard, and passage like ants knew their nest, but the Warrens changed, growing and transforming like mould on damp wood, and I didn't come back here enough to be confident away from the main streets. Sereh had no such problems. Soon, I was thoroughly lost. All I could tell was that we were moving roughly northwest, and I could only tell that from the glimpses I caught of the mountains that flanked the Erastes Valley.

The dog dragged and snuffled behind, slowing our pace and pulling towards scents and sounds in the shadows. I didn't normally get nervous, but this dog was doing a good job of making me think we were being watched from every side. Which we probably were. The Warrens didn't like intruders. But no one interfered. I suspected that was more due to Sereh's presence than mine.

"Where are we going?" I asked.

Sereh didn't answer that. "Why have you got a dog?"

"I think I inherited him."

Which reminded me, Mr. Inles's funeral would be in two days. Three days after death was the city's tradition – unless there was a crime and the Watch or the Ash Guard stuck their oars in – and as the city would be burying him, they would stick to the tradition. I should take the dog along for a last goodbye. Mr. Inles hadn't had many friends – any, possibly – and someone had to be there. One day, someone would bury me, too – unless I was incinerated by an angry mage or eaten by a mad god first. I would want someone there. I would want someone to remember me. Even a fucking dog. Right now, I wasn't sure anyone would. They might hear I had died, think, *Oh, that's sad,* then move on. A memory soon forgotten.

I pushed the thought down. When I was dead, I would be

dead. Why the fuck would I care what anyone thought then? I didn't even care what people thought now.

Except Benny and Sereh.

"What's his name?"

"Don't know. You want him?" A kid should have a dog, right? My mother hadn't even entertained the idea. But not everyone had to have the blessed Countess as a parent.

"No. He would interfere with my intent." Whatever the Depths that meant. Sereh's violin teacher had said something about intent once, too, but neither of them had explained it. Some Dhajawi cultural concept, I supposed. "You should name him, though," she added. "That would probably mean something to you."

"Any ideas?"

"He's your dog."

The path we were following through the Warrens began to rise as we approached the slopes of the valley wall. The warm, fresh, calming scent of cedar trees filtered into the air, a soft, high note above the violent stink of the city.

I knew where we were going, now.

Before long, the salvaged stone and driftwood shacks on the western edge of the Warrens ended, and we came out beside a clear stream that ducked down into the city's bowels beneath the Warrens. The city had never chosen to run clean water pipes into this unwanted part of Agatos, and unless you wanted a long trek through the Warrens to the Middle City or to trust the polluted wells sunk into a few of the courtyards, this stream was the best source of drinking water for the Warrens. It didn't run dry, even in the hottest summer.

Blessed by the Lady, people said, but it was just a mountain spring from higher up the slope.

A handful of residents were already gathering water in buckets and jugs. Sereh led me past them, up the rocky path towards the thick grove of cedars.

Anywhere else in the city, this grove would have long been cut down for building materials or firewood. Not here. The trees, so the story went, were the home of the Lady of the Grove, adopted as patron goddess of the Warrens by those who lived here. The Lady blessed the Warrens, the story said, and a fucking great job she had done of it. Some claimed to have caught glimpses of her, but I never had, and people could convince themselves of any old shit if they needed to believe hard enough. Real or imaginary, no one would be stupid enough to cut a single branch from one of the trees and risk the wrath of the Warrens.

It was always peaceful in these trees, cool in summer, sheltered in winter, but now as we stepped in, it was unusually cold. I shivered, wishing I had worn my mage's cloak after all. I tugged the jacket tightly around me. The dog drew closer to my heels and didn't stop to sniff.

Up ahead, hidden from view from the city below, I saw Benny standing on the bank of the stream, waiting. Beside him, at his feet, lay a body.

You couldn't live long in Agatos without seeing a dead body, particularly in the lower city. Depths, this wasn't my first body this week, and I wasn't particularly surprised. It had become a tradition in the Warrens to leave bodies in the grove overnight before burial to receive the Lady's blessing, before they were carried up to be interred in the caves and shafts above the grove. The city's main burial ground, past the Upper City, was far out of the reach of most people in the Warrens, but as always, the Warrens found its own way.

Most bodies were wrapped in funeral clothes before being left here, but not all, and this body wasn't. Funeral clothes were expensive.

The feeling of wrongness and the chill in the air increased as I trudged my way up. Maybe it was the way Benny was standing over the body or the gaunt, grim expression on his weaselly face. The dog whined behind my legs.

The body was a woman. I thought at first she was young. Her features were smooth, her light brown skin unmarred by wrinkle, scar, or blemish, her long black hair luxuriant on the bare stones. But there was something old about her, too. It was always hard to tell the age of a dead person. Death took away so many things: joy, grief, love, bitterness. My skin itched as I looked down at her, and not just because I was looking at a dead body. There was something *wrong* here.

I turned to Benny. "You didn't kill her, did you?"

"No." He didn't look at me as he said it. He hadn't looked my way once, even as I'd approached.

The air here was fresher than the rest of the city and at once more stale, the colours more vivid and yet dulled. I felt both pulled towards the body and pushed away, like a wave crashing over a top of another withdrawing one.

"Do your thing," Benny said.

"What?"

"Do your thing!" There was so much rage in his voice, I

thought he was going to lunge at me. Did he know her? He had never introduced me.

My thing. My magic, I guessed he meant. I drew in a breath to steady myself, then unfocused my eyes.

Raw magic raged around the body. I threw up a hand to cover my eyes and staggered back, almost blinded. I was used to seeing raw magic. It permeated the air, the land, and the water in Agatos, but it was faint, nebulous, a thin, shimmering mist. This ... this was a furnace. An inferno. It would melt steel, burn bone. I had only seen raw magic even close to this intensity once before, when I had glimpsed the severed foot of the dead god Ethys.

"Is... Is she dead?" There was something in Benny's voice I wasn't used to hearing. Fury. Fear. Loss.

I nodded. Raw magic only came from dead gods. "Is it her?"

Benny's eyes were focused on the body. "The Lady of the Grove."

Denna's mercy.

The patron goddess of the Warrens. Dead. Somehow. I hadn't even been sure she was real until now. She was the one that people in the Warrens looked to for hope, even if they worshipped another god. What would happen when they found out? What would happen when you stripped away all hope from those who already had next to none?

Depths.

"We should call the Ash Guard," I said.

Benny's head snapped around, his face pinched with

anger. “Fuck your Ash Guard! When did you stop being one of us?”

That hit harder than if he’d swung for me. “What?”

“What do you think they’ll do to her? They’ll bury her in Ash. They’ll snuff out every last trace of her. That’s what they do, isn’t it?”

Would they? I knew as well as anyone that dead gods could still be dangerous, and more than that, her body was dangerous. The amount of raw magic pouring off her was stupendous, and it would keep coming for thousands and thousands of years until her body had entirely decayed. The Ash Guard wouldn’t want any mage getting their grubby little hands on it, nor the other things that haunted the shadows and fed on magic. It would be like rolling a barrel of gunpowder into a neighbourhood bonfire. I thought I understood the Ash Guard now, and Benny was right. Better safe than sorry would be their motto, and the Lady would join the remnants of the god of fear and nightmares, the watcher in the dark, Enabgal, in Ash.

“Someone’s going to take her body,” I said. “The amount of raw power it’s giving off, it’ll be a beacon to every mage in the city. And if they’re the only ones who come looking, we’ll be very lucky.”

Benny straightened. He still looked like a long-dead weasel, but he looked like a long-dead weasel that wasn’t going to let a little death stop it. “What do we do? Cos I ain’t letting some mage get their hands on her.”

“I didn’t know the Lady mattered so much to you.”

“She didn’t. Gods, I can leave them or take them. But she

was the Warrens. That matters. It's who we are. Who we were."

And the Warrens would know, somehow. Even without using my magical senses, I had noticed the change in the Warrens. I wouldn't be the only one.

"For a start, we should get her out of sight. One of the burial caves or shafts. Then we need to block her magic. She's a goddess, so we're not going to be able to block her power completely, but we can try to dull it so you'd only notice if you were close. Start with apple tree wood. Surround the body with it. But really we're going to need a sarcophagus lined with volcanic glass, and a lot of it."

Benny's forehead creased. Creased more. It already looked like a drunk ploughman had taken a detour across his head. "I can get the wood right now. The lumberyard on the docks will have it. The rest will take time. Might have to nick it."

I shrugged. "Be careful. Come up with a reason for buying the wood. The lumber yard will report to the Wren, and he mustn't know."

"Like what?"

"Tell them you're doing a job for Mica. A new training room for her mages. That would need apple tree wood and volcanic glass, and a lot of it. The Wren can't exactly ask her if it's true." I knelt by the body. "Now, come on." I hooked my hands under her armpits and lifted, while Benny took her feet. It felt disrespectful to carry her like this, but so did leaving her there. The pressure of her raw magic made my skin prickle and my head thump painfully. Magic wanted to spill from my hands and mouth.

"Keep an eye out," I told Sereh. "Let us know if anyone comes."

She nodded. "I'll watch over the body until dad gets back with the wood. No one will come close."

"Just … take care. Some pretty dangerous people will come for that body if they realise it's there."

Her eyes fixed on me. "No one will come close." Then she was gone.

I shivered.

We made our way up the rocky path beneath the trees. It wasn't easy, and the dead god was unaccountably heavy despite her slender form. Her oiled black hair brushed against my legs with every step. The dog followed close behind, even though I wasn't holding his makeshift leash, a scarcely audible whimpering coming from his throat.

I chose a narrow, sloping cave – more a crack in the rocks than a true cave – just beyond the grove, and we lowered her in. The living trees would provide some magical shielding. All living things held some magic, and it might filter the glare of the Lady's raw magic from a distance. There was no sign of Sereh, but I had no doubt that she was nearby, preternaturally hidden in the shadows, watching.

The whole thing hit me again now that we were done. A shiver ran through me, and I half sat, half dropped onto a rock outside the cave. I should have been sweating, but I felt cold.

I had just carried a dead god up from her grove and

dumped her in a cave. She had died. The hope of the Warrens.

No. She hadn't died. Someone or something had killed her. But how? *Why?*

"What are you going to be doing?" Benny demanded. His voice was full of suspicion, as though he expected me to fuck off to a bar and leave the whole thing to him. Maybe he had justification for that.

What are you going to do? That was the question, wasn't it? Tell the Ash Guard? Just try to bury her and forget her? Benny would hang my guts from the trees if I tried either of those, and the Warrens, fuck knows what the Warrens would do, but it wouldn't be good, not for the people of the Warrens or for anyone else.

"What do you want me to do?"

For the first time, Benny met my eyes. "You're going to find who killed her. Then you and me, we're going to fuck them up. That's not even a debate."

That was the answer I'd been trying to avoid. I didn't want to be part of this. No gods, mages, or monsters. How many times had I told myself that? It was bad enough to get involved with the Brythanii priest. This? This was insanity.

But Benny had been my friend for a long time, and I needed him to be my friend again. I hadn't coped without him and Sereh. *And you thought you were so good at being alone.*

"All right."

"All right," he mimicked. "Fuck's sake. You know what really bends my neck?"

"What?"

"You. All this, 'What do you want me to do?' and 'All right'. It's goat shit."

"I'm just trying to make things right again."

"Well, you can't. Not like this. Just be fucking honest."

He turned away to stare over the trees to the Warrens and ocean beyond.

"Fine." I had let him down. Betrayed his trust. And I wanted to make up for it, I really did. I needed to. But if he wanted the truth, I would tell him. "This is stupid. You want to take on someone who could kill a god. Just you and me, not even the Ash Guard. We haven't got a chance."

I could only think of one story of someone successfully killing a god. When Agate Blackspear, the founder of modern Agatos, had sailed into the harbour at the head of his fleet, he had fought Sien, the goddess of the city, and killed her. In the moment of her death, she had leapt from the top of Horn Hill, at the place now known as the Leap – people in Agatos were imaginative like that – spawning a dozen legends and countless second-rate plays.

Strangely, the Godkiller hadn't left a how-to manual of god killing, and it had been four hundred and twenty-six years ago, so I could hardly ask. But the Godkiller had reputedly been the most powerful high mage the city had ever seen, and going up against someone in that class was madness.

"So, you're not going to help."

"Oh, I'll help," I said. "But it's still crazy, and we'll probably end up dead."

From Benny's reaction, I didn't think one of those deaths would upset him too much. I suppressed a sigh. At least he was talking to me again, and we would be working together. Maybe I would get a chance to make things right after all. Even if I didn't, this was better than the alternative. I could live with him hating me if I could repair some of the damage I had caused.

Which was all very well, but it left me with a question I had no idea how to answer: how did you kill a god?

It wasn't a question most people spent a lot of time thinking about. If you wanted to kill a man, or, I don't know, an otter, it wouldn't be that hard. A knife through the throat, a hammer across the back of the head. But with a god, where would you start? Gods could manifest bodies, certainly, but those were no more the essence of the god than a bubble blown from your lips. Living and dying were abstract concepts when it came to gods. The beast god, Ah'té, had been dead, but it had still ripped a bunch of people to shreds and nearly finished me.

If I could figure out the answer to the question of how, maybe that would be the first step to figuring out who. Narrow down the possibilities, at least. Asking the Godkiller was out of the question – hundreds of years dead was a bit of an obstacle – and even if the existing high mages knew, they would never tell me. I suspected the answer was beyond even Kehsereen's research skills.

But there was someone – possibly a group of someones – who had been poking at the question. This someone might not have the answer, but at least he had theories, and I had to start somewhere. The problem was, this person, one of my old Agatos University tutors, Scholar Longstream, was a self-absorbed, smug bastard. He hated my guts as much as I hated his. When I had gone to ask him for help with the beast god, he had told me he was in a debate with other scholars on how the Godkiller had killed Sien. He'd demanded I raise the corpse of the Godkiller and ask it to confirm his theories in exchange for his help. That was out of the question, and I'd told Longstream where to stick it. I didn't think he would have the balls to try out any of his ideas, even if he was sure he was right, but if I knew what they were, maybe they would lead to someone with a lot more balls than Longstream. Someone who had tried the ideas out and killed the Lady of the Grove.

The problem would be getting him to tell me. He hadn't been willing to part with information to save the city from Ah'té. He certainly wouldn't spill because the patron god of the Warrens was history. I had no intention of even sharing that fact with him.

So, I would have to offer him something he wanted in exchange, something that appealed to his own greed and self-interest rather than the good of the city.

Which begged the question: what exactly did a stuck-up scholar really, really want, other than a punch in the face?

I should have paid more attention in my lectures.

Kehsereen might not know how to murder a god, but I reckoned he knew a whole lot more about scholars than I did. Depths, maybe he'd even discovered something for me about the Brythanii's rituals by now.

"There are some people I need to talk to," I said to Benny.

"You can start with the people of the Warrens. If they'll talk to you." The look he gave me was a challenge, and I read what he meant to say right on his face: *You're not Warrens anymore.* "People come up here sometimes to ask favours of the Lady. Someone might have seen something."

"Is that why you were up here?"

He bristled. "It's none of your fucking business why I'm up here, all right? And no, I didn't see anything."

"All right. All right." I held up my hands. "It doesn't matter anyway. I don't know how you kill a god, but I do know you don't just walk up to it and stick a knife in its throat. When a god chooses to manifest itself, that's not the god. That's the puppet it dangles in front of you. There's power there, but stories about the Godkiller and Sien notwithstanding, no one is going face-to-face with a god to kill them. They're going to do it from where they've had a chance to set up some enormous fuck-off spell and a Depths of a lot of power." More than I could imagine, I guessed. "The people I need to talk to are the ones who might actually know how you would go about killing a god." Unless Scholar Longstream was as full of shit on this as he usually was.

Benny grunted. "All right, then. But you fucking tell me what you find, got it? No more secrets."

"Yeah," I said. "No secrets." Not this time. This time, I wouldn't fuck it all up.

CHAPTER FOUR

It took longer than it should have to reach Kehsereen's apartment. I got lost once in the Warrens, but mostly the dog was to blame. It wasn't only the incessant sniffing and pissing everywhere, or the barking matches with every other dog we passed. When we came within smelling distance of a butcher's stall in a tightly enclosed courtyard, the damned thing wouldn't move on until I had bought it breakfast.

At this rate, I was going to end up broke.

The clouds had begun to come apart above us, slowly separating as if teased apart by fingers, dropping pillars of scarcely moving sunlight onto the city, but the air down here remained still. A thin layer of sweat had built up under my shirt.

Kehsereen opened the door to me with only a brief glance down at the dog. "I don't have your information yet.

I'm going to meet a contact later today. She should be able to tell me much of what you need."

"That can wait. I need something else."

I realised as I said it that it sounded ungrateful, but he stepped aside and waved me in.

I lowered myself into a chair on the opposite side of the room to his desk. It had been a tough morning – emotionally fucking traumatising, as well as all the walking and carrying – and unlike the dog, I hadn't eaten. Mages didn't need to eat or drink as often as other people, and a high mage could probably go for weeks without food. Magic helped sustain us, even heal us when we slept, but it didn't stop us getting hungry.

"What is it you need?" Kehsereen hadn't sat. He fretted restlessly in the space between the desk and the chairs.

"I want to get some information from one of the scholars at the university," I said, "but he's not going to want to give it to me."

"Have you considered torture?"

My eyebrows shot up before I realised he was joking. It had taken me a while to pick up on Kehsereen's sense of humour, and even now, I often missed it. "Don't tempt me. He's a scholar at Pauper's College. I need to offer him something in exchange for that information. Something he would want but couldn't get for himself."

"And you don't know what. What's his speciality?"

Being an annoying, self-regarding arsehole. "Religion, specifically Fatracian and Pentathian gods, I think."

Kehsereen peered off into the space above my head. I resisted the urge to turn to see what he was looking at.

"Agatos scholars don't really undertake original research. They prefer learning from books already written. I doubt I have any that the university doesn't. Perhaps an artifact might pique his interest, if you could find one."

I shook my head. "Not for what I'm asking from him." The fact that he'd demanded that I raise the Godkiller the last time I'd gone to him meant he wasn't selling information for a trinket.

"Then you will want a book or manuscript that he won't have seen."

"I'm not going to be able to pick that up in the Penitent's Ear."

"You would be surprised, but no. It would be unlikely, and I have something specific in mind. The most well-known Fatracian deity was Tulbek the Old. But long before it became Tulbek, it was a tribal god associated with a river called the Eyvonne in northwest Fatracia. It is not so far from Khorasan, and I spent some time in the area. There is a small city there now called Perrammes. The early religions of the area were documented in a volume called *The Silver Oak*, but most copies were destroyed during the Fatracian Ascendancy."

There had been a reason I'd drifted off in my history lessons. I had no idea what most of those things were. I probably couldn't pick out Fatracia on a map.

"Which helps us how?"

"I am almost certain that your scholar will not have a copy."

"Yeah, well, neither do I."

Kehsereen smiled. "But Senator Greenfield probably does. He's said to have the most extensive private collection of religious texts on the continent."

"Great. And he'll be willing to give it to me, will he?"

Kehsereen's smile widened. "Absolutely not. He protects his collection jealously. I imagine you will have to steal it."

THIS DAY WAS GOING FROM BAD TO ABSOLUTELY TERRIBLE faster than a drunk taking a tumble down the Corithian Steps (ask me how I know; my ankle still hadn't recovered all these year later from the wall I had met at the bottom). If this hadn't been about the Lady's murder – no, if this hadn't been about getting back into Benny's good books – I would have laughed it off. My two attempts at burglary so far had led to me being framed for murder and having to flee from a temple I had accidentally burned down. But I wasn't going to be offered many more chances to make things up with Benny.

"I don't think I know this Senator Greenfield."

"You'll like him. He has a palace near the top of Horn Hill. His family were rich, but he cornered the trade in high-value items from Corithia, Myceda, and Kendar after becoming a senator. Marble, gold, craftsmanship in ivory."

Of course he had, the fucker. If there was one thing you

could rely on, it was that senators would enrich themselves before helping the city. Mica's boyfriend – partner, whatever – claimed to be different, and maybe he was, but neither of them were exactly living in poverty.

"He has a personal mage, too."

I stilled in my chair. "Are you fucking kidding me?"

Most mages attached themselves to one of the high mages – my mother, the Wren, or Carnelian Silkstar, until his death. A dozen or so – not those with ambition or particular power – worked directly for the Senate, generally on public works, maintaining the morgue-lamp network, the wards on public buildings, and the city's magical defences, degraded though those had become over the centuries. A small handful took up private employment with wealthy families or businesses, looking after their interests and staying out of the politics of the high mages. Then there was me, of course, Agatos's sole freelance mage, taking jobs from anyone who could pay and who didn't piss me off too much, and struggling to meet each month's rent. Honestly, I was surprised more mages hadn't followed my example.

The private mages weren't going to trouble a high mage in terms of power, but they were well-trained and focused on their one job. In the case of Greenfield's mage, that would include protecting his assets from second-rate mages on the steal.

"That's really the only option?" I asked.

Kehsereen shrugged. "If you want the book. I don't know what else might persuade your scholar."

Yeah. Me neither. Maybe some needles under his fingernails or a ball of fire up his arse. But I'd had enough of being arrested this year. "Fine. Tell me what I'm looking for."

Kehsereen eyed me thoughtfully. "The senator has a large collection, I understand. I think I will need to come with you."

I stared back up at him. A tourist. That was all I needed. Fuck me.

ANY NORMAL TIME, I WOULD HAVE BROUGHT BENNY ALONG ON a jaunt like this. He had been a professional thief most of his adult life, and he still wasn't dead or in gaol. My two attempts had been ... mixed ... to say the least, although I had walked away with my stolen opal from the temple I had burned down, so there was that. Benny had been in on the first attempt – the framed-for-murder lark – so that was a mark against him, too, but overall, he had a far higher success rate than I did. But I didn't know where I stood with him. Would he think I was trying to dodge my part of the deal? Anyway, he had more important things to get on with – procuring apple tree wood and volcanic glass to shield the Lady's body from magical detection – and three people was too many for a quiet bit of burgling.

"We'll do it this afternoon," I said. "Three o'clock. Meet at the top of the Corithian Steps. You know it?" That way I could avoid my mother's palace. Even the thought of going near that made my heartbeat stutter and my skin tighten uncomfortably.

"Why not tonight?"

"The Senate will be in session this afternoon. He'll be out the house, as will many of his staff. If we're lucky, his mage will be with him."

If not, we would have a problem. *Another* problem. I wasn't foolish enough to think I could take on Greenfield's personal mage head-to-head. I was right on the bottom of the scale when it came to power, not much more potent than an apprentice. I had some tricks and plenty of skill, but when it came down to brute power, I wasn't impressing anyone. I had lost my obsidian-headed mage's rod in the explosive chaos and destruction of the city's dockyards. My fault, unfortunately, and they still hadn't finished rebuilding the dockyards, but I'd had a good reason. I hadn't replaced my rod yet. I missed the heft and reach of it when it came to confrontations. I had surprised a few overconfident opponents with a crack across the head or a balls-bursting smash between the legs, and no one wanted that in a fight.

"Then I shall look forward to Senator Greenfield's library," Kehsereen said.

"Yeah. You do that." Personally, I would look forward to us not being horribly killed by the wards, the mage, or the guards.

I wasn't sure which of us was being more optimistic.

It was a long time until my appointment with Senator Greenfield's private collection. It wouldn't hurt to give the place the once-over – check entrances, windows, wards, that kind of thing – but there was only so much I could do without getting inside, and there was no point raising suspicion. Anyway, if I spent too long thinking this through, I would just drive up my anxiety. I didn't operate well when my anxiety took over. And I still had another job.

It hadn't escaped my memory that I had promised to save the Brythanii priest, Cursed Ethemattian, from being murdered by his own congregation. Time was ticking down, and it really wouldn't help my professional reputation if one of my clients was beaten to death. I still didn't have the information I wanted before I tried to investigate the Brythanii temple, and distracting Kehsereen with this Senator Greenfield shit wasn't helping there, but as often as not, in my very limited experience, the people most willing to fuck you over were those who were supposed to be closest to you. I could start with the priest's family.

I headed home to exchange the dog for my black mage's cloak. There was something distinctly more intimidating about looking like someone who could turn your blood into steam rather than wielding a dog that tended to wag enthusiastically at everyone he met. Then I headed for the address in the Stacks that Cursed Ethemattian had given me for his brother.

Over its hundreds of years of existence, the rulers of Agatos hadn't made a great number of sensible decisions. A few days in this chaotic mess of a city would be enough to convince anyone of that. But it just about worked in its own way, particularly if you were rich, and speaking as a chaotic mess of a human being who just about worked in his own way, I fitted in.

One of the few sensible decisions the Senate had made was to restrict the sprawl of city into the Erastes Valley. The valley was bounded by steep, almost impenetrable mountain ranges on either side, and while most of the city's goods arrived through trade, the Senate had understood the need to protect the farmland and natural resources within the valley in the case of blockade or failure of trade. It would be almost impossible to march an army into the valley. The Storm Gate that guarded the narrow northern end of the valley, where the Lidharan Highway marched higher into a narrow mountain pass, was impregnated with old, powerful magic, and if any mage did force their way through, they would find a detachment of Ash Guard waiting. The harbour had similarly potent defences, along with the city's mages and batteries of cannons facing down any fleet. But cutting the city off from trade, well, that would be significantly easier. Thus, the preservation of the farmland, quarries, and forests beyond the city limits. The northern boundary of the city was littered with the torn-down ruins of buildings whose owners had tried to extend beyond. When I needed to feel better about the city, I would go and look at those ruins and imagine the merchants and politicians who'd thought the rule didn't apply to them.

Of course, this policy also meant that those who owned land and property within the city's boundaries – many of them, by an astonishing coincidence, senators themselves – suddenly found themselves several times richer. And, again of course, the very wealthiest had their palaces and estates in the foothills at Carn's Break further up the valley, which by another equally astonishing coincidence appeared to be exempt from the rules.

Funny how things turned out.

It was this policy, though, that had led to the birth of the Stacks.

If they couldn't build into the valley, the citizens of Agatos had shown they would build just about anywhere else, over, under, in between, or up. And so the Stacks had emerged. On the eastern side of the valley, before the cliffs because impossibly sheer, beneath the ominous façade of Ceor Ebbas, houses clung to the steep slopes, piled like toy blocks almost on top of each other, so that the ground floor of one house was level with rooftop of the one below.

I had always liked the Stacks. Along with the Warrens, Dockside, and parts of the Grey City, it was where many of the immigrants to Agatos settled. Unlike the Upper City, I didn't look out of place. If it hadn't been for the precipitous streets that would fuck my bad ankle seven ways, I could happily have lived here.

The part of the Stacks that many Brythanii had made their home was at the northern end, about two thirds of the way up. I noticed that, unlike many parts of the Stacks, which had a good view of the city, the sight of the Brythanii temple in the Street of Gods was blocked here. I wondered which had come first, the settlement or the temple. Either way, their refusal to even look towards their hated god was the type of long-term grudge I could get behind.

I didn't know what kind of country the Brythanii had originally come from, only that it had been far to the south and without much sun, judging by the near-white skin and pale hair of most Brythanii. Their homes and businesses had a characteristic style, painted red and green in sharp, angular, abstract patterns, with the same patterns carved into wood and stone. I didn't know if it originated in their homeland or was something they had picked up or developed in the generations-long migration north. But I knew I was in the right place.

The family address Cursed Ethemattian had given me was a small home with a covered work-yard attached to the side. Lumber was neatly stacked, raised off the ground, and sheltered by the roof and a stone wall. From further back, I heard the gentle tap of a hammer striking something repeatedly and a murmur of voices. I let myself in and made my way around the lumber.

Two figures perched on stools at a workbench, a man of maybe forty and a girl who couldn't have been more than a year or two older than Sereh. Twelve, thirteen, perhaps. Both were working, the man carving a block of wood with hammer and chisel, the girl carefully sanding a nearly finished piece, a face with exaggerated cheekbones and forehead cut from wood. Neither of their pieces seemed particularly Brythanii in style.

"Hello!" I called as I approached.

The man's hammer stilled, and he glanced towards me. "What do you want, mage?"

The black cloak didn't seem to impress him. I supposed

when your entire culture had sworn a vendetta against your own god, a mage was pretty small time.

"Are you Retha Ethemattian?" I could see a similarity between this man and my client. He looked older, but maybe that was just the difference in lifestyle between a pampered priest and a man who worked for a living.

"Might be."

"I need to ask you some questions."

He turned back to his work and gave the chisel a gentle rap with his hammer, then pursed his lips. "If it's about how much it'll cost you to commission my services, go ahead. Otherwise, I'm busy."

I wondered if that often worked as an approach to getting customers. Basically telling them they were an inconvenience and you wished they would go away.

Is that so different to the way you run your business?

"Shut up," I muttered at my brain. Well, it would take more than some amateur-level rudeness to put me off. "It's about your brother."

"Don't know what you mean."

I was certain this was both the address and the name the priest had given me. Was he pissing me about? If so, he was going to get my toe up his arse.

"Ard Ethemattian? The priest?"

"That man's not my brother. Not anymore."

Great. A sibling grudge. But it was interesting. I was looking for people who might have reason to hate my client, and this guy wasn't showing a whole lot of love and affection.

Or was this a cultural thing I was unaware of? The

Brythanii hated their god, and they ritually murdered one of their priests each year. Perhaps disowning the priests was another way of showing their disdain.

"Why?" I asked.

The Brythanii lowered his hammer and chisel. "Who are you, mage? Why are you asking?"

A pretty fair question, all things considered. Most people just saw the cloak and started talking. This guy was going to be less helpful.

I could hardly tell him I was working for the brother he hated. "I work with the Ash Guard." If being an unpaid informant and occasional suspect counted as 'working with'.

"What's Ard done this time?"

"This time?"

He looked away. Unexpectedly, the girl spoke up. "Dad was supposed to be the priest, but Uncle Ard got in first."

Her father's hands tightened on his tools. "He knew I wanted it. He knew that had always been my ambition. But he always wanted what I wanted." He shook his head. "It's ironic. He was always better at woodworking than me. He had the hands of an artist. He should have inherited this place. He had no interest in religion. Then he realised how much power and influence a priest could have. He joined the temple a week before I had planned to. He knew I was going to, so he made sure he got there first. That was Ard every time. He's not my brother."

So, someone who wasn't afraid to clamber over others to get to the front of the queue. My client sounded like a man who would be good at making enemies.

"There can only be one priest in a family," the daughter added. "It should have been dad."

If this was true, then, honestly, my client was a bit of a wanker. He didn't deserve to die for it, though.

"We don't talk about that man anymore."

They had done a fair amount of talking about him, but who was I to complain? I had just poked the boil and watched the pus seep out. The fury this man still held for his brother was palpable. He certainly didn't lack motive. But he was a wood carver. How could he have influenced the selection of priest for this bloody ceremony?

"What are you working on?" I nodded towards the abandoned carving on the bench. Retha Ethemattian looked surprised to see it.

"It's a piece for the new Temple of Gwillan-Whose-Light-Falls-on-the-Few-Not-the-Many. The old one burned down."

"Yeah. I heard that." We didn't need to go into how it had happened. "I'd have thought you would be working on site." I had walked past the ruins a few times out of morbid curiosity. It had always been swarming with workers. If you could say something for the adherents of Gwillan-Whose-Light-Falls-on-the-Few-Not-the-Many, you could say they weren't exactly short of cash, and the merchants of the city were engaged in a self-aggrandising contest to see who could do the most and in the most public way towards the restoration of the temple. If you looked at it right, I had done everyone a favour in burning the place down.

"People don't like having a Brythanii on site. They think it might offend their gods." He turned his head and spat. "It's easier to work here and send my work to the temple."

"You do a lot of work for temples?"

He shrugged. "Enough."

"How about for the Brythanii temple?" I had been wondering how someone like him would get access to the Sanctum where the selection of victim had taken place. But if he worked there...

The man's face twisted into a sneer. "No Brythanii would honour the betrayer god by working on its temple."

Hard to argue with that, from what I had seen. "You know your brother was chosen as sacrifice for your ritual?"

Something passed across the man's features too quickly for me to identify, to be replaced again with the sneer. What was it? Guilt? Fear? Regret?

"What of it? He made his choice. No one has to volunteer."

"Have you ever wondered that if your brother hadn't taken your place, it might be you waiting to be beaten to death in four days' time?"

He snorted, but again there was that fleeting expression.

"You said only one member of each family can be a priest. When Ard is killed, maybe you'll get to be a priest after all."

I wanted to push him. I wanted to see what that emotion really was. I wanted to know if there was enough motive for him to arrange to have his own brother killed.

Maybe I pushed him too far. His hand closed around his

hammer. "That's enough, mage. The Ash Guard has no business here. There's not magic. You're not welcome."

I had stretched my luck enough. If this came to violence, Captain Gale wouldn't be sympathetic to my deception when I was inevitably arrested. I still held out a faint hope that she might one day agree to a date with me, despite all the evidence to the contrary. Anyway, Retha Ethemattian looked fairly handy with a hammer, and I would get nowhere with this job if he knocked a hole in my skull.

Frustration almost won out. I hadn't expected to solve this case here, but I'd hoped ... what? That it would be handed to me like sweetmeats at a Charo celebration? How often did that happen?

I just wanted this job to be over. Benny had handed me a chance to mend the friendship I'd broken, and this job was an obstacle. Maybe I should abandon it and return Ethemattian's payment, tell him I couldn't help him. But if I did and he died, that would be on me.

Having a conscience was a bastard.

I would wait for Kehsereen's information, then I would do my job and hope to fuck it didn't get in the way of what I had promised Benny.

Retha Ethemattian was starting to look twitchy with that hammer. Never let it be said that Mennik Thorn couldn't take a hint. I left.

CHAPTER FIVE

DESPITE THE FACT THAT MUCH OF MY JOB INVOLVED WAITING around, watching places or people, I had never been much good at waiting for things to *begin*. Restlessness built up in me like water in a blocked sewer, backing up, bubbling out, and I couldn't focus. I needed to be moving or my mind would do the moving for me, spinning and darting from one thought to another.

Not so different from Kehsereen. Maybe that was why we worked so well together.

I had arranged to meet Kehsereen at three o'clock. That left me with a couple of hours spare and nothing to do. I should be trying to find out more about Ard Ethemattian and the Brythanii religion or trying to figure out who or what would or could kill the Lady of the Grove. I could do a lot in two hours. Except I couldn't. My attention wouldn't settle.

Why didn't you arrange to meet earlier?

Because if I had, I wouldn't have gone to see Ethemattian's brother. I would have fidgeted and fretted the morning away instead.

My fucking brain.

I headed home to let the dog out before he could trash my place.

I was greeted by a torrent of barking as I unlocked the door.

That's going to encourage new clients, being met by a mad dog.

When I pushed open the door, the dog leapt on me, almost sending me staggering down the steps. I started to throw up a shield before I realised the damned thing was trying to lick me rather than tear my throat out. His tail whipped back and forth. His breath stank worse than Dumonoc's beer. I pushed him back. "What have you been eating? Wait. What *have* you been eating?"

I hurried from my office into my living quarters. My apartment wasn't enormous – just a small bedroom, a living area divided between a couple of old but comfortable chairs at one end and a kitchen at the other, and a privy with a toilet that emptied to the sewers below and a bucket for washing – and it didn't take long for me to find the source of the dog's foul breath. I kept a covered bucket in my kitchen for scraps, to empty into the waste carts a couple of times a week. I didn't cook here. There was no room for that, and I had a bad habit of poisoning people when I tried. But I often brought back food from restaurants. The bucket had been knocked on its side and the contents strewn over the floor.

"Fuck's sake!" I turned on the dog, who flattened himself on the floor. "What were you thinking? I only just fed you."

The dog's tail swept across the floor. Wet, brown eyes looked up at me.

"I don't suppose you're going to clear it up, are you?"

I fetched my brush and began to sweep the remains back into the bucket. It wasn't really the dog's fault. I had left him locked in all morning with something that smelled at least vaguely like food at his head height. I should have known better.

"You're going to have to start thinking if you're keeping this thing," I told myself. And what else was I going to do? Turn him out on the street? He'd already shown he knew where I lived, and anyway, I wasn't that much of an arsehole.

The dog's head snapped up, he gave a little yap, then he sprang to his paws and darted for the office.

"Where are you going?" Had I remembered to close the door? The dog had jumped on me and then... *Bannaur's balls!* I raced in pursuit. I shoved through the adjoining door in time to see the dog's tail disappear out the open doorway. "Get back here!"

The dog was at the end of the street as I came out my front door and was gone before I hit street level.

Pity! I stood, fists on hips, staring the way he'd gone. How about that for gratitude? I had saved the bloody creature, fed him, given him somewhere warm and dry, and the first chance he got, he was off. I should just let him go. He wasn't my responsibility.

And what would Mr. Inles think of that?

"He wouldn't think anything. He's dead."

Son of a goat!

We had played this game before, the dog and I, and I was an old hand. I had practiced this tracking spell enough that it took only a few seconds to get a fix on the dog.

He was heading towards the Warrens. He was going back to Mr. Inles's house. Swearing under my breath, I took off in pursuit, only stopping long enough to lock my door behind me, far too late.

I cut through the lower part of the Middle City, only checking my tracking spell a couple of times to confirm my assumption: the dog was indeed going home. Or what used to be his home.

By the time I was a couple of streets from Mr. Inles's house I could hear the barking. That was going to please the neighbours. The whole time Mr. Inles had employed me to recover his missing dog, the beast had never once returned home by himself.

He knows something's wrong.

Of course he did. He had come to find me. He had brought me back here, expecting me to do something to help his owner, and all I had done was lead him away again. So he'd come back once more.

"I can't perform miracles," I said under my breath.

I was sweating in my black cloak when I emerged onto Mr. Inles's street, just half a block down and on the opposite side of the road.

There was the dog – my dog, now – and the reason he was barking was plain. The door to Mr. Inles's house was open, and two men were carrying out Mr. Inles's table. A third faced off with the barking dog, club raised and ready.

I stormed towards them. "What in the Depths do you think you're doing?"

The man with the club glanced up. "Collecting taxes."

Taxes? "You don't look like you work for the Senate." I knew the moment I said it I was being naïve. They weren't that kind of tax collectors.

"We're under the Wren's protection. Keep out of this."

The other two men manhandled the table into the back of a wagon. It already held Mr. Inles's chairs, his rug, and the portrait of him and his wife.

Every thug and thief in the lower city paid a cut to the Wren to be left alone, to act with impunity. I had grown up down here. I knew the deal. It was the same deal Benny made. But Benny wouldn't be emptying a dead man's house right on the edge of the Warrens. You didn't shit on your own doorstep. But it seemed these guys did. I had met people like them before, people who preyed on their own, and now they were preying on Mr. Inles, a lonely old man who'd only had a dog for company. I wasn't putting up with that. I wasn't.

I stepped forward, summoning raw magic. "You're not under my protection."

I only intended to put on a lightshow, convince these thugs there were easier pickings elsewhere. But the man looked up again and snorted, and my dog took his chance. He lunged. The man's club came down, right for the dog's head.

I reacted before I could think. I threw force at the man. It picked him up and slammed him into the wall with a bone-cracking impact. His head snapped back. He slumped to the cobbles, limp, blood pouring from his head, arms and legs bent unnaturally.

An incoherent shout of fury came from the other men. They charged.

I was more controlled this time. I snatched away their legs. They hit the cobbles face-first. I sent hammer blows of magic onto the backs of their heads.

Controlled, not gentle.

I looked around. No more thugs. Half the passers-by had fled, the others gathering in groups to stare.

Shit.

Fury still pumped around my body. I clenched my hands into fists and forced my breath to slow.

I should not have done that. I should have found a way to resolve it peacefully. Beating the crap out of men under the Wren's protection was stupid.

They attacked my dog. They were robbing Mr. Inles.

The Wren would find out soon. Maybe I should go to him first, put my side of the story.

And it wouldn't help. The Wren wasn't the kind of man you went to for mercy. Anyway, fuck him. If there were consequences, I would deal with them. I wasn't going to go begging. This kind of shit, the impunity these thugs operated under, that was down to him. He should be apologising to everyone else. I forced back a laugh at the idea.

I was busy. I had things to do. The Wren could wait. I

crossed to the dog, who was sniffing suspiciously at the first fallen man.

"Come on, boy. We're done here."

I closed the door to Mr. Inles's house, locked it with magic, tied the string through the dog's collar, and headed out of there.

At least I had found a way to fill that spare time after all.

I HAD LESS THAN AN HOUR NOW BEFORE I WAS DUE TO MEET Kehsereen. I would be there before that, despite how long it would take me to climb the Corithian Steps with my wonky ankle. I would have time to deliver my dog back home first and take a quick look at our target. I still had no idea how we were going to rob the place without being discovered, but winging it usually worked out. Sometimes worked out.

Occasionally.

We reached my apartment at a trudge. For some reason, the dog had been able to reach Mr. Inles's house at full gallop, but when I took him anywhere, it was at a speed a hedgehog would be ashamed of.

"I think you're taking the piss," I told him the twentieth time we stopped, but he didn't answer.

I pushed open the door, and immediately the dog started growling. I surveyed the office. There was no one here, no new client waiting to complicate my life, no former client come to complain about my work. I was often hired to spy on cheating spouses – don't judge me; I wasn't the one cheating or being paranoid about a partner – and no one ever liked my answers, whether their supposedly-loved-one was innocent or guilty. Somehow it was always my fault rather than their fucked-up relationship. I still got paid either way.

But the dog was straining past the office, towards the private part of the apartment, hackles raised, a growl rumbling deep in his throat. I unfocused my eyes. My wards were still up, untouched as far as I could tell. That wasn't good news. There were people and things in this city that could walk through my wards without a trace, and I didn't want to confront any of them.

Surely it was too soon for the Wren to have learned I had attacked the men under his protection?

"The Wren doesn't come to you," I muttered. "You get taken to the Wren."

I should fuck off back out of here, take the dog with me. Go find Captain Gale. I didn't want to face whoever was in there alone.

You've dealt with gods. What's the worst that can happen?

Keeping a firm grip on the dog's collar, I drew in raw magic and passed through my wards.

My sister was sitting at my table, eyes fixed on the doorway, and she didn't look happy.

"Mica." My shoulders sagged. "You almost gave me a heart attack."

We shared a mother, but Mica and I could hardly have been more different. I was tall, often slumped and shabby, and worn. By contrast, Mica was poised, elegant, and controlled. If you hadn't known better, you would have thought her a scion of an old, wealthy Agatos family. It hadn't always been that way. As a kid, she'd been as at home in the alleys of the Warrens as I was. Tough, dirty, knees and fists often bleeding. Look at her now.

She was younger when we left. It was easier for her. She was more powerful, too. Much more powerful and much more the heir our mother had always wanted. She had shed the Warrens like a frayed shirt. I never had. I might not fit in the Warrens anymore, either, but it still had its hooks in me. I didn't belong anywhere. Mica was Upper City, through and through.

"Do you know what they're doing in the Senate right now?" she said.

I opened my mouth.

"Don't say anything sarcastic."

"I wasn't going to." I absolutely had been going to.

"They're discussing my elevation to High Mage."

Ah. I put on an innocent expression. "Shouldn't you be there?"

"Cut the shit, Nik. I know this was your doing."

I snorted. "You think the Senate listen to me? You think they even know who I am? No one listens to me."

"The Ash Guard listen to you. Gods know why, but they do, and the proposal came from the Ash Guard."

"And you think it was me?"

"I know it was. Denna's mercy, Nik. I told you I didn't want it. I told you it would make my job harder. The moment I become a high mage, everyone's eyes will turn on me. Everything Elestior and I are trying to achieve will be seen through the lens of me being High Mage. Mother might not see me as an enemy, but she'll start to see me as a rival, particularly when she realises that my aims and hers are not the same. The Senators who owe her allegiance will drop their support for us. We've worked so hard for this and you've ... you've..."

"Fucked it up? So turn them down. No one can force you to be a high mage."

Her fists clenched, and she stared up at the ceiling. "That would be worse! Powerful people respect power. If I refuse this, I'll lose their respect."

All I could think of was that little kid, determinedly chasing Benny and I around the Warrens, ready to fight anyone, dirty, determined, unafraid. And now she cared about rich people's *respect*?

"Fuck them!"

"No, fuck you, Nik. We could have made this city better for everyone. Now it's going to be ten times harder."

Maybe I *had* fucked up. Maybe I had stalled her plans. But I had still been right. "You know there's going to be a third high mage. The Ash Guard won't leave it at two. They want three. They think it places you all in an impasse, not able to move against each other."

"That's stupid."

"It's the way it is. So, if it wasn't going to be you, who would you choose? Who else would have the power to stand against Mother and the Wren *and* wouldn't use that power for their own selfish self-interest? Who would actually use the influence of a high mage to make Agatos a better place for ordinary people? Name them, and I'll go right back to the Ash Guard and tell them to choose that mage instead." I raised my eyebrows.

"You should have respected my choice, Nik. You should at least have warned me. You told me you didn't know anything about the rumours."

Yeah, I had said that. It was exactly the same thing I had done to Benny: lied and concealed to avoid an awkward explanation. It had fucked things up with Benny, too.

"I'm sorry. You're right. I should have told you."

Mica took a deep breath. Then she slammed a hand on the table hard enough to shake it. "Pity, Nik! You are a massive, massive arsehole."

Fair.

My dog let out a little growl.

"My dog doesn't like you," I said petulantly.

Mica took another deep breath, then carefully inched off her chair into a crouch, holding out the back of her hand. The dog sniffed it tentatively and wagged.

"Traitor," I muttered.

"What's his name?"

"Um..."

"You haven't named him?"

"I only just got him."

A thoughtful expression crossed my sister's face. "How about 'Giuffria'?"

"Like the Spear?" Giuffria's Spear was the wedge of cliff that jutted into the western side of the city, a barrier hiding the Warrens and parts of the Middle City from the Upper

City. In the Warrens it was known more commonly as Giuffria's Cock. "Why in the Depths would you suggest that?"

"Elestior wants to name our child Giuffria if it's a boy. I hate it. But he can't use the name if you've already used it for your dog."

"You're having a baby? You're only..." My mind went blank. In my mind, she was still a kid.

"I'm twenty-three. But no. We're not having a baby yet. One day."

"Fuck."

"Is it a deal?"

Why she couldn't just tell him she hated the name was beyond me. But I didn't really have a choice, and her weird relationship stuff was none of my business. "I'm not going around the streets shouting 'Giuffria' whenever I'm trying to get my dog back."

"You don't have to. You can say 'Fria'. His name has to be Giuffria, though."

I looked down at the hopeless mutt. *Fria*. I could live with that. It was better than 'Dog'.

"All right, High Mage. You've got a deal."

Was that a touch of a grin on her lips?

"Too soon, Nik. Way too fucking soon."

CHAPTER SIX

Coming as no surprise to anyone, I was late to meet Kehsereen.

Shit happened, and it happened to me, and it happened to me particularly when I needed to be somewhere at a specific time.

If I hadn't known Kehsereen, I would have thought he had grown impatient while waiting. He was striding back and forth under a shaded colonnade that ran alongside Agate Way, near the top of the Corithian Steps, fidgeting like he'd sat on an ants' nest. But he knew me too, and I doubted he expected me to turn up on time.

"I have made contact with my Brythanii source," he said as I hurried up, limping on my painful ankle. If I hadn't already been late, I would have rested part way up. "She has promised to provide me with details of their ceremony tomorrow afternoon."

"I didn't think the Brythanii liked to share information."

"Not all Brythanii are dedicated to their religion of hatred. Some – a few – think the obsession with an old betrayal traps them. They consider forgetting and abandoning their god would be a more suitable revenge than spending their days on bitterness."

That made sense. I felt the same way about religion. Gods didn't deserve my time. Funny how I kept getting tangled up with them.

"But she can find out what I need?"

"She is a scholar and a former priest. She will know."

So, I would just have to wait, and my client would have to wait, too. He had four days. Plenty of time.

And how often have you thought you had plenty of time but didn't?

Screw it. This matter with the Lady of the Grove was important to Benny and so it was important to me. More important than a priest of a fucked-up religion getting himself killed. Depths, no one had forced him to become a priest of the Hated God. He could step down, go to the City Watch for protection. But he wanted to hang on to the comfy life of a priest. He wanted the prize without the cost. That was on him.

Senator Greenfield's palace was situated near the top of Horn Hill, about halfway between Thousand Walls, home of the now-dead high mage Carnelian Silkstar, and the Countess's palace. Land at the top of Horn Hill was at a premium, and the definition of 'palace' was often stretched far past breaking up here. I always thought it was an interesting study in how ego and wealth balanced. How cramped and mean a 'palace' would the wealthy put up with in exchange for status and position on Horn Hill when they could instead own an actual palace elsewhere in the city? But Greenfield Palace, despite being neither green nor close to any field, was a real palace. Not quite as large as Thousand Walls or my mother's home, perhaps, but it was still an imposing building built in the Dhajawi style, with three tall stories topped with delicate, non-functional crenellations and pierced with high, onion-bulb arched windows. If it was true to the Dhajawi style, it would be built around an open, carefully cultivated courtyard with the full three stories of cloisters facing into the courtyard. Older Dhajawi palaces featured a small temple in the centre of the courtyard, but that had fallen out of fashion, and anyway, most Senators only worshipped their own pursuit of power.

"Do you have a plan?" Kehsereen asked.

"Find a way in, find the library, find the book, and get the Depths back out again."

"So, no."

I ignored the sarcasm. "There are going to be wards on the building. I'll have to examine them, see how people are entering and leaving." Of course, I should have been doing that for the last couple of hours, rather than chasing after my dog and arguing with my sister. I decided not to mention that. I nodded down the street to where the colonnade ended just opposite Greenfield Palace. "We can watch from there."

I could just make out the very corner of my blessed mother's palace further down Horn Hill, but for anyone there to see me and Kehsereen beneath the colonnade, they would have to crane their head out the last window and squint into the shadows. That was good enough for me. Or, if not good enough, then far enough away that I would be able to operate.

Kehsereen and I took up position in the shelter of the pillars and settled in to watch.

Wards were complicated magic. There was a reason trainees and acolytes spent years practicing and perfecting them. In their most basic form, wards weren't so different from curses, and even a natural, untrained mage with little power could lay a curse. But a ward like that wouldn't be much use. A true ward had to be self-sustaining, powerful, finely tuned to its purpose, and able to allow the right people to pass through. That wasn't the kind of thing you learned in a week, or even a year.

Wards came in a variety of flavours, too, from those that were simply an impenetrable barrier, through those that would give you a painful shock, all the way up to ones that would vaporise anyone who tried to force their way through. The kind of wards that my mother or the Wren or Mica used were enormously complex and powerful spells that drew on sources of intense raw magic. Mine were more the barrier-followed-by-nasty-shock-for-anyone-who-kept-pushing variety, but even so, they took hours of exhausting labour to create.

That was only the start, though. There were probably cases where an impenetrable barrier that no one needed to pass through was a requirement, but for most wards, the ability for the mage to choose who could and couldn't move through them without being turned into a fine mist of blood and bone was kind of important. That meant the ward had to be designed in such a way as to recognise individuals with absolute reliability. A ninety percent success rate wouldn't get you many repeat contracts and would make coming and going from your own home more exciting than most people would be happy with.

There were a bunch of different ways a ward could recognise an individual. The most reliable and secure was to have the magic tuned to the unique magical pattern of an individual. All living things held at least a trace of magic, and their natural state was unique. Tuning the wards to that pattern was beyond most mages. It was, however, something I could do. I wasn't a powerful mage by any standards, but I had compensated with fine control. My wards recognised me and now Fria. Anyone else would come up hard against them. The downside was that most mages in the city could just punch through my puny wards, and the most powerful, as my little sister had just proved again, could walk right through without even disturbing them.

If you couldn't manage detecting individuals' magical patterns, you weren't completely out of luck. Another common technique was for the controlling mage to lay a magical structure – a specific curse in all but name – on anyone who needed to get through the wards, which would be recognised by the wards. This was common, but it was vulnerable. A good enough mage would be able to see that magical structure and duplicate it, making the ward essentially useless. I was hoping this was what Greenfield's mage had chosen, because I reckoned I could make a good enough copy to get us through.

Finally, if a mage wasn't always available to approve every guest or visitor, they could enchant objects to act as keys. An item of jewellery was common. The owner of the home or business could hand them to anyone they wanted to let in. There was a vulnerability in that, too: if you could get hold of one of those keys, you would be essentially invisible to the wards.

The Greenfield palace wasn't busy, but nonetheless, every few minutes a clerk, servant, or tradesperson would enter or leave. The senator undoubtedly had offices lower in the city where most of his business was carried out, and probably an office in the Senate itself, but when you were rich enough, apparently, there was always something going on around you. Lucky I was so poor. It would have bugged the fuck out of me.

I watched with unfocused eyes to see the visitors and staff pass through Greenfield's wards. It wasn't as easy as it sounded. The foyer and front offices were unwarded, and most of those going in and out didn't go anywhere near the wards. But occasionally, someone would pass into or out of the main palace. I watched intently, my head aching and my eyes throbbing from staying unfocused.

"It's a little hard to tell from here," I said to Kehsereen after watching the third person walk through the wards unharmed, "but I think the mage has marked them magically to allow them passage."

"You can replicate that?"

I sucked my teeth, like a landlord renegotiating my rent. "I need to be closer. If I get the pattern of the spell even slightly wrong, we'd be lucky to walk out with all our limbs intact."

Benny would have made a sarcastic remark, but Kehsereen took everything in his stride, always. I didn't know if he was genuinely that sanguine about the possibility of horrible death or was just good at hiding it. "How long and how close?"

"Very close, and at least twenty seconds. Longer would be better."

"Let me know when you see someone."

We waited another ten minutes before I saw a clerk emerge through the wards and hurry onto the street, leather folder clasped in one hand, turning up Agate Way towards the Senate building. "That one."

"Follow me, then."

We trailed the clerk under the shadow of the colonnade until we were away from the palace. It occurred to me that I should have asked Kehsereen his plan. From my experience, he wasn't generally a violent man, but I couldn't forget that we'd first met when he'd drugged me with his *ulu-aru*, tied me up, and dumped me in an alley.

He was stressed. He thought you were involved in the disappearance of his nephew.

I just hoped he didn't have anything similar planned for this clerk. The man hadn't done anything wrong.

"Excuse me!" Kehsereen called to the clerk. "Hello!"

The man turned, frowning. He was short, not much taller than Kehsereen, and dressed in the muddy green and brown Greenfield uniform.

"Me?"

"Yes." Kehsereen drew closer. I followed, trying to make it look like I was just wandering up the street, nothing to do with any of this. "Did you drop this?" He held up a coin. Gold glinted in his hand. A crown. A *god* we called them in the Warrens, because they were about as rare as a god manifesting itself in those tight alleys. The clerk's hand moved towards his waist then froze. Smart move. Every pickpocket knew that trick; make a mark reach for their money to protect it. Then they would know where to target.

The man seemed torn between honesty and the lure of Kehsereen's coin. A god was a lot more than a clerk was paid.

Focus! Or unfocus, more to the point. I was supposed to be examining the spell, not admiring Kehsereen's dirty tricks.

The spell was placed on the clerk's chest, just behind the Greenfield badge. To my magically-sensitive vision, the spell appeared as an intricate knot pattern of yellow, purple, and violet – almost as unappealing as the colours of his uniform – folded over and under itself. I licked my lips. This wasn't going to be easy. But shaping magic was what mages trained to do, over and over again, until our brains wanted to explode. I had been good at it. Not powerful, but good.

My staring must have got the clerk's attention, because he took a step back. Kehsereen interrupted his vision with the coin.

I pulled in raw magic and shaped it. Thin, woven threads.

The Song of a Nightingale in the First Light of the Morning, my tutors had named this technique, which was not only pretentious but also wholly unhelpful, as this had nothing in common with the song of a nightingale, in the morning or otherwise. Maybe to mages who heard magic as music it made more sense.

"If you didn't..." Kehsereen let the sentence trail off and his hand fall back.

"Yes! Yes, I think I must!" The clerk wouldn't have fooled a new-born baby with that lie.

I let the spell I had created hover over the man's chest to compare. No. Not exactly right. I pulled at the threads, rearranging them. Still not good enough. I let it go.

Try again.

"You see, I wasn't sure it was you," Kehsereen continued, waving the coin just out of the man's reach. "It could have been someone else." By now the clerk's eyes were so fixed on the coin, he wouldn't have noticed if I'd taken my clothes off and danced naked in front of him.

"No. No, it was me. I think I heard it fall." He made a lunge for the coin, but Kehsereen didn't release it.

I tried the spell again. Closer. Very close. But not perfect. I fixed the image of the pattern I needed into my head and tweaked the magic.

"A whole crown? It seems a lot to lose."

I heard the frustration in the clerk's voice. "Yes. It is. So, if you please?"

Kehsereen released the coin. The man snatched it away

and shoved it into a pocket tied into his trousers. "Thank you. Now—"

Kehsereen grabbed the man's hand and shook it, pulling him in as though for a hug.

There! I had it. I moved the spell onto Kehsereen and settled it there. I really hoped this was perfect, because we were out of time.

The man jerked away. "Thank you, as I said. But I am very busy..." He tore his hand free and hurried away up the street. We watched him go.

"That's a lot of money to waste," I said. "I'll try to pay you back, but it'll take—"

Kehsereen lifted his hand, the coin clasped between his fingers again. "I wasn't going to let him keep it. I'm not quite as rich as you think I am."

"Impressive," I muttered. I resisted the urge to check my own coins. "Now, stand still."

I replicated the spell and attached it to myself. I fancied I could feel the scratch of the magic against my skin, but there was nothing in the spell that could have caused sensation. "Now." I turned back to look at Greenfield's palace. "How do we get in without anyone noticing?"

The Greenfield palace occupied its own block, separated from a lesser palace above it on the Hill and a grand apartment building below by narrow streets. A few windows looked onto the streets – or would have if they hadn't been shuttered – but the wards pressed right up to the skin of the building. No burglars would find a way in here – unless they had been clever enough to give themselves a pass through the wards. I resisted the urge to dust my fingers on my lapel. I would allow myself to be smug after this actually worked.

"The library is in the corner at the back, on the left," Kehsereen said. "Third floor."

"How do you know that?"

"Someone has to design buildings like this, which means there have to be plans. If you know where to look for them..."

Yeah, all right. Now he was the one being smug. Still, it would save a lot of sneaking around. "That's why I like working with you," I told Kehsereen.

"I thought it was because you didn't have any other friends."

He had meant that as a joke, but ouch. It hit harder than it should. I found a smile. "Let's just do this."

"Second floor window." Kehsereen pointed. "It opens onto a stairwell that will take us straight up to the library."

"I hope you're good at climbing, then."

With a last glance around, I headed out from the cover of the colonnade, across Agate Way, and into the narrow street beside the Greenfield palace. The buzz of the wards in the nearby walls made my skin tingle. Careless construction or a warning? It didn't make much difference. We would have to go through anyway.

We stopped beneath the window. It would be a bit of a scramble up, but there were plenty of handholds. I unfocused my vision again and examined the window. The wards hung heavy on it, but I couldn't see any other barrier. Not a mage lock or a secondary ward. Lazy? Arrogant? My magic found a latch on the inside, but it was easy enough to slide up and open with just a twitch of the spell.

"Want to go first?" I asked.

"This seems more like a job for a mage."

Well, it was my spell that would let us through. Or not. Kehsereen had done his part.

We were still in view of Agate Way here, and although the side street dead-ended at a low wall on the cliff edge only twenty or thirty yards further on, it also branched off between the smaller palace on our left and another building. All it would take would be for one of the passers-by to twist their head or turn down here, and they would see us breaking in. And then what? In the lower city, you would mind your own business if you knew what was good for you. But this was Horn Hill. The crimes that got ignored here and in the Upper City were of an entirely different scale to petty burglary. Steal a silver shield – or a book – and they would have the Watch on your back before you could blink. Steal ten thousand gold crowns through clever accounting and cheating people out of their wages, and they would applaud you in the Senate.

What are you going to do? Go home? We had come too far for that, and I had promised Benny. I reached for a gap between the stones and hauled myself up.

Too many people were too impressed by magic. Mages were to blame for that. When your personal wealth relied on convincing people that your magic was both terrifyingly potent and infallible, you could spout a whole load of unsubstantiated shit. I was as guilty of that as anyone. I often relied on the reputation of mages to bully or threaten my way through situations I wouldn't have otherwise survived. Greenfield's mage was clearly no different, and Greenfield put too much faith in his wards. The wall was easy to scale. The gaps between the mortared blocks were perfectly sized for fingers and toes. He couldn't have made it easier if he'd nailed a ladder to the wall. It only took seconds to scramble up, pull open the shutters, push open the windows beyond, and slip through the wards.

The sensation of magic made my skin tighten, but my spell did its job. The wards recognised me and let me through.

I landed in a marble hallway, near the foot of a set of stairs. A white marble screen, perforated with elaborate, curling patters, allowed glimpses of a room beyond, itself open to the daylight from the palace's interior courtyard. Pot palms, ferns, a couple of large, elaborate vases, and red-and-gold drapes dominated the room, but as far as I could tell, it was unoccupied. Still, I was exposed out here in the corridor if anyone should come by.

I leaned out the window to offer Kehsereen a hand, but he was already up, and he swung in easily. I pulled the shutters closed behind us and gently shut the windows. Kehsereen gestured to the stairs, and we made our way up.

We stopped at a pair of double doors ten feet beyond the top of the stairs.

"This is it," Kehsereen said in a low voice.

I examined the doors. No more wards on them – overconfidence, again – but there was something magical beyond. A spell with a purpose I couldn't discern from here. I unlocked the doors with my own spell, then drew in raw magic and formed a shield in front of us. I wasn't being caught by a booby trap again. "Stay behind me," I said, then pushed the doors open.

Whatever this room was, it wasn't a library. There were no books, for a start, and no shelves, although I could see marks on the wall where they had once been attached.

Instead, four pillars made of some kind of dark, reddish wood – mahogany, perhaps – stood in the four corners of the room, and on a pedestal in the centre sat an enormous emerald. I wouldn't claim to be an expert on giant gems, but I reckoned this one must cost almost as much as the whole Cepra-damned palace. A spell was woven through the four pillars. In my magical vision, blue and purple strands began at the pillars and spiralled in towards the emerald. At first, I wondered if this was the power source for the palace's wards, but there didn't seem to be any connection between this and the wards.

If anything, the magic looked like some kind of trap. I had a heart-fully-jammed-in-the-throat moment when I wondered if we'd got ourselves caught. But the magic was ignoring us. Figuring out what a spell did just by examining it was always a tricky task, particularly when it was something as unusual as this. If I were forced at knife point to guess, I would say this was designed to trap magic of some type and funnel it to the emerald. But it wasn't affecting my shield spell nor was it gathering raw magic the way I had managed with my stolen opal a couple of months back.

The closest similarity I could think of was the spell the Cult of Sharshak had been trying to perform beneath the shoemaker's shop when Kehsereen and I had followed their priest there.

What in the Depths is everyone up to in this city? Could Greenfield have a connection to the cult? It didn't seem likely. *Unless that's the real reason Kehsereen brought you here.* I dismissed the thought. Anyway, they were going about the spell in completely different ways.

What are you trying to trap? If something was going on in Agatos, no one had told me.

"Which is what happens when you don't talk to anyone," I muttered under my breath. Maybe Mica could tell me, but then I would have to explain what I had been doing here, and she thought little enough of me already.

"He has moved his library," Kehsereen said.

"You don't say." The question was, to where? Our luck wouldn't hold out if we had to search the whole palace.

Kehsereen was ahead of me. He drew out a sheaf of papers and laid them on the floor. They were plans of the palace, each sheet showing one of the floors. There was a basement, too, by the looks of it.

"We're here," Kehsereen said, pointing to one corner of the topmost sheet. "If we assume that he moved the library because he wanted more space and that he would not choose to move it further than necessary, that leaves us with a couple of options." He moved to the second sheet. "The room below us would have space, and it is just marked as offices. Easy to move. Or the corner on the opposite side of this level." He returned to the first sheet.

"This level," I said. "If he moved because he needed more space, that room's twice the size, and it's the private part of the palace." There were no offices, meeting or reception rooms, large dining rooms or other places to entertain marked up here, and the hallway outside this room had been empty. It would catch the cool breeze in summer, too.

I wasn't as confident as I sounded. Maybe there was something about this particular corner that he liked, and the room below might scratch the same itch. But we had to choose one, and if the room below really was an office, I didn't want to walk in there in full view of his clerks.

I sent tendrils of magic into the hallway and nearby rooms to make sure no one was around, then beckoned Kehsereen to follow. In theory, a mage should be able to sense the traces of magic in living things, including people. But in reality, they were faint and easily obscured by background raw magic or nearby spells, and I was more likely to see someone coming before I detected their inherent magic. Other than telling whether a body was alive or dead, the ability had little practical purpose. The spell I had employed was designed to actively seek out life magic, and it was pretty effective. There was no one close to us or to the room we were heading for, on this floor at least. The downside of the spell was that it would be a beacon to any mage nearby, and any competent mage would be able to block it. I hoped my assumption that Greenfield's mage had accompanied his boss to the Senate was accurate.

The double doors were again locked but not warded, and when I pushed them open, the library waited within. "Told you," I said, holding the door for Kehsereen. It was always satisfying when a random guess turned out to be right. All the credit with none of the actual work.

The room was large – forty feet by sixty, I guessed – and lined with tall bookcases. Freestanding sets of shelves taller than me divided the room into smaller spaces, several with desks and chairs occupying the area between. Morgue-lamps cast light over the wooden shelves and thick rugs. In the sickly green glow, I couldn't tell what colour the rugs were supposed to be, nor, in fact, whether someone had vomited all over them. Taste and wealth rarely went together.

A large window on the far side of the room was shuttered against daylight. To protect the books, I supposed. And there were a lot of books. Thousands, if I had to guess, most of them bound in green or red leather. Hopefully, Kehsereen could figure out how Greenfield's system worked, because I didn't fancy searching through every one.

I unfocused my eyes.

There was magic everywhere. It lay over the bookshelves like a net wrapped tight around them, a hook buried in each book.

"Don't touch anything!" I warned. I peered closer. I wasn't sure exactly what this spell did. Maybe it was just a filing system to make sure books ended up back in the right place. Or maybe it was an alarm. Or a trigger for a booby trap that would smear the pair of us across the opposite wall. Whichever, I would have to unhook the magic from the book we wanted.

"See if you can find it," I said, "but don't try to pick it up."

The hook would be easy to release, but what would happen to the magical net if it was? Would the whole thing unravel like a knitted blanket with a cut strand?

Kehsereen's voice came from the far end of the shelves. "He has Parsimon's *Malachite*."

"Oh, I'm sorry. Is there a cure?"

Kehsereen shot me a disgusted glance. I tried not to chuckle.

"It is a book. It's said to be the foundational text of Dhajawi magic."

"Never heard of it."

"That's because the tradition was dismissed centuries ago. Supposedly, it simply didn't work."

"Yeah, I can see why that would be a problem." I returned to studying the spell.

I couldn't imagine that Greenfield had his mage present every time he took a book off the shelves, so there must be some flexibility here. But there also had to be some purpose to it. Greenfield's collection was valuable, supposedly, and this had to be some kind of security. Who against? Servants and staff? Not a mage. If you thought a mage was coming for your shit, you put in a lot more security. Mage locks on the doors, for a start, and wards that couldn't be penetrated by someone who chatted to one of your clerks for half a minute.

So, pick up a book and place it on a desk, and the chances

were nothing would happen. Take it out of the library or the palace, and that would set off some reaction.

Unhooking the book wouldn't be enough. I would have to repair the net so the absence wasn't obvious. There were a fuck of a lot of books here. He might not notice one had gone for years. Altering the net couldn't be too hard, because Greenfield must get plenty of new books from the size of the collection, and maybe even get rid of some. They wouldn't rebuild the spell each time.

"It's here," Kehsereen called. He was out of sight on the far side of the library. I hurried over.

The volume we were after, *The Silver Oak,* was less imposing than I had imagined. It was slim, two hundred pages, no more, and had clearly been re-bound in a new, green leather cover. The title was picked out in small, golden letters. Finding this on my own would have taken hours. Grudgingly, I admitted that Kehsereen had been right that he should accompany me. Of course, I only admitted that to myself. Kehsereen was smug enough as it was.

I pulled in raw magic, readying for a reaction. "Very carefully, I want you to remove the book from the shelf."

Moistening my lips with my tongue, I watched Kehsereen slide the book free. The net of magic stretched, as I had expected, hook still in the book.

"All right. Stop there."

Kehsereen froze, book held a foot from the shelf. I took the chance to examine the spell more closely. There had been no reaction to moving the book. No pulse of magic, no trap or alarm triggered. The spell had merely stretched. Now, what would happen if the hook came free?

"Only one way to find out," I muttered.

Kehsereen, whose hearing was annoyingly good, said, "That is so reassuring."

I waved a dismissive hand. There was nothing particularly complicated about the net. The thread of magic was one of the Hundred Key Forms of magic – of which there had been a hundred and forty-seven last time I had bothered to check. The hook was another of them. Even a trainee mage would be expected to come up with these at will. What they connected back to, I couldn't tell from here, but it didn't much matter if I never triggered it.

I formed a thread of my own and wove it into the net, bypassing the book, then used a simple blade of magic to cut away the hook. Released from the net, the hook dissipated, and the net rebounded. The thread I had added took the slack, and the net resettled over the bookcase. A couple of quick adjustments, and there was no sign a book had ever been there.

I grinned with relief. "We're done. We—"

My words were cut off by the sound of the library door opening. I just had time to drag Kehsereen out of sight behind a freestanding bookcase before two men strode in. I watched them through a gap between books and shelf. One wore a blue robe trimmed with angular gold stitching. A white sash with the words, *I am Agatos*, embroidered onto it crossed his chest. That must be Senator Greenfield. The other man wore the very familiar black cloak of a mage.

Bannaur's balls! We'd taken too long, or the Senate had finished early for the day. Either way, we were fucked.

The mage held up a hand. "There's been magic here."

Spells left traces, even the best constructed ones. All evidence of mine would have faded within minutes, but we hadn't been given minutes.

The mage reached out with tendrils of magic, searching for us. It was the same spell I had used earlier. I watched the tendrils reach towards us, then gently diverted them, using as little power as I could. Again, I thanked my own impotence as a mage that had forced me to learn fine control and how to work with very small amounts of magic. Unless this mage was far more adept than most, he wouldn't notice my interference.

But this wouldn't help for long. All they would have to do was round the shelves and they would see us crouching here like rock squirrels startled by a cat. I couldn't turn us invisible nor influence them to turn away. We needed a diversion.

My go-to diversion was my *fucksthat* spell, so-named because everyone's first reaction to it was to say, "What the fuck's that?" But I had used it too often, and people were starting to associate it with me. No point leaving a calling card.

We needed something, though. A modification to the spell. Sound only. Something loud, destructive. Get rid of the lights, the fake wind, the illusion of a demon clawing its way out of the ground. Just noise.

Painfully slowly, I drew in raw magic. Any capable mage would notice a significant flow of power. Even the amount the other mage was using for his simple spell was easy to see. At best, I could pull in a trickle, making it seem like the natural flow and eddy of background power.

The mage let his spell fall. "There's no one here. But there was. We should check for anything missing."

Greenfield's reply was too faint for me to hear, but the mage nodded, and Greenfield headed back out the doors.

I still didn't have enough magic. This was like trying to fill a bath with a teaspoon.

I held a finger to my lips, then beckoned to Kehsereen to follow me. As the mage strode further into the library, we retreated in the opposite direction, while I continued to build up my reservoir.

Perhaps we could slip through the doors when he was out of sight.

The sounds of voices from the hallway put an end to that plan. Greenfield had gone for back-up.

Come on. I was almost there. A few more seconds.

My foot caught on something. It tumbled across the floor and clattered into a bookcase. The mage spun, sucking in power of his own, and I cast my spell.

From the first room we had investigated came an inhuman scream and the sound of an explosion, then panicked shrieks. Whoever was in the hallway did me a favour by adding their own curses in response. The mage hesitated for a second, then took off towards the screams.

There was no illusion to accompany the sounds. The moment the mage reached it, he would see it for what it was.

I grabbed Kehsereen by the arm and tugged him further into the library.

"The door..." he started.

"They'll see us."

At the back of the library, I wrenched open the window, then booted the shutters wide, and peered out.

The back of the palace reached right to the edge of Horn Hill. This far up the hill, the slopes were nearly sheer, falling a hundred and fifty feet before meeting the next set of roofs, then a hundred more to the Middle City below. From where we were, I could see the Agatos Museum, Giuffria's Spear with the Ash Guard fortress as its base, and the Fields of the Dead further north.

"Jump," I said.

"What?"

"Jump. I'll cushion our fall." I had done that plenty of times before, although admittedly not from this height. I couldn't fly, but I could fall less painfully.

Kehsereen took hold of my arm, and we climbed out onto the window ledge. I released the distraction spell – no point wasting power – and together we stepped off. I just had long enough to feel touched at Kehsereen's faith in me before I needed all my concentration to stop us plummeting to our deaths.

We drifted down towards the roofs below. Well, drifted might have been too kind a way of putting it; a controlled fall, more fairly. I was starting to feel rather pleased with myself when a shout of fury came from above. I glanced up to see Greenfield's mage leaning from the library window far above and cursing down at us. I had my hood up, and I hoped we were far enough away that we weren't recognisable, so I risked a little wave.

Mistake.

The mage launched a stream of fire at us.

I shouted, "Fuck," then threw up a shield. The fire blasted off it, but I didn't have the power to maintain both spells. We fell, out of control.

We were only ten feet above the roofs, but ten feet is a long way to fall when you're not expecting it. We hit the tiles with an impact that made my breath explode, rolled, and tumbled over the edge. I managed to get the shield under us, but it wasn't enough. We slammed into cobblestones. I felt something snap in my left wrist and shouted in pain. Kehsereen's face smacked into stone. He came up, blood pouring from his nose and mouth.

"You call this cushioning our fall?" he demanded through bubbles of blood. But at least he was standing, if shakily. I didn't reply.

Together, we stumbled along the steep street heading down to the Middle City. Waves of pain throbbed through my broken wrist with every jarring step I took. My heart thumped double time. Sweat stuck my shirt to my back. I wanted to throw up.

That had not – *not* – gone according to plan.

I had the book, but Greenfield's mage had seen us. Whether or not he'd got a good enough look to identify me, he would start asking questions. People talked in this city, at least if money was on offer, and Greenfield had money. There weren't that many mages in the city.

Nothing you can do about that. I couldn't hide, and I couldn't use my mother's reputation as a shield – she had made that clear many times before. *So, keep going.* I had something to bargain with now. I could go to Scholar Longstream, get the information I needed, find out who might have killed the Lady of the Grove, or at least who knew how to do it.

It would be worth it, I told myself. For my friendship with Benny, for the Warrens, for the whole city. I tried not to notice the blackened cloth down my left leg where my shield had failed to protect me completely from the mage's fire.

Depths, maybe even Kehsereen would forgive me his bloodied face when I finally told him the truth of what was going on.

CHAPTER SEVEN

We parted when we reached the base of Horn Hill, Kehsereen heading for his luxurious Middle City apartment, while I trudged towards my home near Dockside, stolen book tucked under my cloak. Kehsereen complained surprisingly little about his bloody face-plant. Maybe it hurt to speak. I held my injured wrist as still as possible against my side. It wasn't a bad break. A good night's sleep would heal it. Until then, a sling or splint might help. If I had any idea how to make such a thing.

I decided to swing by my friend Holera's restaurant. She and her wife had patched me up more than once, and unlike her wife, Elosyn, she wouldn't give me an earful about it first.

The restaurant was already open when I got there, but it was early enough not to be busy. I made my way around the side and let myself into the kitchen.

The kitchen was already hot and steamy, the air filled

with the smell of frying herbs, spices, meat, and stock. My mouth watered the moment I stepped in. I had left it too long between meals.

"Well," Holera said, as I closed the door behind me, "I haven't seen you for a while. I thought you'd gone off my cooking."

"Too busy." The truth was, Holera's prices were too high for me, and while she and Elosyn were both willing to feed me for free, I didn't like taking advantage. Well, unless I really had to. I had done a job for them once – a curse-breaking – but it had been easy, and they had paid me off a long time ago. I glanced around. "What would you feed a dog?"

"Oh, that's lovely." She dried her hands on her apron and made her way over to me. "He doesn't come here to eat, then he suggests my cooking is only suitable for dogs."

"I inherited a dog. I've no idea what to feed it. It's costing me a fortune." I couldn't believe every dog in Agatos lived the way Fria had this last day and a half.

"Who in their right mind would leave you a dog?"

"I don't think he intended to die."

"Just ask for ends at a butcher's. They should be able to sell you some cheap. You're not trying to hand off the dog, are you? I'm far too busy."

"Nah. I think I'm keeping him. We're starting to understand one another."

"Good." She glanced back at her cooking food, then moved to scatter some more herbs in a pot. "So, what do you want? I've got some soup that's ready."

Why did everyone think I was after charity? Just because, admittedly, I often was. Right now, I was fine for money, and my business was stable. Priests could afford to pay.

"I think I might have broken my wrist."

"Depths, Nik. Why is it that other mages never end up like this?"

All right, I had been wrong that I wouldn't get an earful from her. "They don't have my charisma."

She didn't look impressed. "Let's take a look." She gently pushed up my sleeve and winced. The flesh around my wrist was dark purple-red and swollen. "That looks nasty."

I shrugged with the other arm. "I've had worse. It'll be fine tomorrow."

"Just because you can heal quickly doesn't mean you have to get injured." She drew a bandage out of a drawer along with a flat piece of wood and proceeded to splint the wrist. I won't say it didn't hurt, but I remained stoic. I hardly winced and cursed at all during the whole procedure.

When it was done, Holera said, "I'll wrap some bones for your dog. And now you owe me. Come around to our house tomorrow evening. Elosyn and I are both free. She's going to be pissed off you haven't visited for so long. I want to be there to see it."

The sky above Agatos was darkening and the streets had sunk into shadow, not helped by the thick clouds slung overhead, by the time I arrived home. For once, there were no clients waiting impatiently for me to return. I fumbled my door open, book and wrapped bones jammed awkwardly under my bad arm.

"Fria!" I called. "I've got dinner." For him, not me, but I was too tired to go out again.

I was expecting a clatter of paws or a storm of barking, but there was nothing. Maybe Fria was sulking after being left all afternoon. I didn't think Mr. Inles had left him often. I locked the book in my safe, raised the wards on it, then headed into my apartment from the office.

"Fria?"

Still nothing. I checked all the rooms. *Pity!* Where was the blasted creature? I checked under my bed, and when I still couldn't find him, I checked my back courtyard, but he wasn't there either.

He had got out again. I checked my windows and found one ajar. Surely he couldn't have squeezed out there? But my wards were still intact. No one had broken in. *Unless they were a powerful mage.* I couldn't imagine the Wren being reduced to dog-napping, and I had already tried to palm Fria off on my sister without any luck. *Maybe I need a ward against dogs.*

When Mr. Inles had constantly lost his dog, I'd thought he was doing it on purpose so he had the excuse to seek out company, but the damned thing was slipperier than an eel in a vat of oil.

I left the bones in the kitchen-corner of the apartment, then cast the tracking spell I had long ago perfected to find Fria. I wasn't at all surprised to see that it pointed back towards the Warrens and Mr. Inles's house.

"Ah, fuck," I muttered. The poor old thing still didn't get it.

So much for resting. I wrapped my cloak back around me and headed out again, my wrist still throbbing like a hammer blow.

The Warrens and the area around it were rarely quiet, even at night. Even so, there was something off when I arrived. People were hurrying, heads down, yes, but there was an edge to it, a tension, as though being here was a bad idea. Maybe it was what I had done earlier when I had found those thugs robbing Mr. Inles's house. Maybe the Wren had sent his enforcers out to find who was responsible and introduce them – me – to the blunt end of a cudgel or the sharp end of a knife, reinforce that his bought protection wasn't something so easily scorned. Fuck it. Let them come. I had done what I had to.

The door to Mr. Inles's house was ajar. I had locked it with a spell, but I hadn't put up wards. Someone with a key or just a set of lockpicks had come back. I didn't bother knocking. Mr. Inles lived alone, so any answer I got would either be an intruder or his reanimated corpse, and in neither case did I want to give warning.

The house was stripped bare.

Every picture, every piece of furniture, every household item, his clothes, his memories, his life: gone. Those bastards I had chased off had come back, or maybe another gang of thieves had taken their chance. They had desecrated his home. Magic built up in me, and the almost uncontrollable urge to hunt the Cepra-damned fuckers down made me twitch.

But what would be the point? If it hadn't been them, it

would have been someone else. Or the city would have claimed it all as funeral expenses, even though the funeral they would give him tomorrow would be cheap and perfunctory and all the rest would go to swell the pockets of some clerk or politician. That's all you were in this city if you were poor, if you were from the Warrens: a body dumped in a hole and profit for whoever had bribed their way into the right bureaucratic position. The rage threatened to overwhelm me. My fists clenched, despite my broken wrist.

Why are you so angry?

"Because he deserved better."

No. That wasn't it. He did deserve better, but so many people in this part of the city deserved better, and that wasn't why it had hit me so hard.

Because it's going to be your fate, too. Dead, forgotten, no one to mourn, no mark left behind. A life wasted.

"You've always known that," I said out loud. "Why is it bothering you now?"

Maybe it was the pain in my wrist. Maybe Mr. Inles's lonely death had scraped the scab off a wound. Maybe something else entirely. I had felt ... antsy these last few days. Uneasy.

"Fria?" I called. "Where are you, boy?"

I thought I heard something move in the room above. I headed for the steep steps and up.

Fria was lying where Mr. Inles's bed used to be, flattened on the floor, head on paws. They had even taken the waste bucket, but not before emptying it on the floor. The stink here choked my throat.

"Hey boy," I said, crouching in front of Fria.

His eyes turned up to me, showing crescents of white. His tail gave a single, desolate thump on the floor.

"He's gone," I said. "He can't come back. We'll say goodbye to him tomorrow. Make it official, eh? A good howl at the shaft when they lower him in, you and me. Howl the city down." I didn't know why I was saying that to the dog. But he was listening, I could tell. "Come on. Let's go back home. I've got you dinner."

I reached out a hand, and he licked it, once. Then he clambered to his paws and followed me down. I hadn't remembered his leash, but he showed no signs of running off. His ears drooped.

When I stepped outside, a woman was waiting, fists on hips.

"Who the Depths are you?" Her accent was pure Warrens.

Despite my mage's cloak, she didn't seem intimidated. I had been chased down enough alleys by women like this as a kid that I had to force myself not to take a step backwards. "I'm a friend of Mr. Inles."

Her expression didn't change. "You don't look like a friend."

Nice. Although she wouldn't be the first one to point out my apparent unfriendly demeanour. "So, what do his friends look like?"

"He didn't have any friends."

No. I didn't think he had. "He had me." In a way. Eventually, I had stopped charging him for finding his dog, anyway.

"This ain't a time for strangers here."

I glanced over her shoulder. Most of the people on the street were hurrying past, but a few were hanging back in the shadows, watching. I could feel the animosity and threat. "I'm from here. I'm not a stranger."

She looked me up and down. "Yeah, you are. Take my advice." She leaned in. "Stay away. Thing are going to get bad, and people like you, you're going to make it worse. Don't pretend you can't feel it. If you're really from here, you can."

I could. I could feel the tension, the anger, the suspicion seeping like sewage through the Warrens and spilling out to these neighbouring streets, and I reckoned I knew why, even if they didn't. The Lady of the Grove was dead, and they could sense it. They could sense that hope was gone.

I kept my magic ready all the way back home. Benny was right. We had to find out who had killed the god, and we didn't have long. The Warrens was ready to erupt.

SLEEP HEALED MY WRIST – ENOUGH THAT I ONLY FELT A DULL ache, anyway – but left me exhausted. Mages, even untrained, natural mages, used raw magic to heal while we slept. It didn't take any conscious effort, and I wasn't sure I could prevent it if I wanted to, but it took a lot out of my body. I woke to late-summer sunlight and a cold dog's nose nuzzling in my ear.

"Come *on*," I muttered, trying to pull my blanket back over me. Fria pawed it away.

Fuck's sake. I levered myself up. I felt hungover, and I hadn't even had a drink. My mouth was sticky. I flexed my wrist. Just a twinge. Good enough to remove the splint.

"I suppose you want breakfast."

Fria's tail thumped.

"All right, all right." I swung my legs out of bed and went looking for clean clothes. I was hungry, too. Sustaining myself through raw magic didn't fill the stomach like a good plate of breakfast and a mug of spiced coffee.

I looped Fria's leash through his collar, then we headed down to my regular coffee house. When I had eaten, when I was ready, I would go to the university and confront Scholar Longstream. But not before a lot of coffee.

The coffee house was clean and light, even though the frontage that had stood open all summer had been closed against the wind and cooler days. Blue and white tiles covered the walls, the floor boasted a mosaic showing a scene of the harbour – omitting the filth of the docks and the sewage-soiled water – and several potted trees brought life to the room. Light still streamed in through wide windows.

Ileoni Silver, my favourite waitress, was serving a couple of elderly men I often saw here, and I found myself smiling when she waved a greeting. Somehow, just seeing her made me feel better. Other than clients, suspects, witnesses, and people who were generally fed up with my shit, I didn't talk to a lot of people, and even fewer of them were ever pleased to see me. She was one of the few people I considered a friend just as a friend, not out of duty or history or professional need. Sometimes, finding someone who had no connection to the rest of your life, its complications and traumas, was a relief.

I settled at my usual table under one of the trees and waited for her to become free.

A few minutes later, she brought over my breakfast and coffee and slid into the other chair. She looked tired, although probably not as tired as me. We were similar ages, but I always managed to look a good five years older and twice as exhausted. It was my healthy, stress-free lifestyle that did it.

"You got a dog?"

"Yeah. His owner died. He used to be a client." I shrugged. "His name's Fria. The dog, not the dead owner."

"I assumed." She reached down and offered her hand to Fria. He sniffed it, then pushed his head against her hand. She ruffled behind his ears. "He's lovely."

"That's one way of putting it." Smelly and in need of a bath was another, but that could apply to me as well.

For a few seconds there was an awkward silence. I wasn't used to that with Ileoni. Talking to her was usually easy, but today she seemed nervous, glancing around the coffee house.

"Is something wrong?"

"No." She settled herself with an effort. "Maybe. I don't know." Her hands tightened on her gown. "I really didn't want to ask, but I think I might need your help."

"What's happened? Is someone causing trouble?" I wasn't normally the protective type, but I felt a brief, unaccountable burst of rage at the idea that someone might be threatening her.

It's the Lady of the Grove. With the god gone, everything was thrown out. Like we were in a deep pond, and someone had leaned in to stir up the mud with a stick. *Or pulled something out. Uprooted it.* I wasn't the only one to feel it. We weren't so far from the Warrens here. I would have to watch my emotions. In time, things would settle, but for now…

"No. Nothing like that. It's just…" She laughed self-consciously. "It sounds silly, but last night, I'm sure there was something in my cellar."

"A rat?"

"No." She wasn't laughing now. "Something much bigger. Not a person, either. I could hear breathing, and it wasn't right. I don't know how to describe it. And sharp sounds. You know, like if you scraped a knife on a rock. But this morning, there was nothing there."

"You went and looked?" Why the fuck would she do that? Anything could have been down there. The things I had seen…

Calm.

"With my neighbours and my brother. We brought weapons."

Weapons wouldn't help against some of the things that strayed into this city. Mostly, those things knew better than to risk the fury of the Ash Guard, but sometimes they still came. For a moment, images of her torn to pieces by some monster stamped their way across my mind.

Calm! It's probably a cat or a dog. This is just the Lady's absence affecting her too.

"The thing is," Ileoni said, "there's no other way out of

the cellar, and the door was locked, but whatever it was, it had gone." She met my eyes. "I wanted to think it was just a nightmare, but I could still smell it. Like something really rotten. And there were scratches on the floor. I don't think I—"

Or maybe not the Lady. Fuck. I forced my breath to remain even, a smile onto my face.

"It's all right." I didn't know exactly what had crawled into her cellar or how, but it had fucked with the wrong cellar. No one – nothing – threatened my friends. "I'll come back with you tonight." I had promised Holera I would come around for dinner, but we hadn't said when. I could deal with this first and still have time to go. She would understand. I hoped. "Whatever it is, I'll deal with it. What time do you finish?"

"Six o'clock. I can pay..."

I waved it away. "I don't charge friends." *You don't let your friends down.* I had told myself I lived by that rule, but I had let Benny and Sereh down.

I wouldn't do that this time.

CHAPTER EIGHT

IN THE TIME BETWEEN MY MOTHER DECIDING I WOULD NEVER have the power to succeed her as high mage and my leaving her court for good, I had spent a year at Agatos University. There were, after all, more ways to be useful to the blessed Countess than raw magical power, and being of use mattered very much to my mother. Far more than family.

It hadn't gone well.

I had grown up in the Warrens. *The Warrens run deep*, they always said, and it was true. I had hated it there and loved it, and it was carved into my bones. I had been seventeen years old when my mother had finally left the service of the Wren, claimed the mantle of High Mage, changed her name from Solone Thorn to Anatase Coldrock, moved the whole family – me, Mica, and herself – to her new palace on Horn Hill, and arranged election to the Senate. Mica had managed the move seamlessly. The street brat had become an elegant young lady in a single, smooth step. It had been too late for me, and I hadn't fitted in any better at Agatos University than I had as my mother's junior mage on Horn Hill.

Agatos University catered to the children of the wealthy and powerful of Agatos. The children of merchants, politicians, and the old families of the city. My mother might have been 'the Countess,' a high mage, and a senator, but I was still a child of the Warrens. I did not belong. Their effortlessly superior goat shit itched like a bed full of hot gravel. I'd had two choices: avoid them or unleash my fury and contempt on them. Wealthy and lofty they might have been, but none of them were trained mages. For a year, I had kept myself to myself, following my own interests in the university library. For a whole year.

I deserved credit for that, at least.

A year.

The blood, bruises, and broken bones I had inflicted on the students of Paupers' College when I finally stood up to their bullying of the staff had been entirely their own fault. The university scholars hadn't seen it that way when they threw me out. I hadn't objected. I had already decided to leave, and I hadn't held back on telling them what I thought.

I'd never imagined that one day I would come back looking for a favour, but earlier this year, I'd needed information about the ghost of the beast god, Ah'té, that had been terrorising the city. Their refusal to help had been a lesson, and it was why I hadn't come empty-handed this time.

The university had been closed to students over the

hottest part of the summer. Not because of the heat. The heavy, old university buildings were cooler than most parts of the city, being shaded by trees and surrounded by gardens. But the wealthiest and most powerful families escaped the city's heat in the summer, retreating to the foothills of Carn's Break, and if they weren't going to be there, everyone else would have to wait for them to return. Now that the heat had broken, the university had re-opened and the students were back. The wide avenue of ancient cypresses leading to the entrance of Paupers' College was busy with groups of young men and women and the occasional robed scholar. I had been out of the university long enough that none of the students would recognise me, but I couldn't say the same for the scholars. Words had been exchanged when I'd left, and not many of them had been complimentary. I didn't exactly hurry as I made my way to the college entrance, but I didn't hang around, either.

The mill of students and scholars continued in the large lobby. I had made the mistake when I'd first come here of assuming that my fellow students were here to learn, but I'd been disabused of that early on. With few exceptions, attendance at Agatos University was part of the ritual of rule in the city, where future politicians, merchants, and family heads made the connections and alliances that ensured power stayed exactly where it always had been: in their hands. No doubt my mother had fantasised about my participation in those rituals, cementing her place in the city's political aristocracy. It just went to show how little she knew me.

Attendance at lectures and tutorials was seen as a

distinctly optional activity, which was a good thing, because based on the lectures I had attended on theoretical magic, they were the biggest pile of bollocks this side of a sausage shop.

I wasn't here for advice on magic. I was here to find out if any among the scholars had taken their theoretical arguments on how gods might be killed into more practical realms.

I strode up to the green-cloaked scholar seated at the far side of the lobby and rapped on his desk, making him jump. "Scholar Longstream. Where is he?"

I didn't recognise this man, and he didn't seem to recognise me, but he recognised the black cloak and straightened. "Scholar Longstream is giving a lecture, Mystery. You will have to wait."

I felt immediate sympathy for any poor sod trapped in the auditorium with him. "Excellent. I'll wait in his rooms." I pushed away from the desk and headed for the hallway leading to the scholars' quarters.

"You can't go in there," the scholar called after me.

"I think you'll find I can," I said without looking back.

Longstream's study was locked when I reached it, but a quick spell dealt with that, and I let myself in. I didn't know Longstream well. I'd had a single lecture course with him on the history of religions in the Erastes Valley. We hadn't hit it off. His study was the same mess of haphazard books and papers that I remembered. We had that much in common. The difference was that the college employed cleaners for the scholars' rooms, whereas my apartment only ever got tidied when I had something else really important to do.

His books on theology and the history of religion weren't much interest to me, nor were the artifacts on his shelves, but maybe I would find something in his personal correspondence or notes. If, as he had claimed, the topic of how a god might be killed was a matter of debate among scholars, he might have letters or records of arguments. I had come prepared with my bribe, but anything I could get without having to use it would be a bonus. I settled behind his desk and sorted through his papers.

By my estimation, it took me a good five minutes before I had completely lost the will to live and was suffering from flashbacks to Longstream's interminable classes. His papers were full of notes on his lectures, and while it should have been impossible to write in a monotone, Longstream managed it. Certainly, there was nothing about killing gods. The most exciting thing in his desk was a heavily drafted and redrafted complaint to the senior scholars about the number of students he had been assigned (too many) and the attendance at his lectures (too few). I slid the drawer in and sat back. His door might have been locked, but he wouldn't be the only one with a key. The cleaners and college staff would have access, students were notorious for getting where they shouldn't, and there was always the matter of an interfering mage to whom locks were no barrier. If he really thought his ideas were important or original, maybe he wouldn't keep them where they might be found.

I glanced around. His notes could be hidden in one of the

many books, inside an artifact, in his private rooms beyond… Or maybe there weren't any notes at all. Maybe he kept it all safely in his brain. Contrary to what some people believed, no mage could read another person's mind. There were ways to extract information: compulsions, even torture if you were that kind of mage, but pulling thoughts from someone's brain? Nope. I didn't believe even high mages could do that. I hoped not.

The sound of keys in the door interrupted my thoughts. I just had time to scoot around the desk and settle into the visitor's chair when the door opened and Scholar Longstream strode in. He had taken a moment to compose himself, but his face was still flushed. He must have hurried straight out of his lecture when he'd been told I was here. At least I'd saved whichever students had actually turned up half an hour of tedium.

"Mystery Thorn." Longstream rounded his desk and settled in the seat I had occupied moments earlier. If he noticed the warmth of the seat, he didn't show it. "This is becoming a habit. I have sent for the porters. I will take great pleasure in seeing you thrown out if you are still here when they arrive." His scrawny shoulders were trembling. Anger? Or something else?

"I missed you, too. We'd better get down to business."

"I have no business with you."

I smacked the stolen book on his desk on a pile of papers. A satisfying puff of dust rose around it. "Do you know what this is?"

"It is called a book, Mystery Thorn. You may not be familiar with them."

Smug twat. He knew I came from the Warrens, and he'd never let me forget it. He also knew I was the Countess's son, so he hadn't been able to refuse to teach me, but his opinion of me had never been high. That was fine by me, because my opinion of him was even lower.

"It's one of the few remaining copies of *The Silver Oak*. I have it on good authority that the university doesn't own one."

Longstream's eyes widened, and he reached for the book. I pulled it back and wagged my finger at him. "Uh-uh."

"Where did you get that?"

"Do you care?"

I could see his mind working. The guy should never gamble, because his thoughts were written as clear as a banner across his face. "Is it genuine?"

"As genuine as it gets." Like I would know. But I trusted Kehsereen. "Ready to talk now?"

His eyes hadn't left the book. "What do you want?"

Now wasn't this better? "I want information, that's all. When we met earlier in the summer, you told me that there was debate among the scholars as to how gods could be killed. You're going to tell me all of the theories, and you're going to give me a list of the scholars who've been involved in that debate. Every one of them."

Longstream's thin fingers opened and closed like he was trying to grasp the book. I didn't think he even knew he was doing it. His tongue darted across his lips. "No."

“What?” This time I was the one who couldn’t keep the incredulity from my face. No? After all I’d been through to get this, robbing a senator, being caught in the act and attacked by a mage, breaking my fucking wrist. Kehsereen’s nose had been smashed into the cobbles.

“No. I have already told you the price for my help. It has not changed.”

“Are you serious?” *Bannaur’s broken balls!* I fought the urge to pin him down with magic and rip the information out in blood. Now was not the time to get locked up by the Ash Guard. But fuck me, I needed this. I had promised Benny. I’d wasted so much time and effort getting this book and bringing it here, time I could have spent chasing other clues.

What other clues? I pushed the thought away. I conjured a flame between my finger and thumb and held the book up to it. “You know I could burn this right here and now?”

Longstream’s eyes flicked nervously between the book and the flame. Then his expression hardened, and I knew I had lost. “You can. But my price remains. Raise the corpse of Agate Blackspear so he can tell me exactly how he managed to kill Sien, the Lady of Dreams Descending. Then I will tell you everything you want to know.”

I let the flame die. “You’re crazy.”

“Perhaps.” A smirk touched his lips. “But I will be at the Godkiller’s tomb at two in the morning if you change your mind.”

When I'd set up in business as a freelance mage, I'd lain down three very clear lines that I would not cross, and even though I'd pressed up close to them, I'd never stepped across. Firstly, I would never lay a curse on another person. Break a curse? Of course. All the time. It made up a good chunk of my business. Secondly, you couldn't hire me to hurt someone. People might, and did, get hurt in some jobs, but I wouldn't take a job to do so deliberately. And, finally, I would never raise the dead. I had done it once, during my training, and I had encountered the risen dead in my work, but the feeling of wrongness about them was like salt on a slug. Bringing back the dead always ended badly.

I left the university, passing through the University District – an area not so different in wealth to the better parts of the Middle City, but without that bustle of commerce and business that drove most of the rest of the city – then across the river to join the Royal Highway down past Horn Hill.

What Longstream was asking went against every principle and instinct I had. There had to be another way. There was *always* another way.

And what is it? I had felt the despair and anger in the air near the Warrens. People there knew something was wrong, and we wouldn't be able to keep the Lady of the Grove's death a secret forever. Things like that got out. Without hope, the Warrens would explode. People would get hurt. People would die. If I did do this for Longstream and we found out exactly how Blackspear had killed the goddess, then Longstream should be able to tell me who had proposed or championed that theory.

That was a lot of *ifs*.

"I'll make another way," I muttered.

It wasn't that I was a stranger to failure. Depths, I was a twenty-nine-year-old mage scrabbling to pay my rent in a city that made mages rich. I had fucked up jobs, I had fucked up relationships, and I had fucked up friendships. But this was different. This was my one chance to prove to Benny I wasn't the selfish cunt he thought I was.

Yeah? Aren't you making this all about you right now?

I didn't have an answer to that.

And while I was on the topic of making everything about me, I had done next to fuck all to discover who had set up the priest, Ard Ethemattian, to be beaten to death by his own congregation. I had to do a quick mental calculation to figure out he only had three days left. That wouldn't be long to uncover the truth, even if I didn't have the Lady's murder to worry about.

Not long to live when you know you're going to die, either.

I took a diversion on my way back from the university to check in on Kehsereen. I could say I wanted to make sure he was all right after our escapade and his face-plant yesterday – and I did – but I also needed the information he had promised about the Brythanii religion.

Selfish.

Kehsereen looked like shit when he answered the door, so I let him know that. His nose and mouth were swollen and raw, and he was limping.

"Not all of us heal like mages."

"I could try to..." I gestured vaguely at his face.

"No. Thank you."

Good choice. A skilled and powerful mage could help with wounds, but it was a dicey game to play, and there was a non-zero chance I would do more harm than good.

"Does it hurt?" Stupid question. Of course it hurt.

"I've had worse." His hands moved seemingly subconsciously to his arms. He kept the raw scars beneath his sleeves and bandages covered, but they looked almost like acid burns. Should I have asked about them the first time I'd seen them? Was that what normal people did?

Too late now.

I dropped into one of his chairs and watched him lower himself gingerly opposite. His normal restless movement seemed suppressed.

"Is everything all right? Apart from that?"

He nodded. "I went to see Asarian at the Ash Guard fortress."

"Not good?" His nephew had been tortured for months by the insanity of Enabgal, the god of nightmares.

"He is calmer, but ... listless. He doesn't respond. I know he needs the Ash to remain safe, but it takes so much from him."

Mages, even natural mages, didn't realise how much we sustained ourselves through raw magic. Only when we came into contact with Ash, as I had done too often recently, did we feel how draining that absence was. Asarian was a natural high mage. He had sustained himself on raw magic alone in the grasp of Enabgal. It was unheard of. The impact of having that snatched away must have been brutal.

At least he's alive. Without the constraining Ash, the Guard would have killed him to protect Agatos.

"I'm sorry."

He shrugged. "I will find a solution. I am meeting with the cult of Sharshak later. I have some ideas about Ash."

"You need me along?"

"No. I don't believe they are dangerous."

They were a religion – or a cult; there wasn't much difference. That made them dangerous by definition. But Kehsereen could look after himself, and I was the one who had almost got him killed yesterday.

"I don't suppose you want a book?" I dropped *The Silver Oak* on his table.

His eyes went to it. "I cannot say I am not interested, but I am not sure it would be wise to be found in possession of this book right now."

That thought had entered my head as well. I had thought that Longstream would take the bribe and no more would be said of it. But Senator Greenfield knew he had been robbed – another fuck up – and when he discovered what was missing, well, word would get around, and Longstream would have another lever to turn against me.

Kehsereen looked thoughtful – although it was hard to tell under the bruises. "I was sure he would want this book."

"Yeah, well. He did. He just wanted something else more." At the tilt of Kehsereen's head, I added, "He wants me to raise the remains of Agate Blackspear."

"Can you?"

"In theory. It's been centuries, but that's not the problem.

I'm not sure how much of him would be left to raise, and I doubt he'd be able to communicate. But more to the point, it's not something I do. You raise a dead person, they come back with their memories, but there's something else missing, something that doesn't come back. It always goes wrong, and Blackspear was a high mage. Think how wrong that could go. Think what could happen to the city."

"And that is the reason? The threat to the city?"

"Isn't it enough?"

"Of course."

Ah, and it was bollocks. Of course I cared what happened to Agatos, but I also knew that Captain Gale and the Ash Guard wouldn't let the resurrected corpse of a dead high mage wreak havoc on the city. They would step in before things got too out of hand. "You have to have lines. You have to have principles. If you don't..."

"Then you would not know how or where to stop."

"Yeah. This job... People need things. Desperately. They need answers, they need their problems fixed, their lives repaired. Without lines, how far is too far? When does doing good cross into doing harm?"

He spread his hands.

"Fuck."

"I met with my Brythanii contact."

"I hope it went better than my meeting."

"Perhaps. We talked about the Choosing ceremony and about the time leading up to the ritual murder."

"And?"

"It would be difficult to enter another person into the

Choosing. Entries require the candidates to put themselves forward both in person and in writing. They are delivered to a senior priest – a Most Cursed, they call them – in the Sanctum."

"Unless this Most Cursed is the one behind it. Maybe my client pissed them off." He had certainly pissed off his brother, and while having your own family furious with you didn't necessarily mean you were an arsehole, my own family were often pissed off with me, and I wouldn't want a vote taken on whether I was an arsehole or not.

"Perhaps. But the Most Cursed who draws the name is not the same one who accepts the entries, and the draw takes place in the Sanctum in the presence of the entire priesthood."

Right. So, it would need two of them at least – one to fake the entry and attest to its authenticity, and one to ensure Ethemattian's name was drawn. A conspiracy like that was unlikely. There were easier ways to kill someone. But it wasn't impossible, and I didn't have a lot of leads. "I think I'm going to need to talk to this Most Cursed."

"His name is Most Cursed Coyd Keffen."

Keffen. I had heard that name somewhere before. Where? "I assume it's not easy to access the temple to poke around?"

"You are right. Only Brythanii are allowed in, and even they are not allowed into the Sanctum unless they are priests or temple servants and guards. But I am told many come veiled in the period of the Choosing so as not to favour the god with their faces."

"I'm guessing they're still not allowed in the priests'

private quarters."

"No. The priests have rooms behind the temple, but ordinary Brythanii cannot access those. Just the priests, servants, and guards, again."

'Cannot' was an interesting word. A lot of people used it when they meant 'not allowed to'. They would be surprised at how often those weren't the same things. Ordinary Brythanii and non-Brythanii might not be *allowed* there, but with the right robes, a veil, and an outwards display of confidence, we would see.

I stood. "Thank you. And, you know." I nodded at his bruises. "Sorry again about that."

I SPENT THE WALK BACK TO MY APARTMENT IN THOUGHT. I would have to start talking to the priests. Ethemattian's brother might hate him, but with no access to the private parts of the temple, I couldn't see how he would have had the opportunity to arrange something so complex. The brothers didn't even look that much alike, so he couldn't have pretended to be Ard to submit a fake entry. The veiling in the days leading up to the ceremony – the *murder* – was an unexpected bonus, but the Brythanii were a pale-skinned, white-haired people, and I was ... not. I would have to ask Ethemattian to find me clothes and a veil that would fit in and would cover me convincingly. Maybe even priests' robes. Then, somehow, I would have to make this Most Cursed spill his secrets. Most people wouldn't come out and admit they had set someone up to be murdered, and I wouldn't know how to lean on the man until I met him.

"Wing it again, eh, Nik?" I muttered.

"It's worked for me so far," I said in reply. Within certain definitions of the word 'worked'.

When I reached my office, the door was unlocked. I had locked it behind me, of course, but that didn't seem to deter most people. For a moment, I wondered if Fria had figured out how to pick locks. It would explain his ability to escape every time he was left. Then I pulled in magic and shouldered the door open.

Benny was in the chair in front of my desk, turned towards the door. He didn't look happy, even for Benny. His arms were tight across his chest, his shoulders hunched, and his dried-meat face fixed in a scowl. Sereh was there, too, sitting cross-legged on my desk, expressionless and unmoving. Somehow, that was even more terrifying. If she ever did decide to kill me, I would get no hint of it from her, and I wouldn't get time to defend myself.

"Where the fuck have you been?" Benny demanded.

"Finding out about killing gods. Like I promised."

"Yeah? You know who did it?"

"No."

"You know how?"

"No."

"Any suspects?"

"Not yet. But—"

"Fucking typical. Don't know what I expected."

I thought about edging around him to reach my seat

behind the desk, but I wasn't sure I would make it in one piece, and I would be disconcertingly close to Sereh, so I settled on the couch near the door. "Look, it takes time, all right? People who go around killing gods don't tell everyone."

"Well, there ain't time. You been to the Warrens recently?"

"Last night."

"Things are going to shit down there. People know. They don't know they know, but they know. People are angry."

I had felt that, too. A building fury. One spark, that would be all it took. It had been a while since there had been a good riot, and it was overdue.

"The person who's got the information I need isn't talking yet." Yet. Not talking at all, more like, but I wasn't ready to admit that.

Sereh's head tilted, and those clear, still eyes met mine. "Why don't I ask him, Uncle Nik? People like to talk to me." Her knife had appeared. I hadn't seen her hand move. I shuddered.

"No! I mean, not yet. There's more things I can try."

Her eyes didn't move. I sat there, frozen, for several seconds. Then her knife was gone. "All right."

Fuck.

"There's no time for you to piss around like normal," Benny said. "You remember Jirra Lane's little bakery? The one in the alley behind Rulend's house?"

I nodded.

"Yeah, well, it ain't a bakery anymore. Jirra disappeared a couple of weeks back, and now there's something going on there that's got people nervous. Not Warrens' stuff. Outside stuff. People don't need to be nervous right now. You should look into it."

"I said I could find out what's going on," Sereh protested. "No one would see me."

"Yeah, and I said you're not. Nik can risk his neck if anyone's going to."

"I'll do it." I reckoned I was going to be risking my neck a whole lot before Benny ever thought of forgiving me. "Did you do what I said?"

"*I* always do. Apple tree wood and volcanic glass. Wasn't easy, but no one asked questions."

It would do for now, as long as no one got too close to the god's body. I would need a better solution eventually.

Benny got to his feet, heading to the door. "Don't waste any more time. Anything that happens, it's on you."

Sereh followed him, stopping to peer up at me with those terrifying eyes. "I took your dog for a walk, Uncle Nik. You should do it more. He gets bored."

I stared at her. I'd locked Fria in the private part of my house, behind my wards. I could see them there, still, unbroken. "How did you get through the wards?" I hadn't given her or Benny passes when I had rebuilt them last. I had thought about it in the hope they might come and visit, but I had quashed that.

She smiled. "There are no wards in the shadows, Uncle Nik."

I shivered as she danced down the steps to the street. Why had that sounded so much like a threat?

CHAPTER NINE

I TOOK FRIA FOR A WALK.

Partly it was because Sereh had made me feel guilty, but mostly it was because I needed time to think and because whoever turned up at my office next wasn't going to be happy with me, whether it was Ethemattian wondering if I was actually going to get around to saving his life, the Wren's enforcers come to chastise me for interfering with a gang under his protection, Senator Greenfield's angry mage wanting his book back, or, gods help me, a new client.

We stopped at the Penitent's Ear to pick up some lamb, chickpea, and mint wraps from a stall, then shared them under the small grove of olive trees at the east side of the market. If Fria wasn't used to this kind of food, he kept quiet about it and watched me closely as I ate mine. His own had disappeared with no noticeable chewing.

"You're going to give yourself indigestion," I told him. He

didn't seem bothered, and I used my belt knife to divide the remains of my food. I quickly shoved my last portion into my mouth while he was scarfing down his.

"You know the problem with this job?" I said around my mouthful. Apparently, he didn't, so I continued. "For weeks there's nothing much to do, then it all happens at once, and everyone wants everything right away and it's all urgent."

Fria didn't look sympathetic. Instead, he let out a bark and stared meaningfully at my now-empty hand.

"You ate it. It's all gone."

He barked again.

"You'll just make yourself sick."

He responded by wandering off and taking a shit under a tree. I felt bad leaving it there, but Fria was hardly the only dog crapping in the streets, and it wouldn't be long before Warrens kids came by to scoop it into a bucket and sell it to one of the last remaining tanneries in the corner of the Warrens. In a way, I was just supporting entrepreneurs. In the meantime, if you didn't know well enough to watch where you trod in this city, you deserved everything you put your foot into.

One day, I would take that lesson to heart.

We headed up the Royal Highway, past the Grey City, and into the shadow of Horn Hill until we reached the Street of Gods.

I didn't visit the Street of Gods often. It wasn't that I didn't believe in the gods. I had encountered enough of them to know better than that. It was just that, given the choice, I would take a bout of syphilis over a close encounter with a god. The less I had to do with them, the better. The fact that I had – accidentally – burned down the Temple of Gwillan-Whose-Light-Falls-on-the-Few-Not-the-Many only added to my incentive to stay away. This job I had foolishly taken made that impossible.

The Brythanii temple was a heavy, gloomy bulk of a building, despite being whitewashed like most of the city. Managing to paint something white and still make it look dark and foreboding was quite an architectural achievement. Most religions – those who liked their gods, anyway – tried to make their temples as glamorous and impressive as possible to encourage worshippers, and, more importantly, donations. The Brythanii probably did like donations – who didn't? – but they certainly weren't going to use them for the glorification of the Hated God. The building was a magnificent monument to depression.

Unfortunately, it sat directly opposite the remains of the Temple of Gwillan. I had managed to avoid suspicion for the conflagration. In the excitement of the blaze, no one seemed to have remembered me. I had run into my sister and her partner while I was scoping the place, but as far as I could tell, they hadn't said anything. Maybe Mica had enough residual faith in me to think even I couldn't accidentally burn down a whole temple.

"See, boy," I said to Fria. "Sometimes I do exceed expectations."

Still, I didn't want anyone to recognise me and remember seeing me. I kept my hood up, despite the growing afternoon warmth.

On the plus side, the Temple of Gwillan was a furious anthill of activity. Stonemasons, carpenters, and labourers were everywhere. I was a one-man job creation scheme. You're welcome.

I watched the entrance to the Brythanii temple for a few minutes from just down the street. It wasn't exactly busy, but there was a steady traffic in and out. A few priests, but mostly Brythanii ... worshippers? That had to be the wrong word. Haters? Enemies of their god? As Kehsereen had suggested, many of the Brythanii wore veils – mostly grey, green, or yellow – against the supposed gaze of their god. Pointless, really, because the god was unlikely to be watching, and if it was, a veil wouldn't do much good, but as a symbolic 'fuck you' it had some potential. It would also do a good job of hiding my face and hair, if I kept my head ducked and my hands hidden. I wondered if the colours of the veils were significant. Something to check with Cursed Ethemattian before I tried and put my foot in it. I could put my foot in it *after* I'd got advice.

"Let's check around the back," I said.

Fria didn't disagree – there was an enormous advantage to spending time with a dog rather than Benny – so we followed an alley alongside the temple until we reached the rear. As I'd expected, the front entrance wasn't the only way in. I passed one door leading off the alley, but it was mage-locked, and I couldn't open it. A mage lock was a specialised type of ward usually fixed on a lock or bolt to prevent nosy bastards like me from shifting it. As with any ward, if the mage trying to break through was significantly stronger or more skilled than the one who had set it, they would be able to get through, but mage locks were a tougher proposition than normal wards, being required to only protect a single lock rather than a whole building. I could have taken the door off its hinges, of course, or even made a hole in the wall, but that would hardly be subtle, and I wasn't trying to storm the place.

The back was more promising. A courtyard was enclosed by two wings of the temple, which must hold the priests' rooms, and a wall. It should be easy to enter, either through the arched doorway or over the wall.

The wing to my left would catch the morning sun and keep it through much of the day. The rooms there had balconies and tall windows. The temple might be heavy and gloomy, but the same couldn't be said for the priests' quarters. Those ones would be for the senior priests, the Most Curseds, although they didn't seem to be cursed by their living quarters. For some reason, I hadn't expected there to be quite so many rooms and so many priests. I could hardly start hammering on doors and asking which one of them was Most Cursed Coyd Keffen.

The other wing was more modest. The accommodation for ordinary priests like my client, Ard Ethemattian, I guessed, as well, perhaps, as any servants' quarters. I didn't imagine the priests washed their own underwear. Too busy doing priestly things like ... fuck knows. I certainly didn't.

Watching the courtyard entrance confirmed my suspicions. Despite what Kehsereen's informant had said, while some of those entering and leaving were priests, most of the foot traffic was servants, deliveries, and the odd labourer. And not all of them were Brythanii. It would be an option.

But not yet. First, I would need to talk to Ethemattian.

Finding him in the temple would be a bad move. Whoever had set him up needed to believe they had been successful. I couldn't afford to blow that, or my suspects would shut up and any evidence would disappear.

I would have to let Ethemattian come to me. In the meantime, I had Benny's suspicious activities in the Warrens to look into.

"I don't think you're coming with me on this one," I told Fria. Maybe I was imagining it, but he looked disappointed.

THE WARRENS WASN'T THE KIND OF PLACE YOU WANDERED into by mistake. Not if you wanted to wander back out again with your pockets still full and your limbs intact. Contrary to what most of the city believed, the Warrens wasn't a nightmare of crime and violence. If you were from the Warrens, you would be as safe there as if you were walking through the grand plazas of the Upper City. Safer, in fact, for a Warrens kid in the alleys and the dark corners of the Warrens where there were no City Watch or private guards to chase you off with club or blackjack or flat of the sword.

If you were from the wealthier parts of city, that was another story. Much of Agatos had been rigorously planned and sanitised – the Grey City, when it was built, the Middle

City, Horn Hill, the Upper City, even the Stacks and Dockside in their ways. They had been made grand, or at least respectable, even if some areas had since sunk into tired decay. There was no place in such grand schemes for the poor and the workers who kept the dirty, unpleasant parts of the city running. Someone had to clear rubbish from the streets, unblock sewers, dredge the harbour, carry loads, pick apart ropes, and break stones. Those people had to live somewhere, so the city had brushed them all into the corner, out of sight, and left them to look after themselves. The Warrens was the result. Warrens people knew their place, their place was out of the way, and it was theirs. If you chose to come there uninvited, you deserved anything that happened to you.

I'd found myself in an awkward position when it came to the Warrens. I had grown up there, but I had become a mage, my mother was the Countess now, and I had found myself a citizen of the rest of Agatos as much as I was of the Warrens. I didn't fit fully outside the Warrens, but I didn't fit in there, either. I wasn't in real danger in the Warrens, but I wasn't welcome. I didn't return often, and when I did, I had become used to a degree of suspicion and hostility. Today was different.

The narrow, shadowed streets and alleys felt closer and darker than usual. Men and women hurried past, casting suspicious glances, or hunched in doorways, watching. If I had been paranoid, I would have thought they were all watching me. And truth be told, I did seem to be attracting more glances than most. Whispered conversations stopped as I approached, eyes followed me, muttered curses drifted in my wake.

It's the cloak. It's not personal.

It felt personal.

They know, Benny had said. *They don't know they know, but they know.*

The former bakery Benny had asked – told – me to investigate was in the north of the Warrens, not so far from the Lady's grave.

"It's nothing to do with that," I told myself. "Don't invent trouble."

And how often were my problems unrelated? Everything tangled together in this city, like a cast-off net, and I was a seabird caught in it and slowly sinking.

You're overdramatic, that's what you are.

My route took me along Metton's Run, curving up the gradual slope towards the valley's edge and the mountains beyond. Most streets in the Warrens weren't officially named by the city. They didn't hang around long enough before becoming blocked or diverted by the constant, organic churn of shacks and makeshift houses, and if the city named them, it would have to acknowledge the Warrens' existence. But for as long as I remembered, Warrens kids had called this street Metton's Run.

Up ahead, just before the Run stuttered to an end and spidered into a dozen smaller alleys and passageways, like a river entering a delta, a crowd had gathered at the entrance to a small courtyard. I couldn't see what they were watching, but I could see people craning past each other.

None of your business.

I almost laughed. When had that ever stopped me? *None of my business* was like a baited hook. There was no point pretending it wasn't. No matter how many times the hook went through my cheek and ripped me out of the water, I would go swimming back to it the next chance I got.

I drifted to the back of the crowd. I was taller than most, and above the cluster of heads, I saw a man standing on steps in the courtyard, addressing the crowd. He had been there for a while, I reckoned, because he was gesticulating furiously and sweating, and I felt the anger in the crowd.

"...and it doesn't matter what is yours or what you've earned. It doesn't matter how hard you work. They'll take it all from you. It doesn't matter how much blood and sweat you've spilled. They'll take it. Does that sound right to you?"

I wasn't sure what he was talking about, but as leading questions went, I could hardly argue, and neither could the crowd, who returned an enthusiastic, "No!"

"Them up there on the Hill and the Upper City," the man clarified helpfully. "They don't work. They don't break their backs or twist their hands, but they grow rich, while you whose parents worked and grandparents worked, you're poorer now than you ever were. They take everything. You can feel it. There's nothing they haven't taken, and still they want more. Isn't that right, mage?"

Shit. The man's eyes had found me over the heads of his audience. Many in the crowd, I now noticed for the first time, were holding clubs or knives. Faces turned to me, and they weren't friendly. Most people wouldn't attack a mage. Our reputation was far too frightening. But mobs weren't people. They were their own thing. The Warrens was one stray spark away from going up in flames. I didn't want to be that spark. I raised my hands placatingly and backed away.

The man had made his point, and I heard his voice again as I retreated.

It wasn't that I disagreed with him. The people who worked in this city, particularly those from the Warrens and Dockside and Fishertown, never saw the profit from their labours, while the merchants, businessmen and -women, and politicians grew wealthy. It was wrong, and it had to change. But if he was planning to lead that mob up to Horn Hill or the Upper City, the Watch would descend on them with the kind of brutality that was only ever reserved for those who challenged the status quo.

What he was saying was nothing new. This had been the truth of Agatos for generations. But now things were different. Now, the Lady of the Grove was dead, and every stone and plank of wood in the Warrens knew it.

How did you never believe in her?

"So, find out what happened," I told myself. "Find out who killed her. Give the people a focus for their rage that won't get them killed."

It took me a couple of tries to find the alley that led to the former bakery. A red-doored house that I had always used to orient myself had collapsed or been pulled down, and a couple of scarcely-more-than-shacks had taken its place, jutting into the alley and nearly blocking it, so I had to turn sideways and squeeze past. I slowed as I approached, unfocusing my eyes to 'see' magic and trailing a net of my own magic around me.

And it was a good thing I did. There was an alarm spell set into a wall, stretching its tendrils across the alley. It was good work, but of an unfamiliar build. It took me a while to pick my way past without triggering it, and when I reached the corner beyond which the once-bakery stood, I saw wards on the building.

Not many people bothered with wards in the Warrens, not least because if you could afford wards, you could afford to get out of here. Some of the Wren's mages lived in the Warrens or near it, or had family who did, but the wards set by them had a particular signature that was more effective than the wards themselves at keeping other mages away, and these wards didn't. *Not the Wren's people.*

Who else would be foolish enough to set up in the Wren's territory? It was out of the way, but still. Eventually, someone would find it, and then the Wren would visit. No one wanted that.

I drew closer, keeping to the shadows, with magic ready to detect anyone who looked my direction, and examined the wards.

The first thing that was obvious was that I wasn't getting through them. Whoever had set these wards was more powerful and skilled than I was. Which meant that even if I could have broken through, I wouldn't want to. There was an arse-kicking waiting on the other side of those walls. But that didn't mean I was giving up.

I settled back and unfocused my eyes further, looking

past the red glare of the wards to see what magic was within. It wasn't easy. Imagine trying to simultaneously unfocus your eyes and see something clearly, all the while staring into the sunset. If I didn't give myself a nosebleed, it would be a minor miracle.

There was magic within, a lot of it. I saw at least three sources. Mages, probably, and they were constructing some spell. I couldn't tell what kind of spell from behind the wards. Something powerful.

I let my magical vision drop and slumped. Bannaur's balls, that hurt. My head was pounding. I breathed slowly until the thump of blood in my ears had faded.

Benny had been right. Someone was up to something in there. Who or what, I didn't know.

If I couldn't see, maybe I could at least hear. The best way would be to insinuate taut threads of magic into the building to pick up the vibrations of their voices in the air. But my magic might trigger their wards, and they would certainly sense it.

My magic might not be able to get in, but sound could still get out, no matter how solid the walls, and if it could, I could collect it and funnel it towards myself. I began to shape the air.

It took a while, and my body was aching from the magical strain before I finally gathered enough of the sound from the building to hear it. Creaks of floorboards, the ticking of bugs in the woodwork, and the squeak and scuttle of rats all layered on top of the voices, but I could hear them. I couldn't make out the words, but I could tell they were speaking another language. Pentathian, perhaps? Or maybe one of the variants spoken around the Folaric Sea? Either way, these weren't Agatos mages.

Not that there was any law against foreign mages coming here, if they announced themselves to the Ash Guard, but somehow, I didn't think this lot had or they wouldn't be hiding in a corner of the Warrens.

So, what did they want? Could they have something to do with the Lady's death? A group of powerful, unknown mages. Could they pull it off? Depths, they were as likely as anyone. But if they had, why, and why would they leave her body up there in the grove? The remains of dead gods were among the most valuable items in the world. Even if they hadn't wanted all the power for themselves, selling it would make them unimaginably wealthy.

But that was the same question for anyone who might have killed her: Why leave the body? The only answer I could think of was that they didn't know where it was. As I had explained to Benny, it made no sense to fight a god's manifested body. That wasn't the god itself, just the part it showed you. To kill it, you would have to deal with a whole lot more, and you would want to do that from your own place of power with all your relics and prepared spells to hand. If Benny and I had hidden the body before the murderer could find it, they would still be searching. As would anyone who had felt her death. I wondered if the barrier of apple tree wood and volcanic glass that Benny had created would be enough.

Or maybe these mages had nothing to do with Lady of

the Grove. Agatos had suffered from a power vacuum since Carnelian Silkstar had been killed by the ghost of Ah'té. They might be trying to establish a third centre of power themselves, in balance with the Wren and the Countess. The Senate could proclaim Mica High Mage all it liked, but if these mages succeeded, Agatos would dump her like a cart of waste into the river. The city was as ruthless as it was practical.

Would that be such a bad thing? She didn't even want to be a high mage.

That didn't change the fact that she was the best candidate for the job, the only mage I knew who might – might – put the poor of the city first, and a power move like this would lead to blood before all was done.

And what do you think you can do about it?

I couldn't take on every problem in the city. These mages were clearly out of my class. This was something for the Ash Guard and Captain Gale to sort out. I would warn her and be done.

It had been too long since I'd had anything to pass on to Captain Gale, anyway. It would give me an excuse to visit her. It gave me a warm feeling.

Not yet, though. Ileoni was waiting for me.

I made my way back through the Warrens, hearing shouts in the growing gloom and feeling the anger like shifting fog in the streets. They were a stark reminder. *This* was my real job. Not foreign mages or even Ethemattian's troubles. Helping the Warrens.

You have to do it soon.

Uninvited, the thought of raising the Godkiller pushed its way to the front of my mind. That would be a shortcut to progress, maybe to the answers the Warrens needed. Why not? It might even save lives.

I shoved the thought back. *I don't do that. I won't.*

Ileoni was finishing her shift at the coffee house when I arrived. The sight of her, the idea that something might threaten her, brought fury seething back up in me. It took most of my willpower to shove it back down. Why was I reacting that way? Yes, the death of the Lady was affecting everyone near the and in the Warrens, but that surely wasn't enough to provoke this reaction.

It didn't matter. She was a friend, something had put her in danger, and I wasn't going to stand by. Whatever was in her cellar, I was going to deal with it, and it would fucking regret ever slithering into the city.

The coffee house was sparsely occupied. An older couple under a potted tree, a young woman working on ledgers near the back, and a couple of regulars I recognised from previous visits. The look of relief on Ileoni's face when she saw me made me feel unaccountably guilty.

You let enough people down. Don't feel bad about the ones you don't.

And that was why I did feel guilty. Letting people down was my default state.

"You came."

"I said I would."

She smiled, and I realised then that she reminded me of how Mica had been as a kid. Ileoni was older, but still. There was that openness that Mica used to have. *Not anymore.* Not since I'd let her down and abandoned her. *So don't do it again.* And what were the chances of me learning that lesson?

"You ready?" I asked. "It's starting to get dark, and..." I shrugged. If whatever it was that had found its way into the cellar came out at night, I wanted to be there waiting for it.

Ileoni nodded, then undid her apron, folded it, put it behind the counter, exchanged a few words with the other waiter, and grabbed a thin jacket. We headed out of the coffee house.

A light wind had sprung up with the approach of darkness, and it bullied its way around the streets, stirring leaves and the waste waiting in heaps for the carts to collect. Ileoni pulled her jacket tighter. I didn't know if it was from the cool wind or nervousness about what we were going to do. Well, what *I* was going to do. I didn't want her anywhere near it.

"Where do you live?" I asked, more to distract her than because I needed to know; we would be there soon, anyway.

"With my parents and brother. We've got a little house in the Middle City beneath Giuffria's Spear. Velli Street. You know it?"

"I know the area. It's nice." Not wealthy, but pleasant. It was a wedge of the city that the richest spurned due to the proximity of the Warrens and the looming bulk of the Spear. "Your parents..."

"I told them to stay away until we're done. My brother,

too. He didn't want to, but he knows better than to argue." There was a touch of iron there. *Just like Mica.* I wouldn't have argued either.

"Good."

We walked a couple of minutes north before turning left until we met Sester Street then north again, skirting the edge of the Warrens by a couple of blocks. It wasn't the quickest route, but I suspected we both felt the atmosphere of the Warrens from here.

"You never talk about your family," Ileoni said, as we made our way through the evening crowds. Within a month, the pattern of city life would change. In the heat of the summer, the city rested and hid during the day, emerging only in the evening, but as winter approached and cold winds and snow swept in from the mountains and the Erastes Bay that would flip. "You ask about mine, but you never say anything about yours. Your friends, yes, but not your family."

"No," I said.

She gave me a moment as we parted to let a man with a handcart pass in the opposite direction, then said, "That was an invitation for you to actually talk about them, you know?"

"Yeah. I know. My family..." I rubbed at the side of my nose. It had become unaccountably itchy. "I never knew my father. He was gone before I was born. My mother—" The familiar tightening in my chest – the edge of panic – that came with thinking about my mother made my breath hitch. "My mother never told me anything about him. A sailor from

Tor or Secellia, or a trader passing by, I suppose. Doesn't matter."

"Doesn't it?"

Did it? How the fuck was I supposed to untangle that? "It did when I was a kid. Now?" I shrugged. "You can't miss what you never had, and I wasn't the only kid in the Warrens with one or both parents missing."

"You can. I think you can miss what you never had more than you miss what you did have."

I cleared my throat awkwardly. This was not the kind of conversation I was used to or comfortable with. "My mother was a mage working for the Wren. You know who the Wren is?"

She nodded.

"Yeah, well, she was ambitious."

"And is that bad?"

"No, but... She wasn't there, either, not much. Me and Mica – that's my sister – we were on our own. Particularly after ... after Mica's dad died. He wasn't my dad, but he was, really, and then..." I spread my hands helplessly. "Then his boat sank out there in the Bay, in waters he sailed every day, in good weather, and no one could or would say why."

"And now your mother is the Countess."

I shot her a glance. "You knew?"

"People talk."

Was that why she was being so friendly to me? Because – what? – she wanted a connection to the blessed Countess? "You know I don't have her powers, right? I'll never be a high mage."

"Do you want to be?"

"No!"

"So?"

"Yeah." Why did I resent my mother for passing me over? I had never wanted to be a high mage nor to live as other mages did. That life would have killed me. That was Mica's place, not mine. "The thing is, when Mica's dad died, my mother was already a powerful mage. Not like she is now, but stronger than almost anyone else. She *must* have known what happened to him." Saying this all out loud made me feel petulant and childish. This shouldn't still be eating at me. It had been most of my lifetime ago. But I couldn't stop myself. "I needed to know."

"You asked her?"

"Yeah. And again recently. She just said, 'There are some truths you're not ready to hear'." Fuck it. She had really got inside my head. She'd just been using me in her unending feud with the Wren. What better way to throw me off-balance and distract me from seeing through her schemes? "I don't know what she meant. Did he just leave us, abandon his boat and run? Did my mother drive him off? Or did someone kill him? Someone she knew I couldn't handle? Someone *she* couldn't handle, back then?"

"Like who?"

That was the question. And there was only one answer I could think of. "Like the Wren. But she stayed with him for years afterwards. How could she do that if she knew he had killed her husband?"

"Maybe because she couldn't match him, and she had something else to protect?"

I stared at her, mystified, then when I realised what she meant, I let out an incredulous laugh that startled a couple of kids crossing the street. "Us? Me and Mica? You really don't know my mother." She would throw us to sharks if it was in her interest.

"All right. So, what about Mica? Do you see her much?"

"Sometimes. We didn't for a long time, but we do sometimes now." Mainly so she could chastise me for whatever I was doing wrong right then. Frustratingly, she was usually right.

"That's good."

"Yeah. I guess. She's different, though. She's becoming a high mage."

Ileoni laughed. "Tell me about it. You know how insane my brother is with his schemes. When he was a kid, he was scared to step outside the house."

"That different."

Her eyebrows shot up. "What does that mean?"

"Well…" Depths, how could I explain it? "You're normal."

"And what the fuck are you? Special?"

"I didn't mean that."

"Yes, you did. People are people, Nik, whether they're high mages or street sweepers, and there's nothing special about your problems. There are half a million people in this city with problems they think are as unique as yours. Trust me, as a waitress, you hear enough of them."

I had fucked this up. *As usual, Nik.* "I'm sorry."

"I'm not saying your problems aren't real or they aren't hard. I'm saying they're not special. Just ... just do me a favour. When you look around at other people, try to remember that they've got their own problems, too, and they're struggling just as much as you are."

"So, what? I should just forgive the Wren if he killed Mica's dad?"

"No. No, him you can fuck up any time you want." She linked her arm through mine. "Now, come on. We're almost there. Time to show me what that special magic can really do."

CHAPTER TEN

Ileoni's family home was a small house on a terrace near the foot of Giuffria's Spear. It was well maintained, with clean whitewash on the walls, a blue painted door and shutters, a couple of small olive trees in pots on either side of the entrance, and honeysuckle spreading across a trellis above it. We were close enough to the Ash Guard fortress here that, with a little magical boost, I could have hit it with a thrown rock. Of course, throwing stones at the Ash Guard was rarely recommended. Not that I hadn't been tempted from time-to-time. The edge of the Warrens was only a couple of hundred yards further south, but the contrast was stark. The poverty and desperation that haunted the Warrens was absent here. This wasn't a rich part of the city, but it was the kind of place where most people would be happy to live.

Not today, though. The unease, fear, and anger that now permeated the Warrens were nearly tangible here, too.

Emotions like that spread quicker than cholera and could be just as lethal.

"I want you to show me where this thing was," I said, "then I want you well away from here." Her brow knitted, but I ploughed on before she could object. "I don't know what I'm dealing with. I can't worry about keeping you safe." Sometimes all you could do was try to survive. Ileoni wasn't like Benny or Sereh or Captain Gale who could look after themselves when shit came raining down. And that was a good thing. That was how it should be for almost everyone. That was why I was here, and why the Ash Guard existed. So ordinary people didn't have to deal with things like this. Depths, if you were wealthy and privileged, it was why the City Watch were there, too.

"Fine. Just don't go in my room."

"I..." My jaw worked. "I wouldn't."

"I'm joking. But don't. Come on. I'll show you the cellar."

I didn't see much of the house as she led me through. The last light was fading fast from the sky, and the valley itself had sunk into darkness. Ileoni didn't stop to light candles or lamps but led me confidently through. From what I could see, the house was neat and clean, even if the furniture and wall-hangings were old. When we reached the cellar door, she unlocked it with a key that hung beside the door then unhooked a lamp. I conjured a mage light before she could pick up the matches.

She glanced at me. "See? You're good for something." From anyone else, it might have been an insult, but the smile that accompanied it took away any sting. "Do you need anything? Food? A drink?"

I shook my head. "I'll be all right."

I sent the mage light drifting down the cellar stairs. Tidy shelves filled with jars and small sacks lined the side walls. A chest sat against bare stone at the far end.

"It was here," she said. "I didn't see it, but I heard it, and..." She shuddered. "Anyway, I'll wait with my family in the house at the far end of the terrace. They're friends. Will that be far enough?"

"It had better be." If it wasn't, I was getting myself in far too deep. Again. "If anything goes wrong, head for the Ash Guard. Ask for Captain Gale and tell her what's happening. You'll be safe there."

I waited until Ileoni had left then grabbed the lantern and matches and slowly descended the stairs, feeling step-by-step with my feet, my eyes unfocused. There were traces of magic here, definitely, and not just from my mage light. Something supernatural had been here, but what, I couldn't tell. Powerful, though, to have left traces for so long.

I scoured the cellar. Ileoni hadn't been exaggerating about the scratches on the flagstones. There were dozens, all at different angles, deep and sharp. I doubted I could have made them with a knife. There were no magical sources or artifacts here, though, no unusual levels of raw magic.

The tattered remnants of whatever magic had been here last night were concentrated on the back wall. I dragged the chest away, hearing crockery rattle inside.

There was no hidden gap in the wall nor a secret door.

Not even a drain. I moved the chest over to near the stairs and settled on it to watch. What was behind that wall? Another cellar? A sewer? The remains of an older, collapsed building now buried by time? The ground beneath Agatos was riddled with the ruins of previous generations of the city, as I had discovered to my cost.

Maybe there was just earth behind it.

I doubted Ileoni's family would be happy if I started dismantling their wall, and until I knew what was going on, that would be premature.

I lit the lantern then let my spell fade. The presence of magic might put off whatever had been here – although that would be an easy solution if it did.

As I sat here in the flickering light, I couldn't help but remember the cellar in the Sunstone house where I had gone to exorcise ghosts only to encounter the dead god, Ah'té.

Ah'té is gone. The magic that summoned its ghost is gone. Benny had swallowed the fucking claw that acted as a source of power and a link for the summoning. Ah'té wasn't coming back.

Still, maybe I should have brought silver, charcoal, and arevena flowers in case this was a ghost.

"It's not a ghost," I said out loud. "Ghosts don't leave traces of magic. They leave ectoplasm – ghost-trail – and that would be gone in minutes."

My voice echoed hollowly around the cellar.

"And don't fucking talk to yourself."

Waiting was something I could do. Maybe when people hired me, they had a vision of chases through the city, me flinging spells in every direction, dispatching bad guys – or, more realistically, tracking down lost pets and spying on cheating lovers – but what they were really paying me to do was wait. Sometimes it came down to magic, if we were dealing with a curse or a ghost or there was no other way to spy on someone, but mostly it was about standing in the shadows until something eventually happened. Or didn't. It wasn't what I'd imagined either when I'd set up for hire, but I'd learned to appreciate the calm over the last few months. Far better to be bored than running from an insane or dead god. It gave me time to think, and right now I needed that.

I wasn't making progress on Ethemattian's impending murder nor on the death of the Lady of the Grove, and I was almost out of time on both.

Ethemattian had to have been set up by someone in his temple. Access was too difficult otherwise, and there was the matter of him having to put himself forward in person and in writing to the Most Cursed, Coyd Keffen. So, the Most Cursed was either in on it – bribed, maybe? – or couldn't tell Ethemattian from a beached dolphin. Magic was also a possibility, either to prevent Keffen paying attention to an imposter or disguising that imposter as Ethemattian. Either way would take a Depths of a lot of magic. There were far easier ways to kill someone. A knife in the kidney or a bashed-in skull were always popular alternatives.

And there was the matter of the selection of Ethemattian as the sacrifice. There had been five volunteers. How could anyone be sure that Ethemattian would be the one picked? Again, magic might nudge the choice, but if not, that meant another conspirator at least. From what Kehsereen had told me, this was a ceremony that took place in front of the entire Brythanii priesthood and was carried out by a second Most Cursed. What could Ethemattian have possibly done to piss off so many powerful priests?

I was going to have to squeeze Keffen, and the sooner the better.

Then there was the Lady of the Grove. If anything, I had made less progress there. I didn't know how a god could be killed. I didn't even know the theories. Ash could usually suppress a god's power, and I knew for certain that the Guard had at least one god buried in Ash and helpless somewhere beneath their fortress. Maybe you *could* kill a god trapped in Ash, but there had been no trace of Ash near the Lady's body, and the Guard kept a brutal rein on the possession of it. In any case, the body was just the god's puppet.

And just suppose I could find out how the murder had been achieved? Would that actually take me to whoever was behind this or just to another bunch of scholars who never left their colleges?

I was going to have to get Scholar Longstream to squeal, one way or another.

I couldn't keep my eyes unfocused all night without giving myself a splitting headache. I let myself fall into a pattern of checking every ten minutes or so while I tried to figure my way through my problems, and I almost missed it when it emerged.

The first hint I had was the stench, like a sewer leaking into the cellar. When I let my eyes lose focus, the magic was seeping through the back wall, and by then a shape was already emerging from shadows, becoming like solid smoke. That was the best way I could put it. A shifting, fluid form that sprang momentarily into fixed, hard structures before billowing into new forms. I glimpsed claws in the shadow-smoke, teeth, hints of spikes and matted fur, eyes that blinked like stars between torn clouds and then were gone again. Hulking, bent, then tall and skeletal. The foul sewer smell made me choke.

My first instinct was that it was a tormented ghost. I had seen them like that before, ghosts of the bitter and the angry and the scared, but this wasn't made from ectoplasm. There was magic to this, and solidity drawn from the surroundings. But it wasn't a spell. It was something intrinsic. Not a god, either. The power was wrong.

And while I was busy wondering what in the unholy Depths it was, I had let it finish forming. The last of the magic seeped through the wall and coalesced, then the thing came for me. I threw up a shield, and the shadow-smoke shattered momentarily against it. The impact threw me back off the chest. My head bounced from the stairs, and I saw stars.

Somehow, I kept the shield up, which was a good thing, because moments later, the thing reformed and came after me again.

I had been unfeasibly lucky the shield had stopped it. There were a dozen things that could have passed right through, but this was solid enough – real enough – to bounce right off.

The shadow-smoke pushed against my shield. I felt it driving me down, like I was trying to hold up a collapsing ceiling. Anger rolled off the thing. And now it was spreading across my shield, as though feeling for the edges.

"Fuck's sake!"

What would happen when it found its way around? I wasn't keen to find out. I reshaped my shield into a half-sphere around myself. Still the shadow-smoke spread, squeezing, teeth and claws striking against the shield and then dissipating back into smoke. And, shit, I had been wrong. The shield had held against the first impact, but shadow-smoke was seeping through. Just wisps, but it was coming.

I gathered more raw magic, my body flaring in pain, shaped it into a blade, and slashed through the thing.

The blow didn't kill it. It didn't even hurt it. But for a second, the shadow-smoke parted, and I saw it.

"I know you."

Tendrils of shadow-smoke formed inside the shield. They scratched over my skin like needles, like a hundred paper cuts. I gritted my teeth against the pain.

This thing wasn't a ghost, but I had seen inside it, and it wasn't so different. If you couldn't destroy the source that linked a ghost to a place, you could still unpick the knots that held it together and dismiss it, at least for a while. I had seen the same type of knots anchoring this thing.

I sent my own tendrils of magic into it, searching for the knots of magic and ripping them apart. I wasn't gentle.

The shadow-smoke wasn't gentle, either. Its tendrils tore and stabbed at my skin. But I had it now.

Suddenly, it burst. The smoke dispersed into shadows, which faded in the light of the lamp.

The last of the thing's magic faded. I forced myself up. My hands, my face, and my neck felt like I'd been in a fight with a hundred angry kittens. My skin was criss-crossed with thin, shallow cuts and was coated in blood. Every part of it stung. I cursed creatively. At least it hadn't got my eyes, and at least most of it had been held out by the shield. This could have gone much worse, which made it a victory in my books.

My body didn't agree with me. I was going to have a Depths of a big bump on the back of my head.

I didn't know if this thing would be able to form again like a ghost – a ghost had its source that it was tied to and sustained by – but I wasn't taking any chances.

I let myself settle and my breath slow, then I wiped the blood from my face with a sleeve and set about weaving wards around the cellar and the house that would keep the thing out.

It took me an hour, and I was bone-tired as I struggled up and out of the house, even with my mage-enhanced constitution.

The street outside wasn't busy, but even so, I drew a few frightened glances as I made my way to the last house of the terrace and hammered on the door.

Ileoni must have been waiting just inside because the door slammed open and she stood there, staring.

"Pity, Nik! What happened?"

I shook my head. "Don't worry. It's superficial. A couple of hours' sleep will sort it out."

"Depths. So, there was something?"

"You weren't imagining it. And it's a Cepra-damned good thing you didn't go down there again." I hated to think what might have happened to an unprotected person.

"We need to get you cleaned up. Is it safe?"

"Yeah. It's gone, and I've protected the place so it doesn't come back. As long as the Ash Guard don't come visiting and wreck my wards, you'll be fine. And if they do, I'll set it up again."

I let her lead me back to her place. I was too beaten up and bloodied to object, even when she insisted on wiping my stinging skin with a wet cloth. I realised as I sat there, wincing, that despite my intentions, I wasn't going to make it to Holera and Elosyn's for dinner tonight after all.

You always let someone down.

They would understand. An uneasy voice in the back of my head whispered that maybe this would be the time when they wouldn't, that I would have pushed it too far, like I had pushed Benny too far, like I pushed everyone too far.

But I couldn't go like this. I wouldn't make it. I would have to apologise, beg forgiveness.

Fuck.

"You should borrow one of my brother's shirts," Ileoni said. "Either that or start buying red shirts, because this one is wrecked."

Wasn't that always the way with my shirts? Bloodied and torn and ruined in days. "Your brother's six inches shorter than me," I said. "It would look ridiculous." I tugged the mage's cloak around me. "This hides it well enough."

She didn't look convinced, but she let it go. "How about the neighbours? Are they going to be safe, too?"

"They'll be fine. These things are linked to locations. They can't go far. You just had the bad luck to be in the wrong place."

She let out a sigh and sat in the chair opposite me. "So, what was it?"

"They're called Manifestations. They're similar to ghosts, but they're magic-based creatures, not the remnants of a dead person. They're shaped by strong emotions. Fear, fury, even happiness, although this one wasn't manifested by happiness, I can tell you that." Not unless someone had a really strange idea of happiness.

"There's not been anything like that in this house. I would know. It's been normal. We have arguments sometimes, but nothing much."

"It's not you. It's the Warrens. Things are getting out of control there. People are angry. More than that. Furious and terrified, and it's spilling out of there. If I were you, I would keep well away from the Warrens for the next week or so." I levered myself up. Everything hurt, and it was just going to get worse sitting here. I needed to go home and sleep, even if just for a short while. "I have to get back."

She stood. "I owe you."

"No, you don't."

She eyed me for a moment. "Still, you know you've got me to talk to if you need. About what we said earlier?"

I nodded, although the movement was more of a jerk. I couldn't think about that right now. I didn't have it left in me. I raised a hand, then headed back to my apartment for the sleep I so desperately needed.

I should be so lucky.

WHEN I REACHED HOME, A FIGURE STEPPED OUT OF THE COVER of the steps.

I had seen him already, despite his best attempts to hide, so I didn't meet him with a blast of magic that would have knocked him senseless. I also resisted the urge to turn around and sneak in the back. My visitor's pale skin looked ghostly under his hood.

"Mr. Ethemattian," I said.

"*Cursed* Ethemattian."

I forced a smile. It made the scratches on my face sting. "Come inside."

I needed a better way of running my business. I was always coming home to people hanging around my door. Maybe I needed an assistant. How I would *pay* an assistant, and who would be crazy enough to work for me, well, best not think about that.

I opened the door and let Ethemattian precede me.

"I saw you outside the temple," he said.

"I hoped you would." It hadn't even crossed my mind, but one thing I had learned was never to turn down the chance to look good to a client. The perception of competence paid better than actual competence. “I want to bring you up-to-date with the investigation, and I need to ask you some questions.”

He nodded, but he couldn’t stop glancing around, starting at the sound of Fria scratching at the inner door. I had left Fria home too long again. At least he hadn’t escaped this time. Maybe he was finally settling in.

“Is everything all right?” I said.

He flicked a look at the door, then his shoulders slumped. “I don’t want to be seen here. If whoever set me up knows I’m onto them…” He trailed off.

Whoever was behind this must know he wasn’t going to take this lying down. He hadn’t put his name forward for the Choosing. It was only natural he would be trying to find out who had. But he was right that my involvement would be better kept a secret for as long as possible.

“Where then?”

“There’s a bar I go to when I don’t want to be seen.”

That was no surprise. Everyone had secrets, from the lowest beggar to the highest emperor, and priests were worse than most. It was all that training in being mysterious.

“It had better not be Dumonoc’s,” I muttered.

“What?”

“Never mind. You don’t think your colleagues know about it?”

“Of course they do.” He smiled. It didn’t look natural on his face. “It’s called the art of diversion. You let them think they know what you’re trying to hide. Then, when you do want to hide something, they’re looking in the wrong place.”

Smart. Sneaky, but smart. I would have to remember that trick.

"I'm not the only one," he continued. "I could tell you shameful secrets about every priest in the temple."

Well. That could be unexpectedly useful. "How about Keffen?" If I could get dirt on the priest in charge of the Choosing, I could squeeze him.

Ethemattian tipped his head to one side. "Which one?"

"The Most Cursed— Wait, what do you mean, which one?"

"There's Menatha Keffen as well."

There! Now I remembered exactly where I had heard that name before. She was one of the other candidates for their Choosing. If I hadn't been so distracted by all this stuff with the Lady and Benny, I would have figured it out far quicker.

"Are they related?"

"Uncle and niece."

I clenched my fists so I wouldn't tear my own hair out. "The priest in charge of the Choosing is the uncle of one of the other candidates, the one *you* had a fight with just a week ago. And you didn't think it was worth telling me?"

He shrugged helplessly. "It was nothing… She wouldn't…"

Fuck me sideways. How much time had he wasted?

"Please," he said. "I really don't want to be seen here."

"Fine." It would give me time to compose myself and not tear the stupid bastard's head off and shove it up his own arse. "Where?"

He named a bar in Dockside. "Come in five minutes." He glanced up at me. "Maybe without the cloak?"

When he was gone, I let a furiously enthusiastic Fria out of the apartment. He jumped up, wagging with enough force to stun a bull.

"All right, boy, all right." I should have got a dog a long time ago. No one had ever been this happy to see me. "Wanna go to the bar? We can drink our sorrows away." Maybe alcohol would dull the pain of my injuries. If not, well, I wouldn't look so out of place among the Dockside drunks. "We'll call it a wake for Mr. Inles."

CHAPTER ELEVEN

THE BAR WAS A HOLE. MOST PLACES IN DOCKSIDE WERE. IF THE first thing you did when you stumbled off a ship was head for the nearest bar, you weren't looking for quality. You were after cheap alcohol, and plenty of it. It was a good place for a surreptitious meeting. Most of the clientele were sailors, strangers to the city who would be gone within the week. The few dockworkers who were here weren't focused on anything outside their cups.

I didn't spot Ethemattian at first. I had to elbow my way through the night-time crush of drinkers before I found him at a small table in the shadows. No one peering through the smeared window or around the door would see us. This obviously wasn't the first time Ethemattian had done something like this. I wondered how much dubious crap he got up to. Dubious crap had got plenty of people killed.

But not like this. The plot was too involved to be about some dodgy deal or offended dockworker.

I pulled out the chair and sat, tucking Fria in beside me beneath the table. Ethemattian frowned at Fria for a moment, then nodded. “Good.”

I looked around. People crowded close around the table, but the place was raucous and noisy, and no one would overhear.

“Tell me about the Most Cursed,” I said. “What’s his dirty secret?”

“Why do you need to know?”

“Because if you were falsely entered for this Choosing, he has to be in on it, whether it’s voluntarily or because he’s being blackmailed. I’m going to need leverage to get the truth out of him. That’s if you really want to save your life?”

“Yes. Naturally.” He worked his lips. “Most Cursed Keffen is a gambler, but a bad one. He steals from the temple to pay his debts.”

“You can prove that?”

“I have dates, places, amounts.”

My eyebrows shot up. “Very thorough. And why would you be collecting information like that?”

Ethemattian rolled his neck. Either the pillows at the temple were terrible, or he didn’t want to tell me any of this. “Religion is politics, Mr. Thorn. Not just my religion. All of them. They are about power and influence, not gods, whatever anyone might tell you.”

A server pushed her way to our table. “What do you want?”

"Wine," I said. "Something drinkable." It was going on expenses, anyway. "And a bowl of water for my dog." Fria whined. "Something for him to eat, too."

The server turned away, but not before I saw her roll her eyes. I returned my attention to Ethemattian. "Why did you want to become a priest if it's all so cynical?"

He let out an incredulous laugh. "That is why. People in this city do not much like the Brythanii. Our religion makes others uncomfortable. When they see us and think of how we hate our god, it makes them think, too, of their own gods and how little their gods do for them. People don't like to question their beliefs. It makes them angry, and rather than confronting the lies they tell themselves, they turn their anger on the ones holding the mirror. The more a person has been conned, the more they cling to it and the angrier they are towards those who show them the truth. There is a reason Brythanii never rise far in Agatos. We are not welcome. There are no other routes to power and influence in this city for a Brythanii other than through the temple."

That was ... refreshingly honest for a priest, and I couldn't really argue with any of it. "I want to know more about your religion. What's the point of it? How does it hurt your god in any way to kill one of the priests who hates it?"

Ethemattian leaned forward, pale eyes studying me. "Do you know what gods are, Mr. Thorn?"

I shrugged. The scholars at the university debated it constantly. I had sat through enough lectures on comparative theology to know they didn't know shit.

"They are revenants, faces pressed against the glass,

desperate to find a way in. They are drawn by power. They cannot resist it. Our god betrayed us. A catastrophe struck our people. We prayed and sacrificed for help, and the god ignored us. *You did not help us when we needed you*, we say. Our ceremony puts power into the person of a single priest, and we try to draw the god in."

"Why?" After all this time, did they still expect their absent god to help them? How? It was almost contemptibly naïve.

"Because one day we will manage to summon it, we will trap the god in that body." His eyes didn't blink. "And then we will kill it."

There was a moment of silence between us, almost loud enough to deaden the noise of the bar.

Then I said, "But you haven't managed yet."

"No."

"What makes you think it's going to be different this time?"

Sometime while we'd been talking, the server had brought the wine and the food and water for Fria. I hadn't even noticed her do it. Ethemattian reached for the wine and poured himself a cup. "I do not care if we do. All I care is that *I* am not the body to be murdered in pursuit of this end."

"Right." He wasn't interested in making sure *nobody* should be killed, just that *he* shouldn't be. I was starting to get the idea that my client wasn't a very nice person. Not that it mattered. He hadn't volunteered for this stupid ceremony and the others had. They had chosen to take the risk, and one of them, maybe, had decided my client should die in their place. I wasn't going to allow that. "I need to see the Most Cursed in private. I can go in through the back of the temple and confront him in his rooms. I just need to know exactly which rooms are his, and I need robes and a veil so I can pass as one of your congregation. Oh, and I need your notes on his gambling and theft. The more detail I have, the better. Can you do that?"

"I think so. His rooms are the fourth suite on the northern side of the courtyard, overlooking it from the top floor. I'll bring what you need in the morning. He'll be stubborn."

I smiled. "I'm used to stubborn. I'll have an answer tomorrow, one way or another. You should probably head back to the temple." I pulled the wine bottle over. "I'll stay and finish this." It was the least I deserved after today. And anyway, I wasn't sure I could get up just yet.

I STAYED TOO LONG AT THE BAR. I KNEW I SHOULD DRAG MYSELF back home for rest, but sitting there, sipping the wine, gravity seemed to double, and every part of me felt heavy. It had been a long day of tramping around the city, and the confrontation with the Manifestation had taken what energy remained, stamped all over it, and left me a bloody mess. Only when Fria started whining and pushing at my leg with his nose did I manage to get out of my chair and head through the cool streets for home. It was past midnight, but there were still enough people around that I wasn't worried about being jumped by misguided muggers. I didn't fancy another fight. My body couldn't take it.

My apartment wasn't far from Dockside, and in ten minutes, I was turning in to Corrastar Street.

With the inevitability of a punch in the face, a figure was waiting outside my door. This time I did turn to head for the back yard. But too late. The figure had spotted me.

"Mr. Thorn!"

I didn't recognise the voice. Young, female, Middle City. Reluctantly, I turned and trudged towards the woman.

She was young, as I'd guessed, and an Agatos native, but with maybe a touch of Mycedan. She had that lighter hair and wider shoulders. But more importantly, she was Ash Guard. Even without the uniform, that stance, ready for trouble and violence, the suspicious eyes. Yeah. I would recognise that anywhere. At least she wasn't carrying or wearing Ash. She wasn't here to kill me.

"You're wanted."

That was nice to hear. Or not. Depending on how much trouble I was in. Captain Gale had never sent a minion to fetch me before. Was that a good thing or a bad thing?

"Can it wait? It's late." I was also ready to fall into bloodied pieces on the street.

She eyed my scratched, raw face and hands critically. "No."

For a moment, I was tempted to tell her *tough shit*. But I didn't know this Guard, and I wasn't stupid enough to underestimate her. Even without Ash, the Guard were trained to fight mages.

They moved fast, without hesitation or warning, and they were deadly. A snake-fast kill was best defence against a mage, before we could bring up our magic. Say the wrong thing, and the best I might be able to hope for was being knocked senseless.

I looked down at Fria. He wagged hopefully up at me. "Looks like we're not done yet, boy."

THE LAST THING I NEEDED TONIGHT WAS TO FIND MYSELF IN the Ash Guard fortress. Ash was baked into the bricks and mortar of the building. Like all mages, I relied on magic to keep myself going far beyond normal endurance, at least until I came into the proximity of Ash and all that energy was stolen from me. But the Guard didn't slow as we reached the fortress. She marched me and Fria right inside. In my exhausted state, the effect of the Ash made me stumble, before I regained my balance, and every scrape and cut on my skin screamed. Fria let out a bark of protest.

The Guard left me in a small, comfortable room. I slumped into a chair and laid my head back. I kind of hoped Fria would piss in the corner, although not until I was free to leave, but he was too well trained.

Captain Meroi Gale didn't arrive for another ten minutes, and I had almost fallen asleep by the time she did. I jerked upright as I heard the door open.

She came around and sat opposite me. Her eyes travelled over my wounds. "I'm not going to ask."

"A Manifestation on Velli Street. A nasty one, strong, driven by anger."

"Well, I'm glad you dealt with it. We're run off our feet here. Manifestations are the least of it. Things are coming into the city that know far better than to do so, and half the mages here are being suspicious little creeps."

So how was that different from usual? "Then I've got more bad news for you. I came across at least three foreign mages who've set up a base in the Warrens. I'm pretty sure they're Pentathian, and I'm even more sure the Wren doesn't know they're there. I'll leave it to you to imagine what will happen when he finds out."

"Depths, Nik. How about some good news for once?"

I didn't think I kept the hurt from my face, because she lifted a hand in apology. "No. Not your fault. But what the fuck is going on, Nik?"

"What makes you think I would know?"

She raised her eyebrows. "The city is descending into shit. Are you really going to tell me you don't know anything about it? That you haven't already been dragged right into the middle of it?"

That was quite a talent she had, managing to insult me and be absolutely right at the same time. One way or another, everything from the mood of the Warrens, through the Manifestation in Ileoni's cellar, to the new mages was almost certainly linked to the death of the Lady of the Grove. But I had promised Benny I wouldn't turn the Lady's body over to the Ash Guard. I wasn't going to break that promise.

"You're about to lie to me," Captain Gale said. "I can see it. That would be a mistake."

The threat was there, as clear as she was sitting opposite me.

I owed Benny, but I owed the city, too. How many other people were facing what Ileoni had faced, or worse, and didn't have a friendly mage to turn to? Somehow, I had to balance this.

"It's the Lady of the Grove," I said. "She's been killed. Murdered, I think."

I would give Captain Gale this: she almost managed to keep her expression steady. Just a hardening of her countenance and a twitch of the scar that cut across her face near her left eye.

"Someone murdered a god. In my city. Who?"

"That's what I'm trying to find out. The Lady was the only thing that gave the Warrens hope. Without her, the place is going to erupt into violence. It's not going to be pretty."

"The Warrens isn't my problem. My problem is that every mage and magical creature out there is going to be heading right for that body. You saw what chaos a single god's foot could cause. In fact, if I recall correctly, you managed to destroy a significant chunk of the dockyards with it. Imagine what a competent mage could do." Ouch. To be fair, that destruction hadn't precisely been me, but I didn't think Captain Gale was ready to debate that. "Where's the body?" she asked.

This wasn't going to go well. "I can't tell you."

"You don't know?"

"No. I just can't tell you."

All humour left her face. I had to suppress a shiver.

"There are people in this fortress I do not want you to meet, Nik. People whose job it is to ask questions and get answers. I like you, but you need to understand that it is my job to protect this city, and I will do my job."

This time I couldn't stop the shiver. "I still can't tell you. I really need you to trust me. Can you trust me?" What else was I supposed to say? I was under no illusions about how long I would be able to hold out under questioning without access to my magic.

"Trust is such an interesting word."

"The body is safe, but if you take it, the Warrens really will explode. If they think you or the City are involved, a lot of people will die, people who don't deserve to."

Her eyes didn't waver. Then she said, "Fuck it. We've got far bigger problems than a god's body. But if you screw this up, Nik, you're going to spend the rest of your very short life in an Ash Guard cell. You understand that?"

Some things were better not to reply to. "What do you mean, bigger problems?" The power and wealth implicit in a whole dead god's body, even a minor god like the Lady of the Grove, could destabilise entire countries.

Captain Gale puffed out her cheeks. "I'm going to tell you something very few people know, for extremely good reasons. When a god dies, it's not just the body that's left behind. Try to imagine a stretched rope."

"I think I can manage that."

Not a twitch of humour. I guessed we weren't doing jokes.

"If you cut it, it flies violently apart. You can think of one end of the rope as the god's power in this world. That part of the power is what decays into raw magic. The other end is the god in its own realm, where it exists even when its dead. That's the part you encountered with the ghost of the dead beast god. You know all that. It's basic magic theory. But there's also another part of the god, the power that kept those parts connected, that allows the god to reach between the realms. To be alive, as you might call it. When a god dies, when you cut that rope, that power is violently released. We call it an Eructation."

"Is that even a real word?"

She still didn't crack a smile. "It's an almost unimaginable burst of power."

Fine. "I've never heard of it."

"We don't exactly publicise it, and gods don't die every day. But I guarantee the high mages know about this, and so do several others. The point is, at some point in the days after a god dies, that power will erupt into the world. You want to know where these monsters and mages have come from? They felt this power coming, and they want it."

"All right. I get that. The body is only one part of it. But why is this Eructation more of a problem than the body?"

"Because it's so abrupt and overwhelming. It's not something you'll draw on steadily for years. It'll be a few hours, no more, but in that time, it could reshape the world. If a dead god got hold of the power, that god might be able to reach back into this realm and come alive again. A high mage might be able to wipe out all their adversaries in a blink, or even become a god themselves. We don't know."

I could see that wouldn't be great. Understatement. I wouldn't want my mother or the Wren getting that kind of power.

"All right. But the Lady was only killed a couple of nights back. Those mages in the Warrens came a long way. They haven't had time, nor have those other mages or monsters you talked about." Senator Greenfield's mage had created a peculiar magical construction in his former library. Kehsereen and I had stumbled upon it, and I hadn't had a clue what it was for. Now that Captain Gale had explained the Eructation, I couldn't help but think that it was designed to capture that power. Why else invest so much in it when it so clearly didn't do anything at the moment? But it hadn't been set up in a day or even a week.

"This kind of power is so vast that it echoes back through time. They will have felt this coming for a long time."

"I haven't felt anything." Or was that true? How would I know if I had?

"No, well. But the high mages will have known, I assure you, and they won't be the only ones."

My mother, the Wren, Enne Lowriver, Carnelian Silkstar, my sister, even the cult who had been trying to waken the god of nightmares, Enabgal: had they all known this was coming? Had they planned for it, reached for it? How much of the chaos and conflict in this city over the last few months had come about as a result? And how many others had turned their eyes on that power, gods, people, and monsters alike?

This was far beyond my capabilities.

Yeah? And who else is there?

Well, there was the Ash Guard. A squad of the Guard, smeared with Ash, would put an end to all of it. If they knew who and where and when. Which was a big fucking, city-crushing 'if'. And they hadn't even known about the Lady's death until I'd told them.

This is not your responsibility. I had to worry about the Warrens and Cursed Ethemattian and Benny and Sereh and everyone else I cared for. This Eructation, this was too big. I was one second-rate mage. I would do my job, pass information to Captain Gale if I found it, and I would step aside, like I should have done too many times before.

"I don't suppose you know how to kill a god, do you?" I said.

She faced me with a steady gaze. "Really? Now? One murdered god is enough to be getting on with, thank you. But no. I do not know how to kill a god. We have our own ways of dealing with troublesome gods. You want my advice? Ask yourself who benefits most from the death of the Lady of the Grove."

"That could be any of them."

"Then leave it to us. You should be nowhere near any of this. Do you really want to go up against someone who could kill a god?"

I had asked Benny the same question. I didn't want to be involved at all. But while I could leave the Eructation to the

Ash Guard, my answer to this was the same as Benny's had been: I couldn't just let it go.

"I know you're not going to take my advice." She ran a hand through her hair. She looked tired, worn too thin. I felt for her, and I didn't want to make things harder, but I had responsibilities. "Just be careful," she said. "And don't do anything stupid."

See? She did care for me. Or she didn't want any more disasters to strike the city. If so, she was going to be out of luck, because I had a very big disaster in mind for whoever was behind this. It was just a shame I had lost my mage's rod in the harbour. I really wanted to crack some heads.

"So," Captain Gale said, "when did you get a dog?"

By the time I reached my apartment, it was well into the night, and I was ready to drop. Fria wasn't much better, and he didn't even seem interested in stopping to sniff trees or kerbs on the way back.

Captain Gale might want me to leave all this to her, but by the sounds of it, she had enough on her back. I couldn't do anything about her Eructation, and I wouldn't be much help against all these mages and creatures that were searching for it. She might say she would find the Lady's killer, but when it came down to the blade, it was going to be right at the bottom of her list of priorities. And she was right. It wasn't her job to stop the Warrens tearing itself apart, even if the original cause was the murder of a god. The Ash Guard took their remit in the city seriously. They wouldn't overstep it, for very good reasons. That meant if I wanted to find the killer before it was too late, I was going to have to do it myself.

"And how's that going?" I asked.

Fria let out a little whine.

"Yeah, exactly."

I had made no progress. Two days of poking at this problem, and I hadn't stuck a single hole in it.

Fucking Scholar Longstream. If he hadn't been such an arsehole, I might have an answer by now. I could have given the Warrens a target for its anger. Instead, what? People might die because of him.

I knew he wouldn't care.

I unlocked my door and ushered Fria into the apartment. He headed straight for the bedroom.

"That's my bed!" I called.

Or are they going to die because of you? Because of your principles.

All I had to do was raise one dead body, let Longstream talk to the resurrected remains of the Godkiller. Depths, maybe it would give me the information I needed, too.

And you take one step across the line. Then it's behind you, and you've lost sight of it. The next step is easier and then easier still.

I wanted to scream into the empty room.

Just once, then never again. When I knew how a god could be killed, Longstream would be able to tell me which of his correspondents had championed that idea. I would have someone to challenge. I would be one step closer to the truth, and the truth mattered.

So much for principles. So much for lines.

But first I had to sleep. I couldn't try magic in this state.

Just an hour. That was all.

Fria had spread across the bed. I shoved him over and pulled my blanket across me. It smelled of dog.

I was asleep before I could even kick off my boots.

CHAPTER TWELVE

I woke feeling shit. That was the downside of mage-healing while asleep; it took all the benefit of sleep, shoved it into healing, and left you feeling worse than when you'd started. Tentatively, I ran my fingers over my face. The scratches were healed, but it had been too long since I'd shaved. Rough stubble felt like the bristles of a brush to my touch. A beard didn't suit me.

It was still dark. I cast a mage light. The scratches were thin lines on my hands, but they didn't hurt and they weren't bleeding. It would do for now. Fria shifted in the light, but he didn't wake.

All right for some.

I wouldn't say the sleep had made me think any better of this plan. It had never seemed like a good idea, and that hadn't changed. But the sleep had added to the weight of my reluctance. I felt like a dockworker staggering beneath a bale of cotton.

None of that changed what I had to do. I rolled my shoulders, trying to work out the knots and cricks, then gave it up as a bad job.

I didn't know what time it was, but I did know it was later than Scholar Longstream had told me. I wondered if he would still be there, waiting next to the Godkiller's tomb in the blackness. It would have freaked out anyone with an imagination.

Depends on how much he wants it.

I donned my black mage cloak to put off potential muggers or drunks, then slipped out the apartment, leaving Fria asleep on the bed.

Agate Blackspear, the Godkiller, had, if you believed the story, founded the city of Agatos four hundred and twenty-six years ago, battling and eventually killing Sien, the Lady of Dreams Descending, at the top of Horn Hill.

That founding of the brand-new city of Agatos had come as a surprise to the residents who had been happily living in a city here for centuries, but no one wanted to argue with a high mage who had just killed their patron goddess, and so the pirate had become a king, the city had become Agatos, and for decades, Agate Blackspear had ruled over his own city.

Eventually, even high mages died, and the Godkiller had been buried beneath a suitably garish monument in the Fields of the Dead. In the dark of the night, beneath heavy, running clouds, the Godkiller's monument loomed like an upraised fist against the mountainside.

There were guards at the Fields of the Dead, of course. People often buried their loved ones with jewellery, as though a rotting corpse was going to look any better with a shiny necklace or gold-buckled belt. I didn't really understand people. I did, however, understand the thieves who sometimes snuck in to redistribute wealth from the dead to the living.

I also understood the guards, who had long ago decided life would be much easier and probably longer if they all stayed in the guardhouse and didn't go confronting the kind of person who would rob corpses, because those people had no problem dropping a corpse or two more down a burial shaft.

No one, however, thief or guard, wanted to be anywhere near the Godkiller's tomb at night.

No one except Scholar Longstream, who emerged from behind the monument, wrapped in a thick coat, as I approached.

"Mystery Thorn. You are late. I was beginning to think you were not interested in your answers, and I was wondering if the rumour I heard of someone stealing a copy of *The Silver Oak* from Senator Greenfield could possibly be true. I was wondering if I should do my civic duty and come forward."

Civic duty, my arse. This man wouldn't help if he saw an orphanage burning.

"Let's just get on with it, shall we?"

Longstream gave a little bow. It would have been the perfect opportunity to knee him in the face, but I resisted the urge. See how mature I was getting?

"After you, Mystery."

Go fuck yourself.

The monument stretched maybe fifty feet into the air. An iron door led through to an inner chamber. It was locked and rusted shut, but a couple of spells saw the lock click and the rust around the jamb and hinges flake away. I pushed it open with a creak of metal that would be enough to scare the shit out of anyone nearby.

The interior was ominously lit with morgue-lamps, the green glow making Longstream's face look dead as he followed me in.

The walls were gilded – no one would be stupid enough to rob *this* monument – and illustrated with suitably epic scenes of the towering Godkiller battling the goddess then ruling over the city. If the artists were to be believed, the Godkiller had been a seven-foot-tall, heroically built man of Torian or Secillian descent, with an aggressively jutting beard.

Depths, maybe we were related. You know, apart from the heroic build and beard, and that he was a high mage from four hundred years ago.

Despite the size of the monument, the Godkiller was buried in a shaft, like most citizens before and since. This shaft was capped with a beautifully carved alabaster lid.

I turned to Longstream. "I don't know how much of the body is going to be left after all this time. I will raise it, but I can't say whether it will be able to speak or if you'll be able to understand a four-hundred-year-old language, but that's your problem. Agreed?"

"Yes, yes." He waved a hand contemptuously. His eyes were fixed on the shaft. He was almost vibrating with excitement. A wave of apprehension swept over me. Was this such a good idea? I was resurrecting a centuries-old mage. His own followers hadn't done that. They had known better. *All* mages knew better.

Of course it's not a fucking good idea.

If this went wrong, Captain Gale was going to kill me.

"Help me with this," I said, indicating the cap on the shaft.

"Can't you use magic?"

"I'm saving my power for the job."

With a lot of grunting and really very minimal help from Longstream, we shoved the cap aside, revealing a deep, dark shaft. I took an involuntary step back. The last thing I wanted was to fall down there, break my neck, and end my days in the Godkiller's skeletal embrace.

I wasn't scared of dead bodies or bones. Depths, I wasn't *scared* of dying, although I would rather not do it yet. But this was *wrong*, fundamentally, on a level I couldn't elucidate. And I still had to do it.

I felt sick.

I knelt on the lip of the shaft.

"Try not to fall in," I told Longstream, who was leaning over the edge, an eager expression on his face.

The shaft was no different to any other I had seen. *Dead is dead. No special privileges anymore.* It was cut smoothly from the rock, sloping slightly so that the body could be slid down rather than dangled, banging off the side like a drunk in a hallway.

The shaft had probably been excavated with magic, as most were. *Fun job for a mage, there.* At least I hadn't been reduced to that.

The green light of the room didn't penetrate deep into the shaft, and the blackness beyond seemed to stare back up at me, as if the Godkiller had tilted his skull back to fix those eye sockets on me.

I hated the dark under the city.

There were some religions that left their dead exposed on the mountainside for scavengers to consume or that burned the bodies. Both were so much better than being lowered into a dark hole.

What does it matter when you're dead?

Except I wasn't dead, and if I did this right, the Godkiller wouldn't be dead soon, either.

"What's the delay?" Longstream demanded.

"Nothing."

I formed a mage light and slowly floated it down the shaft. Inch by inch, the smooth rock emerged from the dark.

It was deep, this shaft, deep enough for a dozen corpses. I felt an undeniable urge to lean further in, over the edge. I steadied myself and unfocused my eyes. No magic down there except my mage light.

The light came to a halt. It had reached the bottom.

"Well?" Longstream said.

I squinted. "I can't see the body."

"What do you mean?"

I gestured to the shaft. "Take a look."

Longstream craned his neck over. "Brighten the light."

I fed in more magic. It didn't help. The glare of the light at the bottom of the dark shaft made it hard to see anything at all.

"You're going to have to go down there," Longstream said.

I turned my head slowly to face him. "Why don't *you* go down there? You're smaller. You'll fit more easily."

He lifted his chin. "Do you want your answers?"

"Do you want yours?" Maybe I should just push the bastard down. He'd find out quickly enough that way.

He shrugged. "You came to me."

Bannaur's bitter balls! I was going to have to go down there, wasn't I? Gather up the remains, bring it all back up... The revulsion I felt was so great I almost strode right out of there. But I couldn't. I stared down into the depths, my mage light glowing like ghost trail far below.

I sat on the edge, easing my legs in. The hole was narrow, wide enough for a body not to get stuck, but not much more. My pulse was rising, my chest growing tight. Sweat gathered on my palms, but my skin was cold. My vision narrowed so it was scarcely wider than the shaft.

Not now. Calm. You've got magic. You can do this.

I couldn't.

I drove my thumbnail deep into the flesh of my thigh until the pain bit through my panic.

You can do this.

Fuck.

I lowered myself in.

You might have thought that a narrow space and a slight incline would make things easier, but they didn't. There wasn't enough space to brace my hands and feet properly against the opposite side. In the end, I had to use my forearms and knees on the rock and slide, foot by jerking foot, scraping my skin.

How in the Depths are you getting back out of this, Nik?

My muscles ached, and sweat stung my eyes, but I couldn't wipe it away. The shaft felt like it was going down forever.

Maybe it is. Maybe I was sinking below the city, beneath the chambers where I had found the god of nightmares, Enabgal, beyond history and memory.

What if Longstream closed the cap above me? What if the walls closed in tighter until I was wedged?

Get a grip!

My feet hit something hard. I froze. I realised I had squeezed my eyes shut. I blinked them open.

I was right on top of the mage light. I dimmed it, then floated it above my head so I could see properly. Very carefully, in case I had just hit some temporary obstruction or ledge, I lowered my feet and let them take my weight. My body shuddered. At last, I could get a real look.

The base of the shaft was empty. No body, no bones, no remnants of funeral wrappings. I dropped to my knees, running my fingers over the floor.

Nothing. Not a scrap. Not even dust in this sealed shaft.

Certainly no body of the Godkiller. I rapped my knuckles painfully on the stone below, in case it was a false floor, but there was nothing.

My muscles turned weak. I slumped, leaning my head against the cool rock.

Maybe someone had already tried to resurrect the Godkiller or moved his body. More likely, he had never been buried here at all. His burial spot must be elsewhere, somewhere anonymous and undistinguished, purged from all records. This place was no more than a distraction, to attract the attention of thieves and graverobbers and fucking stupid mages who wanted to resurrect Blackspear.

"Well?" Longstream called.

"I'm coming back up."

If getting down had been difficult, climbing back up was brutal. I couldn't get leverage on the walls, and I kept slipping back. If I hadn't been able to draw on magic to push myself up a few feet at a time, I wouldn't have made it at all. Maybe that was why they buried people in shafts: so they wouldn't come crawling back out.

I felt almost like a corpse myself by the time I flopped over the edge onto the floor. I was soaked in sweat, covered in scrapes, and panting.

"Well?" Longstream demanded again. He was frowning, his hands working together.

I pushed myself up then clambered to my feet. I had taken kickings that hurt less than this. "He's not there."

Longstream's brow creased. "What?"

"It's empty. There are no remains. This isn't the real burial place."

"You're lying."

"Want to check for yourself? Because I will quite happily help you down there." This whole thing was his fault, his fucking stupid scheme that could have put this whole city in danger, that violated my strongest-held principle.

He scrutinised my face for a few seconds. "Then we are done here." He turned to leave.

I grabbed his shoulder and spun him around. "No, we are not. I've done what you asked. Now you're going to tell me what I want to know." I could feel the rage bubbling in me like a pool of magma.

Still his expression was of amused superiority. "Have you, Mystery Thorn? I asked you to raise Agate Blackspear. Is he raised?" He made a show of looking around. "I don't see him. Perhaps he is invisible."

I couldn't keep my fury under control any longer. I had been through so much shit for this bastard. Stealing from Senator Greenfield, escaping from his mage, compromising my beliefs, climbing down that cursed shaft...

Magic exploded out of me, slamming Longstream into the wall and sliding him up until he was dangling high above the floor.

"Denna save me, I will rip you apart and leave your body in that hole where no one will ever find it."

His eyes widened, his face slackened. He struggled against the magic, but it was driven by my rage, and I pressed it into him, squeezing.

"Did you think I wouldn't tell anyone I was meeting you?" he gasped. "If I don't return, they'll go to the Ash Guard."

Fuck. He really wasn't going to crack. Nothing I could do was breaking through that overweening arrogance. And what in the Depths was I doing? This wasn't how I operated. Revulsion swept through me, at him, at myself, at whoever had been stupid and selfish enough to kill a god. Suddenly, I was tired, too tired to keep this up.

I let my magic fall. Longstream dropped, crashing to the stone floor with an impact that made him yell in pain.

He scrambled to his feet, limping to the open door. "You'll pay for this, you lowlife, good-for-nothing, gutter shit."

No *Mystery Thorns* anymore, it seemed.

"Fuck you," I said. I thought that just about summed it up.

I WOKE THE NEXT MORNING TO THE SOUNDS OF SOMEONE pounding on my door and Fria barking. For a moment, I wondered if it was the City Watch trying to beat down my door and arrest me for one of the many laws I had undoubtedly broken over the last couple of days, and I considered heading out my window instead. Except if I was going to be arrested, they would send the Ash Guard instead, and I wouldn't wake to a knock on the door but to a sword against my throat.

"All right, all right!" I rolled over and out of bed. My

trousers and shirt were frayed and stained with dried blood from my time down the shaft. To think, I'd changed into a clean shirt after my encounter with the Manifestation in Ileoni's cellar. I should put a clothing allowance in my fees; these jobs went through my outfits like broken glass through skin. My injuries had healed, but I still felt like I'd been dumped out the back of a waste cart. And, yeah, I did know how that felt.

When I opened the front door, Cursed Ethemattian was outside, fist raised to hammer again. He was dressed in an enveloping cloak and hood, which made him far more conspicuous than if he'd dressed normally.

"Wake up the whole neighbourhood, why don't you?" I grumbled as I stepped aside.

"It's ten o'clock. The whole neighbourhood is already awake."

I closed the door behind him. "You have what I need?"

He passed over a bundle. "The robe and veil mark you out as a retired priest. You won't look out of place in the temple. You have a similar build to Cursed Agondra. He left the priesthood five years ago, but he still visits from time-to-time. He wouldn't usually wear a veil, of course, but many do in this period of the Choosing. Don't get too close to anyone, though. You are not that similar, and up close, your face will be clear through the veil. You are not Brythanii." He handed over a small notebook. "This has a record of all the thefts and payments of debts by Most Cursed Keffen that I have been able to discover, along with information about the other priests. The Most Cursed has no duties until midday, so you will find him in his rooms."

Ethemattian wasn't any keener on staying than I was on talking to him before breakfast. I waited until he was gone then hooked Fria to his leash and headed out to eat.

Fria whined when I closed him back in the apartment afterwards. I couldn't say I blamed him. He hadn't signed on to spend his days locked inside. "We'll go out later," I told him, but he didn't look convinced.

I waited until I was close to the Street of Gods before I found a quiet alleyway and changed into the robe and veil Ethemattian had provided. I didn't like the feel of the veil on my skin, and it restricted my vision enough to make me twitch when people loomed unexpectedly into sight. One man I passed spat and muttered something about the Brythanii. I didn't respond, but I did toss a spell at him that made him trip and collide with a wall. I continued serenely on.

Last night had been a disaster. Two days trying to find answers, and they had led to absolutely nothing. I was no closer to finding out who had killed the Lady than when Benny had first showed me the body.

Maybe I had been going about it all wrong. The idea of discovering how a god might be killed and who might be discussing the topic now seemed desperate at best. A half-dozen scholars might have stumbled on a way of doing so, but that didn't mean any of them would actually have gone through with it, nor that whoever *had* killed her had known anything about their arguments.

Who benefits most from the Lady's death? Captain Gale had asked. And it could be any mage who wanted the power, but was that it? Could a mage who killed a god really guarantee that *they* would be the one who captured the power of the Eructation when every other potent mage knew it was coming? That seemed ... optimistic at best.

Maybe it was something else. Who would benefit from the Lady being taken out of the picture? Certainly not the people of the Warrens. But maybe someone who wanted the Warrens crushed. Without the Lady's protection and the hope she brought, what did the Warrens have?

Perhaps the question was, who would want the Warrens broken? People in the Upper City and the Senate hated the Warrens. They saw it as a stain on their pristine, glowing city, but they also knew its value. Who else? I didn't like the presence of those Pentathian mages, but I couldn't image they had travelled all this way to rule over the poverty of the Warrens.

Or maybe the Lady hadn't been killed by a person at all. Maybe it had been another god. That thought made cold fingers scratch up my spine. Gods played games, and people died. I'd had my fill of dealing with gods. If another god was involved, I should get out of this as soon as I could and run the opposite direction. Misbehaving gods were the Ash Guard's problem, not mine. Even Benny would understand that. Wouldn't he?

I avoided the front of the temple and came up on the rear courtyard through the back streets. Again, steady streams of people were entering and exiting the courtyard, the odd priest among them. I waited until there were no priests in sight, checked that my irritating veil covered my face completely, tucked my hands into my sleeves to hide my very un-Brythanii skin, and strode confidently into the courtyard.

Confidence was the key in situations like this. I had been in a lot of places I wasn't supposed to be, and for the most part, as long as you looked calm, confident, and as though you were about some task, most people wouldn't bother you, even if they didn't recognise you. Few people enjoyed confrontation or awkwardness, and I had strolled into some surprising places. If people did object, well, that was what my now-lost mage's rod had been for.

Ethemattian had said that Most Cursed Keffen's rooms were on the top floor – the third floor – on the north side of the courtyard – the left side, from here – and I identified a doorway leading in. Through the doorway, steps led up, and I followed them. I passed couple of servants coming down and a priest emerging from the second floor onto the stairs, but slight bows from the servants and a nodded, "Cursed," from the priest and I was past.

The security in this place was shit. So much for Kehsereen's contact claiming that only priests and their servants could get in here.

While the temple itself had been dour and stolid, the same couldn't be said for the senior priests' quarters. Elaborately painted murals lined the walls. Marble columns and floors were polished almost to mirrors. Elegant statues lined the walls in alcoves. None of the statues or murals showed religious scenes, I noticed. Nothing to glorify the god or its deeds. I wondered if all this luxury was an elaborate fuck-you-we're-doing-just-fine-without-you to the god or whether they just liked high living. The air was perfumed with the scent of out-of-season flowers.

I reached the third floor. The fourth set of rooms, Ethemattian had said. I came to a halt. The hallway was seething with priests and servants, and they were all clustered around Most Cursed Keffen's doorway.

Now, I wasn't going to say I was the most popular person in Agatos, but in my experience, when a large number of people turned up at your door, they weren't there to wish you a happy birthday, unless the happy birthday came wrapped in clubs, fists, and knives. Either way, I didn't see any presents, and as I approached, I noticed several City Watch-women and -men and a couple of temple guards holding the little crowd back from the door.

They had better not be there to arrest Keffen for fixing the Choosing, because I was relying on Ethemattian's payments.

Ethemattian had warned me about getting too close to anyone if I wanted to stay hidden by this disguise. But I would have to rely on everyone being more interested in what was going on in the Most Cursed's rooms and not looking too closely at me.

"What's happening?" I asked as I reached the back of the crowd, trying to make my voice old like the former priest I was supposed to be impersonating. I only managed to sound like a dehydrated frog.

One of the servants glanced back. "Cursed," he said, with

a little bow, and it took me a second to realise he was referring to me rather than reporting on what had happened. "It's the Most Cursed. He's dead."

~

It took me another full second to process what the man had said. "What do you mean, 'dead'?"

The servant's head bowed further. "I know, Cursed. We are all shocked."

Shocked wasn't the word I would have used. Mine would have been a lot more obscene.

"When?"

The servant looked confused. "Cursed?"

Why was that so difficult? "When did he die?"

"We found him this morning when we brought him breakfast."

Which wasn't what I'd asked. Luckily, others had heard. A priest near the front turned and said, "The Watch say he must have died yesterday evening."

Right when Cursed Ethemattian had come to see me. Maybe even when we'd been sitting in that Dockside bar discussing how I might blackmail the old bloke. I swore silently. I had delayed and delayed this job, and now I had missed my chance to question him.

Maybe Ethemattian had been careless. Sneaky he might be, but he wasn't a professional. Maybe he had poked too sharply or been followed when he came to visit me. Maybe someone had simply got nervous. Whichever, someone had decided the Most Cursed was a loose end. I didn't believe this was a coincidence.

If nothing else, at least this confirmed that the Most Cursed had been involved in setting up Ethemattian. But how in the unholy Depths could I prove that if the man was no longer around to talk?

You could raise him, like you were going to raise the Godkiller.

No. This was what happened when you crossed a line. You were tempted to do it again, just because it was easier. But I *hadn't* crossed the line. My toes might have touched it, but I still hadn't crossed.

You would have.

But I hadn't.

There was always another way. Every time someone covered their tracks, they revealed more of themself elsewhere. I hadn't known for sure that Keffen had been part of this plot, but now I did. I *had* been on the right trail. The Most Cursed had fixed the Choosing. He must have done it to protect his own niece from becoming the sacrifice. The question became whether the niece had been working with him, the one who had decided her involvement needed to stay hidden, or whether she was an innocent beneficiary.

I tapped the servant on his shoulder. "I would like to offer my condolences to the Most Cursed's niece. Could you show me where her rooms are?"

The junior priests – the Cursed – had accommodation on the opposite side of the courtyard, and it was considerably less glamorous. Bare, sandstone walls, narrow hallways, and closely-packed doors contrasted with the generous and airy quarters of the Most Cursed. No wonder so many junior priests were willing to take the gamble of volunteering for the Choosing in order to get promotion. It made sense. Squeeze the junior priests, reward the senior ones, and volunteers would pop out. Priests whose desire for power and luxury led them to take such a gamble. It said something about Menatha Keffen that she would be willing to do that, and even more if she would arrange a conspiracy to kill another priest to keep herself safe. In some ways, I was surprised Ethemattian hadn't volunteered himself. He hadn't made any secret that he had joined the priesthood for power and influence. But then you didn't have any power or influence if you were dead, and the odds weren't great for that kind of gamble.

Not such a gamble if your uncle is in charge of the Choosing.

Of course, Cursed Keffen *could* be entirely innocent. Perhaps she put her name forward and her uncle decided to help her without her knowledge. He couldn't have arranged the whole set-up by himself. Someone else in the process, some other senior priest, must have been involved. Most Cursed Keffen could have put Ethemattian's name forward without his consent, but it still had to be chosen, and that wasn't Most Cursed Keffen's job. I would have to find out exactly who else was involved in the process and how it was carried out. But why would the Most Cursed choose to frame the priest his niece had just been involved in an argument with? Wouldn't that just make her look suspicious? Was it coincidence? Dislike? Bad luck because the Most Cursed wasn't aware of the argument? Coincidences happened every single day, but it was still curious.

None of which would matter in just a few days' time, when Cursed Ethemattian would be beaten to death to really show their god what they thought of it.

The servant stopped outside a door that was indistinguishable from twenty other on this hallway. "This is Cursed Menatha Keffen, Cursed."

This whole 'Cursed' thing was getting on my nerves. I nodded and waited for the servant to leave. Then I knocked loudly.

Keffen didn't take long to answer, which wasn't surprising. It would have been generous to describe her room as a cell. It had a bed, a desk with a single shelf above it, a chair, a chest of drawers, and that was about it. Even the room I had occupied in the Countess's palace as a junior mage had been less meagre than this. There wasn't even a window.

The woman herself had the white skin and almost colourlessly-blonde hair of most Brythanii, but her eyes were unusually dark and her face almost flat. The look she gave me wasn't welcoming.

"Cursed Keffen?" I said. "I heard about your uncle." I tried to sound old again, without noticeably more success than the first time. "We knew each other." At least the veil hid the way my eye twitched when I told the lie. "I wonder if I might have a word?"

I wouldn't normally have intruded upon the family of someone who had died so recently. But then I didn't normally have reason to suspect that most relatives had done away with an uncle to cover up a joint crime. My sympathy was a little thin.

"If you must."

With an invitation like that, how could I resist? I stepped inside. "Were you close to your uncle?"

She didn't look close. She certainly didn't look like she'd been crying.

Not everyone cries. Grief came in different ways, and it came unexpectedly, not according to demand or expectation.

"Of course! He was my uncle. My mentor."

And conspirator? She didn't add that. "Do you know who might have wanted to hurt him?"

"You think he was killed?"

I shrugged. "It's a possibility."

She leaned in, squinting. "You're not Brythanii!"

Balls! I had pushed too quickly, got too close. I pulled off the veil. Depths, that felt better. I couldn't think with that thing scratching my face.

"Get out of here! I'll call the Watch!"

"I work with the Ash Guard." It was my default not-quite-a-lie. I *did* work with – or maybe just nearby – the Ash Guard, but Captain Gale certainly hadn't told me I could name-drop. *All in a good cause.*

"Then why were you in disguise? And why are the Ash Guard involved? Was magic used?"

All excellent questions. I couldn't forget that this woman might have set up one murder and carried out another. She was smart. And if she *had* killed her uncle, she would know there was no magic used. "The Ash Guard are always involved in serious crimes related to religion, and we prefer that people not know we're investigating." That sounded plausible, right? I had no idea if it was true. It probably wasn't. The Guard had better things to do, but everyone was scared of the Guard, and scared people were less likely to argue or question. I didn't give her time to think it through. "Was your uncle involved in anything he shouldn't have been?" *Like setting up one of your rivals for the fall.*

"Of course not! He was a Most Cursed. He was a good man."

And while people might not argue with or question the Ash Guard, they would lie to them. Captain Gale had told me that. "We know he had been stealing from the temple to pay off gambling debts."

She glanced to one side, just for a moment, but I caught it. *Aha! So you did know.*

"Do you think that was why he was killed?" she asked.

Maybe she had used it to blackmail him into going along with her scheme. "We can't rule it out." I took another look around her room. There were no clues here, or at least none I could find with her standing there. "Just for our records, where were you last night?"

"Here. In my room. Where else?"

"Was anyone else here with you?"

She looked shocked. "No! That would be entirely against our rules. All the Cursed stay in their rooms at night."

That was a steaming pile of bollocks. I knew at least one Cursed who hadn't been on his own in his room last night, because he had been in a shitty bar with me. But if the rest of them were all locked up in these little rooms, it would make it very easy to reach the Most Cursed's quarters without being seen.

"All right. We will have more questions. In the meantime, if you hear anything, please send a message to Captain Gale at the Ash Guard." I was certain she wouldn't be doing that. It would be embarrassing if she did. I pulled my veil back on. "Don't tell anyone I was here. If someone did kill your uncle, we don't want them to know we're looking."

I was going to have to come back when she wasn't here to see if she had left any evidence lying around. In the meantime, I needed to find out who else would have been involved in the Choosing, and preferably before they turned up dead, too.

CHAPTER THIRTEEN

THERE WERE MANY WAYS TO DIE IN AGATOS, BUT THERE WERE only two ways to be dead: poor and not poor.

If you were not poor, then you could arrange your own or your loved one's funeral. You could have it be moderate or lavish. You could be buried in a family shaft or carried through the streets in a procession, like the Stypilians, or burned on a communal bier. You could even have your body preserved and shipped abroad, although I suspected the chances of your body making it depended a lot on how angry and vengeful your relatives abroad would be when you didn't turn up. Otherwise, your body would be taking the direct route down to the Depths.

Being not-poor in the Warrens was a relative thing. The respectable, decent parts of the Fields of the Dead were not open to even the wealthiest of Warrens residents, but the same principle applied. If you could afford it, the shafts above the Warrens, above the Lady's grove, were an option.

But if you were poor, or if you had no one who cared enough to spend the money, then you would have to suffer one of the public shafts the Senate maintained in a corner of the Fields, right next to where the beheaded criminals were buried. There was no elegance there, no grand monuments, no memorial at all, just a numbered stone by the granite cap of each shaft.

Most Cursed Coyd Keffen wouldn't find himself in one of those public shafts, but Mr. Inles would. At this time of year, when it could still be unpleasantly hot in the middle of the afternoon, that was when the paupers' burials would take place, one after another, like sacks of flour unloaded from a ship, but with less care and attention.

I had plenty of time to spare before the day's round of funerals began. Even returning home to fetch Fria, I could still be back at the Fields of the Dead with an hour to spare.

I was tempted to find Benny to discuss our progress – or lack of it – and plan our next steps. But I had made that mistake before and ended up missing things I'd committed to. The idea of missing Mr. Inles's funeral, of letting him be buried alone in an anonymous shaft, without witness from me or Fria, left me feeling unexpectedly hollow.

"Why do you care now?" I said. "He's dead. It doesn't matter to him anymore."

And yet I did, and it did. I didn't understand those feelings. Maybe I would understand at the funeral. Maybe I never would. But I didn't think I had a choice.

I picked up Fria, changed into my best clothes, and headed back out.

I was only a street from home when two mages stepped from an alley in front of me. The weight of inevitability was like a dead body draped over my shoulders. There was always something. Always.

I recognised one of them, but not the other. I'd tangled with the first one before. She was one of the Wren's acolytes, and we hadn't parted on good terms. Both of the mages had already drawn in magic and held spells ready to let fly. I wasn't fooling myself. I was outclassed here. I didn't have surprise on my side nor my trusty mage's rod to smack someone with. I still wasn't going down easily. I pulled in my own magic.

"The Wren wants to talk to you," the first mage said, taking a careful step forward.

"He knows where to find me." It was bravado, but that was half my appeal.

"He does indeed. You don't want the Wren paying you a visit."

"I didn't want you paying me a visit either, but here we are."

The mage's magic flared, shaping itself into a spear. "This is not a request."

I responded with a shield. This mage was stronger than me, but she would have to do better than that. Fria growled beside me, and I froze. Getting into a magical fight on my own was one thing, but Fria couldn't protect himself from stray magic.

"All right," I said, letting my shield drop. "I'll come with you. I just need to put my dog back inside and—"

"You'll come with us now," the second mage interrupted.

My eyes met his, and I didn't like what I saw. Arrogance. Contempt. I could tell we weren't going to be friends.

My own voice flattened. "After I put my dog inside."

The bastard had been looking for an excuse. His magic formed into a net that came spinning down the street towards me. He was fast, but not fast enough. I shaped a blade and sliced through the net, collapsing it. At the same time, I threw myself sideways, just as the first mage's spear cut through the space I had occupied.

I didn't know if Fria could sense magic – animals sometimes acted as though they could – but if he couldn't, the sudden movements were enough to startle him. The moment I let go of the leash, he darted aside. Then he went for the first mage.

She saw him coming and swung a blade of her own magic down at him. I took her feet out from under her before she could connect. Her head bounced off the cobbles.

The second mage hadn't stopped to watch. He threw a wall of force at me, and I had no time to block it. It hit me like a runaway carriage. I tumbled back, blood bursting from my nose, scraping over the cobbles. From somewhere nearby, I heard shouts and screams.

I came to my knees, shield already up, head spinning. "Get out of here!" I shouted at Fria.

The second mage approached, magic gathering around his hands. There was nothing subtle about this guy. He was all brute force, a magical enforcer for the Wren. No real skill, just power. The problem with that was in a fair fight I wouldn't last long.

So don't make it a fair fight.

Being powerful had its advantages, but it also made a mage lazy. They started to think that direct magic was the answer to every problem. I'd caught more than one overconfident mage with the heavy end of my mage's rod. That was lost now in the harbour, but it wasn't the only weapon around. I held my shield steady as my eyes searched for a good candidate.

There. Behind him. His wall of force had ripped up part of the street. As he strode towards me, he left scattered cobblestones behind him.

I formed my magic and reached for one to smash him over the back of the head. He would never see it coming.

He wasn't the only one. Magic closed around me. It wasn't the second mage, and the first was still unconscious.

The magic tightened. I just had time to think, *That's not fair. There's another of them*, before everything went black.

I HAD BEEN HERE BEFORE.

For the first five years of my magical career, I'd managed to avoid the Wren completely. This summer, however, I seemed destined to run afoul of the criminal high mage at almost every turn.

It wasn't the first time I had woken from unconsciousness in this chair.

I was in the Wren's office in his warehouse on the docks. My chair was drawn up in front of his desk, but there was no sign of the man himself. I worked my mouth to rid it of the taste of chalk and garlic that being hit with magic always left then scanned the room.

To my left, a tall window looked out over the harbour. The light, insistent wind and low clouds had turned the water to rumpled green depths. Fishing boats rocked on the waves, nets dragging behind them. Like Mica's dad's boat had once done. Before it sank on a day clearer than this. Before our family had fractured. I wondered if the Wren had watched it sail out and then … ended it all. My fingers dug into my palms. If he had…

What? What would you do to a high mage?

"Over here, Mr. Thorn."

The voice came from my right. I turned to see the Wren's second-in-command, Melecho Kael, standing in the entrance to the inner courtyard of the hollowed-out warehouse, framed by the small jungle the Wren had established there.

Painfully, I stood and made my way across. I ached everywhere. I didn't know what spell the Wren's mages had used on me, but I suspected they had put the boot in when it was done.

The smell of the jungle-filled courtyard was unlike anything else in Agatos. It was rich, loamy, damp, and scented with the mass of living things. Agatos was dry and parched during summer, icy and snow-driven in winter, and always saturated with the underlying smell of the ocean and the city's shit. There was none of that here. I unfocused my eyes and examined the magic enclosing the courtyard. It was far greater than anything I could have managed. I couldn't even see how it was done. *High mages and their tricks.*

"It controls the humidity, the heat, even the light and rainfall," Kael said.

I couldn't quite place Kael's accent. Agatos, mostly, but with something else beneath it. He was a tall, bulky man, one of the few I'd met who was taller than me, and his skin was darker. From somewhere on the western shore of the Yttradian Sea originally, I guessed, but where exactly, I couldn't tell. He was holding gardening scissors in one hand, and his knees were dirty from the muddy soil of the miniature jungle. He beckoned me towards him, then stepped back beneath the canopy.

"I was taken from my home when I was quite young," Kael said. "But I still remember the smell and feel of the jungle. I allow myself this indulgence" – he indicated the mass of plants and trees – "and the Wren finds it relaxing."

Which was all very nice, but I doubted I was here for a tour. "Where's the Wren?"

"He is busy. He asked me to talk to you."

"Talk?"

"Mm." He reached out and clipped leaves from a bush, then looked at it critically. "We always liked you, the Wren and I, even when you were a kid running around the Warrens. We thought you had potential. Not as a mage, of course. That was your mother's romanticism. She was naïve about you, but everyone else could see."

Romantic? My mother? The blessed Countess? Had he *met* her?

"It is a shame you ended up in opposition to the Wren," Kael continued.

I shrugged. It hid the nervous shudder that ran up my back. "I just do the jobs I'm paid to. I'm not on anyone's side."

"Hmm. And were you paid to assault the gang under the Wren's protection?"

I had known this was coming. "No. That one was for free."

"You know, the Wren once planned for your mother to take his place when he stepped down. Unfortunately, your mother chose another path. The Wren never wanted her as an enemy."

Why the fuck was he telling me this? I didn't give a toss about their rivalry, except that it kept them off my back.

"Yeah? And what did he do to make her an enemy? I know my mother. She's not forgiving, but she's not a fool. She's practical above all else. She wouldn't choose to be the Wren's enemy for no reason." What would make my mother dedicate so much of her power and so many of her resources to opposing and undermining the Wren? I could only think of one thing. I leaned forwards. "Was it something to do with my stepfather? Did the Wren kill him?"

Kael stopped, scissors around a twig. "Take care. People make decisions. There are consequences to those decisions. That is as inevitable as the tides."

Was that an admission? Or a warning? Consequences

for what? What could my stepfather have done that would make the Wren kill him, knowing full well it would cause enmity with my mother? Or was he talking about something that had happened between the Wren and my mother?

Why did everyone have to be so fucking cryptic?

"That gang were robbing my friend's house," I said. "Are you saying the Wren's protection extends to not defending my friends?"

The scissors closed, clipping off the twig. "Choices and consequences, Mennik. There must be consequences, and they must be visible consequences."

And there we had it. The reason the Wren had brought me here. The consequences. I still didn't regret it.

"Why don't we just get on with it, then?" I didn't think he would kill me, but I did think this was going to hurt.

Maybe Kael was enjoying himself too much. However polite he might be, I couldn't forget he was second-in-command of a brutal criminal gang.

"Last night," he said, "you went to Agate Blackspear's tomb to raise his body."

I gaped. I couldn't help it. I couldn't even speak for several seconds. Eventually, I sputtered out, "How in the Depths did you know that?"

"The Wren has eyes and ears everywhere. There are no secrets from him."

That was as much goat shit. Which meant that Scholar Longstream had talked to the wrong person, gloating or boasting or complaining.

"It is never wise to raise the dead, and even more reckless to raise something that old."

"He wasn't there."

"Of course he wasn't. No one would be foolish enough to bury Blackspear where his body might be found. You would have wasted your time, anyhow."

"The body wouldn't have been able to talk?" As I had suspected.

Kael didn't confirm it. "You wanted to find out how a god might be killed so you could discover who killed the Lady of the Grove."

All right, that shouldn't have been a surprise. One of his people had definitely been talking to Longstream, and Captain Gale had said powerful mages would have known this was coming. The equation wouldn't have been hard to solve. Even so, I couldn't prevent myself starting at his words.

One thing I was damned sure he didn't know yet, though, was where Benny and I had hidden the Lady's body, and there was no way I was telling him.

"Blackspear could not have told you that," Kael continued.

"What do you mean?" I wasn't following this.

Kael folded his scissors and placed them in a pocket. "Agate Blackspear did not kill Sien, the Lady of Dreams Descending. He threw her down and tore away most of her power, but he was not able to kill her. It suited him to be known as 'the Godkiller' and to promulgate his myth, but it was a lie, and he no more knew how to kill a god than I do."

I took a step towards him. "How would you know that?"

Kael smiled. Whatever else, he certainly didn't feel threatened by me. "There have been Wrens in this city since the end of Agate Blackspear's reign. The title is handed down, but records are also passed on. We have records of Agatos here that the university could only dream of. In fact, the first Wren was a mage from Blackspear's court."

Well, that was all a big fucking revelation. This city was built on the reputation of Agate Blackspear, the pirate who became a king. The Godkiller. Only, if Kael was right, Blackspear had never been that. How many people would fear his reputation if they knew the truth?

"What happened to Sien?"

"You don't know?"

"No," I said, raising my chin, even though I suspected I did.

"She diminished and became the Lady of the Grove, patron god to the last of the city's inhabitants who still held to her, in the Warrens."

"And now she's dead. Now someone has done what the fucking Godkiller himself couldn't. Killed her."

Kael nodded.

"Who in the unholy fucking Depths could do that?" I exploded.

He tilted his head. "I thought you would have known that, too, by now."

This time I really didn't. I shook my head mutely.

"Sien was a dual god. Her twin was Niarret, who you know as Enabgal or Enhuin. They sustained each other. When Sien was weakened in her fight with Blackspear,

Niarret sustained her. When Niarret was lost beneath the city, forgotten, Sien, the Lady of the Grove, sustained him.

"Then you found Niarret, you took him, and you buried him in Ash beneath the Ash Guard fortress. Niarret could no longer sustain Sien.

"You want to know who killed the Lady of the Grove? You did, Mennik Thorn. You killed her."

CHAPTER FOURTEEN

I DIDN'T REMEMBER MUCH OF MY WALK HOME THROUGH Dockside and the lower part of the Middle City. I supposed the streets were busy. I had vague recollections of bouncing off shoulders and hearing curses follow me, but I wasn't paying attention. The Lady of the Grove had been Sien, the patron god of the city, reduced, diminished, but still a symbol of hope for the Warrens. I had told myself I was on the side of the people there, that the Warrens flowed in my veins as deep and as hot as blood. That I would fight for the Warrens whenever I could.

And I had killed her.

The words didn't make any sense. How could I, one of the weakest and most impotent mages in the city, have killed a god?

You know how. By breaking her link with her twin so she faded and was eventually ... gone.

I couldn't process it.

What was I going to tell Benny?

I'd wanted to find a target for the Warrens' fury. Well, I'd certainly done that. And if I told anyone, they would rip me apart.

What the fuck was I supposed to do?

I reached my front door just in time to see it burst open and for Fria to leap on me in a frenzy of barking.

I dropped to my knees. Suddenly, I wanted to scream and weep and shout. I wrapped my arms around the frantic dog. He was warm, soft despite the short fur. "Thank Pity you're all right," I whispered into his neck. If he was, maybe everything was. Then I straightened. "Who let you back in?" He had been out in the street when I'd been taken.

The answer wasn't hard to spot. The door had been kicked open, the wood around the lock splintered violently. I eased carefully inside, magical shield raised.

My office desk had been overturned and smashed. The rug on the floor was shredded, my couch eviscerated, the chairs not much more than kindling. Only my heavy iron safe had survived the assault, and it had taken a couple of solid blows that had bent the metal.

The damage didn't end there, either. My wards had been taken down, leaving only tatters of magic. The inner door was completely off its hinges.

The destruction continued inside the apartment. The furniture, my few pieces of crockery, my bedsheets, my clothes: all torn, smashed, and ruined.

Consequences, Kael had said. *Visible consequences.* The fucker.

There wasn't much I could do about this now. I put up new wards. They weren't powerful or elaborate, but they would hold. Then I led Fria out, locking the front door behind us with a spell, and headed for the Fields of the Dead.

The paupers' funerals had already begun when we arrived, but a quick question of a waiting undertaker told me that Mr. Inles's turn hadn't yet come around. So we waited, Fria and I, under the low grey clouds as bodies were lowered, relatives wept, and the restless wind buffeted around us. At last, the city official called, "Inles," and the body was brought out on a stretcher, wrapped in cheap linen.

I couldn't make out the body through its wraps, but Fria did. He strained against his leash.

"Easy, boy," I muttered.

The service was short. A generic prayer to gods who didn't care, uttered in the same monotone the city official had used for the last dozen burials. There was no one there to witness it other than me and Fria and the bored undertakers. Surely there should have been *someone*, if only out of curiosity? His whole life brought to this, burial under a flat sky with no one who had known or cared for him, not a single person to mourn his passing. Gone without a ripple on the world. If I died today, would anyone come to stand holding Fria's leash? Or would it be as empty and forgotten as Mr. Inles's passing?

As the body was tipped and slid into the shaft, Fria

howled, startling the city official, his voice echoing from the valley wall. Then it was done, the body gone, and the next was on its way. Over. Finished. So little, the punctuation at the end of an already forgotten sentence. I'd never even known his first name.

It wasn't enough, but it was all there was.

WHEN WE REACHED HOME, THE PLACE WAS STILL TRASHED. THE afternoon was drawing on, and getting all this fixed up today was going to take longer than I had to spare. The furniture was firewood, and my business might be doing well, but not so well I could replace all of this. A carpenter to fix the front door should be a priority, then a new mattress. A desk and chairs for the office. That would blow everything I had put by.

I kicked the broken items to the side, did my best to re-hang the inner door with the help of a couple of spells, and examined my bed, while Fria sniffed around the apartment. My bedframe was history, but while someone had taken a knife to the mattress, if I stuffed it back and flipped it over, it might serve for a day or two.

A few clothes were salvageable, and I found a plate and a bowl that were chipped but which I could use.

"See?" I told Fria. "It's not as bad as it looks."

Fria didn't look convinced. Perhaps he was just hungry.

"Oi!" a voice called from the office. "Nik. Where are you?"

I hurried out to see Benny standing in the debris. "What the fuck have you done?" he demanded.

I winced. "I think I've pissed off the Wren."

Benny prodded a broken chair with his foot. "Got off lightly, then."

"Yeah. I suppose."

"Same inside?"

I nodded. "Gonna need to replace some stuff. Know anywhere I could get a mattress, some chairs, and desk cheap?"

"No questions asked?"

"Yeah."

"Might know someone. Won't be today. We've got bigger problems."

He didn't know the half of it.

"You can't keep a dog in here," a soft voice said just behind my ear.

I started and let out a little squeak. Sereh was so close behind me, I could have felt her breath. Her eyes were flat, unwavering, and terrifying. I took a step away.

"Pity, Sereh! How long have you been standing there?"

"I've always been here, Uncle Nik."

Fuck's sake. "Just…" I clenched my teeth, then tried a smile. "He'll be fine. He's a dog." As if in response, Fria came trotting over to nuzzle Sereh's hand.

"I'm going to take him home until you sort this out. He can't sleep here."

The words sent an unexpected twinge through my chest. Depths, I'd only had Fria three days. I'd been fine for years on my own. I could manage a few nights without him.

"What about me?" I grumbled.

"It's your home, Uncle Nik. If you didn't want it this way, why did you let it?"

I was jumped, I wanted to say. *There were three of them, at least.* But Sereh wouldn't have allowed herself to be jumped. If they had tried, they would have been dead.

"We don't have time for this," Benny broke in. "I've just come from the Warrens. People are gathering. They're angry. They figured out what happened, and they blame the Senate. People aren't backing down this time. It's going to get ugly."

Had they worked it out, or had someone told them? Someone who saw it as an opportunity to sow chaos and hide their schemes?

Benny went on, "You better have found out who killed the Lady, or they're going to march right up to the Senate and try to burn the place."

Yeah. About that...

"I talked to the Wren's assistant. Melecho Kael. Remember him?"

Benny nodded. "Yeah, I know him. Dangerous piece of work, people say. I keep my distance."

With the implication that I should have kept my distance, too.

"He knows the Lady is dead. Everyone knows." I held up my hands. "I didn't tell them."

For once, Benny didn't seem inclined to blame me. "Was always going to happen."

"Yeah, well, he had some things to say, too."

"I bet he fucking did. I don't suppose he came out and said the Wren did it, right? Because that would be really fucking convenient now."

For a second – just a second – I was tempted to say that was exactly what Kael had admitted, to kick the Wren right into the path of the Warrens' avalanche of fury. But you didn't send people up against a high mage unless you wanted them dead, and it would be cowardice.

"Not exactly. He said Agate Blackspear never killed Sien. The Godkiller wasn't a god-killer at all."

"And what? How the fuck does that help us?"

Now that it came to it, I didn't know what to say. The words stuck in my throat. Benny's fury at the murder of the Lady was something overwhelming and visceral. If I told him I was the one who'd killed the hope of the Warrens, he might just go for me. He might bury a knife in my stomach. Even if he didn't, it might be the end of any chance of repairing our friendship. He would *hate* me, even more than he already did.

You don't have a choice. It'll come out eventually. Secrets don't stay hidden forever. And Benny would never forgive another lie, that was for sure. He wouldn't take being betrayed twice.

Fuck this!

"Kael said the Lady of the Grove was a diminished version of Sien, the Lady of Dreams Descending. He said she was a twin of that nightmare god I tangled with when..." Back when Benny and I had fallen out. When I had let him down. I took a slow breath. "He said I was the one who killed the Lady of the Grove through what I did to her twin."

I waited for Benny's reaction. Faced with the truth, would he cut my throat? Turn me over to the mob? Had I just signed my own death warrant? Or was there enough residual friendship to keep quiet, to just turn away?

Benny's sun-dried face broke into a grin. "You?"

"Yes." That wasn't the response I had been expecting.

"He told you that you killed a god?"

"Yes."

"You." He let out a guffaw and slapped his leg.

"*Yes!*"

"And you believed that shit?"

Now I was starting to feel offended. "It made sense when he explained it."

"You are so far up your own arse, Nik. I've known you for, what? Twenty-five years?"

"Give or take."

"That is the biggest load of bollocks I've heard in all that time. Fuck me, mate."

"I gave Enabgal to the Ash Guard. They buried it in Ash. They cut off its powers."

"And you think that killing a god is that easy? You know what I heard? I heard there's half a dozen gods trapped, helpless, in that fortress, but I never heard any of them were dead."

Captain Gale had said much the same thing, too. They didn't know how to kill gods.

"So why did he tell me I had?"

Benny laughed again. It sounded bitter this time. "To throw you off your game. You're a pain in the arse. You get in the way, you cause trouble, you draw attention, and he knew you were full enough of yourself that you'd believe it. He wanted you out of the way for some reason."

And I *had* believed it. I had been stupid enough to think that anything I could do could threaten a god. It was absurd. Only last night, Ileoni had told me I wasn't as special as I thought I was, and I'd nodded resentfully along, but I'd gone on believing it, deep down. What a twat.

"I think I might know why," I said, slowly.

"Yeah? This one I wanna hear, too."

"I talked to the Ash Guard."

Benny's face hardened at that.

I held up my hands again. "Captain Gale said all the mages already knew the god's death was coming. They felt it. But I didn't tell her where we put the body. Thing is, apparently when a god dies, it's more than just the raw magic from the body. There's this power that connects a god in this world to whatever realm they properly exist in. When a god dies, she said, there's a bit left here, their presence and their body, and there's the god in its own realm, and then there's the connection. The power that connects them is what every powerful mage in the city and beyond is after. Apparently, it could be enough to bring a dead god back to life or even let a high mage become a god. If that power is up for grabs, the Wren wouldn't want anyone getting in his way, would he?" A little lie from Kael to send me spinning into self-recrimination or even a suicidal admission of guilt, and all my interference would be out the way. He didn't even need long, if Captain Gale was right.

"If you had that power," Benny said, thoughtfully, "you could bring the Lady back to life, right?"

I shrugged. "Theoretically, I guess. I reckon that's what the cult of Sharshak are trying to do with their god." I had seen their magic beneath the shoe shop when Kehsereen and I had followed the cult priest back from Kehsereen's apartment. I just hadn't realised that was what they were up to.

"So do it."

I stared at him. "What?"

"Do it. Take that power and bring the Lady back to life. That would fix all of this."

I would have been less shocked if he had punched me in the mouth. "Benny, what in all the dark Depths makes you think I've got the power or strength to do that?"

"Then what fucking use are you?"

That wasn't fair. "I never claimed to be able to resurrect gods. I don't even know if it's a good idea to try. With that much power, anything could happen. It could be a catastrophe. It *would* be a catastrophe."

"You don't know that."

"Yeah, I do. The absolute best that could happen – the *absolute* best – would be that I was torn to bits."

From Benny's look, he didn't seem that upset by the idea. "Then you'd better think of something else before we get over there, because the Warrens is done waiting. There's going to be blood."

CHAPTER FIFTEEN

We left Sereh and Fria at Benny's house, along with instructions to stay exactly where they were, although neither exactly had a good record for doing that. The house wasn't far from the Warrens, but I didn't think trouble would be coming this way. If it did, well, Sereh could look after herself.

What Benny expected me to do, I was less sure. My skills centred around spouting goat shit, using some clever tricks, and performing wholly inadequate magic. Calming angry mobs wasn't really my speciality.

I wasn't the only one feeling the unease in the air. As we headed for the Warrens, I saw people hurrying in the opposite direction or bolting doors and closing shutters. Trouble breathed on the back of the lower city's neck.

I couldn't stand in the way of a mob. I couldn't turn them

back or drain away their fury. I certainly couldn't intimidate them. So, what did that leave me?

The truth. The Warrens knew the Lady was dead, and they needed revenge or a release of the anger and despair her death had caused. I didn't blame them. The Lady was theirs, all they had, and she'd been taken away. Useless and self-serving as gods were, they offered something to pin hopes and dreams on, even if the gods themselves wouldn't piss on you if you were on fire. The reaction of the Warrens to the Lady's murder wasn't so different to the reaction of the Brythanii to their god's betrayal. The only truth I could offer the people of the Warrens was the truth of who had killed their god before they took out their rage on the rest of the city, and that truth still eluded me.

Who had killed her? Not me. Benny was right to puncture that bladder. And that meant it hadn't been the Ash Guard, either. Depths, Captain Gale hadn't even known the Lady was dead. *Unless she was lying to you.* But why would she do that? Why would she or they throw the city into magical chaos and allow so much power to come up for grabs? If they wanted a god out the way, they would do it the same way they had with Enabgal, in a prison of Ash.

So, who else?

A high mage or wannabe high mage? Blackspear might not have been able to kill a god, but that didn't mean someone hadn't figured it out since. Both the Countess and the Wren might have reasons, but I couldn't believe Mica would do anything so reckless.

How do you know? You don't even know her anymore.

I did.

Or maybe my first hunch had been right: some interfering scholar up at the university. They wouldn't care about the chaos and death as long as they were proven right.

Then again, it might be someone I had never heard of, let alone met. A god, a mage, some twat with a holy relic. I just didn't know. I had run through the possibilities again and again, and I had no more to go on than I had when we'd started. This wasn't going to just come to me in some bolt of divine inspiration.

"Well?" Benny demanded as we plunged into the narrow, dark alleys of the Warrens.

I shook my head.

"Then we stop everything going to shit for as long as we can, however we can. All right?" He lifted his chin in challenge.

"Yeah," I said. *Somehow.*

We weren't the only ones heading through the tight streets. Men and women, cloaked and tightly wrapped with face scarves and hoods, clubs and stones and knives in hand, filtered through the Warrens, all converging on the northeast corner where it bordered the Middle City.

We heard the crowd before we reached it. Resentful, muttering voices, louder shouts, anger so thick you could have bitten it, swallowed it down like heavy, rancid soup.

A couple of thousand people, at least, had jammed into the courtyards, choking the streets and alleys, leaning from doors and windows, with more arriving all the time. They were so closely packed I could have walked across their heads. If I had fancied being dragged down and kicked to death.

"Change of plan," Benny whispered. "No way we're stopping this lot. Unless you've got some spell?"

I gave him a look.

"Yeah, well."

"So, what do you want to do?" I asked.

"Follow along, I guess. See if we can head off the worst of it." He turned his face up to me, and I saw the same rage in his eyes. "Nah. That's a lie. I want to pick up a length of wood and beat some fucking bastard in the Upper City to a pulp."

I got that. Here, even on the edge of the crowd, fury swirled around us, sucking at me like a wave running back from a beach. All I had to do was stop resisting and let it carry me away.

I knew as well as Benny did what a bad idea that would be.

From somewhere near the front of the crowd came a roar of voices. I couldn't make out what they were saying, but it didn't matter. I could *feel* it. The crowd around us picked it up and roared in response. The whole body of people surged forwards. Benny and I went with them.

We spilled out of the tight confines of the Warrens onto the wider streets of the Middle City, like blood pouring from a cut vein.

Everyone who lived here on the margins of the Warrens must have known what was coming. Doors and shutters were a blank face onto the mass of humanity emerging. But the crowd – the mob, now – wasn't aiming for here, and I saw more than a few people slip out of nearby homes to join the horde, the rush of anger pulling them in. We were heading for the Upper City and Horn Hill.

The Senate wasn't going to let that happen.

Now we were out of the Warrens, the crowd was looser packed. I tapped Benny on the shoulder, indicated with my head, and weaved my way towards the front. The men and women here were more focused, faces harder, and better armed. Long, solid clubs, knives, tools.

I didn't know if anyone was guiding this mob or whether it was going on instinct, but even though it would have been a more direct route, we were steering a course that gave a wide berth to the Ash Guard fortress. Hundreds of years of reputation was buried deep in the animal brains of the citizens of Agatos.

The Ash Guard won't get involved. There was no magic being used, and a riot was none of their business. I wondered briefly if I should start chucking magic around to get them off their arses, but all that would lead to was me getting put down by the Guard while the crowd went on its merry way.

The noise of the crowd was a constant rumble, now, like an earthquake or a rockslide from the side of the mountains. We were moving faster, too, building into a charge, although what exactly we were charging at I didn't know. I suspected many of the crowd had never been to the Upper City.

We came out into Curmer Plaza, a large, cobbled square not far from the foot of Horn Hill, and spread again.

The front of the crowd slowed, and as I pushed my way through, I saw the reason why. At the far edge of the plaza, blocking the streets out, was a line of City Watch. They had come prepared for violence. The clubs they usually wore at their belts were replaced by spears and shields. At a guess, a couple of hundred Watch faced the crowd.

Even though the front of the crowd slowed at the sight, more kept pouring into the plaza behind, pushing those in front forwards.

I had known this was going to get ugly.

An officer stepped from the line of Watch and surveyed the crowd. His voice boomed out, magically amplified. “This city is under curfew. Return to the Warrens.”

I checked for a mage among the Watch, but there was none. Just a spell carried by the officer, tied to the medal he wore around his neck. The Ash Guard’s prohibition on the use of violent magic against people, except in self-defence, was as severely enforced on the Watch and the Senate as it was on anyone else, and the Watch didn’t employ mages.

“Return to the Warrens,” the officer bellowed again. This time, the line of Watch took a pace forwards. Spears crashed on shields. The sound rolled across the plaza. It felt it like a punch in my stomach.

The move was a mistake. This wasn’t an ordinary mob. This was drawn by the vacuum left in the Lady’s absence. *The Warrens run deep,* and the Lady had been the life that filled it. I just had time to think, *Shit!*, then someone in the crowd shouted, “For the Lady!”, and suddenly stones were flying through the air. A couple of Watchmen went down under the barrage, despite the raised shields.

No one in the Warrens was under any illusion that they

lived in anything other than the arse-end of the city, where all the waste was flushed, often literally, and that their betters considered them part of that waste. Sometimes it was a source of resentment, other times a source of pride, but at most times a source of both resentment and pride simultaneously. The people of the Warrens responded by making their place theirs alone and enthusiastically robbing the rest of the city when the chance presented itself. Mostly, though, they accepted it with a long-suffering fatalism. Not anymore. Agatos had dealt a fatal insult to the Warrens. It had taken the Lady from them. The crowd surged towards the Watchwomen and -men.

Spears lowered to meet the crowd.

People were going to die. Men and women of the Warrens. Men and women of the Watch. This mob would overwhelm the Watch, despite their spears and shields, and tear them to pieces, but not before hundreds were killed or injured. And there was nothing I could do about it.

"Fall back!" the officer bellowed, and the Watch retreated a few quick steps.

The crowd roared in victory, charging forwards, before what was waiting beyond killed the sound in their throats. A line of soldiers waited, kneeling, muskets raised. The moment the Watch were out of the way, the officer shouted, "Fire!"

A volley of shot hurtled towards the crowd, the noise like thunder echoing from the Leap and the surrounding buildings. I threw up a magical shield in front of me, Benny, and the people around us, but I couldn't cover the whole crowd.

Bullets ricocheted off in front of me, but twenty feet away, I saw a bullet catch a woman in the throat. Blood sprayed as she fell back and down. The shouts of anger became screams of pain and fear.

Through the drifting smoke of the guns, a second line of soldiers stepped, muskets already raised. I heard twin shouts of "Reload" and "Fire", and then more bodies were falling. A few stones flew in reply, but not enough to slow the soldiers.

I pulled in magic and used it to amplify my voice into a roar. "Get out of here! Get back to the Warrens!"

That was all it took. The massed crowd sagged and broke. People ran. I grabbed Benny's arm. "Come on!"

Another crash of spears on shields, and the Watch advanced at a trot.

The plaza was wide and open, and the crowd had spread out, but the streets would funnel them and slow their exit. It would become a bottleneck, and the Watch did not look merciful.

"Fuck this," I muttered. I let my shield fall. I was going to need all my power for this. I sucked in raw magic, shaped it, and threw the spell. A wall of fire erupted across the plaza, between the Watch and the crowd. It was an illusion, of course. I didn't have the power to do this for real, but I did feed in a little heat, too. It wouldn't hurt anyone, but it might slow them down. Then I turned and sprinted after the fleeing crowd.

I had underestimated the Senate. All of us had.

Up ahead, more screams and shouts sounded, and the crowd reeled back. I shoved my way forwards. Over the heads of the people, I saw another line of soldiers had cut off the street out of the plaza. I turned and saw that all the exits were being closed.

"Fire!" someone shouted from the ranks of the soldiers closing the street, and a volley hit the crowd.

They had trapped us, closed us in. They were going to kill everyone, or at least enough to make this a lesson the Warrens would never forget: Know your place. Don't step out of line.

These were my people, people who had grown up like me and with me, but without the privilege of magic to get them out of there. I had played with some of them as a kid, fought with others, lived with them. I couldn't let this happen. I wouldn't.

I fought my way through the panicking crowd. I saw men and women coated in blood, supporting and even carrying one another. I saw hungry, drawn faces, thin bodies clad in rags and patched clothes. I saw fear and desperation.

Then I was out of the crowd, and the soldiers blocking the street were raising their muskets again.

I charged and threw a wall of force at them. It hit like a storm wave, tossing them back and down. Blood poured from my nose, and my muscles felt like they were tearing.

"This way!" I shouted.

My fire illusion was flickering and failing on the other side of the plaza. Gritting my teeth against the pain, I fed more power into it.

Shown a way out, the crowd converged on the open street. I saw soldiers trying to get to their feet, then going down under punches and kicks. There was nothing I could do for them, and I didn't think I would have if I could. They had opened fire on fleeing women and men. They had chosen their own fate.

The soldiers at the other points of the plaza weren't done. More volleys sounded, pounding into flesh and filling the air with stinging smoke.

I couldn't fight them all. Depths, I couldn't fight more than a dozen without surprise on my side. All I could do was wait here, try to keep the way out open, and slow down the pursuing Watch. When the crowd reached the Warrens, they could disappear, and I didn't think the Watch or the soldiers would pursue into the tight alleys and courtyards now that night had drawn in. If they did, they wouldn't come out again.

As the crowd withdrew, many limping or staggering, I saw the aftermath of the assault. Seventy, maybe eighty bodies sprawled on the cobbles, some moving but most not, the stones slick in the green light of the morgue-lamps.

I turned and followed the last of the crowd into the streets.

No more gunshots sounded as we fled back to the Warrens, but the Watch didn't slow their pursuit. Even as the crowd exploded outwards like a flock of birds beneath a plunging hawk, some sprinting ahead, others limping behind, spreading into the side streets and alleys in desperate attempts to escape the armed men at their backs, the Watch pursued in small squads, savagely beating anyone they caught up to, whether they had been part of the mob or not. I heard shouts of pain from the streets around.

Not everyone could run. Some were wounded, others just worn down. I stayed on the main street with Benny, at the rear of the retreating crowd, helping where we could. Whenever a Watch squad came into view, a show of magic warned them off, but I couldn't be everywhere, and I couldn't save everyone. Screams still sounded out of sight, too often cut off abruptly.

I might not have killed the Lady of the Grove, but this was my fault. If I had bent my whole effort to discovering who was behind it, all of this could have been avoided. The Ash Guard would have made an example of them, and the Warrens would have been satisfied.

Even as I thought it, doubts ate away at me. *Would they? Would that really fill the loss? Would anything at this point?* Maybe not. But maybe, also, the Warrens wouldn't have turned such fury against the Upper City, and the Senate wouldn't have had the excuse to show exactly whose side they were on.

At last we reached the boundaries of the Warrens, and Benny and I helped the final stragglers into the safety of the narrow, dark streets. I didn't know how many Warrens people were left out there, alive or dead or dying, but the squads of Watchwomen and -men, backed up by soldiers, were beginning to appear in the surrounding streets. Benny and I followed the injured in.

"That was a fucking disaster," I said, as we stopped in the shadows to peer out.

"Could have been worse."

I turned on Benny. His thin, weaselly face was hard. "What the fuck do you mean it could have been worse? There could be hundreds of people hurt and dead out there."

Benny's eyes turned on mine. "You've forgotten what life is like in here. People die all the time in the Warrens. Some of those we brought back are going to die anyway, because there's no surgeons here, no clean bandages or clean water. That's how it is. If you hadn't been here, *that* would have been a disaster."

I squinted at him. "Excuse me?"

His expression hadn't softened. "I'm not saying I forgive you for what you did to Sereh, but here, you saved people. You put yourself at risk for them. That's what you do. Maybe if you stop putting others at risk along the way, you'll be all right."

"Yeah." I turned to look out the alley, not least so I didn't have to keep meeting Benny's eyes. Maybe it was the trauma of the evening, but I was having a hard time controlling my emotions.

The Watch and soldiers were gathering and forming lines along the boundary to the Warrens. In the dark, many of the Watch carried burning torches instead of spears now, the orange light throwing sinister, flickering shadows over faces.

"What in Pity's name are they up to?" I said. "You reckon they're actually going to storm the Warrens?"

"They'd be crazy to try." Benny indicated the deeper alleys behind us with a flick of his head. "Back there, they lose every advantage. We'd rip them to pieces."

We. Benny didn't live in the Warrens anymore, either, but we were both products of the place, Warrens' kids at heart, when you stripped everything else away. *We.*

"Maybe they're just making sure it's over, that no one tries again." I didn't think that would happen. I reckoned a lot of corpses of Watchwomen and -men and soldiers would turn up in the harbour over the next few weeks and months, but not a mass attempt to attack the Upper City or Horn Hill. The Watch and the Senate had seen that coming, and it had only gone one way.

A shouted command from somewhere in the Watch's ranks saw them all take a dozen steps forward.

"On the other hand..."

Benny's fingers closed on the knife at his belt. I readied magic. They wouldn't be coming down *this* alley. I had no doubt the homes and alleys of the Warrens were filled with men and women preparing themselves, too. We might have been chased out of the Middle City, but it would be different here. This was *our* place. The soldiers' muskets would do them no good here. I could almost feel the readiness, the *anticipation*, of the Warrens. A lot of people would be looking for revenge if the Watch was foolish enough to offer it to them.

"Throw!" the command came, and suddenly dark objects were flying over the Warrens' low roofs. One hit the rooftop near us and split. Something dark and wet dripped into the alley. Benny knelt by it, touching it with his fingers, then sniffing at the residue.

"Oil..."

"Light it up!" This time it was torches spinning through the night. Where they hit, flames shot into the air. Screams sounded.

"They're burning the Warrens!" Benny shouted.

A torch came towards us. I punched it back with magic, but it was no good. The Warrens was already on fire. The prevailing wind would drive the fire deeper. These buildings of salvaged wood, brick, and clay would catch easily and burn fast.

Figures burst from nearby alleys, trying to flee the flames, and were met by the savagery of the Watch, beating them down and driving them back.

In the Upper City, people thought the Watch were there to uphold the law. Down here, we knew better.

More screams and shouts came. This time I could hear children, too.

I grabbed Benny. "We have to help. Get people down to Dockside. The city won't let the docks burn." Too much money involved there.

A building further down our alley burst into flames.

"Bannaur's bloodied balls!" I spat. I ran towards it, drawing in raw magic. I cast the spell, pressing down on the fire, smothering it. The effort made me stumble, and Benny caught me before I could fall. The fire went out, but already the next building was engulfed, and the sky flickered sunset-orange from the light of the burning Warrens.

"I can't stop this," I gasped. The air was growing thick with smoke.

"I ain't letting anyone else die."

"Me neither." I modified a shield to form a bubble around us, pressing away smoke and flame and drifting ash. There was nothing I could do about the heat. "Come on."

We pushed into the Warrens.

I heard shouts from a nearby burning building. Benny kicked the door open, and we shoved inside. The ceiling was on fire. Flames dripped like liquid from the beams. Sweat coated my skin. Even with the bubble around us, the air felt thin and too hot to breathe.

There was a family in the back room, pushed up against a wall, as far from the flames as possible. I extended the bubble to cover them.

"Get up!" Benny shouted above the roar of the flames. "Get out!"

Every part of me hurt. I wasn't used to using this much magic for this long. It felt like a million needles were being driven relentlessly into my skin, my muscles, my joints. But I couldn't let it drop. None of us would survive in here.

We lurched to the door, the parents and Benny supporting the kids. A burning beam fell from the roof. I caught it on the shield, grunting.

When we were free of the flames, Benny gave the family a push. "Get to the docks. Don't stop." Then he and I plunged further into the Warrens.

We weren't always as lucky. In one house, I found a woman trapped beneath a fallen, burning roof, life already fled from her. At another, the building fell as we tried to force our way in, and the screams ended abruptly. At a third, a man stumbled out, clothes and hair blazing, skin melting, an unearthly shriek tearing from his throat, before he fell and moved no more.

I didn't know how long it went on nor how many we saved or failed to save. We were in a daze, pushing our way over and over again into the growing inferno. We weren't alone. But even with the other rescuers and those tossing water onto the flames, we couldn't stop it spreading. By now, half the Warrens must be on fire. I was stumbling more than walking, and I couldn't tell in the light of the flames if the wetness on my skin was sweat or blood seeping from my pores from the effort of the magic.

I staggered again towards the burning buildings, and Benny grabbed my shoulder. "We have to stop!"

"What?"

"Look." He jabbed a finger above me. It took me a moment to realise my bubble had gone and ash and soot were falling around us. I would have charged into the flames without noticing. I tried to form it again, but I couldn't. I had nothing left.

The Warrens was still burning. The fire was still spreading. I had failed. I hadn't been strong enough. Again.

Benny pulled on my arm. "We're going to be trapped."

He was right. The flames still leapt from building to building, driven by the late summer wind over dry roofs. We retreated.

A new set of shouts sounded from the south of the Warrens. There was something different about these. Less fear, more ... celebration. The sky was darker there, too. We turned in that direction, teetering towards the shouts until finally I saw what was happening.

The Wren was striding through the burning district, and everywhere he went, the flames were dying. As he walked, he reached out, pulling the fire from the sky and the burning buildings, extinguishing it entirely through sheer magical power. I watched, gaping, eyes unfocused to watch the display. If I had trained for a thousand years, I could never have done that. He didn't even spare us a glance as he strode by, followed by cheers and applause from the survivors.

Within twenty minutes, it was done. The fire was gone. Only the smell of smoke and burned wood, brick, and flesh hung in the air. Benny and I looked at each other. Neither of us spoke.

CHAPTER SIXTEEN

We shambled from the Warrens back to Benny's house, which stood untouched from the chaos nearby. I expected to be greeted as enthusiastically as ever by Fria, but he just lifted his head from where he was lying on the floor next to Sereh then lay back down with a sigh as we staggered in.

At least one of us had been having a good time.

Benny and I flopped on the couch. I was coated in soot, ash, sweat, and, yes, blood, now dried and flaking on my skin. My clothes were charred in places, despite the magical shield I had used.

This couch was going to be wrecked.

I could still smell the fire. I wondered if I would ever get it out of my skin and hair and clothes. My body throbbed with pain, and my bones ached deep inside.

That's what you get for overusing magic.

When Sereh was done fussing over Benny and shooting murderous glances at me, as though I had been the one who had got us into this instead of the other way around, and when we had both had a drink, Benny said, "You know what I've been wondering? Why did he wait so long?"

I blinked away the black needles that kept sliding into my vision. "Who?"

"The Wren. Why did he wait so long to step in? He must have known the Warrens was going to riot. Everyone knew. Even if he didn't know the Watch was going to burn the place, he had to know something bad was going to happen. So why wait so long? He could have ended it any time."

I didn't care. All I wanted was to fall asleep and let my body recover. "Hard to be a hero until everything has gone to shit first."

"Yeah. That's what I've been thinking. The Wren always wanted to be the king of the Warrens like he's king of Dockside, but the Warrens had the Lady, and in the end, that's where people turned."

I sat up straight. As straight as I could with every muscle feeling like it had been stripped apart. "But now the Lady is dead, the Warrens burned, and the Wren steps in as a saviour."

"You heard the cheers. He finally gets what he always wanted."

"You know, when I talked to Captain Gale about the Lady's murder, she said look for who has the most to gain from it. I couldn't tell who that was. The Lady's power could go to anyone." And it still would. But the Warrens, the Warrens would go to the Wren.

Benny's fists clenched. "He did it, didn't he? He killed the Lady of the Grove. I knew it. Back when you fucked us over, he was ready to send people to kill me and Sereh. I always knew he was a cunt. Of course he would kill the Lady."

I had seen that look in Benny's eyes before, and it never ended well. "We don't know that. He might just have been taking advantage of the situation."

Benny wasn't listening. "The fucker."

I loved Benny. He was my oldest friend. He was closer than family. But when he built up a resentment, it would take an ocean to wash it away and a sledgehammer to break through to him. He had clearly been stewing on the Wren for months.

"Benny." I moved so I was right in front of him. "We can't go after him ourselves. We have to find proof and take it to the Ash Guard. They're the only ones who can handle a high mage."

His eyes lifted to my face. "Yeah. Yeah, all right. I want to nail the fucker to his own door. This is personal."

I settled back, still uneasy.

Benny twisted to meet my eyes. "You asked why I was up there in the grove when I found the Lady's body."

I had forgotten I'd asked him that. "It doesn't matter." It wasn't like he could have witnessed anything useful. If the Wren had killed her, he would have done it from his centre of power, not up in the grove.

"You remember Alena Sand? We used to know her when we were kids."

"Of course. I bumped into her a couple of months back." I hadn't recognised her at first. The Warrens did that to you. They drained you and left you old before your time.

"She died."

"Shit. How?"

Benny shrugged. "How does anyone die in the Warrens? Hunger. Accident. Sickness. All the shit of the city gets shovelled in there, and there's no one to help if you fall. She's buried in the shafts up there. I've been up a couple of times. Pay my respects, you know? This time, the Lady was lying on the path on the way up. Never got as far as Alena's shaft. Going to be a lot more in those shafts these next couple of days."

I didn't know what to say.

Benny perked up. "I got you something."

"You what?"

"Wait here."

He limped across the room then returned carrying a long shape wrapped in cloth.

"What is it?"

"Open it and see, you twat."

It was heavy, solid. I unwrapped the cloth to reveal a polished length of walnut wood with a chunk of obsidian embedded in the end. "My mage's rod! Where in the Depths did you get this? I lost it in the harbour."

"Must have washed up. Saw it on a stall in the Penitent's Ear and recognised it."

"You bought it for me?" I ... hadn't expected this. The mood he'd been in with me, I would have thought he would have burned it.

"Don't be fucking insulting, mate."

Then he'd stolen it. But was it really stealing when it belonged to me all along? I wasn't going to argue. "Thank you." I'd missed having this.

"Don't make anything of it. It doesn't mean anything."

It did to me. It meant so much that for a moment I couldn't breathe. I had to swallow to speak and force back tears from my eyes. These last few months, with Benny hating me, had been harder than I'd been willing to admit, even to myself.

"Yeah, all right." I stretched, and my back protested. I focused on the pain. Far easier that than the emotion that threatened to drown me. "I have to get home. I need to sleep."

"Use the couch. You're not making it back like that, and you've already wrecked it." He raised a finger. "Just tonight, right?"

"Yeah," I said. "Just tonight."

By the light coming through Benny's shutters, mid-morning had come and gone again by the time I awoke. My burns, bruises, and whatever internal trauma I had given myself seemed mostly healed by sleep, but I was exhausted, and I had gained a bonus bad back from sleeping on the too small, sagging couch. It hadn't occurred to me at the time to wonder why I wasn't being offered Benny's spare bedroom. I guessed I wasn't completely forgiven yet.

The house was quiet. Benny would be sleeping in preparation for a night of redistributing wealth from the rich to his own pockets, and Sereh was … well, I never knew where Sereh was, unless she was holding a knife to my throat. I rolled off the couch with a grunt then stood. Fria let out a complaint from where he'd wormed his way under my legs during the night. And I'd wondered why I had put my back out. I crossed to the kitchen, helped myself to a cup of water, then chivvied Fria off the couch towards the door.

I was only two feet from it when a voice directly behind me said, "Not there, Uncle Nik."

I forced a grimace onto my face before turning – it was supposed to be a smile, but you try smiling when a miniature psychopath sneaks up behind you. "Why not there?"

Sereh was only feet away from me, hands clasped behind her back, looking up at me with innocent eyes. "Don't tread on that plank. I installed a new trap. It would break both your legs."

I couldn't even hold onto the grimace. "You know I left wards on the house, right? Good ones."

Her expression didn't change. "How many people in Agatos can get through your wards, Uncle Nik?"

Other than the Ash Guard, that would be every mage who was more powerful than me. "I don't know. A hundred. Two hundred."

"So, I need to be ready to kill two hundred people."

How the fuck did she manage to say that so calmly? And why did it make me shiver? "They won't all come at once."

"I will not let anyone hurt Dad." She took a step forwards, and it took all my willpower not to step back onto her booby-trapped plank. "Anyone." Suddenly, she grinned. "You can step on it if you like, Uncle Nik. I didn't set the traps while Fria was here."

I examined her face closely, but no. I really couldn't tell if she was lying. Carefully, I turned and stepped over the plank to the door. The burst of laughter that followed didn't reassure me in the slightest, nor did her voice that drifted after me out the door: "Fix up your apartment, Uncle Nik, or I'm going to take Fria back for good."

"She doesn't mean it, boy," I told Fria. But I reckoned she did.

Outside in the street, the smell of burned buildings hung in the air. There was no breeze today, and the air felt heavy and low. An unbroken layer of thin cloud filtered the sunlight like a sheet draped over a lamp. There was something subdued about the city. There were people about, but no one was speaking loudly. Heads were down.

I couldn't resist the urge. I turned right out of the door and tracked the half block to the edge of the Warrens. The place was destroyed. Stones lay blackened, bricks burst from the heat, wood charred. The stink of smoke was strong here, although the flames were long gone, ripped away by the unimaginable power of a high mage. Every now and then, I forgot just how much more powerful high mages were than the rest of us. The narrow alleys were filled with rubble.

Exhausted people in rags picked their way through the piles, looking for the remains of their lives or the bodies of loved ones. Somewhere deeper in the ruins, a lone voice wailed in grief.

The Warrens had been closely packed, but it had never been an enormous part of the city. Even so, many thousands of people had lived here, and by my reckoning, a good half of it had burned. Benny and I had saved dozens. How many hundreds of others had we not been able to help? The city had done this, deliberately, to teach a lesson. I wondered if my mother had been part of the decision, or Mica's partner, Elestior. Had they seen it as a necessary sacrifice, something not to waste their political capital preventing? They hadn't warned anyone. Mica and my mother hadn't stood there in defence of the Warrens, the place in which they had both been born and grown up. They could have done the same as the Wren, snatched the fire from the air and extinguished it. They hadn't. Maybe they had been cut out of the decisions, not told what was going to happen. If so, that would be a catastrophic loss of influence for my mother. My mother did not allow herself to lose influence.

"What does it matter?" I said to Fria. "The Warrens know better than to expect help from the Upper City. You know that, don't you, boy?" Whatever they might once have been, the Countess and Mica were Upper City now. The Warrens were on their own, as always. And in a few short months, winter would be here. Thousands of people would have no shelter as ice and snow blew down from the mountains and people froze.

I turned away.

My clothes were ruined. Burn holes, patches of soot and ash, patches of … other stuff I couldn't identify. And most of what I had at home had been destroyed by the Wren's thugs. Time to spend some of my meagre savings.

I headed for the Penitent's Ear.

Agatos was a city built on commerce, and while most of the profit might funnel its inevitable way to the wealthy merchants who controlled trade, there was little short of an earthquake that could close the city's markets, and even then, the Penitent's Ear would spring up around the cracks.

I searched out a couple of cheap, second-hand outfits that almost fit, then made my way to the northwest corner of the market where tradespeople advertised their services.

A couple of carpenters were in attendance, hawking their skills from small stands that displayed samples of their work.

"I need a door repairing," I told the first one as I approached. "Today."

She sucked her lips. "It's going to cost. In case you hadn't heard, the Warrens burned down. There's a lot of demand for repairs right now."

"Goat shit. Almost no one in the Warrens can afford a carpenter at the best of times, and certainly not now. If anything, you've got less work than normal."

She shrugged, not offended at being caught in a blatant lie. "Three o'clock, then. Two watchmen, half up front."

I handed over one of the silver coins. It wasn't a bad price. I could probably get it cheaper, but it wasn't worth wasting half a day to find someone willing. "Materials included." I gave her the address. "Don't go poking around inside. There are wards that'll fry your brain if you try." They wouldn't do any such thing, but I still didn't want her nosing into my business.

Fria and I got breakfast and ate where we had before, under the olive trees at the east of the market. I divided the pastries in two with my knife. They probably weren't healthy for a dog – or for me – but Fria didn't complain. Even here, I could smell the smoke and ash of the Warrens. Maybe I was just smelling it on my skin and hair and clothes.

When we were done, I headed back to my apartment to change and make sure my wards were still up, then took Fria for a walk through the Middle City. I couldn't prove the Wren had murdered the Lady of the Grove. Perhaps he had just taken advantage of a situation he had seen coming. In many ways, the urgency of finding out had passed. The worst had already happened. The Warrens had rioted, the city had put the residents down brutally and left them traumatised. It would be a long time before something like that happened again.

It still didn't seem right.

I knew who had turned massive violence on the poor of the city: the Senate, the Watch, the army. The Warrens would take its revenge as it always did, with thefts and the killing of anyone from the Upper City stupid enough to intrude. But I didn't know who had killed the Lady. Ultimately, whoever had done it was to blame for all of this, and they deserved to pay. I would find out, eventually. I hadn't been quick enough, and we had all seen the consequences.

In the meantime, I had another pressing matter. Cursed Ethemattian was almost out of time. If I couldn't prove he had been set up and by whom, he would die tomorrow night, beaten to death in his own temple in the latest long-failed attempt to murder the Hated God.

I had been certain – *was* still certain – that Most Cursed Coyd Keffen had falsely entered my client into the Choosing, probably to protect his niece, but I didn't know how he had ensured Ethemattian's name was chosen. I *did* know he must have been working with someone else or he wouldn't have been killed to stop him talking. Whether that was his niece or whoever had helped him fix the Choosing, I didn't know.

I didn't know enough about any of it. I would have to turn to my most reliable source of information once again.

I found Kehsereen hard at work in his apartment. A bright lamp stood on his desk, next to a microscope. I wandered over and peered down.

He had been studying a fine, white powder under the microscope. I eyed it warily.

"Do not tell me that's Ash." I fucking well knew it was. I could see the void of magic around it.

"A trace, mixed with chalk and ordinary ashes."

"Denna's mercy!" I threw myself into a chair. "You know that doesn't fucking matter, right? If the Ash Guard finds out, it's a death sentence."

"I am careful."

"Just get rid of it. Dump it in the harbour or down a drain."

His shoulders slumped. "I cannot. I must find a way to

protect Asarian from his own powers. He cannot spend his whole life locked in that fortress."

Yeah. I understood that. His nephew was too powerful and too damaged not to be a danger to himself and everyone around him. If I'd been in Kehsereen's position, if it had been Benny or Sereh, I would have done the same. Depths, I would have gone further, ripped up the whole city to save them, no matter the cost. In the end, we all took the risks we had to.

I forced down the lump in my throat again. Last night had left me ... fragile, in danger of spinning out of control. "I need more information about the Brythanii. Can we meet that contact of yours? It's pretty urgent."

"Of course." He managed to look guilty. "I will have to ask a favour in return."

Fair enough. He had done a lot for me since that unfortunate day when he'd drugged away my magical powers with *ulu-aru* and left me tied up in an alley while a rat tried to eat my face.

"What do you need?"

"I'm going to want you to apply different types and strengths of magic to the Ash so I can see how it reacts."

Magnificent. It would be just my luck if the Ash Guard turned up while we were in the middle of it.

"Fine. If the Ash Guard kills us, at least they'll kill us together. I never wanted to die alone." That didn't get a response. No one appreciated my sense of humour.

Kehsereen tidied up his desk and put the Ash in a

strongbox in a drawer. "Let's find my contact now. She will ask for payment."

Everyone did. I leaned over and scratched Fria behind his ears. "Time for another walk, boy."

Kehsereen's contact had an apartment on a small, shabby plaza in the Grey City, not far from where I'd lived for almost five years, before the Wren had got me evicted. I should have seen the warning signs back then. I should have run, got as far away from the city's mages as possible again, like I had when I'd walked out of my mother's palace. If I had, maybe none of this would be happening. Instead, I'd pushed my way closer and closer into their business. But every time, it had seemed like I had no choice, that it was the only option open to me, that the problems I had to solve justified another step back in. Now look at me.

Kehsereen's contact opened her door to Kehsereen's knock, and I saw a short Brythanii woman with dyed brown hair and a brutal scar on her face that had taken out one eye.

"Price of being a Brythanii in this city," she said, as she caught me looking.

"I'm sorry."

"Wasn't you." She turned to Kehsereen. "What do you want, Jettuk?"

"Information. More about the Choosing."

The woman looked back at me. "This your friend?" She tilted her head. "Hm. All right." She gestured us in.

Her apartment was cramped but better maintained than mine had been when I'd lived in the Grey City. A window looked over the plaza to the flat, green waters of the Erastes Bay. Fishing boats, sails limp in the still air, dotted the water. Like my stepfather's boat had before the Wren had sunk it and drowned him

You don't know that.

I didn't know he *hadn't*. What I did know was that now the idea had lodged in my brain, I couldn't let it go.

"Hey. Tall guy."

"Sorry?"

The Brythanii woman was looking up at me, head tilted to one side. "Take a seat. You're making my room look small from up there."

"Right." I eased into a low chair. It wasn't good for my backache.

"Information costs money, you know that, yeah?"

I nodded.

"Good, because getting work as a one-eyed Brythanii isn't easy, and I have rent like anyone else. A king'll buy you what I can tell you."

I winced at that. A gold crown – a king, in Middle City slang – was pretty much everything I had. Ethemattian had better be ready to part with more money. I reached into my purse and counted out the shields and oars. It looked pretty empty in there. After I had paid the carpenter, I was going to go hungry.

It wouldn't be the first time.

"I need to know the whole process of the Choosing, all the way through."

The woman shook her head slowly, rubbing at the scar around her missing eye. "Fucking dumb tradition. All right. Any Cursed can put themselves forward. Normally it's only three or four, but the more there are, the better the odds. The temple caps it at eight a year. You wouldn't want everyone doing it at once or you'd only get one brutal murder in exchange for a whole temple full of Most Curseds, and then how would you get someone willing to be killed the next year?"

Smart. I supposed. I wondered how many priests sat there calculating the odds each year, waiting to see who else would put themselves forward, counting to see when the odds fell enough in their favour to take the risk. Or not, if their plan was to frame some poor bastard to take their place if they lost. I wondered how often that had happened over the years, how many priests had not been able to find someone like me to save them.

If you save him.

"So, how does it actually work?" I asked.

She waved a hand. "We're getting there, tall guy. If you want to put yourself forward, you go to the relevant Most Cursed – last thing I heard it was Coyd Keffen, the little shit."

"Not anymore. He's dead."

"Natural causes?"

I shook my head.

"Probably had it coming, the miserable old bastard. Anyway, you have to swear to the Most Cursed that you're volunteering of your own free will, and you have to put it in writing, too, signed, so there's no doubt."

It was a pretty robust system. All the way up until the Most Cursed decided to fix the whole thing. Never trust a priest. "And then what?"

"At the end of the week, the signed statements are brought in sealed envelopes to the Sanctum. All the Curseds and Most Curseds are there to witness. The high priest – they call her the Cursed of God – picks one, opens it in front of the witnesses, and reads out the name. It's not fucking pretty, I've got to tell you. You're reading someone's death warrant, and they fucking volunteered. I don't think most of them ever think it's going to be them. Whole lot of fucking tears and snot and screaming and everyone else sitting there smug because it wasn't them. Anyone who wants can check the statement, and believe me, they check."

I wondered if Ethemattian had checked or whether he had been too shocked when he heard his name read out knowing he hadn't submitted himself. "Doesn't anyone ever try to run? It's not like the volunteer is locked up." Ethemattian seemed free to walk around and do whatever he pleased, even if he was being watched, and I didn't even know that for sure.

She shrugged. "Occasionally. But it doesn't last long, because they'll be a target for every Brythanii in the city, and a lot of the stupid fuckers really believe they're getting revenge on the god. Anyway, if they do, their family won't get the compensation given to relatives of the sacrifice. It's generous."

"Really." That was interesting. Ethemattian's brother and niece really hadn't liked him, but revenge for stealing the brother's place in the temple hadn't seemed enough of a motive, and supposed lack of access meant I had ruled them out. Perhaps I should look again at Retha Ethemattian. In the meantime, "I think I'm going to need to see those statements." Perhaps Most Cursed Keffen had substituted all the other entries with duplicates of Ethemattian's fake statement. That would mean no one else had to be involved, except the person who had killed Keffen, and I had his niece lined up for that one. "Do they keep them?"

"Until after the sacrifice, so that anyone who queries the Choosing can verify it. There's a room behind the Sanctum, but you won't get in."

I'd heard that before. "We'll see. One last thing. Any chance Keffen and the Cursed of God might have collaborated to fix the Choosing?"

She laughed. "Those two couldn't collaborate on the breakfast menu. Keffen hates her. Hated her. They'd always been rivals, I remember that, but Keffen thought the Cursed of God fixed her own promotion. After that, he wouldn't pull her out of a bath of shit if she was drowning."

Which meant that if Keffen did have help, it wouldn't be her. But it was interesting information. Keffen had resented the Cursed of God for cheating her way to the top job. How would that have influenced him? Would it have made him more or less likely to fix things for his niece? I supposed that depended on what kind of a man he'd been.

"You didn't think much of Keffen?"

“I didn’t think much of any of them.” She fixed me with her single eye. “You’ll find more care and loyalty in a pack of starving rats than in that lot. Never become a priest.”

“I wasn’t planning to.” I stood. “Thank you.”

That gave me a lot to think about. Whether it got me any closer to proving Ethemattian had been set up, well we would have to see about that.

CHAPTER SEVENTEEN

Kehsereen's contact might not think I had much chance of getting into the Sanctum and the room behind it, but she had said I wouldn't get into the accommodation, either, and I'd managed that.

You were still spotted.

Eventually. And only after I'd got too close to Menatha Keffen. I wouldn't make that mistake again, even if the Sanctum was more carefully guarded.

Ethemattian would be able to view the statements, but that wouldn't be enough. *I* needed to see them. Perhaps I could get Ethemattian to steal them. Except there was a damned good chance he would be caught, just like he must have been spotted coming to consult with me, leading to the death of my best suspect. Anyway, the moment the statements were removed from that secure room, whoever was behind this would be able to claim they had been forged or replaced to clear Ethemattian, and I might as well just burn them.

No, I was going to have to get in there myself.

I headed back to Kehsereen's apartment to carry out my part of the deal, our progress slowed by Fria's insistence on sniffing every Cepra-damned stone and doorstep on the way.

I spent the best part of an hour summoning, manipulating, and releasing magic in various forms and at various strengths, while Kehsereen squinted and hmm'ed at his sample of Ash. Half the time, I expected the Ash Guard to come bursting through the door, and the other half I spent desperately trying to figure out how I was going to get into the most holy – or unholy – part of the Brythanii temple and examine those statements unnoticed. Benny might have found a way, but I wasn't sure we were on firm enough ground yet for me to ask favours. Sereh would agree if I asked, and I had no doubt she would be able to steal anything she wanted, unnoticed and uninterrupted. But if there was anything that would be guaranteed to rip off the fragile scab forming over the wound in Benny's and my friendship, it would be putting Sereh into even theoretical danger again. I was going to have to do this my usual way: bluster, goat shit, and a projection of confidence I absolutely didn't feel.

By the time I made it back home, the carpenter was just finishing up my broken door. She might have overcharged me and tried to rob me blind, but she had done a good job. I paid her the remaining coin and headed in with Fria. My purse was noticeably light.

"You know, boy," I said to Fria, "today might be the day we take up Holera and Elosyn's offer of a meal." If the offer was still open. Whether it was or not, I was going to have to apologise for standing them up.

Should have done that already. But there always seemed to be something else pressing on my time. *Or you always find an excuse to avoid awkward conversations.*

I collected up the Brythanii robes and veil that Ethemattian had given me and set out water for Fria in my surviving bowl. "Please don't escape this time. I'm really not going to be gone for long."

Fria whined.

"Fine. At least find Sereh if you do run away. I can't go searching the whole city for you."

Fria didn't answer. I hoped that was dog for 'yes'.

THE BRYTHANII TEMPLE WAS AS BUSY AS IT HAD BEEN LAST time. Enough people were wearing the same robes and veil as me that, with luck, I wouldn't seem out of place. The weight of my mage's rod under my cloak – yes, I knew how that sounded – reassured me. A few priests weren't getting in my way.

A whole lot of priests, well, then we would see.

It wasn't news that I wasn't a fan of the gods. As far as I could tell, they never did a thing for their worshippers. Yes, sometimes people invested their hopes, dreams, and whole identities in the gods, like the citizens of the Warrens had, but in return, the gods did a whole barrel of fuck all. You might have thought, then, that I would have had a lot in common with the Brythanii, whose entire religion was based on telling their god how much of a shit it was. But, in truth, it just left me depressed. The Hated God didn't *deserve* the attention. A far better fate would be for it to be forgotten, as most gods were in the end. The ruins of earlier cities and towns beneath Agatos were full of broken temples to lost gods, and it was what they deserved. Forgotten. Ignored. Instead, the Brythanii had built this dour edifice of stone to the god they hated, and everyone still knew of it.

Sadly, no one was asking my opinion.

I checked my robe and veil were covering me, then strode into the temple.

Most temples, whatever the religion, were focused on a single point, or several points, where the god could be glorified through statues, raised daises, shitty art, altars, relics, or sometimes a cluttered mess of all of them. In the end, the Brythanii weren't so different. A single altar occupied the centre of a circular chamber maybe a hundred feet across. The altar was placed at the end of a platform that jutted out over a dark, elongated pit. I couldn't see into it from here. Faceless statues stood on either side of the entrance, and I noticed that many of the Brythanii entering and leaving turned their heads to spit on the statues as they passed. The statues were stained, and a slowly dripping layer of spit and phlegm coated most of the stone. My stomach turned, and I was immediately grateful I hadn't stopped for lunch. Although maybe throwing up on the statues would have given me bonus points, I decided not to risk lifting my veil to join in with the ritual.

The air of the temple was putrid and bitter. I had grown up near the last of Agatos's tanneries, and there was more than a hint of those places in here. Moments later, I saw the reason why. A priest climbed up to the altar and shouted something in Brythanii. I didn't speak the language, but I recognised insults when I heard them, no matter what tongue. The next moment, the priest upended a bucket of something nasty into the pit. I wasn't close enough to see exactly what it was, but I could make some educated guesses. Cheers sounded from the small crowd of Brythanii watching. I heard one of them shout, "You did not help us when we needed you."

Someone's going to have to clean that up later, I thought. Not one of the priests, though. A servant, no doubt, down in the pit scrubbing away whatever shit they'd dumped down there.

Ignoring the stench, I drew closer to look into the pit. There was another faceless statue down there, this one lying on its back, the blank head directly beneath the altar to catch everything the priests could toss in. The statue lay in a soup of piss, shit, and rotting food. I thought there might be rancid blood down there, too. My stomach clenched again, and I took a step back.

I would give it to the Brythanii: they knew how to hold a grudge.

I looked up and saw a priest watching me from the far side of the temple, a thoughtful look on her face. I recognised her immediately as Menatha Keffen. She was the only one who had seen me without my veil, and I had to admit I stood out here, even disguised.

Time to get moving before she decided to make my life difficult.

Kehsereen's contact had said the statements I needed would be in a room behind the Sanctum, whatever the fuck the Sanctum was. As a priest, I would know. As a mage pretending to be a priest, I didn't have a clue and couldn't ask. Somewhere private to the priests where not everyone could come and go.

The circular chamber was surrounded by a pillared cloister, and above that a balcony that ran the whole circumference of the chamber. A dozen doors opened off the cloister. I couldn't try them all or someone would get suspicious.

Where would I put my most holy – or unholy – room? In most temples, it would be central, the heart of the building, but I was starting to get a feel for the Brythanii religion by this point. If everyone else did it one way to glorify their gods, then the Brythanii would do the opposite to highlight their contempt. Off to the side, then. Something small, cheap. Like the door furthest left. I saw it open and a priest duck out.

"As good a choice as any," I muttered.

A Brythanii man looked up. "Cursed?"

I shook my head. I *had* to stop talking to myself.

The door was at least a foot shorter than me, the wood rough, crudely cut, and stained with something brown. Paint, I hoped. I had to pull my hand out of my sleeve to open the door. In the shadows, I hoped no one would notice my un-Brythanii skin.

Beyond the door, I found myself in a smaller but still sizeable room with a raised platform at the far end. No altar here, but there certainly were statues. Again, they represented the faceless figure of the god, but that was where the similarity ended. Someone had got very, very creative here.

The statues formed a procession around the room, and each one was the subject of intense violence. One was pierced through with spears, another disembowelled with its stone guts spilling over its belly, a third was crouched, head beneath arms, while disembodied clubs and hammers rained blows upon it. Almost every form of vicious murder was depicted in carved stone. The sculptor had been talented and enthusiastic. The way the brutalised figures seemed to writhe and twist was startling.

I couldn't help but wonder how it must feel to hear your name read out as sacrifice while surrounded by these depictions of horror and to know that you were going to suffer the same fate, all in the hope that it might somehow do the same to your god. For the first time, I admired just how calm Ethemattian had remained while understanding this would be his fate if I failed to save him. I could almost – almost – sympathise, too, with Keffen if she truly had set up Ethemattian to save herself. Except she'd had the option of not putting herself forward, a choice she had denied Ethemattian.

If she's behind it.

I *had* to solve this. If Ethemattian ended up like one of

these statues, it would be my fault. I didn't want that on my conscience.

I wasn't the only one here. A couple of priests sat on absurdly high chairs that made them look like kids perched up there, heads bowed in hands. Praying, or maybe cursing, or whatever they did. A single door led out behind the platform. That must be the room Kehsereen's contact had mentioned. I straightened, and keeping my hands hidden in my sleeves, headed for it.

"Can I help you, Cursed?"

I turned to see one of the priests had looked up from his ritual cursing.

Time to see if my information was good. "I am going to inspect the candidates' statements," I said, trying my old man voice again. Nope. I still didn't have it.

The priest frowned. "You know I will have to fetch a Most Cursed, of course?"

Nope. I did not know that. That bit of information would have been very useful. Maybe I should ask for a refund.

The last thing I needed was to be quizzed or supervised by a high priest. My disguise – and my faked voice – wouldn't hold up to close scrutiny. I nodded my head gracefully, making sure the stupid veil didn't tumble off and leave me face-naked.

I waited until the priest had left, then promptly headed for the door at the back of the platform.

"Cursed!"

For fuck's sake! The other priest was staring at me now. These bastards were far too easily distracted from muttering insults at their god. It was almost like their hearts weren't in it. I gave her a nod, then displaying a very un-old-man dexterity, leapt up onto the platform, pulled the door open, ducked through, and locked and jammed it behind me with a spell.

I had expected an office, but this was more like a library or archive. A couple of tables with morgue-lamps above them had chairs drawn up and were thankfully unoccupied. The walls were lined with shelves stacked with books and ledgers, except at the back where half a dozen filing cabinets occupied the space. A spiral staircase led up to a second, balcony level that held more shelves of books. A door at the end of the balcony led to elsewhere in the temple. I would have to be quick. As soon as the priests realised they couldn't open the door I had used, someone would remember the upper door, and I would be trapped.

So, where in the Depths did I start?

The priest rattled the door then hammered on it. "Cursed? You must wait."

I ignored her. Short of kicking the door in, she wasn't getting through that.

The statements would be letters, essentially, not books, written and signed in the presence of Most Cursed Coyd Keffen. Single sheets of paper. I could rule out the bookshelves. That left the large filing cabinets.

Anyone could check these statements, supposedly, and equally supposedly, they frequently did so in the week before the holy murder. The priests would want them easily accessible. No one wanted to be kneeling on the floor, scrambling about at the back of a drawer every time some nosy, untrusting git asked to check their paperwork.

The knocking came again. "Cursed. I must insist!"

Insist away.

The two top drawers of each cabinet would be my best bet.

I pulled off the irritating veil and opened the first drawer.

Single sheets of paper, with or without their envelopes, that was what I wanted. I flicked through the filed paperwork, ignoring the bound reports and everything else that didn't match. I even resisted the urge to read the random letters I came across, just scanning them quickly to be sure, then moving on.

Even so, it took too long, a couple of minutes just to get through the top drawer. I moved on to the next one down.

I was halfway through when another knock sounded and a different voice called, this one more authoritative and used to be being obeyed. "Cursed. You do not have permission to be in there. Open this door immediately."

The new priest – a Most Cursed, probably, from the tone of her voice – might not be used to being ignored, but I was used to ignoring the fuck out of people, and I had ignored far more important and dangerous people than her.

There were other voices out there, too, talking urgently. A moment later, a key rattled in the lock. *Good luck with that.* How long, though, before someone thought of the other entrance? I sped up my search, hoping against the gods that I wouldn't miss the papers in my hurry.

Something thumped against the door, shaking it in its

frame. I placed another spell on it to hold it steady. *You're wasting your time trying to break that down.*

I finally found the papers in the fifth drawer, and by that time, the shouts and running feet outside were becoming harder to ignore. Someone *must* be on their way to the other door soon. It was true that people didn't think clearly in a crisis, but not everyone would remain flustered forever. I could lock the other door as well, but I would just be imprisoning myself here until someone came along who got through my spells. Not many priests could wield the power of their god, and I doubted the Hated God shared its power, but there were always a few mages in every temple. They might not think of themselves as mages. They might not even realise they were using magic rather than the blessing of their god. But that didn't make them any less effective.

I grabbed the papers and spread them out on the nearest table. Five statements. Five different names, including Keffen and my client, Ard Ethemattian. *Bannaur's balls!* I had really hoped Most Cursed Keffen had substituted four duplicates of Ethemattian's fake statement. But these were all different.

Unless he substituted the other four back. It would be easy for him to slip in here, remove four duplicates and place back the originals. I could never prove it, but he would be a fool not to if that had been how he'd framed Ethemattian. *Shit!*

I picked up Ethemattian's statement and stared at it. It was a fake. It had to be, because Ethemattian had never submitted it. But how could I convince anyone of that? Most

Cursed Keffen claimed to have witnessed it, and now he was conveniently dead.

How easy would it be to fake the statement? If only I had a way to compare the statement with Ethemattian's handwriting. But if I took it out of here, no one would believe I had the real one.

You do have a way.

Ethemattian had given me his blackmail notebook detailing the sins of all his fellow priests. I had brought it along in case I needed it to leverage my way in here. I opened it on the table next to the statement.

The handwriting was similar. Very similar. If I hadn't had the notebook right here, I would have assumed it was Ethemattian's writing. I wondered if he had looked at it and been bewildered to see his own hand condemning him. But when I compared them more closely, the o's didn't quite match, and neither did the d's. Someone had worked very hard at this forgery. They must have practiced for a long time. But they hadn't been perfect.

"Got you," I said.

My next thought was, *It's not enough.* The Brythanii wouldn't uproot their whole ritual over some shaky handwriting. He was nervous, they would say, or drunk. Whose word would they take? The mage who had impersonated a priest and broken into the temple, or the dead and much-mourned Most Cursed? And it didn't tell me *who* was behind the fake.

Fuck!

I scooped up the statements, returned them to their

drawer, and headed for the stairs, pulling my veil back on as I went.

The crashes on the door were getting louder. The priests had found something heavy to hammer against it. Maybe they had repurposed one of the tortured statues of the Hated God as a battering ram. At this rate, they really might smash the doorframe out of the wall. Short of setting up full wards, I couldn't keep them out.

I let the spells fall as I reached the upper door. Without the spells to hold it, the lower door exploded into shattered planks, splinters, and a tumble of overbalanced priests. The upper door was locked, but I tripped it with a spell, threw it open, and came face-to-veiled-face with another priest.

I didn't know which of us was the most startled, but I had practice at this, and I reacted faster. I shoved him back into the hallway beyond, tangled his feet with magic, then leapt over him and ran.

If I was right, this hallway led deeper into the temple, maybe even to the residences behind. I would get lost in there. Instead, I took a branch to the right. Another locked door led out onto the circular gallery that ran around the main temple chamber, twenty feet above it. I could *see* the exit from here, but the chamber was frantic with priests, servants, excited Brythanii visitors, and temple guards, with more spilling into the space every second, like bees emerging from a hive at the arrival of a hornet. I would never make it through.

"Up there!" someone shouted.

Mara's piss! I ducked down, too late, and peered through gallery posts.

Priests and temple guards streamed towards the sides of the chamber. Stairs, I guessed. No point hiding.

I took off at a run again.

I was halfway around the gallery when a man stepped out from a side door, and we collided.

This time, neither of us had time to react. I sprawled on the wooden floor, snatching to keep my veil in place, then rolled to my feet. The man I'd hit was not a priest, he was winded, and I recognised him.

Retha Ethemattian, my client's resentful brother. He had been carrying a section of newly carved wooden relief – walnut, maybe – when we crashed into each other, and it had fallen and cracked.

You told me you didn't work for the Brythanii temple. You fucker. The archive where the statements of entry were stored was only a couple of doors away.

Locked doors.

Yeah? And how hard was it really to pick the locks or wait until they were left open? How hard was it to get a key?

The sound of footsteps clattering on the wooden floor brought me up and running again. *Escape first, then figure out what it means.*

Enthusiastic shouts from the floor below followed my progress, and now I saw priests in the gallery both ahead and behind me around the curve. I was going to get trapped here.

I shouldered open a door, raced through what appeared

to be a storeroom, then out into another hallway. I was thoroughly turned around now, but I kept running.

A couple of servants leapt out of my way as I charged past.

The corridor curved to the right. Paralleling the gallery? If so, any of the doors on my right could open and disgorge furious priests at any moment.

I barged through a door on the left instead.

This time, the room beyond really was an office. Cabinets, a few shelves, desks with pens and ink. Luckily for me, it was unoccupied, and on the far side was a window. I crossed to it and peered down. An alley ran below.

Time to get out of here.

I pushed open the window, clambered onto the windowsill, and jumped out, cushioning my descent with magic. When I reached the flagstones, I closed the window with another spell.

I slumped against the temple wall, allowing myself a moment for my heartbeat and breath to slow.

I really was shit at this breaking-into-places thing. Benny would be utterly ashamed of my efforts if I ever told him, which I had no intention of doing.

It would take the priests a while to establish that I wasn't in the temple anymore, and they would spread out, looking for me. If I had any sense, I would be out of here well before that happened. I had been close to being caught half a dozen times. This was my chance to get away clean. But Retha Ethemattian, who so bitterly resented my client and who stood to receive very generous compensation when his brother died, had been there. I could track him down later, but there would be nothing to stop him denying the whole thing.

I guessed I wasn't getting away after all.

I removed my robes and veil, bundled them into a corner in a small alley that branched off this one, then headed to the back of the temple to wait.

Retha Ethemattian didn't emerge from the temple for another hour, and as I expected, he came out the back, hurrying with a hooded cloak pulled down tight. In that time, the area around the temple was alive with scurrying, searching priests. Even when one of them found my abandoned robes and veil and a shout of excitement went up, no one made the connection with the tall, dark-skinned mage propped casually opposite the temple's rear entrance. After all, what kind of idiot would hang around the place they had just broken into? I had been concerned that Cursed Menatha Keffen might identify me after she'd spotted me in the temple, but either she hadn't been sure, or she hadn't wanted the attention.

My client's brother, when he scurried out the temple, no doubt thought he was being inconspicuous, but that kind of thing took practice, and a bowed head, close hood, and a bent, nervous scuttling, like a cockroach making a dash across a restaurant floor, drew more attention than if he'd jumped up and down shouting, 'Look at me.' I stepped out in front of him as he headed for a dark alley, holding up my hand.

"It's not a good idea to lie to the Ash Guard." Every word the truth. It was a terrible idea to lie to the Guard. That I wasn't Ash Guard was neither here nor there.

He stumbled. I grabbed his arm to steady him then ushered him the rest of the way into the alley.

"What do you mean?"

"Come on, Retha. You told me you didn't do work for the Brythanii temple. You told me no Brythanii would honour the betrayer god – your words – by working on it. That was a lie, because you were working on it all along."

He had regained his composure now. His chin lifted. "I don't see any reason why I should tell the Ash Guard anything. I'm not a mage. I don't use magic. What I do is none of your business."

"You'd be surprised what can be Ash Guard business if the Ash Guard decide." I pushed him back so he hit the wall. I was done with people lying to me.

"You're Mithalii," he spat.

"What the fuck does that mean?"

"It means you're not Brythanii. It means I don't trust you."

"Yeah? And it means you'll answer my questions now, or you'll answer them from an Ash Guard cell. Understand?" I loomed over him, using my height as an unfair advantage. For a moment, I thought he was going to tell me where to stick it or make a break, but then he slumped before the Ash Guard's reputation.

Maybe I could get Captain Gale to deputise me. It would make my investigations a lot easier.

"I didn't want anyone to know I was working there, all right? Especially not my daughter. I'm not proud of it, but I have bills, and half the time someone finds out you're Brythanii, they won't employ you. So, yeah, I've been working for the temple, and, yeah, I've been lying about it. So what?"

"So, it seems to me that it would be Cepra-damned convenient for you if Ard got beaten to death in the temple. You would get the compensation, you'd have revenge for the way he betrayed you, and Depths, maybe you'd get to be a priest after all, like you always wanted."

He pushed away from the wall. "Why would I want to be a priest if it's the kind of place Ard would fit in? You know what I think? I think they're all like him. A bunch of self-centred, treacherous bastards. But I still wouldn't hurt him. He's my brother."

Like that made a difference. The gaol was full of men who had killed their brothers or spouses. "You told me he wasn't your brother anymore."

"I wouldn't get him killed. That's the kind of thing Ard would do, not me."

Ironic, then, that Ard Ethemattian was the one having it done to him. Maybe Retha was right. Maybe all the priests were like that. It wasn't like they were there for the love of their god. Still, Retha had motive, and now I knew he had the opportunity, too. I wasn't letting it go so easily.

"You were working only a few corridors away from the

office where all the paperwork was kept. It would have been easy for you to sneak in and meddle with the statements at any time, add a fake entry statement for your brother." Although it still wouldn't explain how he ensured his brother was the one chosen. *I'll figure that out.*

A smirk spread across Retha's lips. "Not as easy as you think. I was working on Senator Farstone's palace at Carn's Break until the day after the Choosing. I wasn't anywhere near Agatos. You can confirm it with senator's Master Servant if you want."

Bannaur's balls! If that was true, there was no way he could be involved. Carn's Break was too far, even if he had a carriage, and he wasn't the kind of person who could afford a carriage. I tried to keep the disappointment off my face, but I didn't think I managed it. I jabbed a long finger in his face. "I will. Don't leave the city again until we're done."

I watched him hurry off into the gloom of the alley. If his alibi held up, this trail ran headfirst into the side of a cliff. If he wasn't just lying to me again. But why would he? This would be easy to confirm.

Maybe he's fleeing back home to grab his daughter and his money and get the Depths out of Agatos.

I didn't believe it. Retha Ethemattian might be a lying shit, and he might be disgusted and bitter at his brother, but I believed him. There were too many holes in the theory. How would he persuade Most Cursed Keffen to help him out? How could he ensure Ard was the one chosen? No. He had told me the truth about this, at least. He hadn't framed my client. I didn't know whether to feel relieved or frustrated by that.

I settled for both.

It wasn't all bad news. His sudden appearance at the temple had been a complication and a distraction. If I had kept chasing it, I could have wasted time I didn't have. My main suspects remained Menatha Keffen and her dead uncle, along with whatever conspirator they had worked with. My problem was, I couldn't prove any of it. Everything I had as evidence could still be dismissed as coincidence. There had to be more, some way to tie them irrevocably to the fixed Choosing. Any conspiracy involving more than one person would have loose threads, and if I kept plucking at them long enough, they would come free.

I was running out of *long enough*.

CHAPTER EIGHTEEN

I LEFT THE STREET OF GODS AND HEADED FOR MY APARTMENT.

Maybe Menatha Keffen's uncle had worked without her knowledge. Maybe the fight she'd had with my client really was no more than an intellectual difference. Maybe the Most Cursed's death was solely the work of some conspirator among the other Most Curseds deciding to cover their tracks. If so, Ethemattian was fucked, because I had no idea who that co-conspirator might be. The most useful candidate would be this chief priest, this Cursed of God, who was responsible for drawing the name. But Kehsereen's contact had said Most Cursed Keffen and the Cursed of God loathed each other.

So, maybe Keffen had blackmailed her. Maybe he had proof that she had fixed her own promotion to chief priest. The first thing I should do when I got home was sit down and see what Ethemattian had gathered on the

Cursed of God in his little book of blackmail. If there was something, Most Cursed Keffen might have known it, too.

I reached Corrastar Street, in sight of my office and apartment, and felt the weariness settle over me. Tomorrow night, Ethemattian would die, and I had no proof he had even been set up. I was almost out of time.

"Hey!" someone called from just behind.

I turned, wondering what the Depths it was now, right into a swinging club.

I jerked back, and it caught me on the shoulder, spinning me. Pain burst in the joint, and I staggered into another man. I had no time to react before he punched me in the stomach, knocking the breath out of me. Someone shoved me, and I sprawled on the cobbles.

A moment later they were all around me, boots thumping into my sides and stomach and back. I wrapped my arms around my head as pain blossomed everywhere like Missos flowers.

A boot caught the back of my head, smashing the side of my face into the stone.

Fuck this!

I ripped in raw magic and exploded it out. It caught my assailants and threw them back like rags.

I pushed to my hands and knees, biting down on my lip. Bannaur's broken balls that hurt! My breath caught as I struggled to my feet. My ribs protested. *Oh, fuck.*

I wiped blood from my face and looked around.

There were four of them, typical Dockside thugs. They

were trying to stand, groaning, reaching for dropped weapons.

Suddenly, I was furious. I'd had enough. Too much. Everything – *everything* – was going to shit faster than a drunk falling into the sewers. And some low-rent fuckers thought they were going to make my day even worse?

I limped over to the nearest of them and slammed magic into her, driving her into the cobbles. The second was fumbling for his knife when my mage's rod caught him across the head. He fell, limp.

The third tried to run. I took his legs away, lifted him with magic, and threw him back down.

The final one backed away, hands held out in front of him. He had dropped his club, but if he thought that would spare him, he had picked on the wrong mage. I pulled in more power, felt every bruise protest, and smashed him into the nearest wall. His head bounced off and lolled. I held him there, his feet off the ground, and slapped him around the face. "Hey. Wake up." I slid him further up the wall. "Who in the Depths are you? What do you want with me?"

His lips worked soundlessly.

I reached up and slapped him again. He blinked, slowly, coming back to consciousness. "What do you want with me?" I repeated.

His mouth opened and closed for a moment, then he said, "Paid."

"Paid? Someone paid you to attack me?"

A nod.

"Who?"

"Didn't give a name."

"Then describe them."

He winced, his arms and legs twitching helplessly. "A woman. Brythanii."

"A Brythanii woman paid you to, what? Kill me?" I knew precisely two Brythanii women. Cursed Keffen and Kehsereen's contact.

The thug's eyes widened in fear. He jerked another nod.

I leaned closer. "How many eyes did she have?"

"What?"

"How many eyes?"

"Two! Of course!"

Not the contact. Keffen! She'd seen me at the temple. She must have known I was onto her, so she had hired thugs to dispose of me. Bad move. You don't come for a mage like that.

I let the man drop. "Get out of here. Take your friends. If I see any of you again, I will rip the bones from your body and use you as a fucking carpet. Got it?" I flared magic around me.

He nodded, then helping his fallen comrades, stumbled and tripped away down the street as fast as they could. One of them was still unconscious. I watched them go. *Bad mistake, Keffen. Now I know it's you.* It was the last mistake she was going to make. She had fucked around too long, and now she'd made it personal.

"Nik!"

I turned at the shout, readying more magic, only to see Ileoni Silver hurrying towards me. I tried to straighten. Jabs of pain shot through my chest. Those thugs had done a number on me. I was tempted to go after them to give each a couple more kicks just for the sake of it. If I hadn't ached so much, I might have.

"I saw what happened. Are you all right?"

Apart from a barrel-load of bruises and a bit of blood? "I'm fine. I've been through worse."

"You shouldn't have to."

I couldn't disagree. "It's the job I'm working. I've got too close, and someone's panicked. Make a move like that, though, and if you miss, you've exposed yourself." I straightened my clothes. "I need to go and finish this."

She stepped in front of me. "You're not going anywhere like that."

"What do you mean?"

"You look like you've been pulled out from under a landslide. How far do you think you're getting? You'll collapse before you reach the end of the street."

That was an exaggeration. I would get at least to the middle of the next street. But I was certainly feeling it, and it hurt to move, more than I wanted to admit. I would do ... poorly if I hit any more problems like this.

"Come on." She took my arm. I tried not to wince as she led me to my door. "Let's get you cleaned up and rested, and then you can do what you need to do."

I could see the sense behind that. I just hoped the thugs didn't report back to Keffen that they had sold her out. I wouldn't if I were them. I would disappear.

"What in the Depths happened here?" Ileoni said, as I gave her a pass through my wards – a painful spell in my condition – and let her into my apartment. In the midst of having the shit kicked out of me, I'd forgotten my apartment had been trashed. I was spared having to answer immediately by Fria arriving in a rush and almost knocking me flying.

"Careful, boy," I said. He smelled better than I did. A cosy mustiness of fur, rather than stale sweat and blood. I pushed him down and rubbed him behind his ears.

"Sit," Ileoni said, firmly, and both Fria and I obeyed. "How long has it been like this?" She indicated the apartment.

"Since yesterday." It seemed longer.

"The same case?"

I shook my head.

"Pity, Nik. This job is not good for you."

"Yeah, well. Someone has to do it."

"Hm." She crossed to my kitchen space, poured water into my one good plate, and dampened a rag. "And it has to be you?"

I raised my hands. "I don't choose this."

She came over and dabbed at my cheek. I flinched.

"Don't be a baby."

Time to shift this conversation away from my flaws. "Is everything all right? The Manifestation didn't come back, did it?"

"No. Everything's fine. I was worried about you. I haven't seen you at the coffee house since you helped me, and you were a mess when you left." She raised her eyebrows at me. "A *different* bloodied mess."

"I'm doing fine."

She patted the wet rag at the blood on my nose. "I can see that."

Depths, that hurt! "I've just been busy. This case has been murder, literally, and then there was the riot."

"You were there, of course."

"Someone had to help."

"Yeah. My dad and brother went to see what they could do, but the Watch wouldn't let them through."

"Figures."

"But you've solved your case?"

"This one? Kind of. I know who's behind it, but I haven't figured out how to prove it."

She finished wiping the blood from my face then offered me a hand up. "Do you have anything clean to change into? That outfit's a bit..."

"Bloody and torn? It was new this morning." I gritted my teeth as I got to my feet. Luckily, I had bought more than one outfit. "I'll get changed."

I avoided looking at my bruises as I peeled off the destroyed clothes and climbed into new ones. I needed to wash properly, but that would mean going out to the public pipe half a block away to fetch buckets of water, and I couldn't face that.

When I came out, Ileoni was rubbing Fria's belly as he rolled delightedly on the floor. That dog was far more popular than I was, to no one's surprise. Ileoni stood when she saw me emerge. "Let's get you something to eat. You look like you need it, and Fria certainly does."

"Yeah, about that… I'm kind of broke. I was going to see my friends Holera and Elosyn for dinner." To *beg* for dinner. Assuming the invitation was still open, and assuming they would forgive me for not turning up when I'd promised and not having the decency to come around and apologise before now. They were more tolerant than I deserved, but there were limits.

"Good. You can tell me about your case on the way. My dad always says if you want to solve a problem, tell someone else about it, and half the time you'll realise you had the answer all along."

I cleared my throat. "You don't have to do this, you know."

"Nik, you saved my family. What would have happened if you hadn't stopped that Manifestation?"

It would have got nasty. With the power from the dead god feeding it and anger from the Warrens shaping it, no one in that house would have been safe.

"That was—"

"That was what friends do. So is this."

I surrendered. "All right. The case. I've got a client – a Brythanii priest – who's due to be ritually murdered tomorrow. The only problem is that the priests are supposed to volunteer, and he didn't. Someone set him up." I explained what I had discovered so far. "I'm certain his entry to the Choosing was faked, but with the high priest dead, I can't prove who was behind it."

"But you think it was this other priest—"

"Menatha Keffen."

"Yeah. So, you think someone faked the entry statement."

"It had to be one of the Keffens. Ethemattian's handwriting didn't match. It was a good forgery, but not perfect."

Fria stopped to piss on the corner of a house. I pretended not to notice.

"Did you compare it to either of the Keffens' handwriting?"

"What?"

"If one of them forged it, maybe there's a trace of their handwriting in it."

Why hadn't I thought of that? "I didn't have time. The priests were onto me."

Menatha Keffen's statement had been right there, too, but I'd hardly glanced at it. Had the handwriting been similar at all? I couldn't remember.

I wanted to tip my head back and scream into the night. I had been *right there*. The answer could have been in my hands.

Fuck!

I was going to have to go back.

"I'll never get into their archive, again," I said. "They'll be watching."

"But you know where they have their rooms, right? You told me you'd been to them. I don't know about you, but if you searched my room, you would find quite a few things I've written down."

And both Keffens were priests. Priests spent a lot of time writing. Didn't they? In between the rituals and all that stuff. Ethemattian certainly had, a whole notebook of blackmail material, for a start.

"You're brilliant!"

"I know."

I cleared my throat. "Um... Could you look after Fria for a few hours?"

I wondered if I could remember the forged letter well enough to recognise the letters that had been wrong. *The o's and the d's.* I pushed Fria's leash into Ileoni's hand.

"How about dinner?" she called after me as I broke into a run.

"Another time. I promise."

CHAPTER NINETEEN

In the hour and a half since I'd left the Brythanii temple, the furious bustle of priests hopelessly searching for their intruder had subsided. Daylight had gone from the valley, even from the mountaintops, and the Street of Gods was now illuminated by the sickly green glow of morgue-lamps and whatever godly luminescence the various temples were able to cajole, bribe, or wheedle out of their gods. The breeze had risen, bringing the salt smell of the Erastes Bay and the stink of the harbour into the streets as well as a damp chill that had me wrapping my mage's cloak tighter around me. The sound of competitive evening praying echoed from the open doors of the temples.

Things were quieter and dimmer in the alleys and side streets that ran behind and beside the temples. Displays of sound, warmth, and light were paper thin façades to tempt passers-by in and to get one over on the other temples. You would find the same thing at every bar and brothel on Dockside. The small open space behind the Brythanii temple – not substantive enough to be called a plaza – was lit more practically for the priests and their servants, as was the temple courtyard overlooked by the priests' accommodation.

The gate wasn't yet closed or guarded for the night, but the illumination in the courtyard meant that I would be seen by anyone looking out. None of which mattered. I wanted to do this before Keffen's thugs decided to report their failure, and I had run out of my weekly allowance of fucks to give. The sooner I got this done, the better.

So, which Keffen first?

The high priest was the most likely to have forged the entry. He had managed the whole process. He had access to all the statements throughout. But he had been found dead yesterday. A Most Cursed wasn't a random citizen of the lower city. Even though the Brythanii weren't much liked, the Watch would take his murder seriously. They would have swept through his room, scooping up everything that might be a clue. They might even have left a guard. There would be samples of his handwriting elsewhere in the temple but finding them would be difficult.

The younger Keffen, by contrast, occupied a single, anonymous, untouched room. It would be easy to search. I had wondered once if her uncle had worked without her knowledge. The moment she had sent those thugs after me, that idea was over. I suspected she was the force behind this whole thing. It was her life on the line, after all. Chances were, she had murdered her own uncle to keep him quiet.

Perhaps she would have insisted on making the forgery herself to get it right.

Mind made up, I strode into the courtyard and to the door leading to the Curseds' rooms. A few heads turned to watch, but I ignored them.

I hit the stairs at a run. I couldn't help myself. Something was bubbling up inside me. Fury. This priest, this person, had tried to kill me. She had set my client up to die in her place. She had murdered her own fucking uncle after he'd helped her. And if I couldn't prove it, she would get away with it all. Ethemattian would be viciously beaten to death, and she would become a Most Cursed, with all the privileges and wealth it gave her in Brythanii society. That was wrong. It offended me.

A priest stepped out onto the stairs, holding up a hand. I brushed past him and kept going.

Now, which was Cursed Keffen's room?

It took me a moment to recall the right door, and I found it locked. That delayed me all of two seconds before I was through and locking it behind me again.

I had forgotten how bare this room was. There weren't many places to hide things, but why would she hide her own writing?

The desk, then, and the shelf.

I pulled out all the papers and dropped them on the bed. No point trying to conceal what I was up to. She already knew I was onto her. What was she going to do? Send thugs to murder me?

Most of the papers were useless. Religious proclamations.

Stern notes about leaving the kitchens clean. The bureaucracy of the priesthood. I tossed them aside.

Here! Her own notes. A half-finished letter to a merchant in the Middle City – she had been unhappy about the quality of her tea, apparently, and who could blame her if the letter was half true?

Focus.

A notebook, filled with her religious thoughts rather than the blackmail Ethemattian had filled his with.

I spread them out and examined the writing. She wrote in a controlled, precise way. *A good skill if you want to copy another person's hand.*

The o's and d's. I peered closer.

Maybe. I could see the resemblance to the forged statement. The shape and formation of the letters was similar. But…

"It's not proof," I muttered. "It's not enough." I slammed a fist into the bed. It shook and shifted. *Calm!* If I took this to their head priest and presented it, it wouldn't convince her, or anybody.

Depths, maybe Cursed Keffen hadn't forged it. Maybe her uncle had done it. I swore.

Someone knocked on the door. "Cursed Keffen? Are you in there?"

Bannaur's bloodied balls! I didn't need this. I wasn't ready to be interrupted again so soon. All I had was a statement supposedly from Ethemattian where the handwriting was just a bit off and some script from Keffen where the o's and d's might or might not match the forged statement. My word that Keffen had sent thugs to kill me. Even if I could find them again, who would believe the word of Dockside murderers?

It still wasn't enough. Ethemattian was still going to die. I swore, again, under my breath. Time to search the Most Cursed's rooms after all. I grabbed a couple of pages of Cursed Keffen's notes and shoved them into my shirt then stood abruptly.

The bed clunked behind me, as though it had fallen slightly. I pushed it, and it rocked, thumping gently on the floorboards. It had been steady when I'd sat down, I was sure, and no one would choose to sleep on a bed like that without attempting to level it.

"Cursed Keffen?" the voice came again. "I can hear you. You're due in temple."

I ignored the voice and lowered myself to the floor. I conjured a light to see under the bed.

One of the legs was shorter than the others. Something had been shoved under it to prop it up, and when I'd stood or when I had thumped the mattress, it had come free. I reached under, through the dust, and pulled the item out.

It was a sheet of paper, folded repeatedly and jammed under the bed leg. I opened it and flattened it on the bed.

I couldn't help the laugh that burst out of my mouth. "I've got you! I've fucking got you!"

Keffen had used this paper for practice. She had written the same sentences over and over again. The first ones were poor efforts, her own handwriting clearly recognisable, but as it went on, it became more and more like

Ethemattian's handwriting until it was almost indistinguishable.

Except the o's and d's. Except the o's and d's.

This was the proof I needed. There was no arguing with it. Keffen had forged Ethemattian's statement, and along with her uncle, she had ensured that he would be entered and chosen as ritual sacrifice instead of her. Whether it was dislike and rivalry that had driven it or whether he was just a convenient scapegoat, she had selected him to die.

Just like I had once been framed for a Master Servant's murder.

Leaving the page on her desk, I opened the door and stepped right out into the waiting priest who was just about to knock again.

"Take me to the Cursed of God," I told him.

He puffed up. "Who in the Depths are you? What are you doing in Cursed Keffen's room?'

I didn't have time for this shit. "What's your name?"

He blinked.

"Your name."

"Cursed Luethan What are—?"

I held up a hand then pulled out Ethemattian's little book of blackmail. "Luethan, Luethan. Let's see. Ah, yes." I met his eyes. "A prostitute in Dockside, is it? Jina. I think I might have met her."

I'd never thought Brythanii skin could whiten any more, but this priest's did. I was going to hazard a guess that the Brythanii temple didn't think much of their priests visiting prostitutes.

"The Cursed of God?" I prompted.

All argument had gone out of him. I locked the door behind me with my strongest lock spell. It would take a decent mage to get through that. Then I followed the priest into the temple.

I drew a few curious looks as I followed the priest through the temple's corridors, but if anyone associated me with the robed and veiled intruder who had escaped hours earlier, they said nothing. After all, why would an intruder be strolling through the temple accompanied by a priest, rather than in chains with the City Watch? The mage's cloak didn't do any harm, either.

When did you start relying on the cloak?

I had always hated the deference afforded to mages in this city. And yet I wore this almost constantly now to bully or intimidate my way through awkward situations.

If you didn't, you couldn't do your job.

I wondered how many other mages told themselves that as they slipped through the world in their privilege.

You're a hypocrite.

Focus! Ethemattian's life was on the line. I did what I needed to save it. Anything else would be self-indulgent.

Eventually, we came to a solid, carved cedar door at the end of a marble-floored, fresco-decorated hallway, and the priest knocked, shooting me a bitter glance.

"Come!" a voice called.

The priest opened the door, and I followed him in, ready in case he was about to do something stupid like leading me into a guard room.

A priest was sitting behind a desk, working on papers. He looked up as we entered. He was a young man, not fully Brythanii from the light brown hair.

"We need to see the Cursed of God," my blackmailed priest said.

"It's urgent," I added.

The new priest – a secretary, perhaps – examined me with a look of distaste. "She's busy."

"We're all busy." I took a step forwards. "She'll want to see me." I wondered if I was going to have to resort to blackmail again, but he stood with a sigh and turned to the double doors behind him, cracking them open.

"Cursed Luethan and a Mithalii to see you, Cursed of God. They say it's urgent."

I didn't wait for a reply. I shouldered my way past and through the doors. The two priests followed behind me, making ineffectual and half-hearted grabs at my cloak.

The Cursed of God was an older Brythanii woman, with long hair tied up on top of her head. Despite her age, she looked fit and muscular, more like soldier than a priest. Maybe she needed to give her junior priests a good kicking from time to time. They probably deserved it.

"You fucked up," I announced.

Her eyebrows rose, but other than that, she didn't react. You didn't get to be head priest of a whole religion by being easily shaken. Religion could be vicious, and she had risen right to the top.

"Have I?" Her voice was calm and commanding, hinting at derision. But I had grown up with my mother, the blessed Countess. This woman was an amateur.

"Cursed Ethemattian didn't volunteer for your Choosing, but you selected him for death anyway."

With a sigh, she pushed the book she had been reading away. "The Cursed has already made this claim, but his statement was verified and sworn to by Most Cursed Coyd Keffen. Cursed Ethemattian is not the first to make such a claim after they were Chosen. No one wants to die. The remorse they feel for volunteering manifests itself in denial."

Someone else had to be involved in the Keffens' plan. The most likely candidate was the woman in front of me, even if she and Keffen had been bitter rivals. How she reacted to my evidence would tell me for sure.

And if she is, what then? I would have to take the proof to the other Most Curseds and hope to convince enough of them.

"Coyd Keffen is dead. Conveniently. And the statement is a forgery."

Her head tilted. "You're the one who broke in, aren't you?"

I shrugged. "So call the Watch. And while you're at it, you can explain to them how you're planning to murder someone who never volunteered. We'll see who ends up in the cells first."

That would probably be me, because the Watch hated

my guts – not without reason – and they would be looking for any excuse. But she didn't need to know that.

"If what you're saying is true, who is responsible?"

"Keffen's niece, Menatha Keffen, of course. She and Ethemattian detest each other. She volunteered for the Choosing, too. What better way of protecting herself than to get her uncle to set up a rival? When she discovered I was poking around, she sent thugs to kill me." I leant with my fists on the desk. "That was a very bad idea."

The Cursed of God remained unperturbed. "That is not proof. Those are just words. Cursed Ethemattian could have paid you to say this. Many of the Chosen become desperate as their time approaches."

"Yeah, well, maybe if you didn't beat them to death, none of this would happen. But if you want proof, I can give you proof. We're going to need the statements from the candidates, and we're going to need to go to Cursed Keffen's room."

Then we would see.

"Very well." She nodded to the priests still hovering behind me. "Accompany us."

This was it. If she saw the evidence and she was involved, she would have to make a move. If she thought the two wet sails bobbing hopelessly at my shoulders would be any help, she would be in for a big surprise. I gathered raw magic and held it ready as we made our way through the temple.

It wasn't just glances we drew this time, but an ever-growing wake of curious priests. The Cursed of God didn't send them on their way. Back-ups? Maybe they didn't realise I could knock the lot of them flying.

We collected the statements – and a few more priests – in the archive with its now smashed door then followed the stairs and hallways to the Curseds' residential wing behind the temple.

By the time we reached Cursed Keffen's room, we had gained a mini crowd of chattering priests as well as a few servants, and the commotion caused several doors to open as we passed, only adding to the crowd.

If they were expecting a show, this was going to be a disappointment.

Keffen's door was still locked – thankfully – and I released the spell then gestured to the Cursed of God. She looked back and seemed to notice the gawping crowd for the first time.

"Back to your duties." She turned her gaze on Cursed Luethan and her secretary. "You two wait out here."

Looked like it was just me and her. Did that mean she was going to try and cover this up? She had the wrong mage-for-hire if that was the case.

"Here," I said, showing her the paper on the desk. "You can quite clearly see where Keffen practiced copying Ethemattian's handwriting. Compare it to her statement and the forged statement attributed to Ethemattian."

The Cursed of God leant over the paper, studying it.

"And compare it to Ethemattian's actual writing." I laid the little book of blackmail on the desk beside the papers, careful to open it to the page detailing the Cursed of God's own shortcomings. She raised her eyebrows at me again, but she didn't comment. In truth, her listed sins were minor. A few lies, a couple of hangovers during ceremonies. Nothing that would work as blackmail material. I reached past her to point out the difference between the writing in the statement and in the book.

She stared at the papers for a long time, until I was starting to wonder if she'd fallen asleep where she stood. Then she straightened. "You are right. We have made a terrible error. Please gather the papers and follow me."

Now would be the most dangerous time. She had seen the evidence and seen that it was enough. If she was part of the conspiracy, would she try to destroy the papers, have me arrested, or stick a knife in my back? If she tried to take me down to a murder cellar, we were going to have issues.

"You two." She addressed the priests waiting outside. "Summon all the Most Curseds – *all* of them, no exceptions – and bring them to the Sanctum, then fetch Cursed Keffen and Cursed Ethemattian." She pursed her lips. "Bring a couple of temple guards with you when you fetch Cursed Keffen. She may try to run." She gestured to me. "Come. This will take a vote of the Most Curseds. It is unprecedented."

THERE WAS NO DARK CELLAR, NO KNIFE IN THE BACK, NO Watch to arrest me. We waited in the Sanctum as the senior priests arrived in ones and twos. My presence beside the Cursed of God generated a few glances but no comments as the Most Curseds settled themselves.

Both Ethemattian and Keffen looked bewildered as they

were escorted in, although Ethemattian's expression turned to one of relief when he saw me waiting, and Keffen frowned.

I counted nearly thirty senior priests, along with Ethemattian and Keffen, and a couple of temple guards who positioned themselves surreptitiously at the door.

Now we would see whether the Cursed of God planned to condemn me or tell the truth. I held magic ready, feeling every bruise and scrape amplified by the pressure.

"Most Curseds," the Cursed of God said, quieting the room with her voice. "It has come to my attention that our most profound ritual, the Choosing, has been interfered with."

A babble of voices rose in response. I watched Ethemattian and Keffen. Ethemattian's face stayed still, but Keffen's frown deepened. The Cursed of God waited until the noise subsided.

"You were all here when I drew Cursed Ethemattian's name as sacrifice. You will remember that Cursed Ethemattian protested vigorously and claimed that he had never entered himself into the Choosing. Like me, you will have dismissed his claims as the fears of a condemned priest, and you will have heard such claims before. However, it seems that he was telling the truth. His name was falsely entered, his statement forged, and our late brother, Most Cursed Coyd Keffen, lied when he vouched for the entry."

This time the noise was louder. Shouts, curses, disbelief, and condemnation. The Cursed of God waited again. Keffen was shaking her head, but no one was paying attention.

"It is my belief that the Most Cursed did this to protect

his niece from being Chosen. It might have been the actions of a loving uncle who then decided to take his own life out of guilt. But we have discovered evidence that Cursed Menatha Keffen was the one who forged the statement, that she was behind the scheme to send her brother Cursed to the sacrifice in her place, and I believe she murdered her own uncle to cover up this plan."

Again, shouting, outrage, and above it all, Keffen's shout of "No!" I watched her shake her head violently. Then her eyes found mine, and I saw the fury in them.

Yeah, that's right. I've got you. Perhaps if she hadn't sent those thugs after me, I would never have been sure she was behind it.

"This is an unprecedented situation. Cursed Ethemattian was Chosen, but he did not volunteer. I propose that the Most Curseds examine the evidence, then we will vote on replacing Cursed Ethemattian with Cursed Keffen."

"No!" Keffen shouted again. "I didn't. It's not true."

Oh, but it was. She had been clever. I still didn't know how she had ensured Ethemattian's name was chosen instead of hers. I was certain, though, that the Cursed of God wasn't involved. If she had been, what would there be to stop Keffen condemning her here and now? It wasn't like Keffen had anything to lose.

It took a long time for the Most Curseds to examine and discuss the evidence. There was far more arguing and jabbing of fingers at the papers and sometimes at each other than was really warranted by how clear the proof was. I saw Keffen slowly slide down the wall and settle, head in hands, not watching. Ethemattian stood unmoving. If I had been in his place, I would probably have collapsed like Keffen.

At last, the Most Curseds returned to their seats, and the Cursed of God called for a vote. One by one, the Most Curseds called out their decisions.

In the end, it was closer than I had expected. A full ten Most Curseds voted to leave Ethemattian as the Chosen sacrifice. Whether that was stubbornness, stupidity, malignancy, or an inability to change their minds in the face of evidence, I didn't know. But they were outvoted.

The Cursed of God nodded. "It is decided. Cursed Ethemattian is no longer Chosen. Cursed Keffen will take his place. Cursed Keffen, prepare yourself. Open yourself to the betrayer god in the hope that it will come into you and in your death, hope that the god who failed us dies too."

"You did not help us when we needed you," the Most Curseds responded.

I let my shoulders slump. Fuck me.

"As a consequence of your deceit and untrustworthiness, Cursed Keffen, you will be confined to your room until the time of sacrifice, and your room will be guarded. There will be no escape for you." She turned to me. "This has been a hard lesson for the temple, but we thank you for your part in helping us see the truth."

I shrugged. "I did my job."

As the Most Curseds drifted from the room in small groups, deep in shocked discussions, Ethemattian joined me. "Thank you. I was beginning to have my doubts. Forgive me for that."

He hadn't been the only one. I wouldn't have been happy putting my life in the hands of a second-rate mage either. "I'm curious. What would you have done if I had failed?"

He glanced around. No one else was close. "Fled the city. I had already reserved a place on a Pentathian ship leaving Agatos tomorrow."

Somehow, that made me feel better. Even if I had fucked up, he would have been all right.

"I guess they're not making you a Most Cursed in compensation?"

"No. I am still a Cursed. I did not enter the Choosing, so I cannot ascend to Most Cursed. Perhaps I will enter the Choosing next year."

I stared at him. "Are you serious? After all this? Are you insane?"

His lips turned up. "I can't be unlucky two years in a row. Just as long as I book passage on a ship in case."

Some people you just couldn't help. "And what if the sacrifice works this time around? What if you trap and kill your god? Do you have a plan then?"

Ethemattian snorted. "No one believes that will happen. And if it does, the religion will continue on as it always has."

I knew I should leave it. I knew I should take my money and go, be well rid of this whole absurd thing. Leaving well alone was not my strong point. "Then what the fuck is it all for?"

"It's a game, Mr. Thorn. No one here cares about the god one way or another. It's a gamble for power and influence, and the stakes are the lives of the losers. That is all religion ever is. The gods are an irrelevance."

Hadn't I always said that? But fuck it, it was one thing for me to say it and quite another for a priest to admit it so shamelessly. It left me feeling dirty. Was that all this had really been about? Not saving a man's life but playing their Cepra-damned stupid political games. I wanted to punch someone. Anyone.

Let it go.

"How much do I owe you, Mr. Thorn?"

I had been going to say five gold crowns to cover my time, expenses, and effort, but fuck that. "Ten crowns."

He nodded. "I will not argue the price of my life." He reached into a pocket and counted out the money.

I took it, and I got out of there as quickly as I could.

I should have asked for twenty.

CHAPTER TWENTY

I HAD LOST TRACK OF TIME IN THE BRYTHANII TEMPLE, BUT BY the fading crowds on the street, it was well into late evening. In the heat of the summer, people would have just been emerging, but it had been dark for hours, and there was enough of a chill in the air to discourage loitering outside coffee houses, tavernas, and inns. I stopped at the Penitent's Ear to collect enough dinner for me, Fria, and Ileoni, in case she was still waiting.

I intended to head back home to wash the dirt – real and psychological – from me before going to look for the two of them, but when I reached my apartment, the lights were on in the office, and I found Ileoni and Fria waiting. She had tidied up a bit, and a couple of new chairs faced each other across the broken desk.

Fria looked up at me, gave a half-hearted bark, then

slumped back down. That dog was a massive traitor whenever he got the slightest chance.

"How did you get in? I left it locked."

"Your friend Benny was here when we came around looking for you. He let us in."

Of course he did. Benny had never seen a lock he didn't want to pick.

"He says he's got a new desk for you if you don't ask where it came from. How did it go?"

I dropped into the second chair. "Good. I guess. I cleared my client, and he's free. I got paid."

She tilted her head. "So why don't you look happier?"

I puffed out my cheeks. "Tired, maybe." Which I was. But that wasn't it. "I still don't understand how Keffen did it. I understand how she forged the statement, and I understand that her uncle swore it was genuine. But I still don't understand how she ensured that Ethemattian was the one chosen. If her uncle only entered copies of Ethemattian's statement, that would have been an enormous risk for both Keffens. Someone might have inspected the statements before they could switch them back, and they would have been caught. Someone else must have been involved, and I don't know who. I thought it must be the Cursed of God, even though she and the Most Cursed hated each other, but then she wouldn't have dared accuse Keffen in case her own part in the plan was revealed. Unless she and Keffen had a plan to let Keffen escape..."

"Does it matter?"

I blinked. "I'm sorry?"

"Your client is free. He's not going to be murdered. You did your job, and you saved his life."

I tipped my head back and ran a hand over my face and hair. "I just can't help but think someone has got away with it."

"Nik, people are getting away with things every minute in Agatos, some with far more terrible things than setting up your client. You can't be responsible for all of them. No one can. You'll drive yourself insane. You won. Take it." She stretched. "Now. You seem to have brought food, and I'm starving, so let's eat." She nudged a package at her feet. "I brought you some plates."

When we were settled in the kitchen with food and Fria was happily wolfing down his portion without bothering to chew, Ileoni said, "I have a question for you."

"What's that?"

"How do you manage to run a business at all like this?"

"What?"

"I've been waiting for you here for - what? - an hour and a half? In that time, two people have been here looking to hire you."

Huh. "What did you tell them?"

"Well, the first one had a grudge with his neighbours. He wanted you to set a curse on them or burn their house down or something, so I told him to fuck off."

"Good call."

"The other one, she thinks her husband is having an affair. She wanted you to use magic to prove it."

"That's not how it works."

"Anyway, I told her you'd take the job."

"You what?" I started forward. "I can't take on another job right now, particularly not one like that! That kind of thing takes hours, days, of following people around. I don't have time."

She didn't look perturbed. "You won't have to. He's definitely having an affair."

I resisted the urge to bury my head in my hands. *She's just trying to help.* "How in the Depths would you know that? I can't just make stuff up. I have to be right." There were definitely people who would tell a client any old shit they thought would get them paid. A few former City Watch selling their dubious skills as investigators sprang to mind.

"She had a painting of her husband to show you. I've seen him before. He comes into our coffee house at least once a week with a woman who is definitely not his wife, and they are *very* friendly. He's having an affair. I can probably even give you a couple of dates and times."

I settled back with a grunt. Hard to argue with that.

"So, same question. How do you even get work if you're not here when people come around?"

I shifted in my chair. Not that I was feeling awkward. I just wasn't used to this chair yet. "Some of them come back."

"But not all. I know you've been busy these last few days, but don't pretend you always are. Some days, some weeks even, you struggle to make enough for your rent. I know that, because you tell me, and sometimes you spend hours sitting in the coffee house with only a single coffee. If you're not here, you don't get the work."

"If I am here, I'm not *doing* the work."

"So employ someone to assist you, to be here arranging jobs, weeding out the clients you don't want."

I was shaking my head before she even finished. "I can't afford to pay someone. I can't afford to pay myself half the time."

"But if you had someone here, you'd have more work, and you would be able to pay them and make a better living."

Have someone here, the whole time? The idea made me shiver. I did not get on with many people, and almost none that I wanted hanging around my home all day. I could count on the fingers of one hand, not including the thumb, the number of people I would be willing to work with. "You want a job?"

"Yes."

I sat back. That wasn't the answer I expected. "Really? You have a job."

"You think I want to work in a coffee house all my life?"

I sucked my lips. Was she serious? I had always done this on my own. This was who I was. Yeah, sometimes Benny and I did the odd thing together, or Kehsereen gave me information, but this was still just me. When I had walked away from my mother's palace, I had told myself I wouldn't be controlled by anyone else. I would stand alone.

And then what? Die alone? Be forgotten?

"It doesn't have to be me," Ileoni said. "But you need help."

"Everyone tells me that," I muttered.

"Just think about it. You can't go on like this." Her eyes travelled across my broken office then rested on Fria.

I grabbed a lemon pastry from my plate and shoved it in my mouth. If I was eating, she couldn't expect me to reply. I just had to keep my mouth stuffed for the rest of the evening.

Ileoni hadn't stayed much later after that, instructing me to get some sleep and check in with her the next day. It was ... strange having someone looking out for me. My mother hadn't, even before she'd changed. She hadn't always been the way she was now. Before my stepfather's death, she had often been absent and distracted, but afterwards she had become cold and single-minded. His death had hit me hard. I had been too young to realise how hard it had hit her, too. Even though she hadn't become a high mage and announced herself as the Countess until years later, I thought that was when she'd become that person. But she had never been exactly warm. And Mica was my little sister. I had been the one looking out for her.

Benny and I had each other's backs, of course, always. Well, until recently, and maybe – maybe – that was coming back. But that was different. We had been Warrens' kids, and that taught you to be hard. There had been nothing we wouldn't do for each other, but neither of us had truly stopped the other pushing too far.

This ... this was something new, and I didn't really know what to do with it.

When I woke the next morning, Fria was whining at the bedroom door. Either he was hungry, thirsty, or needed the back yard. His getting off the bed had woken me. Somehow, I hadn't noticed him getting on.

Too tired. Or just getting used to it.

Groaning, I swung out of bed. It was bright outside. Not early-morning-bright, but full morning. I didn't normally sleep this late.

I tested my bruises, but they were gone. At least that was something. And my head would recover with food and drink.

What I could really do with was a couple of days off to rest, sort out my apartment, and not have anyone try to kill me. But while I might have resolved Ethemattian's case—

Did you?

Even though I *had* resolved his case, I still needed to find out who had killed the Lady of the Grove if this shrinking rift with Benny was ever to be completely healed.

The Wren was still our most likely suspect but proving that would be an order of difficulty harder than catching out Keffen. For all the cleverness of her plan, Keffen didn't have decades of criminal experience to draw on and the power of a high mage to back it up.

Fria barked.

"All right, all right."

I opened the bedroom door, and he rushed out – ignoring the door to the back yard and his bowl in the kitchen space – into the office and up to the front door, where he stopped and snuffled at the gap beneath it.

"Either you're trying to escape again or someone's out there."

I took hold of Fria's collar and unlocked the door. A short, older man with a smile that revealed brown stumps of teeth and awful breath peered up at me.

"See, that's magic that is, knowing a bloke's here before he even knocks."

"Squint? What are you doing here?"

"Didn't think I'd see you around Dumonoc's after what you did to his place last time you were there."

I stepped aside. "I saved his bar from complete destruction."

"You also gave him a bloody nose and got his door kicked in. You ain't popular." He shuffled past me.

Squint was one of the Wren's information brokers. I had used him before when I'd needed information I couldn't get elsewhere. He was reliable if you paid, with the understanding that he would just as happily sell your information to anyone else and that anything you told or asked him would get back to the Wren sooner rather than later.

"What's this about? You need something?"

He peered around the office. "This is a state, ain't it? I heard you pissed off the boss."

"It's what I do. What do you want?"

"Me? I want to do you a favour."

Bollocks. "And how much is this favour going to cost me?"

"This one's for free." He leaned closer, his rotten teeth gleaming wetly in the light. I preferred him in the dark of

Dumonoc's bar. "What with us being friends, and you always letting me finish the wine." Squint was the only person who both enjoyed and could survive the rancid liquid that passed for wine at Dumonoc's.

"I'm generous that way."

"Good. Then here's what I've got for you: your mate Benyon Field is going around telling everyone the Wren killed the Lady of the Grove. The Wren ain't happy. If Benny doesn't stop, there are going to be consequences."

I felt a fist clench inside me. Why in the Depths would Benny do something so stupid? He must know the Wren would find out. You didn't piss off a high mage if you had any sense at all.

"Did he? Kill her, I mean?"

Squint grinned. "None of my business, and I wouldn't tell you if I knew. We're not *that* good friends. Warn him off, Mennik Thorn, or you're going to have one less surviving friend in this city." Squint nodded. "That's me done. That's my freebie for the year." With a glance down at Fria, who was sniffing nervously at Squint's trousers, he turned and left.

Fuck's sake, Benny. Why couldn't he have waited? Why couldn't he let me find the truth safely?

Whatever he thought of me, however he would react to me interfering, I couldn't let him do this to himself. That wasn't what friends did.

"Come on, Fria," I said. "We need to make a visit."

THE SMELL OF SMOKE FROM THE WARRENS STILL HUNG IN THE heavy, unmoving air. From outside Benny's house, the burned timbers and blackened stones from the inferno that had engulfed the place were a stark reminder of what had happened. What the Wren had *allowed* to happen, maybe even caused. People moved over the wreckage, no longer looking for survivors or bodies, but sorting through the rubble to salvage materials. That was what happened in the Warrens: buildings crumbled, and what was left was repurposed into ever more rickety shacks. This time would be different. Too much needed rebuilding, too much had burned beyond repair, too little time remained before winter arrived. Turning, I saw a glade of sunlight piercing the blanket of clouds over Horn Hill. If the gods wanted to send a sign, this was an unsubtle 'fuck you' to the Warrens. The fuckers on the Hill didn't even have to share the same repressive weather as the rest of us.

Benny answered the door when I knocked, rubbing his eyes. "Mate, have you got any idea what time it is?"

"No clue."

"Me neither, but it's too fucking early."

I stepped past him, carefully avoiding the booby-trapped floorboard Sereh had warned me about. Benny snorted as he watched me.

"Is there actually a trap there?" I asked.

"Don't know. But I don't step there, either." He glanced back at where Sereh was sitting in the back doorway, looking out over the shared courtyard. She didn't react, but I was absolutely sure she was listening. "Want a drink?"

I accepted a cup of water then settled on his couch. He sat opposite.

"So, why'd you wake me? It better be important. You don't get this beautiful by missing your sleep."

"This is serious, Benny. I heard you've been going around telling people the Wren killed the Lady."

His face hardened like sun-cracked leather. "Well, he fucking did."

"We don't know that for sure, and that's not the point, anyway. The Wren knows what you're doing. You think he's going to sit by while you spread that kind of rumour?"

Benny's hands stilled and a dangerous look entered his eyes. "I was in the Warrens yesterday, seeing if there was anything I could do to help. Someone's built a shrine to the Wren there. A fucking shrine. He kills her, the Warrens gets burned, and people start treating him like a god? I'm not having it."

"You can't go up against him. He'll kill you." It occurred to me then that, if the Wren had killed my stepfather, my mother had done exactly the same to me as I was now doing to Benny: trying to keep me away, trying to stop me asking dangerous questions.

That's different. I'm not being reckless like Benny.

"I'm not walking away," Benny said. "Not from this. I had friends in the Warrens. You did, too, remember? That was our home, our place. He took the Lady from them, and then he let it burn until most of it was gone. He only stepped in when he could look like a Cepra-damned hero, and now they're starting to think he's a god? Don't think he didn't start *that* rumour."

It was hard to argue with any of it. But the Wren would kill Benny as easily as snapping his fingers.

And had my mother told herself that when she'd refused to tell me the truth?

That's different.

"We need proof. We need to take it to the Ash Guard. They're the only ones – the *only* ones – who can handle him.

Benny snorted again. "Mate, just because you've got a crush on that Ash Guard captain doesn't mean they'll help us."

"That's not it." Was it? "They deal with rogue magic, no matter what."

"If you say so. Doesn't make a difference, because you don't have proof, do you?"

I wetted my lips. "Not yet."

"Exactly."

"So I'll get it."

"I ain't holding my breath."

I let myself fall back in the couch. *How?* That was the question, wasn't it? How could I prove what the Wren had done? He was too smart and too powerful to leave anything obvious like Keffen had done.

"Kael," I said.

"What? The Wren's second-in-command?"

I nodded.

"Why the fuck would he tell you anything?"

"He'll know. The Wren doesn't do anything without Kael knowing. All we have to do is get him away from the Wren."

"Right... You know he almost never leaves that warehouse? And even if he did, people say he's almost as dangerous and ruthless as the Wren. You think you can handle him, because I don't? You think you can capture him and put enough pressure on him that he'll betray the fucking Wren?"

Kael wasn't just the Wren's assistant. If the rumours were true, he was the Wren's bodyguard and chief enforcer, although why a high mage would need a bodyguard was anybody's guess. Someone to watch his back, maybe.

"If we had Ash..."

"We don't."

I had stolen Ash from Captain Gale once before, and I was still alive. I didn't think she would tolerate it twice.

Maybe Kehsereen had discovered the secret of Ash and could whip up a batch for me.

Maybe the gods will come down and bring peace to the world, too, while we're about it.

"Then what?"

"You tell me."

I rubbed a hand across my face. Stubble itched against my skin. I was tired, dirty, stretched to breaking. "We could just let it go. Let the Ash Guard and the Senate do their jobs and investigate."

"Fuck's sake, mate. Not this again. If you think they'll bother, you're an idiot. It was just the Warrens. They'll cover it up and bury it. They're not going to disturb their precious balance for the scum in the Warrens. The only people who care about this are us, because it's personal for us."

Was he right? I wanted to believe that Captain Gale would do the right thing. She was ruthlessly wedded to the principles of the Guard. But taking out the Wren would destabilise the city. Losing one high mage had set things on edge, and they were only just beginning to rebalance now that Mica had been made the third high mage. If Agatos lost the Wren, who would there be who could oppose my mother? I doubted the positions of Countess and Senator were enough for her ambition. Agatos didn't need another king. The Guard might take the view that stability was more important for the city than justice.

I had known Benny for a long time. I knew that look in his eyes. He was a stubborn bastard when he got something in his head. He would keep on telling people the Wren had killed the Lady, no matter what I said, and then the Wren would kill him. The Wren didn't make idle threats.

Find out the truth. Find the proof. Go to the Guard. That was the only way Benny was walking out of this intact.

Reluctantly, I said, "If there's proof, it's in that warehouse of his." There were also wards that could tear me to shreds before I could blink, a couple of dozen of the Wren's mages, and the man himself. If we wanted to commit suicide, this would be a quick way.

Benny chewed on his lip. "You think he's kept something that could incriminate himself?"

"Honestly? Probably not. He's not stupid."

"But he might?"

"Yeah. He might." The Wren had been around a long time. Whether he or my mother was the most powerful mage in the city was up for debate, but certainly no one had challenged him directly in all the time I'd been alive. Maybe he had become lazy or arrogant. Maybe, behind those wards, with his own power to hand, he assumed no one would try to get in.

Because it would be fucking crazy. He wasn't just a high mage. He was the undisputed king of the city's underworld. People who went against him died.

"So, we break in," Benny said. "Find what we need. Go to the Ash Guard, and they go fuck him up, is that it? That's the plan?"

I hadn't meant it as a plan. I hadn't intended to have a plan at all. All I'd wanted was to warn Benny that he had drawn the Wren's gaze. I shrugged.

"You reckon we can get in?" Benny asked.

"I don't know. And if we do, I don't know if we can get out again. The whole warehouse is warded, but most of those wards are kept suspended most of the time. A lot of people come and go. The problem is, those wards can come down quicker than you could react. Any one of his people could have the ability to trigger them. If we were seen at all, we could be trapped."

"You can't get through them? The way I heard it, you've got through wards before."

"Not like these. Most wards, there's a way through them." Like there had been at Senator Greenfield's palace. "Not a high mage's wards, though."

"I'll go," Sereh said. I hadn't noticed her leave her position in the doorway to drift over. "Wards don't see me. No one sees me."

"No!" Benny and I both said at the same time.

Sereh pouted.

"We go in when the wards are suspended," Benny said, "and we don't get seen."

I was shaking my head already. "It doesn't matter. The Wren will know we're there." I was damned certain my mother had always known when I was in her palace, even if she had chosen to ignore me.

"Anyone would think you're not up for this, mate."

"I'm not up for having my balls fried on an open fire."

"Not that there'd be much to fry," Benny muttered.

"I'm serious, Benny. If we try to do this and we get it wrong, we're dead. Both of us. He might even come for Sereh."

Sereh's eyes settled on me. Her knife was in her hand. "That would be a mistake."

A shiver ran up my spine. But it was the only thing that could get through to Benny.

"Then what do we do?" he said. "Because we've got to do something."

I could have argued with that again, but it wouldn't have done any good. "We have to get the Wren out of there and far away. We have to have him focused on something else entirely, and we have to pray that we can hide from the rest of his people."

"All right, mate. Now, how do we make the Wren leave his warehouse? Burn the Warrens down again?"

"We offer him something he can't resist."

"Ha! Don't know about you, mate, but I don't think I've got anything the Wren would get out of bed for. That guy could buy everything I owned without bothering to put it in his ledgers. And if he couldn't, he'd just nick it."

"We do have one thing he'd want."

Benny frowned, then his frown shifted into a scowl. "You'd better not be talking about what I think you're talking about."

"We don't have to give him the Lady's body. But he knows it's out there, he doesn't know where it is, and if he thinks it's up for grabs, he'll go for it. He'd be stupid not to, because he wouldn't want my mother getting hold of it."

"And when he finds out it's lie?"

"Then he'd better not know the information came from us."

"I can arrange that."

I tilted my head, trying to read him. "You sure?"

"Yeah. Trust me. I've done this kind of thing before."

Trust him. I didn't know about that. I trusted that he'd done it before, but there was a world of difference in tricking some merchant or senator and tricking the Wren. I couldn't say I didn't trust him, though. Benny might not mean this as a test, but it was, anyway. Our friendship was as fragile as a paper lantern in a storm. A single gust could rip it apart again, and you could only patch it together so many times.

"We'll have to be in and out quick," I said. "We need to

get him as far away as possible, but a high mage can move fast when they need to. The moment he realises he's been lied to, he'll tear back, and if we're still there..." I let it trail off. "We should say that the body is being taken out of Agatos in a carriage in the north of the city. Maybe say it's been claimed by mages from one of the northern cities. He won't try anything in the city, because the Ash Guard would find out. He'll wait until it's outside the city, out of sight."

"Except it won't be there."

"Exactly. It should give us an hour to get in, search, and get out and away again. We'll head to the Ash Guard fortress where he can't get us. It'll be over fast."

"If we find anything."

"Yeah. If." If we didn't, we would have to pray the Wren didn't trace this back to us.

"Seven o'clock," Benny said. "After dark. We'll meet back here, then aim to be at his warehouse just before he's supposed to intercept the cart." He took my gaze. "Don't let me down, mate. Not this time."

CHAPTER TWENTY-ONE

I LEFT BENNY'S HOUSE WITH A SENSE NOT JUST OF FOREBODING but of failure mixed with a thick undercurrent of dread. I had come here to warn Benny off. Instead, I'd ended up agreeing to something far more dangerous. Even without his magic, the Wren had levers he could pull. All it would take was one person to notice what Benny was doing, crumble under the weight of the Wren's persuasion, and he would know.

As for the plan itself, I didn't like it. Benny and I had broken into a high mage's palace once before, and we'd only just managed to survive the experience. The Wren was far more ruthless than Carnelian Silkstar had ever been.

Even if we succeeded, even if we got in and out unnoticed, the chances of us finding anything were slim.

You can still pull out. Tell Benny no, you're not doing it.

But if I did, it would be the end of us as friends. Ironic that Benny's resentment and anger at me had come about because I had put Sereh in danger, yet here he was risking far more for all of us. I should have realised earlier on that his fury at that danger to Sereh hadn't just been directed at me. It had been directed at the Wren, who had sent his people to Benny and Sereh's house, willing to kill them if I didn't do what he said. I had known Benny long enough to know he would never forgive something like that. Just as he never forgot a favour, he never forgave an insult or threat. If I hadn't been so far up my own arse, I would have seen this coming. But it was too late now. If I didn't go along with it, we would be over, and Benny would do something even more stupid.

What matters most? Benny's friendship or avoiding risk?

I could hide from danger and die alone in thirty or forty years. Or I could step up to the execution block and hope the executioner had taken a quick break for a pint down the local bar.

It wasn't even a question, really.

Everyone has to die sometime. Better to do it for a reason. The truth mattered. We might not agree on everything, Benny and I, but we agreed on that.

The truth about the Wren was what mattered to Benny, but if I was going to go down like this, there was another piece of truth I had to know for myself. How *had* my stepfather died? For years I had tried to push all thought of it down, but it kept bobbing back up.

Unlike Endir's boat.

"For fuck's sake," I muttered.

I didn't believe his boat had just sunk out there on the

bay. Endir had been an experienced fisherman from a long line of fishermen. The day had been calm.

Kael had hinted that the Wren had killed Endir, but he hadn't quite come out and said it. We might – *might* – find something that pointed to the Wren's involvement in the Lady's death, but the drowning of a fisherman almost twenty years ago? Not a chance.

The truth of what had happened to Endir mattered more to me than the Lady did. In the end, a god was a god, and I had no time for any of them. But Endir had been my father in all but blood. He had made us a family for a while. If the Wren had taken that from us, I wanted to know before I risked my life to bring him down.

So, who would actually know, other than Kael or the Wren himself?

You know who.

Fuck that. There had to be another way. I doubted the Wren's information brokers were privy to such secrets, but perhaps another fisherman was, someone who had been out on the water that day, who had seen what happened.

And how do you find them? Why would they tell you after all this time? The residents of Fishertown kept their secrets, and doubly so if the threat of the Wren's anger hung over them.

I felt sick, hollow inside, like an oyster shell scooped out and left on the dockside.

There was no one else. No one except my mother, the blessed Countess, up there in her palace, above it all.

I couldn't go back there. Not again. Not after what she had done to me.

Then forget all about it. Move on. You might not die, anyway.

I couldn't do that, either.

Perhaps Fria could read my emotions, or maybe I was holding his leash too tight, because he let out a whine.

"Yeah, you're right. Now or never." In the end, I had to know. Somehow, I had to brave the trauma she'd left me and get her to tell me. Somehow.

I trailed my reluctant way below Horn Hill, letting Fria's insistence on sniffing every corner and doorstep be an excuse for my slow progress.

I had plenty of time until I had to meet up with Benny. Most of the day. There was nothing I could do to prepare. We either managed it or we didn't.

Eventually, I reached the foot of the Corithian Steps and stared at where they switched their way up the steep flank of the hill. That was going to fuck my ankle badly.

So take your time. Take rests.

Or I could go the long way around.

Yeah? And maybe a few more diversions until you're out of time.

I wasn't too far from the Street of Gods here. Tonight, just before midnight, the Brythanii would gather in their temple and beat Cursed Keffen to death. It was her fault, of course. She had volunteered, and then she had set up Ethemattian in her place. If I had failed, it would be my client in there, falling under a brutal hail of blows, pounded into a pulp, every bone broken, flesh split, life draining from him. She had chosen that for him. She had made sure he would die. Even so, there was something – maybe guilt? – playing at me.

No. That wasn't right. Not guilt. Sympathy, perhaps? But it wasn't really that, either.

Why did I feel so unsettled about it?

"Because you don't want to see anyone die like that, arse-hole or not."

That still wasn't it. She had brought it on herself. Plenty of people in the city didn't deserve to die but were dying anyway. People in the Warrens. Workers on the docks. Those who were alone or sick or lost. She wasn't one of them. So, what then?

It's because you didn't find out who else was involved.

Truth matters. The Keffens *couldn't* have reliably pulled it off on their own. Someone else had to have helped them, someone high up in the temple, and that person had walked away free. Much as I wanted to take Ileoni's advice and let it go, I couldn't.

You never can. That's why you always end up sinking in the shit.

I had time. I could go over there now, poke the nest of snakes. See what struck back.

I almost laughed. *You're doing it again*. This was what I always did. Whenever there was something I didn't want to face, I let myself get distracted, told myself that *this other thing* was more important, that it had to be done first, that I had plenty of time... If I went to the temple, something else would come up, then another thing, then before I knew it, my appointment with Benny would have come around, and I would never have talked to my mother. My brain was a fucking traitor.

"You need to know." I might never get another chance.

Fria gave me an enquiring look.

"Not you." Dogs didn't need to know anything, the lucky bastards. Just where the food was, where to sleep, and when the next walk was coming. People overcomplicated things.

The climb up the Corithian Steps was steep enough that I could tell myself it was to blame for my racing heartbeat, the sweat on my palms, and the narrowing of my vision. The pain in my bad ankle – I didn't take my time; I didn't take rests – acted like a needle jabbing at my awareness, keeping me distracted. Despite that, by the time I reached the top of the steps and started down Agate Way towards my mother's palace, I was dragging the weight of half the city behind me. Even Fria turned his head up to me, puzzled, as I slowed more and more.

Do it!

I realised I had stopped.

Why aren't you over this? Why did the thought of facing my mother still fill me with all this dread? All those things she'd done to me, all the suffering she'd weighted me down with to turn me into a high mage was over. She could never do it again.

It was no good. My legs wouldn't move. Blackness closed my sight.

Fria whined again.

I fumbled for the knife at my belt, tightened my fist around the hilt, then jabbed the point into my thigh hard enough to draw blood. I muffled a cry of pain as I bent over.

Fria's head pressed against mine, his bad breath washing over my face, his tongue wet on my neck.

"It's all right, boy. It's all right."

Shaking, I slid the blade back into its sheath. The blackness had fled my vision, and I could move again.

"Let's get this over with."

I had faced down monsters, and I had faced down gods, but none of those took as much courage and willpower as stepping back into the Countess's palace once more. It didn't matter how many times I did it, it didn't get any easier. When I had walked away from here for what I'd thought was the last time, I hadn't realised how broken I was. The years of pain, abuse, and failure had been so ingrained a part of me, I hadn't consciously known they were there. All I'd known was that I couldn't stay here and live. Every time I came back, it all closed around me like an embrace.

Get in, get out, don't think about it.

I strode through marble lobby, past the pointless fountain, the potted palms, the statues of the blessed Countess, up to the mage waiting at the desk.

"I'm here to see the Countess."

The mage looked me over. I recognised her, vaguely. She had just started as an apprentice mage when I'd left, although I didn't know her name. She recognised me, too, I thought, but she didn't show it.

"The Countess is busy."

I had been through this goat shit before. "Watch me not give a fuck. Now, you can tell her I'm on my way, or I can march straight up there. Your call." My mother had given me a pass through her wards in the summer. I hoped she hadn't revoked it.

The mage didn't reply, so I headed for the stairs.

"Mennik." The cold voice stopped me mid-stride. I turned to see that my mother had emerged from the door behind the mage's desk. "Please do not harass my mages." She raised an imperious hand and beckoned me to follow.

Well, that was a dilemma. Did I let myself be summoned like I was still an apprentice? The only other alternative was to head on up the stairs like a twat.

I followed my mother.

"I am supposed to be supervising my senior mages' training."

"Far be it from me to take up any of your precious time."

"Don't be tedious, Mennik." She opened a door into a small, enclosed waiting area near her throne room. She waited until I was seated with Fria beside me before saying, "What is that?"

"He's a dog, Mother. You may have heard of them."

"He doesn't look clean."

I bit back several of my favourite swear words. "You grew up in the Warrens, Mother. You were a street kid, like me."

Her eyes tightened. "And I took you out of there. I offered you all of this."

"I didn't want it. Any of it." I drew in a slow breath. This wasn't how this was supposed to go. "I need to know something."

"And what is that?"

"The truth. About Endir."

She stiffened.

"I have to know. I tried to let it go, but I can't. It just won't leave me."

She seated herself carefully, almost fragilely, opposite me. "There is nothing good that can come from this."

"I don't care. I need to know if the Wren killed him."

She watched me for a few moments. Then she said, "If I told you it was true, what would you do, Mennik? He is far too powerful for you to handle, despite my best efforts to train you."

Best efforts? As though pain and abuse were ever going to do anything except break me in one way or another.

"I wouldn't have ignored it, I can tell you that much. I wouldn't have kept *working* for him."

"Precisely."

"So, it's true?" That bastard had done it. He had taken everything from me.

"I did not say that. I simply posed a question."

"I've met the Wren. I've seen his power. You're more powerful."

Her lips bent, but it wasn't a smile. "You have not seen the extent of either of our magics. Regardless, how do you think your Ash Guard friends would react if two high mages went up against each other with their full powers?"

She was right, but I still couldn't get the bitterness off my tongue. "That's a really convenient excuse."

She sighed. "You still do not see past the horizon, do you? The Wren's empire begins to crumble. His businesses fail, his support drains away. He has lost a dozen mages in the last month. When these things fall, they fall fast and with little warning."

Was that what this was all about, then? His last throw of the dice? As the Wren's power in the city collapsed, had he killed the Lady in a desperate gamble to use the Eructation to wipe away his rivals? To become a god?

I shook my head. "It's not enough."

My mother's eyes were hard. "It is what there is." She stood. "Now. I have neglected my duties for too long. You may show yourself out."

I SCARCELY NOTICED AS MY LEGS CARRIED ME OUT OF MY mother's palace, down Agate Way, towards the Upper City. What had I expected? That the truth would free me, somehow? That it would carry away a weight from my back? That I would be dancing through the fucking streets?

But I did know, and now what?

My mother hadn't come right out and said it, but she didn't have to. She'd said enough. What had only been a thought, an idea, a suspicion scratching at me was now as unavoidable as a mountain and no easier to lift.

You wanted to know.

And what the fuck good had it done?

At least I knew now why my mother had dedicated so much of her effort and wealth to her feud with the Wren. She was trying to bring him down as revenge for what he had done.

That might be her kind of revenge, but it wasn't mine.

If I could find proof that the Wren had killed the Lady, if I gave it to the Ash Guard and they took him, would *that* be enough? I didn't think so. I needed him to admit what he'd done to Endir. I needed everyone to know. I needed him to pay.

I heard my mother's voice in my head again. *It is what there is.*

Before I knew it, I found myself striding past Cheap Gate Market, through the grand plazas of the Upper City, ignoring the glances Fria and I were attracting. It wasn't until I reached Highstar Plaza and saw Mica's grand mansion before me that I realised where I was going.

I hated this monstrosity she called a house, because it wasn't a house. It was a palace. *Not somewhere for people like us.* But somewhere suitable for a high mage. The place was bustling with clerks, servants, and mages.

My kid sister. The girl who had run and chased through tumbledown alleys, over piles of filth and rubble, who had dared everything that Benny and I had dared, in the grime and blood of the Warrens. Look at her now. She really was a high mage. How had we ended up on such different paths?

What was I doing here? Did I mean to tell her the Wren had murdered her father? Try to recruit her for this mad attempt at his warehouse? She couldn't move against him directly any more than my mother could. All I would be doing would be sharing my misery and helplessness. Look at the life she had here now. She was happy. She had a purpose, a partner, maybe a family of her own soon. One of us had got out of this intact. I couldn't destroy it, not for any amount of vengeance.

I waited for Fria to piss on a tree, beneath its yellowing leaves – it was the least I could do for the Upper City – then turned and headed away, back towards the lower city where I belonged.

"Nik!"

I stumbled to a halt then turned. Mica had appeared on the steps of her palace and spotted me.

Bollocks. Shoulders slumping, I waited until she crossed the plaza to me.

"What are you doing here?"

Now or never. The urge to tell her everything was almost overwhelming. I shoved it down. *Let her live her life.*

"Just taking Fria for a walk. Thought he might want to see the better parts of the city."

She gave me an odd look, but all she said was, "Then bring him inside. He looks like he needs a drink."

She was right. He was panting, his head hanging. The heat of the summer might have faded, but we'd been out for a while, and we'd been walking fast since leaving my mother's.

"All right. Not for long, though. I've got a job starting soon." Maybe my last job ever if we fucked it up, and I had a horrible feeling that was exactly what we were going to do.

I followed Mica through the busy outer rooms to her private courtyard, where we sat on the marble bench beside the pool. The jasmine and honeysuckle had lost their summer flowers, and the only scent here was of baking bread from a nearby kitchen. I forced my stomach not to rumble.

A minute later, a servant brought a bowl for Fria and yellow tea for Mica and me. *A servant.* I would never get over that.

"Looks like being a high mage is keeping you busy." I nodded in the direction of the chaos in the outer rooms.

"Hm? Oh, no. It's not that. This is something you might actually approve of."

I frowned. "What do you mean?"

"We're rebuilding the Warrens. The Senate went too far this time. People in the Upper City don't like thinking about the Warrens, and they would rather it wasn't there, but they like to think of themselves as civilised, and this time they couldn't ignore it."

"Poor them."

"The point is, wealthy people are competing to contribute to the rebuilding."

"Fuck me." I shook my head. "And they get to feel all virtuous and smug about how generous they are, and then what? Forget all about it. Leave it to rot again." Until the next time they decided the Warrens had stepped out of line and they stamped back down. The charity of the rich always ended up with a kick in the balls.

Mica leaned forward. "You're right. This won't last forever. But Elestior and I can use this to get reform. We can get representation for the Warrens in the Senate, and not just for the Warrens, for Fishertown and Dockside, too."

Looking into her eyes, I could see the passion and fervour

there. She believed it. And maybe she could do it. But how long before the rich of the city corrupted it and that 'representation' was bought? It always ended the same way.

Maybe for a while it'll be better. For a while, people won't have to suffer quite so much.

"Did you know this was going to happen? Did you know they were going to burn the Warrens? Did Mother?"

"I'm not in the Senate." I noticed that wasn't a denial. "As for Mother, all I can say is that she didn't stop it. She understands people, though. She could have predicted the reaction."

That was the difference between me and Mother and Mica. They would see this coming, and they would let it. They would see the opportunities. Me, I would stop it if I could. My way would see the Warrens preserved and its citizens survive. Their way might see it rebuilt better, it might see representation and reform for a while, and it would see the corpses forgotten. Maybe, from a distance, their choice was better. But I had been there, the fire all around me, seeing people die in pain and terror. *I* couldn't forget the bodies. In the end, I could only make my choice, not theirs. It was why I didn't belong here. I belonged in the lower city.

I stood. "Thanks for the tea, and the water for Fria. I really hope you're right about all this. Now, I've got a job to do."

I left Mica's palace behind, with her servants and mages and grand plans for the city. I didn't think I would be coming back here again, no matter how this ended.

~

I didn't often have the chance to contemplate my imminent death. When I had faced down gods and mages before, it had all come upon me with the speed and impact of a rockfall. I didn't usually have four or five hours to kill before the event, and now I wished I didn't this time. All I could think of was everything that could go wrong, and all those things ended in my and Benny's violent deaths. I worked better in the moment, batting away the shit thrown in my face, relying on instinct and desperation rather than plans that seemed as full of holes as a fishing net.

I found myself walking the streets of Agatos again, as though trying to outpace my doubts or maybe experience the city one last time with its stink of rubbish and dead things, the crowds, the packed markets, the elegant and less elegant plazas, the grand mansions and crumbling tenements, and beyond it all, the deep, green waters of the Erastes Bay where Endir's life had ended at the hands of the Wren.

He had to pay. That was all there was to it.

My path took me through the Upper City and the Middle City, through the Grey City, past Dumonoc's bar and the apartment in which I had spent my first five years as an independent mage, to the foot of the Stacks and the ominous sealed doors of Ceor Ebbas in the cliffs above, then down to Fishertown from where Endir had set out on his boat, and up again to the Street of Gods, where Fria and I came to a halt within sight of the Brythanii temple. How *had* the Keffens pulled it off? It didn't matter, in a way, because Ethemattian was free, but in another, it did.

And there's nothing you can do about it.

Maybe there was.

Maybe Cursed Menatha Keffen would talk. She was marked to die. What did she have to lose? She was locked in her room, guarded, but that shouldn't pose too much difficulty.

And what did she have to gain? Talk or not, she would die. The only thing I could offer her that would matter a damn would be her freedom, and I wasn't giving her that. She had no reason to toss any remaining conspirators over the sea wall. If she wanted to talk, she could have done so by now.

You could make her.

And who would believe it, anyway? The desperate claims of a condemned woman.

How about Coyd Keffen? The Most Cursed was dead, killed either by his niece or another conspirator. But being dead wasn't necessarily an obstacle.

You could raise him, question him. You could have raised the Godkiller if you had found him.

"No." I squeezed my hands into fists. Fria nuzzled his cold nose against my hand until I opened it and rubbed him behind his head.

That line had grown thin. I wasn't crossing it for this.

I turned a last gaze on the Brythanii temple and the growing crowds gathering for their brutal ceremony.

This wasn't right. The whole thing didn't fit together.

Someone in that temple was getting away with attempted murder. It didn't sit well with me.

It is what there is.

Fria was starting to droop again. It had been a long day, and his part in it was just about done.

"Let's get you something to eat then back home," I said.

We stopped at our favourite stall in the Penitent's Ear for food, then settled again under the olive trees to eat.

"This isn't really fair on you, is it?" I said to Fria. "One owner dies, you hook up with another, and then he tries to get himself killed, too. You don't have much luck." It was almost enough to make me call the whole thing off. Almost.

Fria wagged enthusiastically then stared at my food. I passed it over.

"I'm not hungry, anyway."

The sun was dying behind the clouds, the diffused, white glow settling like bright snow over the mountains. Maybe this would be the last sunset I would see. It stood to reason that it would be hidden by clouds.

Pull yourself together.

It was a job, that was all, not suicide. If there were wards or magical booby traps, I would see them, and we could back out. More mundane obstacles – locks, guards, that kind of thing – Benny could deal with like he did on every job he carried out. Benny was thirty years old, and he still hadn't had his hands cut off. That was a pretty good record for a thief. Between us, we were good at this stuff. I couldn't guarantee we would find anything that would incriminate the Wren, but we could do this. *I* could do this. I could show

Benny I was on his side. I could make everything right between us.

"You never have to go through this shit, do you?" I said to Fria. "You just wag your tail and give us the soulful eyes, and everything's all right."

He tilted his head then licked the last crumbs of our meal off his mouth.

"Yeah, exactly. Time to get you home."

For once, Fria didn't look disappointed to be left in the apartment. He headed for the mattress and sprawled across it.

"Didn't we have rules about the bed?"

A single thump of the tail was the only answer I got.

Looking around my apartment just made me feel depressed again. Despite my half-arsed tidying, the place was still trashed. Almost thirty years of life, and this was what I had to show for it.

Fria let out a long, put-upon sigh.

"Yeah, there's you, too. And right now, you want me to fuck off so you can get some sleep." Fair enough.

If I got out of this clean, whether I found proof or not, I was done with all this. I was going back to cheating spouses, lost pets, and curses to be broken.

You've told yourself that before.

This time I meant it. No more gods. No more mages. No more monsters. Better to be poor than this.

I carefully checked the windows were closed, examined my wards, and locked the office door behind me. I still had time to kill, but I couldn't do it sitting in my ruined apartment, staring at walls. I headed to the coffee house.

Ileoni was coming to the end of her shift as I arrived, as I had known she would be. Was I hoping she would talk me out of this? Maybe I just needed to see a friendly face, someone who wasn't permanently pissed off with me.

I waited while she served the other customers then brought over my usual spiced coffee and slipped in opposite me.

"You're looking sombre."

"It's just my face."

"Yeah, goat shit to that," she said cheerfully. "I've known you long enough, Nik Thorn. You look like a slapped fish. I take it you're not here to offer me that job?"

"What?"

"Your assistant? Someone to actually turn your business professional?"

"No. I'm not..." I rubbed my hand over my mouth. "There's something I have to do soon that I may not come back from."

She peered at me. "Then don't do it."

"I have to. If I don't, Benny will do it on his own, and he'll definitely die." At least this way I wouldn't die alone.

"Benny. Of course."

"I owe him."

"I know, and he owes you, and you keep pulling each other deeper into whatever disaster you've created this time."

She wasn't wrong, and I wasn't going to argue, but Benny was my real family in a way that my mother and Mica had stopped being a long time ago, and you don't walk away from your real family. "There's something I need you to do for me. If I don't come back, I want you to look after Fria. He doesn't deserve any of this." I put my key on the table. "Fria's in my apartment. I've given you a pass through the wards, so you'll be safe."

"You really don't think you're coming back, do you?" Now she was the one looking like a slapped fish.

I shrugged awkwardly. "If everything goes according to plan, I will."

"And how often does that happen?"

I forced a smile. "There's a first time for everything."

We sat and talked for a while longer as I watched the light fail outside the coffee house, about her family and neighbours and some of the other regulars here, but as time ticked down, I couldn't help but feel the tension grow in me. By now, if our plan had worked, the Wren and maybe half the rest of the city's mages would be heading out of Agatos to waylay the rumoured body of the Lady and claim its power for themselves.

Ileoni laid a hand on mine. "You're going to be all right. Whatever this is, you'll get through it. The way you've told it, you always do."

And I had. Gods, mages, monsters. I had survived them all. Why should this be any different?

Because no one gets lucky every time.

So, get lucky one last time. For Benny. For the city. For Fria. For yourself.

I stood. "I have to go. I'll see you tomorrow."

"You'd better, because I want that job, and if you get yourself killed, I'm having a mage raise your body so I can tell you exactly what I think of you. All right?"

"Yeah. Fine." What else was there to say?

I left her there and headed out into Agatos to find Benny and do what we had to do.

CHAPTER TWENTY-TWO

The coffee house Ileoni worked in wasn't far from Benny and Sereh's home. That was why I had ended up there the first time with one of my clients when I had been lying low at Benny's. What had been his name, the old man I had gone there with?

Does it matter?

Mr. Mirian! That was it. I wondered how he had done since I'd last seen him. His wife was dead, his brother-in-law, too, but at least he had known the truth by the end.

Fuck! My mind was spinning out of control.

"Nor surprising when you're going to break into the Wren's centre of power," I muttered.

And it would get me killed. I squeezed my hands so hard my nails dug into my palms, using the pain to focus, to push away the panic creeping towards me. I still had my knife if I needed more.

Darkness had engulfed the city. Light slipped from around shutters and doors, but down here, there were no morgue-lamps, and the clouds hid the stars.

Tension made the atmosphere taut, itching, scratching at my skin, making it prickle and my hairs stand on end.

It's just your nerves.

"It's not." I could reach out my hand and tear a chunk of it from the air.

There was no breeze, scarcely any sound, as though a mouth were about to open and swallow us all.

Something's wrong.

"It isn't. Stay calm. You're no use to Benny like this."

Something's wrong.

I broke into a run.

People leapt out of my way as I rushed down the street. My mind screamed at me to calm down, slow down, gather myself, prepare myself, but I couldn't.

Something's wrong.

Benny's street was empty. Too empty. Light from his open doorway painted the doorstep and the cobbles beyond yellow.

No!

I reached the house at a dead sprint and came to an abrupt halt.

There were bodies everywhere, heaped, sprawled, floorboards wet with blood. The air stank of voided bowels and charred wood.

The first man had fallen through the trapped floorboard and broken his legs, then his throat had been opened in a clean slash. But he was only the first. More had followed, dozens of them. Their bodies lay, flesh parted and cut, arteries opened with clinical precision, faces twisted in shock and fury. I stepped around them, my boots squelching in the sticky blood, magic held tight and ready.

My wards had been shredded. Someone had torn them down and left them in tatters. The couch I had slept on held a woman, the tendons sliced at the back of her ankles, a blade stabbed into the top of her skull. Blood and some other liquid had flowed through her hair and over her face to where it still dripped onto the couch cushion.

The first mage was just past her. A knife still jutted from his eye. The wall was burned where his magic had hit.

In sudden rage, I slammed a boot into his side, flipping the body.

Benny. Sereh. These bastards had come for them.

There were more bodies on the stairs, more mages, and the wood was slippery with blood. The stink made my throat tighten and my stomach convulse. The stabs and slashes in their flesh were rougher now, less exact. More desperate.

I tried to pull the bodies aside, but there were too many of them. I clambered over them, feeling the flesh give, blood and piss and shit soaking through my trousers and slickening my hands.

It's still warm.

They had come while I'd been sitting in the coffee house, chatting. I should have been here. I should have helped!

Bodies slipped under me. I kicked and stamped over

them, trying to hurry but just sliding back when I did. I grasped the banister to pull myself up.

The bodies continued in the hallway, thugs and mages tangled together, indistinguishable in death other than by the mages' black cloaks.

I realised I was sobbing, gasping. Tatters of spent magic played over the walls, sparking and dying.

Benny's room was just ahead, and here the bodies were heaped highest, a wall of brutalised flesh almost blocking the doorway. I grabbed them with my magic and flung them away.

Sereh sat just inside the room, blade still grasped in one hand. Blood soaked her skin and clothes and hair. Eyes stared at me like chips of marble from an oil slick, unblinking.

The blood wasn't hers. I could tell that at a glance. She had cut her way through – what? – forty, fifty men and women, and it wasn't hers.

It was Benny's though. My oldest friend lay unmoving on the floor, his head on his daughter's lap. Blood pulsed slowly, reluctantly from a dozen wounds. His eyes were closed, his breath trembling and weak.

Surely he'd never had so much blood in that scrawny body.

In my mind, I saw Sereh slipping out of the shadows, slicing and cutting the wave of people coming at her dad, too many even for her, while I sat drinking my coffee. I imagined Benny fighting, too, knifes, magic, and clubs impacting his flesh while Sereh kept on killing, retreating, and killing again.

"Uncle Nik," Sereh said, her voice as hard and cold as a glacier. "Help him."

I had been standing there staring like a fool, unmoving, too shocked to think, while my friend's life bled away. I hurried into the room and dropped beside Sereh. Benny's arms were covered in cuts, some deep. A burn ran the length of his bicep, up to his neck, the clothing charred away. But those weren't what was killing him. A wound in his chest bubbled with every struggling breath. Blood leaked in slow ripples from a cut in his stomach and from his flank.

"Benny!" I took his face and shook it. No reaction. Fuck.

I shaped magic and reached for the chest wound. What the Depths was I supposed to do here? I had never trained as a healer.

I let magic trail into the wound, probing the damage. It went deep, into the lung. I felt severed tissues, veins, muscle, but I couldn't see how it all fit together. Blood welled up everywhere, into the lung, out over the skin. I didn't even know what things were supposed to look like in there, but I knew it wasn't like this.

I pulled on the edges, knitting the flesh with my magic, trying to hold things together. The blood slowed, at least, and the bubbles ceased, but I was under no illusions. I hadn't fixed the damage. I was just holding it closed, like a man trying to grasp an oily plank as he sank beneath the water. I felt it slip even as I clutched harder.

The stomach injury. There was no point staunching the

chest if he kept bleeding out elsewhere. Again, I reached in and pulled the parted flesh together. I could do nothing about whatever vein was cut in there.

My head thumped. Shivers of pain raced through me.

His flank. Gritting my teeth against the damage being done to my own flesh by the flow of magic, I extruded more power and did the same again.

Already, I felt my grip on the chest wound loosen and blood well up again. I fed in more power.

My breath was harsh and loud, my pulse thrumming and skipping madly, dark spots swirling in my closing vision. I wasn't even healing Benny, just maintaining him in a precarious stasis. Soon, my grip would fail.

I raised my eyes to Sereh. "I can't do this. I need help."

If anything, her eyes hardened further. "Then get it."

I tore what was left of Benny's shirt off him and balled it up. "Press this against..." Roll a die. It wouldn't do much good however it landed. "Against the chest wound."

When she had, I released the magic holding it. Immediately, blood bubbled up around the cloth, soaking it. Ignoring the pain that was tearing me apart inside, I gathered more magic.

I hadn't done this for a long time. I'd never wanted to do it again. I didn't even know if it would work. It was an invasion, a violation, far worse than standing naked in front of a crowd.

I dropped my barriers, opened my mind, and reached out. *Mica!*

Instantly, she was in my mind, her power like a volcano

burning inside, stripping away my thoughts and memories, laying them bare. *Nik?*

Benny's dying. I can't save him. Help me. I let her see what I was seeing. Then I let the connection fall and sagged forward. My mind felt raw, scraped over.

I reached once more for Benny's wound.

I didn't know much about the abilities of high mages, but it was only minutes before I saw magic bloom outside the house, and then Mica was there, her power clearing a path through the bodies as easily as a brush through dirt.

She took in the scene with a glance, then elbowed me out of the way. With my eyes unfocused, I saw her magic reach out, overwhelming yet controlled. I had always prided myself on my fine control of what little power I had, but I could scarcely follow the complexity of my little sister's magic. With a sigh, I let my own magic drop and hers take over.

I stood. "He'll be all right now," I told Sereh. I hoped it was true. "I have to go."

Sereh's eyes didn't waver from mine. "Uncle Nik. You are going to find who did this. You are going to tell me. And then I am going to kill them."

I nodded. I wouldn't expect anything else from her. But I didn't need to find out. I already knew. I even recognised some of the bodies. The Wren had sent them. He had seen through our laughably obvious ploy and sent his people to do this. When the shock wore off, Sereh would realise it, too. She would go after the Wren with her knife and her fury, passing his wards, stepping out of the shadows, unseen.

It wouldn't be enough. High mages didn't die easily. I had to finish this before she could make her move.

"Stay with your dad," I said. "He'll need you." That would hold her for now.

I took off at a run.

Our plan had failed. There would be no proof of the Wren's guilt now, no Ash Guard coming to arrest him. There would just be me, a second-rate mage against one of the powerful and dangerous people in Agatos, perhaps the whole world. I couldn't overwhelm him. I couldn't put my magic against his. Even if I dug up the body of the Lady of the Grove, I couldn't handle enough power to hurt him. He could kill me with a blink.

I knew what I had to do. I headed for Holera's restaurant.

The streets were still busy. The dark did a bit to hide the state I was in, but whenever I drew close, people shied away from the blood soaking my clothes and coating my hands and the stink of death that clung to me.

Holera's restaurant was packed, so I headed for the back door and barged into the kitchen.

All action halted as I stumbled into the brightly-lit room. Four pairs of eyes fixed on me.

Holera stepped forward. "Narth's tits, Nik. Are you all right?"

Sweat ran down my face, streaking the part-dried blood. I nodded. "It's not my blood. It's—"

She cut me off with a raised hand. "Everyone out."

She waited until her staff were gone then nodded.

"Look," I said. "I need a bottle of wine. The best you've got. I can pay."

"Nik..."

"I'll explain later." If I got the chance. "It's urgent."

She looked at me critically. "Whatever you're up to, you can't do it like that."

For a moment, I didn't know what she meant. Then I glanced down at my stained and stinking clothes and my reddened hands. I could smell myself, too, and feel something congealed in my hair. I had the sudden urge to summon up mage fire and burn it all off, hair included.

"I don't have time—"

Again, she cut me off. "I'm sure we have spare clothes around here. Kitchens are messy places." She pointed to a bowl of soapy water. "Get undressed and wash yourself off."

While Holera searched the drawers at the back of the kitchen, I awkwardly peeled the clothes from my body. The blood and other fluids had started to dry, and pulling the clothes free felt like every hair was being ripped one-by-one from my skin. But what was a little more pain? It kept me focussed.

I washed myself down as best I could with a cloth. My clothes were done for. They needed to be burned. Only the blasted mage's cloak had survived. I rinsed it as best I could and laid it to drip from the counter.

Holera walked over with a pile of clothes and gave me a critical look. "You're a mess, and you need to eat more. These aren't going to fit well."

Self-consciously, I took the proffered clothes and dressed

as best I could. Holera was right. The trousers and shirt were a couple of inches too short, but when I wrapped the damp cloak around me, it wasn't too obvious. Maybe I would start a new trend.

"You never came around for a meal," Holera said while I dressed.

"Yeah. Sorry. Things got ... complicated."

"They always do with you. It's not me who's pissed off. Elosyn wants to cut your balls off and shove them up your arse. Her words, not mine. When I saw you come in like that, I thought she'd caught up with you. Nik, what are you up to?"

"If I tell you, you'll try to stop me, and I don't have a choice."

She shook her head, but all she did was hand me over a bottle of wine. "This stuff is worth more than you are. *Don't* waste it."

I wouldn't have known the difference. I'd had good wine in my time, and bad, but apart from Dumonoc's poison, they were all much the same to me. I would take her word for it. The person this was for *would* know.

"Thank you," I said. "For everything."

Her eyes narrowed. "You're doing something really stupid this time, aren't you?"

I shrugged. "That's all there is left."

I tucked the wine carefully into my shirt and headed once more into the city.

There was one more thing I had to do.

Kehsereen's apartment might not have had the glamour and spaciousness of my mother's or sister's palaces, but it was better than I could ever aspire to. Sometimes, when I was feeling down and desperate, I fantasised about moving in here with him, but somehow no one ever wanted a disreputable mage and the trouble they brought shacking up with them, and anyway, my clients would never come here.

Unusually, the guard who occupied the small hut outside the building was absent, so I let myself in and headed up.

For a brief moment, I had considered asking Kehsereen for the sample of Ash he'd been working on to use as a weapon against the Wren, but it was so tiny and so diluted and its range so limited that even if I'd managed to get close to the Wren while carrying it, he could drop a ceiling on me before I could throw it. And I wouldn't get close.

My plan was for something else entirely. It didn't have much chance of working, but as I had told Holera, it was all I had left.

Kehsereen's door was locked, and he didn't answer to my knock, but that didn't matter. It would be easier with him here, but I reckoned I could find what I was looking for if I had to. I let myself in.

I was wrong. Kehsereen was here, but he wasn't alone. He was backed up against the wall, a richly-dressed man holding a knife to his neck. The man was caught in the act of turning towards me. I didn't recognise him, but I did recognise the mage beside him, and I was too slow to react.

Magic hit me, staggering me back then closing around

my limbs, immobilising me. I tried to throw my own spell, but he shattered it before it could finish forming.

Bannaur's balls! The last time I had seen this mage, he had been throwing fire down on me and Khesereen as we drifted to safety from Senator Greenfield's library window, stolen book in hand. Which would make the richly-dressed man Senator Greenfield.

I did not have time for this.

By now, Mica could have healed Benny. Sereh could be putting two and two together. She could be moving out, disappearing into the shadows, heading for the Wren's warehouse.

"Well, this is convenient," the senator said, stalking towards me, leaving Kehsereen to slump. "We were just about to torture your friend to discover your identity. Now we can get right down to business."

"If you want your book back, you can have it. I have no use for it."

A smile twitched one side of his mouth. "Oh, I will have it back. First, there are debts to pay."

He nodded to his mage, and heat seared up my limbs. I bit back a scream. I tried to fight the spell, to redirect or unpick it, but he was stronger than me, and I was helpless. I ground my teeth and clenched my fists until the pain passed.

"Can we do this later?" I said. "I'm busy."

This time, the heat was worse, and this time I couldn't control my grunt of pain. I blinked my vision clear and caught Kehsereen's gaze across the room, trying to indicate his desk with just my eyes.

"If you think this is a joke," Senator Greenfield spat, "you won't be laughing for long."

"I'm not laughing now. I'm giving you one chance, then you're going to regret this." He knew it was a bluff as much as I did, because I was helpless against his mage. But that didn't matter. All I needed was to keep his attention. "My mother will turn you inside out." She wouldn't do a fucking thing, I was certain of that. She had left me to my own fate long ago. "You might have heard of her. The Countess."

Briefly, doubt crossed his face, and he exchanged a look with his mage. Then his expression hardened. "All you're doing is giving me a reason not to let you live."

Kehsereen had moved away from the wall to his desk and now was looking at me again. Depths, I hoped he knew what I was trying to communicate. I managed a brief nod.

"You don't have the balls," I said. "You've been seen coming in here and so have I. The Ash Guard will shove an Ash-coated spear up your arse."

This time the mage did hesitate. The senator didn't. "It will be self-defence. You attacked my mage. They will take my word for it. I am a senator. You and your friend are nothing."

He might be right about that. Captain Gale knew me. In theory, that might mean she was instinctively on my side, but it also meant she knew what I got up to – some of it, at least. It would provide enough doubt. But I wasn't trying to scare them off. I was playing for time, and Kehsereen had finally taken the hint. He carefully picked up the glass dish of Ash and threw it at the mage.

There wasn't much Ash in there, and its range was only a few inches. But it was enough to disrupt his spell. As the magic faltered and broke, I surged forward, tugging my mage's rod from my belt and swinging it down to slam onto his head.

The effect of Ash was never nice. The weakness, confusion, and nausea were enough to stun him for long enough until the lump of obsidian on the end of the rod cracked his skull.

Senator Greenfield backed away, hands held before him. I was in no mood for mercy. Sereh could be out there right now, looking for revenge against the Wren. These fuckers had slowed me down. They had put her life in danger. I wasn't having it. My next blow caught the senator on his jaw, spinning him around into the table. He slid to the floor. I put in the boot just to be sure.

I looked up and met Kehsereen's eyes. He was still behind the desk, hands resting on either side of his microscope. Guilt hit me. That experiment had been his chance to help save his nephew. "I'm sorry about your Ash."

Kehsereen shook his head. "It doesn't matter. It was not working. Even if I could have duplicated the effects of Ash, Asarian could not live under its influence forever. I will have to find another answer." He came around the desk and joined me over the unconscious bodies. "What shall we do with them?"

I shrugged. "Restrain them and call the Ash Guard. Toss them naked into the street. Slit their throats, if you want."

The fury had burned deep into me, and I felt cold. "I can't stay to help, but I do need something from you."

The clouds had parted by the time I reached Dockside. Stars like silver dagger points pierced the black sky. The air still held a scratchy tension, like it might tear into a million pieces.

This had taken too long. It had been – what? – nearly an hour since I'd left Sereh, Benny, and Mica.

She'll stay with her dad. He'll be weak. He'll need her.

If he wasn't dead.

He won't be. Mica will save him. She's a high mage.

But she wasn't a god. He had lost so much blood. I tightened my fist around the handle of my dagger until the pain calmed me and I could breathe again.

Finish this.

The Wren would listen to me, talk to me, if only out of curiosity. I could end this whole thing now.

Straightening, I headed for the Wren's warehouse.

A couple of mages stood unnecessary guard by the entrance, watching the docks. As though anyone sane would try to break into the Wren's warehouse. I forced back the bitter laugh that threatened to spill out.

The docks were still hectic, despite the lateness of the hour. Agatos was a busy city. Goods flowed in and out as relentlessly as the tide, supplying not just this city but also the cities to the north via the Lidharan Highway. Merchants from around the Yttradian Sea and beyond traded in goods for and from the north and the Folaric Sea. In the glow of ships' lanterns and warehouse lights, dockworkers loaded and unloaded. The smell of sweat, spices, and the sewage-filled harbour choked the air. The thump of bales on cobbles, the shrieking and roaring of caged animals, the shouts of workers, the creak of ships and cranes all continued unabated, whatever the Wren or the other mages and politicians might be up to. Only by midnight would the activity cease, to start up again at first light. In some ways, it was reassuring. Dying gods, feuding mages, and still the city kept breathing.

You're putting this off, I told myself. *You have to do it.*

I approached the mages at the door. "I need to talk to the Wren. Tell him it's Mennik Thorn. He'll know why I'm here." And he would either kill me where I stood, or his curiosity would get the better of him. I hoped it was the latter, for my sake and for Sereh's.

He didn't keep me waiting long. One of the mages led me up the stairs to the Wren's office. She didn't bother searching me. Why would she? What could I do against a high mage?

The courtyard jungle that the Wren's assistant maintained was dark beyond the office, and there was no sign of Kael himself. The Wren, though, sat at his desk, writing in a ledger. He was an old man. He looked maybe sixty, but high mages lived longer than most, and he had looked the same twenty years ago. Grey hair, pale skin, washed out eyes. I had often wondered if he had a bit of Brythanii in his ancestry.

He put aside the pen as I sat opposite him and waited for the other mage to leave.

"You made a very foolish mistake today," the Wren said. "Your friend has paid for it."

Acid rose in the back of my throat. My eyes swam. Yeah. Yeah, we had. "I know."

"I wonder. What did you hope to achieve?"

No point lying anymore. "Benny was sure you killed the Lady of the Grove. We wanted to find proof, one way or another. We thought it would be easier if you weren't here."

The Wren tipped back his head and laughed. "If I had the power to kill a god, I would not be sitting here. I would be ruling this city."

"If the Ash Guard let you."

He acknowledged the point with a nod. "Indeed."

"So, did you?"

His grin widened. "I did not."

Did I believe him? It didn't really matter anymore. We were beyond that now. Sereh was all that mattered. I wouldn't – I *couldn't* – see her dead. "I want to bring this to an end," I said. "Your people, they—" I swallowed so I could continue. For a second, all I could see was Benny's body sprawled on the floor, bleeding, dying, and Sereh sitting behind him, soaked in other people's blood. "If Benny isn't dead, he's near to it, and I don't know if Sereh will ever recover from this. They've paid the price."

"Have they? Your friend was warned, and he ignored it. I have nothing against his daughter unless she chooses to become involved."

She already had.

"And what of you, Mennik?" His eyes turned to diamonds. "What have you paid?"

What had I paid? Everything that mattered. "I want to make a deal. You leave Benny and Sereh alone. They keep well away from you and your interests." I had to swallow again, this time in disgust. "And I'll be in your service. I know you and my mother have an ongoing feud, and I know she's got the advantage. I know you are losing support and influence. I can help you turn that around. I can undermine her plans and pass you information."

He eyed me thoughtfully. "Last time, that didn't work out so well."

"She was using me. She's not using me this time."

"And how about your friends? How will you ensure they stay away?"

At least he was considering it. That was something. I looked down. "That'll be on me. I'll make sure it happens. If not, I'll take the consequences."

The Wren tapped his fingers on the desk.

Come on. Take the deal. End this.

"You will not like what I ask of you."

I shrugged.

"Very well. You will be mine, forever. Whatever I ask, you will do. There will be no morals, no qualms, and no hesitation. If I tell you to kill, you will kill. If I need you to die, you will die. There will be no debate."

I took a slow, controlling breath. "All right."

"Good."

I pulled the bottle of wine from inside my shirt. "Why don't we drink on it?"

He let out another laugh. "Really?" He took the bottle and examined it. "From Malaru. A good year. I had this smuggled into the city only six months ago. How did you afford it?"

I shrugged. "I've been doing all right."

He reached down, pulled out a couple of glasses, broke the seal, and poured the wine. That was at least a month's rent in each glass.

He pushed a glass over. "You'll forgive me if I ask you to drink first."

"Of course." I took the glass and drank it down. He watched carefully. It wasn't good. But would I have known if it was? I felt it burn its way down, the numbing effect spreading through me. I placed the glass back.

The Wren watched me for a minute, then another, then reached for his own glass and took mouthful. He grimaced. "It's corked." He laughed. "You couldn't even buy wine without getting conned, could you? To think, I once thought you had potential. Ah, well. You'll do." He finished the wine and placed the glass beside mine. "Our deal is sealed. You will receive your orders."

I nodded, I felt dizzy, sick. "I do have a question for you."

He sighed. "Very well."

"Did you kill my stepfather?"

The Wren rolled his shoulders, as though he'd been sitting hunched up too long. "Endir was a good man. A principled man. He should have stayed in Fishertown. But he asked too many questions, he pushed too far. He was warned, many times, because I valued your mother's service and allyship. But he would not stop."

"So you killed him."

The Wren raised his gaze again. "He killed himself."

That was all I needed to know.

The Wren frowned, suddenly. His hand gripped the table. He blinked. "What have you done?"

Ulu-aru wasn't like Ash. Ash destroyed magic. It took raw magic and spells, even the power of gods, and wiped it away. *Ulu-aru* was different. It drugged the brain, stole the ability of a mage to control magic until it wore off. The part of the mind that could grab, shape, and release magic was incapacitated as completely as if a knife had been driven into it. I had added it to the wine after getting it from Kehsereen. It had taken all my magical skill to repair the seal on the bottle.

The *ulu-aru* had stolen my power seconds after I had drunk my glass of wine, but my power would have been useless against the Wren. His power, on the other hand...

I had lied to the high mage. I couldn't stop Sereh. No matter what, she would come for him for what he had done to Benny, and she would die. Maybe he would die at the same time, maybe he wouldn't, but she would. The only way to save her was if he was dead already.

The Wren staggered to his feet. The dizziness was affecting me, too, but at least I'd been through this before. I knew what I was facing.

Then I felt the Wren reach for his power. I unfocused my eyes and saw him draw in raw magic. He was struggling, fighting for it, only pulling in a trickle, but he was managing it.

The wards around the building crashed down, raging red and black around us.

Bannaur's fucking balls! He shouldn't be able to do this. *Fucking high mages!*

If he formed the magic into a spell, I was dead.

I lunged across the table, stumbling, almost sprawling, tugging the knife from my belt and plunging it into his chest.

He staggered, fell, losing control of the magic, and I followed him down. I plunged the knife in again and again. *For Benny. For Sereh. For Endir. For the Warrens.*

Blood flowed like a dozen red springs from his chest and stomach and his arms where he had raised them in futile defence. It came up over his lips. His shocked eyes stared at me. His lips moved, but I couldn't hear what he was trying to say.

"You killed yourself." Fear and rage and disgust poured out of me. "You could have left us all alone. This is on you."

His lips moved again. What was he trying to say? *Sorry? Help me?* There was nothing he could say that would save him. Savagely, I wanted to hear him plead anyway.

I leaned close. His breath shook, frothy and weak. At last, I caught the words.

"I am not the Wren," he said.

CHAPTER TWENTY-THREE

I STARED DOWN AT HIM. "WHAT?"

But his lips had stopped moving. The blood no longer pulsed from his chest nor ran over his lips. His eyes had stilled, turned glassy. He was dead.

I am not the Wren. What the fuck was he talking about?

I tried to understand, but the vertigo and light-headedness from the *ulu-aru* overwhelmed me. I slipped back down, almost falling on the body. Soon. I would get up soon.

Power grabbed me. It wrenched me back and up, lifting me effortlessly into the air.

I was helpless. Even if I'd had my magic, I would have been helpless. When I unfocused my eyes, the magic that rushed around me was like being suspended in a waterfall. I had to blink it away so it didn't burn out the backs of my eyes. This wasn't like Senator Greenfield's mage, who had simply overpowered me. This was high mage power.

My body rotated in the air. Striding towards me from the jungle courtyard came Melecho Kael. A small box hung from his neck by a chain, and it blazed with raw magic. A relic of a dead god. Powerful mages kept them for when they needed access to more raw magic than the environment could provide. The city was saturated with raw magic from the gods that had once been worshipped here and had died, but it was diffuse. Fine for the likes of me, but less so if you wanted to tear a mountain in half.

Kael stalked past me, not sparing me a glance, and stood over the body of the Wren. No, not the Wren, if what the man had said was true. My mind was still so scrambled from the *ulu-aru*, I struggled to think.

Kael knelt beside the body and touched a hand to the man's head, then straightened. He turned to the table and picked up the bottle of wine.

Drink it, you fucker.

He sniffed it, touched his tongue to the rim, then placed it back down. "*Ulu-aru*. I haven't seen this for two hundred years. I thought it was forgotten. You are resourceful." On that last word, his magic constricted. My bones creaked. Pain engulfed me, like I was pressed under boulders. I would have screamed if his magic had let me. Tears gathered in my eyes. I couldn't even breathe.

The magic eased. I wrenched in a breath. Blood flowed from my nose, over my lips, to drip from my chin. My ears were bleeding, too.

Kael looked down at the body again. "He was a good Face of the Wren. He served me well for a long time." Now Kael did turn to look at me. "He should have been the face for decades more." He came around the desk, grabbed me with one enormous hand, tore me out of the air, and flung me into the floorboards. My head cracked against them, sending stars spinning across my vision. "Get up."

I forced myself to my feet, even though my legs shook. I thought about reaching for my mage's rod, but this wasn't some amateur I could get a cheap shot on. His magic roared around me.

"He was a friend," Kael went on. "You don't know how rare that is in this city."

"You're the Wren," I forced out, more to keep him talking than because it mattered.

He waved a hand. "The Wren is a fiction. It was a useful legend to build. Now I will have to choose a new Face of the Wren. None of the candidates are adequate. I had once planned that your mother would be the next face, but she proved as stubborn as you." His magic took me again, lifted me, squeezing, slowly this time, but growing tighter. "I am going to kill you, Mennik Thorn. I should have done it a long time ago."

My knife whipped up from the floor beside the body and slammed into my shoulder. This time he let me scream.

How fucking stupid had I been thinking I could walk in here, kill the Wren, save Sereh, be a hero? There were no heroes in Agatos. Just people who got themselves killed. I hadn't even known who the Wren really was.

The knife rotated in my shoulder, scraping across bone, tearing through flesh. The pain was like nothing I'd felt before. Fire raged in my shoulder, shooting down my arm and across my chest. My throat tightened to a fist.

Bannaur's bloody, broken balls!

"Nothing to say, Mennik? You always have so much to say."

He reached up and yanked the knife from my shoulder. I bit my tongue, choked. Blood flowed down my side and arm. Drops fell from my fingers, but he still he didn't let me move. *Motherfucker!* I hated being so helpless. More than the pain, more than my imminent death, not being able to do *anything* about it wrenched at me.

He really was going to kill me. There was no trick I could pull, no surprise, no desperate surge of magic.

He buried the knife in my thigh.

Please, gods, stop. I couldn't speak. He wouldn't even allow me that. Kael seemed to have lost interest in speaking, too. He withdrew the blade and turned it thoughtfully in his hand, examining me.

Get it over with, you bastard.

Something struck his wards.

The building shook. The wards flared angry red and black.

A second blow landed. I felt it through my bones. Dust drifted down from the ceiling. Magic spun and rushed through the air as the wards responded. The Wren turned from me, watching, but he didn't let his magical grip go.

A third blow fell, harder than the first two, like a sledgehammer brought down on an egg, and the wards shattered. Stray magic ripped through the building, smashing glass, sending cracks racing through walls. Something subsided, and the wall dropped to my left, the floorboards tilting. A wave of the hand from Kael stabilised it.

My mother strode into the room, magic raging around her. She was carrying a relic of her own around her neck. I had seen my mother angry before – fuck me, I'd seen her angry – but never anything like this. Power burned through her, radiating in waves that could burn a man to ash.

Kael's head tilted to one side, and he smiled. "Are you finally ready to test your powers against mine, Solone?"

My mother's eyes were as cold as I had ever seen them. Even though they weren't directed at me, a shiver moved through me. "We had a deal, Agate. My children's lives are off limit."

"Then you should have taught them better. Mennik has overstepped." He waved a hand to the body. "He has forfeited his protection."

"That is not for you to decide."

"Then show me your powers, Solone." With that, Kael drew in raw magic. It streamed in a great torrent into him from the relic he carried. My mother responded.

At last, Kael released me, his magic falling away, and I slumped onto the floor, forgotten, as the two high mages turned their full focus on each other. I wasn't foolish enough to think I could interfere. The magic around Kael would flay the skin from my body, flense the flesh from my bones. I scrambled away from between them.

Raw magic still poured into each of them. Their power built like tidal waves approaching on the horizon. *You have not seen the extent of either of our powers,* my mother had said, and I'd dismissed it, but now I saw the truth of it. It was like being caught between two mountain ranges leaning towards each other, rising and rising from the earth, ready to clash and annihilate everything between them. Space itself seemed to distort around them, like a rubber sheet pressed on by a fist. Stone groaned. Magical discharges leapt between them and to the walls and ceiling and floor, and still they pulled in more power.

Stop! I wanted to yell. They would destroy the whole city, rip it apart, drag it beneath the ocean, shatter the mountains around us, if they let their power meet. But I couldn't find air, and their eyes were fixed only on each other, almost two decades of hatred and rivalry finally unleashed.

Even where I lay, unnoticed, away from them, the pressure of their magic threatened to crush me. My brain was being squeezed between rock-hard hands.

Into that overwhelming pressure, another voice spoke. "Stand down."

I twisted my head, my neck creaking, to see Captain Gale advance from the door towards the high mages.

"In the name of the Ash Guard, stand down."

She wasn't wearing Ash! Why in all the cursed Depths wasn't she wearing her Ash? With Ash, she could have destroyed their magic, taken away their power, left them helpless. The courage it must have taken to walk into the middle of this without Ash to protect her would have stolen my breath if I'd had any to steal.

The two high mages stilled. They didn't drop their power,

but they stopped building it, never letting their gazes leave each other.

Captain Gale positioned herself between them, between the twin, vast columns of feverish magic. It would take my mother or Kael less than a thought to reduce her to mist, to remove her so thoroughly from existence that no trace would remain.

Her hand dropped to the hilt of her sword. "I will not warn you again. Stand down."

The ground bucked, shifted to one side, fell, making everyone stagger. Briefly, I thought one of the high mages had made their move, but the power wasn't coming from them. It was coming from somewhere else.

What now? Not Mica, please. She might be a high mage, but she was no match for these two. If she tried to get involved, she would die.

The ground shook again.

"The Eructation," Captain Gale said. "It's begun."

An instant later, both high mages dropped their magic and took off at a run, Kael heading for the courtyard jungle, my mother for the stairs.

"What the fuck?" I managed. In seconds, only Captain Gale, the dead body, and I were left in the Wren's office.

"I told you. The high mages have been waiting for this moment for a very long time. Even their..." She pursed her lips. "...even their rivalry won't get in the way of that. Do you know you're bleeding?"

"Yeah, and it fucking hurts." Kael's knife – *my* knife – seemed to have missed any arteries, but the wounds were still deep, they hurt like they were filled with fire ants, and they didn't want to stop bleeding.

Captain Gale knelt beside me and pulled bandages from a pouch at her belt. Quickly, she bound my wounds. She looked like she'd had practice. Despite my state, I couldn't help but shiver when she ripped away my shirt to expose my shoulder wound.

"You need to start carrying your own bandages, or I'm going to charge you for Ash Guard supplies."

I laid a hand on her forearm. "Thank you, Meroi. Again." She didn't object to my use of her first name.

"It's my job. Anyway, I can't go losing my best trouble-dowser. I'd look unprofessional. Can you stand?"

I nodded and let her help me up. I was a lot taller than her, but she was much stronger.

"I have one question for you," she said.

I nodded.

She indicated the body. "Did you kill him?"

"Um."

"Did you use magic?"

I snorted. "Kind of the opposite."

"Then it's none of my business. If the Watch want to pursue it, that's up to them, and you'll have to face it. But I doubt there will be any evidence if they turn up. Kael won't want it thought that his puppet was killed so easily. It would destroy the myth of the Wren. Let's get you out of here."

So easily... That was a joke.

Captain Gale hooked my arm over her shoulder and

helped me towards the stairs. I didn't really need the help, but I wasn't complaining.

"What are you going to do?" I asked. "About the Eructation? If my mother or Kael get that power..."

"Our best. We've planned for this, too. The Ash Guard has plans for everything. All the powerful mages in the city, as well as several other entities, will be reaching for that power. We keep records. We know who most of them are. We'll disrupt as many as we can and hope the rest fail." She stopped and peered at me. Our faces were uncomfortably close. "Tell me you're not stupid enough to be one of them."

"Depths, no. I know my limitations."

Her eyes examined my face.

"You don't believe me?" For some reason, that thought hurt more than it should.

"I do. I just wish you would stay within them a little more often."

I didn't know what to say to that, so instead I said, "Did you know about Kael? Him being the real Wren, I mean."

"Of course. We're the Ash Guard, Nik. Mages' secrets are our nourishment." She raised her eyebrows, and I immediately started to think of all my secrets. I wondered how many of them she could arrest me for if she chose.

"I don't get it," I said quickly. "Why did he do it? Why pretend someone else was the Wren? Why not just fill the role himself?"

"The art of diversion. Everyone was looking at the Face of the Wren, not at him."

I frowned. "You're the second person who's mentioned

the art of diversion to me this week." Ethemattian had said something about it. Something about showing people what you were hiding so they wouldn't notice what you really wanted to hide. I didn't really see how it applied.

"You haven't heard of it? It's a principle from Xehartes' *The Politician.*"

I shrugged, or as best I could with my arm over her shoulder and several painful injuries.

"The Kendarian philosopher? About three hundred years back. No?"

"No."

"Fuck me, what exactly did you learn at that university?"

Not a lot, was the answer to that.

"Xehartes was most famous for writing *The Politician.* It was a critique of political manipulation, but every power-hungry lunatic since has used it as a manual. It's all about manipulating your opponent into doing what you want without them realising you're doing it."

So, why had Ethemattian quoted that to me? Why would a priest even know that?

Because it's all about power. He told you that himself.

Power and manipulation. If he quoted it, it was because he expected me to not know the reference. And he'd been right. Had he been taunting me?

I had never figured out how the Keffens had pulled off their set-up of Ethemattian without help from the Cursed of God.

Perhaps they hadn't.

Something else came back to me, too, something Ethemattian's brother had said. *He had the hands of an artist.* I had thought it was just simple resentment of the brother who had stolen his place in the temple. What if it hadn't been? What if it was just a statement of fact?

"You know," Captain Gale said, "we could really do with your help if you're up to it. We've got our targets, but we won't have found everyone. You could help us search and send back messages to the fortress if you come across anyone."

"I can't." My pulse was hammering so hard I could scarcely hear my own voice. "You should check out Senator Greenfield's mage, though." If Kehsereen hadn't slit his throat. "He was definitely preparing for it." I hadn't known at the time what the spell in Greenfield's palace had been for. "And so was the cult of Sharshak. They've got a place under a shoemaker's on Tarragon Street in the Middle City. If I see anything else, I'll let you know, but I have to go." My throat was tight with dread. "I think I've made a terrible mistake."

I unhooked my arm and set off at a limping run towards Dumonoc's bar.

CHAPTER TWENTY-FOUR

In the Wren's warehouse, the only sign of the Eructation had been the earth shocks that had nearly knocked us from our feet, but out here on the streets, the signs were far more noticeable. Sheets of green, red, and yellow light cracked across the sky above the valley, throwing the city into ominous and sickly light. Shivers ran over the waters of the harbour, rocking ships at their moorings. A low rumble and, oddly, the scent of spring, filled the air.

The residents of Agatos, who, if nothing else, would run towards an approaching river of lava just so they could say they had been there, filled the dockside and the streets, pointing, looking up, and shouting to one another. A few were trying to see how panic might add spice to the situation by screaming, pushing, and running about.

I bowled my way through them, no doubt adding to the panic, shoving bodies aside, first along the docks, then up the

Royal Highway, and into the Grey City. Watchwomen and -men, who should have been trying to keep order, were using the excuse of the chaos to lay about them with clubs. Maybe burning the Warrens had given them a taste for violent over-reaction. A passing Watchman swung a club for my head. I didn't break stride as I sent him flying with a blow from my mage's rod. My tolerance for the Watch had fallen a long way this last week. If the fuckers got themselves killed, I wouldn't be mourning.

The crowded streets slowed me and made progress hard. The effects of the *ulu-aru* still hadn't completely worn off, and every step sent pain lancing through the injuries in my thigh and shoulder. I had to gasp for breath. Despite Captain Gale's competence with bandaging, my wounds had begun to leak again. Sweat plastered my clothes to my skin and streaked my face.

"Watch the fuck out," a man with a handcart shouted as I swept by him, sending him staggering, but I didn't slow. The suspicions whirling through my brain didn't let me. If I had got this wrong. If I had got this wrong...

The little plaza in front of Dumonoc's was packed. I recognised a few of the local residents and a couple of the regulars from the bar, but Dumonoc was nowhere to be seen – it would take more than the imminent destruction of the city to penetrate the miserable old fucker's foul mood – and nor was the man I was here to see. If he was elsewhere, I was screwed.

Dumonoc's bar was down a set of steps and through a solid wooden door. The door had been patched recently, probably after the gang of smugglers who had been chasing me at the time had smashed it in. One of the very many reasons I wasn't popular with Dumonoc.

Dumonoc's didn't advertise itself with any sign. I had discovered it by accident when I'd first moved into the Grey City. I had never found out why Dumonoc had opened a bar, seeing as he hated all his customers with a passion that could defy the gods and did his best to drive them away.

I pushed open the door and stepped down into the dingy, poorly-lit bar. A scatter of tables stood empty in the gloom. Only a single customer sat at a candlelit table at the back of the bar. Squint.

Dumonoc saw me coming and stepped around the bar. "Fuck off out of here, Thorn. You're barred."

I guessed he hadn't appreciated the broken face I'd given him when I'd saved his bar from the Jaunt's Ghost. Admittedly, the place had probably taken a fortune to fix, but it could have been worse.

That could be my new slogan: *Hire Nik Thorn. It could always be worse.*

I jabbed my mage's rod towards him. "Settle the fuck down."

The *ulu-aru* was fading fast now and my concentration was returning, but I'd rather not use magic just yet.

He seethed at me but retreated back around the bar, and I crossed to Squint.

"He don't seem happy to see you," Squint commented as I drew out a chair and sat. "Where's the wine?"

"No wine." He had half a bottle of his own, anyway,

amongst half a dozen candle stubs. I wasn't feeding his toxic habit. "And he's never happy to see anyone."

"Not a happy man, our Dumonoc." Squint flashed me a grin of rotted teeth. "Bit exciting out there, sounds like."

"You want to know what's going on?"

He considered. "Nah. Reckon everyone's going to know soon. Not worth paying for."

I could tell him I had knifed his boss, too, and while he might pay for that information, I didn't want it spread. I didn't know what Kael would do when the whole Eructation excitement was over, but I wasn't poking the shark.

"You know I got attacked yesterday?"

Squint chuckled. "I heard. Gave you a bit of a kicking."

"I need to find them."

"You sure about that? Way I heard it, you gave better than you got. People might not look too favourably if you go back to give them more. There's a code to this stuff."

I didn't have time to argue. I didn't know how late it was, but I knew it was late. If I had been wrong, I had to make this right, soon. I slapped a gold crown on the table. "Where can I find them?"

Squint rubbed the side of his nose. "Your call, and I ain't saying no to a bank." His fingers closed on the coin. "They're holed up in *The Whale's Head*. It's a tavern in Dockside. You know a couple of them still can't walk, right?"

They had tried to kill me. I had as much sympathy for them as for a streak of piss in the gutter. "You know who paid them?"

"Nah, but I can find out. Come back tomorrow, and I'll let you know."

"Tomorrow's too late. I'll do it myself." I stood. "I wouldn't stay in here too long. Things are going to get worse out there. Ten to one, this place'll come down." I glanced across to where Dumonoc glowered at me from behind the bar. "Get the miserable old bastard out of here, too, even if you have to stick him with a knife to move him."

THE WIND HAD PICKED UP WHILE I WAS IN DUMONOC'S. LEAVES and waste from the streets swirled through the air. A tile slipped from a nearby roof to impact with an explosive crack on the cobbles. High above, against the flickering lights that chased across the sky, what looked like an awning from a coffee house or market stall whipped past. The ground grumbled almost constantly. All across the city, mages and other power-greedy arseholes would be trying to grab the force behind this Eructation and bend it to their own ends, and the Ash Guard would be shutting them down as fast as they could. And me? Me, I was going to intimidate a gang of Dockside thugs. It was the glamour of my job that made it such a pleasure.

I hit the Royal Highway at a run, heading down to the docks. The crowds had swollen, most people having more sense – or more curiosity – than Squint and Dumonoc when it came to staying inside during an earthquake. If only it had been just an earthquake. At least the City Watch had stopped hitting everyone, self-preservation winning out over the chance to beat the shit out of innocent people, at least for now.

A reverberation sounded, and the ground kicked. I stumbled, then pushed my way on. A rolling crash told me a building had collapsed some streets over. The modern Agatos was built on the ruins of older cities, homes and temples fallen into cracks in the earth. How many times had this happened before, a god dying, the resulting Eructation tumbling the city into the earth, only for a new city to rise, the cause forgotten?

Or had it been whoever had taken the power of the Eructation who had caused the cities to fall?

How much worse would this get?

When I reached the docks, I almost gave up the whole thing. The harbour had been shaken into a frenzy. Waves crashed over the quayside, sending spray across the cobbles. A waterspout spun over the harbour until it hit a ship, and the ship disintegrated, wood, canvas, and cargo thrown into the air. Moments later, the waterspout impacted a warehouse. Bricks and tiles followed the remains of the ship. I thought I saw bodies flung up, too, but I didn't stop to watch.

I ran over the slick stone. Wind battered me. A wave smashed over the docks, almost snatching my legs away.

The Whale's Head was on a small street just back from the quay. I staggered up the steep incline, away from the water and flying debris.

The tavern's windows were shuttered and the door

barred, but I was finally free of the *ulu-aru*, and I used magic to smash it open.

A couple of men hunched by the bar, drinking. They looked up as I burst in, and I recognised one of them. He recognised me, too, because he tried to run but stumbled and fell. Bruises stood purple and black against his pale skin. I hauled him up. This was the guy I had interrogated before. I could see from his face that he hadn't forgotten. He looked terrified. Normally, I would hate the fear mages caused in the city, but this fucker had tried to kill me.

No. If I was right, he had just attempted to make it look like he was trying to kill me.

If I was right, I had been a fucking idiot.

I slammed the man against the bar. "You lied to me." I sent magic coruscating across my body. The thunder behind me from the Eructation and the sickly, shifting light around the shutters didn't do any harm, either.

"No!"

"You did." Fire erupted in my eyes. It was a neat effect, but if it had been real, it would have burned my eyes out. "Who hired you?"

His mouth opened and closed.

"Who hired you?" This time, I let heat wash over him.

"All right, all right! I'll tell you. He said he'd pay more if we did you and then said it was a Brythanii woman that paid us. We weren't asking questions!"

"So, it wasn't?"

A shake of the head.

"Then who did pay you?"

"Never got his name. Brythanii, though, so that wasn't a lie."

No. A good lie always had a bit of truth in it. I wondered if that was in *The Politician*, too.

I let the man drop. "Find a better job. Next time, you might not get so lucky."

I EMERGED FROM THE TAVERN TO THE SOUND OF ANIMALS howling, squawking, and shrieking. I made out dogs, cats, and some large predator – a lion, perhaps – from near the docks. It must have been brought in as cargo on a ship, along with the parrots, monkeys, and exotic birds from across the sea. A rat raced in front of my feet and disappeared frantically into the dark.

Spray from the waves that pounded the quayside whipped up the narrow street. Something massive protested as stone slid against stone. The air was filled with electrical potential, ready to crack between buildings. The ground vibrated, and the sound of shifting bricks and slipping tiles was almost constant. Too much more of this, and the city would shake itself to bits. It wouldn't just be the Warrens in ruins this winter.

It won't last long. Either someone would grab it, or it would dissipate. *I hope.*

That was the Ash Guard's problem, not mine.

Mine was that Ethemattian had used me. He had lied to me, and I had fallen for it.

Ethemattian had entered the Choosing hoping to attain the luxury of being a Most Cursed, but he had a plan in place in case it all went wrong. He had come to me with his tragic tale of being set up. He had pushed me ever so gently towards Menatha Keffen. It wasn't her, he'd told me, knowing I would be suspicious. Whether he really had a feud with her or whether he had staged it as a clue for me to follow didn't matter. What did matter was that she had an uncle in charge of the Choosing, someone for me to turn my suspicious eyes on. He had fed me clues like a puppy following a trail of treats. But Most Cursed Keffen had been a problem: he would have known that Ethemattian *had* entered, and he would have sworn to it. It would have been his word against Ethemattian's, a Most Cursed against a lowly Cursed. So, Most Cursed Keffen had to die.

He had the hands of an artist.

Ethemattian must have known I would need proof if I was to convince the Cursed of God that Keffen had set him up. A few deliberate little mistakes in his own handwriting on the statement he had provided for the Choosing to throw doubt, and then the proof itself: a piece of paper on which Keffen had supposedly practiced forging Ethemattian's handwriting but which Ethemattian himself must have written from bottom up, slowly transforming his own writing into Keffen's.

The hands of an artist.

What kind of idiot would practice forging handwriting like that and then use the evidence to prop up the leg of their bed? What kind of idiot would believe it? But I had been so keen and so rushed to prove Ethemattian's innocence that I had bought it as easily as a fish gulping down a worm on a hook.

And when I had been too slow, when I might have stopped to think, he had sent thugs armed with a false description of their paymaster to attack me and make me forget all logic.

He had played me. But he had made a mistake. He had been too impressed with his own cleverness. He had mocked me with a principle from a book he had been sure I wouldn't know. And he had been right.

He'd hadn't figured on Meroi Gale knowing it and talking to me.

And now, in the Brythanii temple, in the middle of the Eructation, the priests and worshippers were preparing to beat Menatha Keffen to death. All because I had been stupid enough to believe a priest.

I wasn't going to let that happen.

It might already have happened.

"It fucking hasn't," I said, my voice lost in the chaos. I wouldn't *allow* it to have happened. Shaping my magical shield ahead of me like a wedge, I sprinted towards the Street of Gods.

IF THERE WAS ONE THING RELIGION LIKED, IT WAS EVERYTHING going to shit. The deeper the shit, the wider the temple doors, and the bigger the donations, and by the looks of it, a lot of priests were getting rich today. As long as their temples didn't collapse on top of them. The crowds outside the temples were the thickest I had come across so far, the press almost too great to force my way through, a panicked, sweaty mass of humanity desperate for reassurance or divine intervention.

They were going to be out of luck. If their gods were paying attention, it would be to the Eructation. *Revenants, faces pressed against the glass,* Ethemattian had said of the gods. *Drawn by power.* He could have been describing himself.

The cult of Sharshak had been preparing for the Eructation to claim the power for themselves or for their god. How many other temples I shoved past were doing the same? There weren't enough Ash Guards to cover them all. I hoped all the religions were as incompetent as Sharshak's lot.

Inch by inch, I pushed my way towards the Brythanii temple.

At last, the looming bulk appeared before me. The Brythanii hadn't been waiting for the Eructation. Their ritual sacrifice to the downfall of the Hated God had always been scheduled for tonight, as it was every year, but I wondered if the excitement of the event had drawn out more adherents than usual. The road in front of the temple was packed with veiled and robed figures, and the door was jammed with pushing bodies trying to force their way through. Menatha Keffen was in for a bad night if I didn't get in there.

The lights in the sky were swirling now, dragging streaks of cloud with them, to form a funnel above the entire city.

Wind gusted through the streets and over the rooftops. The rumbling beneath the city came in almost constant waves, and somewhere under everything, a low, hollow howl seemed to echo from every corner.

Stonework from a temple further up the street cracked and slipped into the street, scattering the crowd. I heard screams of pain and terror.

You can't help everyone. This was happening all over the city, but there was only one person about to die because of what I had done. She was the one I had to save.

You have no proof.

It didn't matter. I would stop it anyway.

I gathered raw magic, felt the wounds in my shoulder and leg flare with pain, then shaped my shield again and pushed into the crowd.

My shield could stop a lot of things. Fire, falling beams, even bullets. But the packed throng was too tight. Shouts came from the crowd as I pushed, but there was nowhere for them to move to. All I was going to do was crush them, and still there was no way through. I let the shield drop.

What else? Fling them out of the way one at a time like sacks of flour? I wouldn't manage it.

Chanting drifted through the doorway. The words were Brythanii, and they were angry.

Fuck.

I needed another way in. I headed for the side alley running along the edge of the temple. I had seen a door down here somewhere.

The crowds were avoiding the alleys. Not surprising. The

flagstones showed enough broken tiles and shattered stones to make being here a bad idea. I specialised in bad ideas.

The door was mage-locked, but they hadn't bother to protect the hinges. I split them with a burst of magic that sent black specks swirling across my vision, then kicked the door in.

The chanting filtered down the hallway from my right, so I followed the sound.

It didn't take me long to find my way to the main, circular chamber. The stench from the statue pit below the altar in the centre of the chamber was matched by the stink of too many bodies pressed too close together.

But there was one clear space, across the pit from the altar. There, Menatha Keffen stood flanked by temple guards, her head drooping while the crowd surged and withdrew around her like the sea.

The chief priest, the Cursed of God, stood at the altar, her hands flung out, her long hair loose and whipping about her as though she stood in the centre of a storm.

I unfocused my eyes.

Magic raced around the chamber in a rush of blue and purple flecked with gold. Four pillars that hadn't been there before marked the compass points and acted as focus for the spell. At the centre of it was the Cursed of God, shaping and controlling the magic. She was a fucking mage. Of course.

This spell was similar to the one I'd seen in Senator Greenfield's palace and felt in the Cult of Sharshak's basement. These fuckers were making a move on the Eructation, too.

Where the Depths were the Ash Guard? I looked desperately around, but no Ash-coated figures waited in the wings and there was no sign of Ash deadening the magic within the chamber.

How long would it take me to get out and send a message to the Guard? How long would it take for them to get here?

Longer than Menatha Keffen had left.

I elbowed my way into the crowd, shoving bodies aside, trying to fight my way through.

"Stop!" I shouted, amplifying my voice with magic so that it slammed into the space, overwhelming the chanting. The chief priest's head turned to search me out. "I made a mistake! Ethemattian was the one who was really chosen. Cursed Keffen didn't set him up. He planted false evidence. You've got the wrong person."

The Cursed of God's eyes settled on me. Around me, the Brythanii crowd kept chanting. Keffen's head rose, her gaze desperate, hopeful, afraid.

"It's too late," the Cursed of God said.

"What do you mean, it's too late?"

In response, her back arched, and her mouth stretched into a soundless cry of pain. I unfocussed my eyes again.

Power poured into her. Vast oceans converging on her. I had thought the power my mother and Kael had wielded had been unthinkable, but it had been nothing compared to this. The Eructation. The power that allowed a god to pierce the barrier between its realm and this, released as the Lady of the Grove had died and now captured by the chief priest of the Brythanii.

Then the power surged out of her, across the pit, to hit the captive form of Menatha Keffen. Her limbs spasmed, her head flipped back, and she fell. Purple light churned under her skin like roiling fluid, bleeding from every pore.

I tried to push forwards again, but hands grabbed me. "Stop!"

"Can't you feel it?" the Cursed of God shouted. "The god is here."

The air in the temple had become oppressive. A presence grew, like a gigantic weight, pulling everything towards it. Drawn by the power of the Eructation, the Hated God had arrived. Slow, ponderous, but inevitable, like a deep-sea predator cruising through the dark waters. Shadows gathered. Space itself distorted, like a lens focused only on the writhing, burning form of Menatha Keffen.

Then she stopped moving. The light beneath her skin shut off. Slowly, like an insect pulling itself from resin, Keffen rose. Except it wasn't Keffen anymore. The god was within her.

For hundreds of years, the Brythanii had bent their will to this moment, to summon the god who had betrayed them into a human body. And now, now they would kill it.

Still the power of the Eructation poured into it.

The crowd seemed stunned, but for how much longer? This was what they were here for. To bury the Hated God in a frenzy of violence that would annihilate it. And annihilate Menatha Keffen along with it.

My fault. My fault.

I wanted to throw my magic at the god to drive it away or

at the chief priest to stop her, but the power there would sweep my poor magic away like a puff of breath in hurricane.

Someone at the back of the crowd shouted. I didn't understand the words, but I understood the hatred. Generations of bitterness and the need for revenge all condensed into this moment.

Other voices took up the shout. In amongst the Brythanii language, I heard words I did understand. "You did not help us when we needed you." The Brythanii prayer. After all this time, they had their god in front of them, the god who had ignored them and let them suffer catastrophe. The god who had turned away.

It couldn't turn away now.

The crowd shifted, pushed forwards. The temple guards stepped back.

Still the Eructation came, pinning the god with its own mindless need for power.

I couldn't stop the god. I couldn't stop the high priest.

I wrenched my arms free and spun. The Eructation poured in from all directions, focused and captured by the spell woven into the pillars.

I pulled in every trace of raw magic I could grasp. Pain sliced through my body like a rope studded with razor blades. I could hardly see. I couldn't speak because of the scream fraying my throat. I focused the magic into a spear and flung it at the nearest pillar.

The wood split, far more violently than my spell should have caused. Splinters sprayed in every direction. Several people at the back of the crowd fell or stumbled away.

Untethered from the pillar, the spell spun out of control. Its grip on the Eructation slipped. A surge of power hammered into the Cursed of God, and the chief priest simply exploded. Her body was shredded. A mist of blood, shards of bone, and gobbets of flesh sprayed the crowd.

Menatha Keffen fell. In less than a second, the god was gone. Shrieks of horror filled the temple. Moments later, the shouts turned to fury. I dropped to my knees, done, bleeding, too weak to stand.

The crowd around me stared down at where I slumped, slow realisation overcoming them. The fury and hate directed towards the god had a found a new target: me.

Shit. Oh, fucking, bollocking shit.

The remains of the spell weren't done, and neither was the Eructation it had shackled.

Walls creaked. Plaster rained down. A chunk of ceiling fell, hitting the crowd below. More screams of pain followed.

It was enough. The crowd scattered, shoving and fighting towards the entrance. People fell, trampled beneath feet, and no one stopped to help them.

They had gathered here to murder one of their own. They hadn't even stopped when they knew she was the wrong person. I had no sympathy for them.

Groaning, I staggered up and across the rapidly clearing chamber to where Menatha Keffen lay motionless on the floor. If someone else had been Chosen, she would have been in the crowd, joining in with the brutality. It made no sense, but I had come here to save her, and I would do that, at least.

Still the magic ran out of control, and the power of the Eructation built. The air felt too thick to breathe.

I reached Keffen and dropped beside her. She was breathing, faintly, but not moving. She lay awkwardly, as though something was broken inside, as though her bones had been snapped and rearranged. If I tried to move her, I could cause her untold damage. *More* untold damage.

Bannaur's balls!

The power intensified. Light arced through the air like lightning trapped in the temple. Wind howled. A deep, heartbroken keening seemed to rise from beneath me, ripping into my soul, a feeling of utter loss and sorrow.

The temple burst. Like a bowl dropped onto a stone floor, it fragmented. The roof, the walls, the pillars, everything erupted, spraying out into the night, an explosion that shook the ground. Masonry, beams, tiles, and shattered furniture were flung in every direction.

I pulled a shield in over us and hung on while debris rained down.

Eventually, the pain overtook me, and everything turned black.

CHAPTER TWENTY-FIVE

I DIDN'T KNOW WHO PULLED ME FROM THE RUBBLE, BUT THE sky was already lightening when I blinked my eyes open and saw a woman in the robes of a doctor peering down at me.

I hurt. I hurt like I been trampled by a runaway bull. But I had slept, and the worst of my wounds had healed. I was covered in dust, congealed blood, and dried sweat. My mouth was dry, and my tongue tasted of chalk and garlic. The doctor leaned over, offering me a cup of water, and I gulped it down.

Pity, that had been some night. I hadn't felt like this since I was sixteen and drinking too much wine with Benny.

Finally, I noticed the sky was clear of the sheets of light. The rumbling beneath the ground was gone. The unholy howling had quieted. The Eructation was over.

I tried to speak, swallowed, then tried again. "The woman who was with me? Is she all right?"

The doctor shrugged. "No idea." She waved a hand, encompassing the area around us.

I lifted my head, ignoring the thumping headache. I was in a large plaza. It was filled with makeshift beds. Doctors and other helpers moved between patients.

The Eructation. The earthquakes. The exploding temple. How many people had been hurt or killed? All because some wanker wanted the power of a god.

"If you can walk, I'm going to need that bed."

"Yeah." I pushed myself upright, feeling every muscle and joint protest. I could walk.

The plaza I'd been brought to wasn't far from the Street of Gods. Not my part of the city, but Horn Hill on one side and the Ependhos mountains on the other were enough to orient myself. There were signs of damage everywhere. The odd building collapsed, paving stones shoved up and cracked, debris everywhere. But, overall, the city had done better than I had thought. No landslides from the mountains, that I could see, no vast chasms opened to swallow whole districts.

The same couldn't be said of the Street of Gods, or at least the bit of it I'd been involved with. Where the Brythanii temple had stood was little more than mounds of rubble. The explosion had torn through neighbouring temples, too, buckling walls and bringing down roofs. The new Temple of Gwillan-Whose-Light-Falls-on-the-Few-Not-the-Many, which had begun to rise in place of the one I had accidentally burned down, had taken a hit, too. Scaffolding was strewn across the street, and half the walls had been reduced once more to ruins.

Served them right.

Eventually, I made my way back to my apartment at the bottom of the Middle City, passing through the already bustling Penitent's Ear. Stalls had been damaged, but that hadn't stopped the market traders. Quick bodge jobs of repair were everywhere, and a few traders were reduced to using cloths spread on the ground, but other than that, the Eructation might as well have never happened. Not much slowed Agatos down.

In violation of my usual luck, my apartment didn't seem to have suffered any damage at all. Maybe it helped that my furnishings had already been trashed.

There was no sign of Fria. I hoped that meant that Ileoni had come to fetch him. I couldn't see how he could have escaped on his own, although that had never stopped him before.

I would get him later. Right now, I could scarcely take another step. I fell onto my mattress and was asleep within moments.

"Asleep on the job, I see."

I woke to a feeling of utter exhaustion. It was dark again. I must have slept all day, at least.

I rolled over and blinked through sticky eyes. Ileoni was standing in my bedroom door, holding Fria on a leash.

"Ugh," I said, showing my usual sharp grasp of the situation. I patted the bed next to me.

"That had better be aimed at the dog, not me," Ileoni said.

Before I could protest, she let go of the leash, and Fria leapt forwards, jumping up onto me and knocking me back flat. I eventually managed to fight free. "Are you all right? Your family?"

She nodded. "I was worried about you."

I waved a hand. "I'm always all right."

"Good. Then get up. You're late."

It would be fair to say that I wasn't completely with it yet, but I was fairly sure I didn't have any jobs today. "What?"

"For dinner. You need feeding." She looked at me critically, then tossed over a bundle of clothes tied in a package. "Get dressed. I'm not taking you anywhere like that. I'll wait in the office."

There was fresh water in my little washroom, so I cleaned myself as best I could and dressed in the clothes Ileoni had brought me. They weren't my usual style – too colourful and too fashionable – but at least they fit.

I tested my wounds. The extra sleep had all but healed them. I was stiff, but I suspected that was from lying so long unconscious. I made my way to the office.

The place had been tidied ruthlessly, and a new desk had appeared where my broken one had stood. Ileoni was sitting behind it, arranging the drawers.

"How long have you been here?" I croaked.

"Since this morning. I didn't want to wake you. You looked like shit. The desk arrived a couple of hours ago."

I had slept through the whole thing. Pity, I must have been exhausted. I kind of still was.

"Thanks, I guess."

"Damned right." She peered around the office. "I'm going to want my own desk when I start working here."

Had we agreed that? I couldn't remember. My brain felt tired. It didn't sound like the worst idea, though. My stomach rumbled, and I took the hint. "Come on then. Where are we going?"

"Your friends, Elosyn and Holera. They dropped by, too. Apparently, you stood them up a few days back then turned up at Holera's restaurant looking like – and this is a quote – a rat that's been dragged backwards through a slaughterhouse drain."

Ah. I hoped Elosyn didn't punch me when we got there. I was feeling delicate, and even at the best of times, she was stronger than me. All day kneading dough and lifting heavy trays in and out of ovens would do that.

Ileoni led me through the Middle City, through the evening crowds. Everywhere we walked, there were signs of the destruction caused by the Eructation. Broken windows, cracked walls, slumped roofs, holes gaping in streets. Piles of rubble stacked everywhere. But it wasn't as bad as I'd feared. The damage in the Street of Gods looked like it had been most extreme, although I didn't know how much devastation the wind and waves had caused to Dockside. But the city was carrying on around it all. Workers were already starting to repair the streets and buildings. Agatos persisted, like it always did.

Elosyn and Holera's house didn't seem to have suffered too badly, other than some cracked away plaster and whitewash.

They weren't the only ones waiting when we arrived. Benny, Sereh, and Mica were there, too, as well as Kehsereen. Benny was even standing, even if he had to lean on the back of a chair.

I could hardly believe it. The last time I'd seen him, he'd been bleeding to death on the floor. I hadn't truly believed he could survive. I hurried over and stopped a pace away, worried that even touching him might cause him pain or split open a wound. "Benny! You're all right." I turned to Mica. "Thank you." I was always underestimating my little sister's magical power.

She shook her head. "I didn't have to do much. He healed himself."

"That's not possible." He had been on the edge of death. "I saw him."

Mica didn't look as happy as I'd hoped she would. "There's something in him, Nik. Something powerful, and it didn't want him to die."

That didn't make any sense. Something in Benny?

"Remember that claw I swallowed?" Benny said. "Turns out it had some side effects. Who knew?"

I had almost forgotten about that. Benny had once swallowed a claw of the dead beast god, Ah'té. That action had saved us both, and the claw had never … re-emerged. I had thought it was done.

Mica met my eyes. "It worries me, Nik."

"I'm just glad to be alive," Benny said. "Because when the Wren's people came for us, I didn't think I was going to make it."

He shouldn't have. Not even with Sereh on his side.

"I'm going to want to examine Benny a lot closer," Mica said.

"Not happening." For a moment, Benny's grin was almost wolfish. "I ain't having the kid who used to follow me around the Warrens poking at me."

We would talk about that later, whether he wanted to or not.

I glanced around, wondering if Meroi Gale had been invited, too, but there was no sign of her.

"Sit down," Holera said. "You look like you're about to fall. And tell us everything."

I was outnumbered and outclassed. With a sigh, I dropped into a chair and told them everything. Everything except the true identity of the Wren. I didn't think that was a secret that should be shared. I wondered if that had been the secret Mica's dad had discovered that had led to him being killed.

Sereh didn't look happy when I told her what I'd done to the man we had thought of as the Wren. I suspected she would have killed him very much more dead if she'd had her way.

"What I don't know," I said, "is how my mother and Captain Gale turned up at the Wren's warehouse."

Mica had the graciousness to look guilty. "That was me. When you reached out to my mind, I, ah, had a little poke around in yours. I saw what you were planning. I didn't think you'd actually manage to kill the Wren. That's ... something. I let them both know. I hoped one of them would stop you. I was kind of busy myself."

"Enough of this," Elosyn said. "We didn't spend all day cooking so you could waste the evening chatting. Come on." She hustled us to the table.

I didn't speak much as we ate. It was enough to sit there, listening to my friends laugh, joke, and gossip, and to feed Fria under the table.

Maybe when I inevitably got myself killed, someone would come to the funeral after all. It made me unexpectedly emotional. Maybe that was just the aftereffects of what I'd been through.

Eventually, the meal was done, and I made my way back home. I might have slept all day and most of last night, but I was still absurdly tired.

I went to bed.

I HEADED TO THE ASH GUARD FORTRESS FIRST THING THE NEXT morning. I suspected the Eructation and everything around it had kept them busy, but there were still too many things I didn't understand, and I wanted answers.

Captain Gale looked as tired as I was when she emerged from the fortress. She gave me a critical look. "I heard you survived. Which is more than can be said for the Brythanii temple. Why is that you're always at the middle of the chaos in this city?"

I smirked. "Just trying to help."

She shook her head. "Come in."

"Um..."

"It's not going to kill you, and I promise I'll let you out again."

The last thing I wanted was to enter the Ash-infused walls of the fortress, but if she wanted me in there, there wasn't much I could do to stop her.

She led me to a comfortable room and indicated a chair then sat opposite me. "You have questions."

"How did you guess?"

"You only come here for two things, Nik. Questions or favours, and I know even you're not asking for a favour right now."

Fair enough. "I've been thinking about the Wren and Kael."

"I'd rather you didn't."

"Too late. When my mother turned up, she didn't call him Kael. She called him Agate."

Captain Gale pursed her lips. "You really want me to answer that?"

I nodded.

"Then, yes, she did."

"Agate as in Agate Blackspear, the Godkiller."

"Yes."

"You're telling me that Kael is Agate Blackspear, the same guy who founded Agatos over four hundred years ago? The same fucker who killed the Lady of Dreams Descending?" Except he hadn't killed her. He had just cast her down and left her diminished, haunting the Warrens like the ghost of hope. "That would explain why his tomb was empty. How is it even possible?"

"I'm going to pretend I didn't hear you say you were poking around the tomb of Agate Blackspear. But, yes. High mages can live for a long time, and Blackspear has always been obsessed with immortality. We suspect he's always wanted to become a god. He undoubtedly tried to kill Sien to take her place, but he wasn't able to."

"So why in the Depths is he skulking in the lower city instead of ruling Agatos?"

Captain Gale observed me across the table. "You really have to ask? We are the reason, Nik. The Ash Guard. The Guard made a deal with Blackspear. He would step down, his death would be announced, and he could continue as a high mage as long as he kept in his place. The Wrens that control the criminal underworld have always been under his control. Neither Blackspear nor the Guard wanted a war. It was a good compromise. The city moves on, out from under the heel of its conqueror, and Blackspear pursues his quest for immortality, something we will never allow him to achieve. Don't worry. We've talked to Blackspear. He won't come after you or your friends over the death of the Face of the Wren, and you, in turn, will stay out of his business. And you *will* stay out of his business, Nik." The tone was unmistakeable, and I wasn't arguing. I was done with that shit.

I shifted the subject. "Did you figure out who killed the Lady? Was it Kael?"

"No. We think it was the chief priest of the Brythanii temple. She was a powerful mage in her own right, and the Brythanii have spent hundreds of years discovering how to kill a god. Whether it was a dry run for murdering the Hated God or just to get that power to tempt their own god to be present, we don't know, and I guess we're never going to." She raised her eyebrows at me. "I hear she exploded."

And very messy it had been, too. If she was behind all this, she'd escaped too easily. "What happened to the power of the Eructation?"

"With luck, it's dissipated. It doesn't stay for long. The Brythanii were the first to grab it, and by the time they were done, hopefully it was too late for anyone else. We checked out your tips, by the way. Senator Greenfield's mage seemed to have taken a kicking, and he wasn't up to much. The temple of the Cult of Sharshak had collapsed from the Eructation. Don't have your temple in a basement would be my suggestion."

"And if that power hasn't gone?"

"Then some other fucker has got it, and we'll deal with it when the time comes. That's the fun of the Ash Guard. There's always another bastard waiting around the corner to try their luck."

Right.

"If that's all?"

Was it? There was one more thing. My mouth was dry, my heart beating a thousand times a minute, my vision turning black. But if I didn't do this now, I never would.

"Um." I cleared my throat. "I, ah, I don't suppose you'd want to go on a date with me, would you?"

Her lip pulled up on one side, her scar twisting her smile. "Maybe in a different life." She must have seen the disappointment in my face. "Nik, I like you. You're a good person, in your own way. But I am the Ash Guard. This is what I want to be. This is the life I chose. And one day, I may have to kill you."

~

It took me almost a week to track down what had happened to Ethemattian.

I didn't recall ever actually employing Ileoni, but somehow she moved into my office and started organising my work. I couldn't complain. I had never been so busy, nor, I had to admit, so well paid, despite her drawing her own salary. It turned out that having someone in the office to actually filter and accept work really did mean a lot more jobs, and none of them involving some fool who'd got caught up in the machinations of gods or mages. I scarcely got a moment to stop and think. I suspected Ileoni had arranged it that way deliberately.

I hadn't even figured out what I was going to do with the Lady of the Grove's body, but that could wait. She was safe where she was, for now, and in the end, that would be Benny's decision as much as mine.

Eventually, though, I tracked Ethemattian to Dockside, and a few bribes and favours-promised brought out the story. Ethemattian had reserved a berth on a ship heading for Melaru. He had turned up the night of the Eructation, right when the winds were shuddering the bay and waves hammering the sea walls. Perhaps he had been in the temple when I'd arrived and started shouting about Keffen's innocence, and he hadn't waited around. The captain hadn't wanted to sail, hadn't even wanted to board his ship in that chaos, but eventually Ethemattian had bribed him enough. I didn't know where he'd got so much money. Stolen it, blackmailed someone for it. I wouldn't put it past him.

The ship had set sail, but it hadn't made it past the sea wall. It had been torn to pieces by the fury of the Eructation. More lives lost to Ethemattian's scheming.

I headed back to my office, where Ileoni had lined up enough work to stop me worrying about it for the next month.

The city was recovering. Work had even begun on rebuilding the Warrens. In weeks, I suspected, a visitor to Agatos would never be able to tell anything had happened. It was how the city worked. You could beat it down, but it always got back up and kept going. And maybe, sometimes, it got back up stronger. Sometimes, things got better. For all of us.

- End -

AUTHOR'S NOTE

THIS IS THE FINAL MENNIK THORN NOVEL.

For those of you who've followed Nik through his adventures, thank you! I hope you've enjoyed reading these books as much as I've enjoyed writing them.

I must admit that I am sad to leave Nik and the city of Agatos behind me. I've lived with Nik and his friends for a long time now, through a pandemic, through learning how to publish books myself rather than through a big publisher, and through connecting with a book community I scarcely knew before.

Although this is the last Mennik Thorn novel, that doesn't mean there won't be any more stories in Agatos or starring Nik. He still has a living to make, the mages of Agatos will never stop scheming, and there is enough shit out there in the city to drown anyone. But these stories are currently much more likely to be short stories and novellas rather than full-length novels.

It's time for me to move onto new books. I hope when they come out that you'll join me in those stories, too, but in the meantime, all I can say is, again, thank you for joining me on this journey.

If you would like to keep up to date with my new novels and stories, please subscribe to my newsletter: patricksam phire.com/newsletter/

I'll see you again, in Agatos or beyond.

- Patrick Samphire, August 2023.

APPENDIX 1: THE REGION OF AGATOS

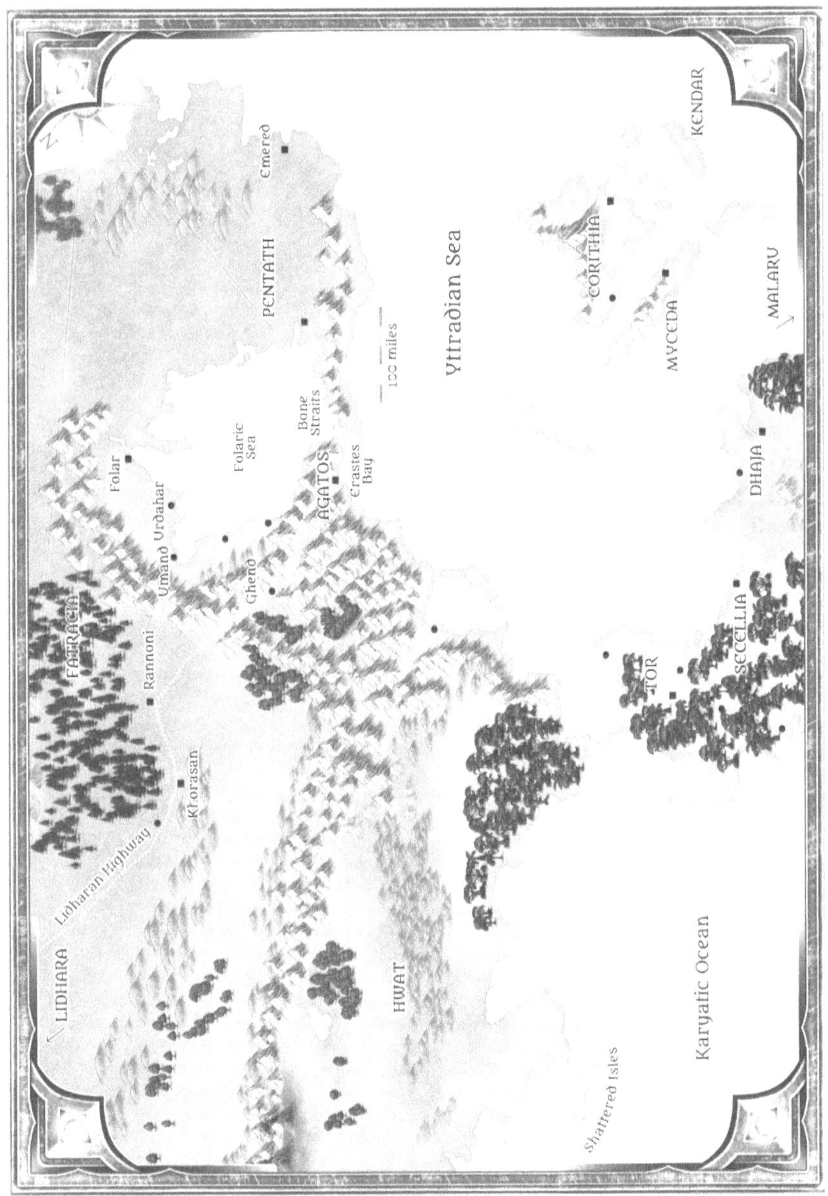

See larger map: patricksamphire.com/agatos-region

APPENDIX 2: THE GODS OF AGATOS

There have been many gods worshipped in Agatos. Some of these are dead, some living, and some whose status is pointlessly disputed. Some, although not all, are associated with particular aspects or locations. Here are some of the gods you may encounter in the Mennik Thorn books.

Karchek: Beast God (Dead)
Bellamer: Beast God (Dead)
Mur: Beast God (Dead)
Ah'té / Nimha'té: Beast God (Dead)
Gwillan-Whose-Light-Falls-on-the-Few-Not-the-Many: God of Commerce and Wealth (Living)
Belethea: Goddess of Bees (Dead)
The Lady of the Grove: Patron God of the Warrens (Dead)
Sharshak: Sun God (Dead)

Mara: Sky God (Living)
Kethcal: Sky God (Dead)
Talifa: Mycedan God (Dead)
Sien, the Lady of Dreams Descending: Patron Goddess of Eras / Agatos (Dead)
Stypar: Sea God (Living)
Yttra: Sea God (Living)
Denna: Lord of the Depths (Living)
Cepra: God of Death (Living, ironically)
Tulbek the Old: Fatracian God (Dead)
The Nameless God / the Hated God: Brythanii God (Living)
Lord Ensio: God of Luck (Living)
Oleos: Eel God (Dead)
Shapray: God of Arbitrary Decisions and Unjustifiable Demands
Chaerd the Unkind: God of Missed Opportunities
Niarret / Enhuin / Enabgal, the Watcher in the Dark: God of Nightmares, Sea God (Living)
Ethys: War God of Melaru (Dead)
Bannaur (Disputed)
Narth the Sleeping (Disputed)
Putchek (Living)
Felen (Dead)

APPENDIX 3: CURRENCY

CURRENCY IN AGATOS IS ACTUALLY QUITE SIMPLE, CONSISTING of four basic units: the piece, the oar, the shield, and the crown. However, the residents of Agatos don't make anything easy, so I am including a guide to help you follow the ins-and-outs of money in Agatos.

Value

Piece (iron): comes in units of ½, 1, 2, 5.
Oar (copper): 1 oar = 10 pieces
Shield (silver): 1 shield = 40 oars
Crown (gold): 1 crown = 12 shields

Slang Terms

½ piece: Cut, waste, splinter
1 piece: Penny
2 pieces: Pair
5 pieces: Hand
Oar: Sailor's hand, round
Shield: Watchman, silver
Crown: God, king, gold, bank

APPENDIX 4: MONTHS OF THE YEAR

1. Elletos
2. Mael
3. Unchera
4. Fichera
5. Missos
6. Eppos
7. Keratos
8. Thieth
9. Enetha
10. Irratos
11. Imminas
12. Coel
13. Andaros

KEEP IN TOUCH

Subscribe to my newsletter to get a free short story in the world of SHADOW OF A DEAD GOD and NECTAR FOR THE GOD, and to be the first to find out about future books: patricksamphire.com/newsletter/

You can find out about all my other books and stories at my website: patricksamphire.com

You can often find me on Twitter

(twitter.com/patricksamphire) as well as on my Facebook page (facebook.com/patricksamphireauthor/).

A REQUEST

PLEASE REVIEW THIS BOOK!

Reviews help authors more than you probably imagine, and for independent authors, they are everything. It would mean an awful lot to me if you could leave a brief review - a sentence or two is perfect! - wherever you bought this book or on a service like Goodreads.

READ MORE

THE CASEBOOK OF HARRIET GEORGE

Mystery, murder, and adventure on Mars...

Mars in 1815 is a world of wonders, from the hanging ballrooms of Tharsis City to the air forests of Patagonian Mars, and from the depths of the Valles Marineris to the Great Wall of Cyclopia, beyond which dinosaurs still roam.

Join Harriet George and her hapless brother-in-law, Bertrand, as they solve mysteries and try to save their family from ruin.

Volume 1: The Dinosaur Hunters.

Volume 2: A Spy in the Deep.

Available in paperback and ebook.

ABOUT PATRICK SAMPHIRE

Patrick Samphire started writing when he was fourteen years old and thought it would be a good way of getting out of English lessons. It didn't work, but he kept on writing anyway.

He has lived in Zambia, Guyana, Austria, and England. He has been charged at by a buffalo and, once, when he sat on a camel, he cried. He was only a kid. Don't make this weird.

Patrick has worked as a teacher, an editor and publisher of physics journals, a marketing minion, and a pen pusher (real job!). Now, when he's not writing, he designs websites and book covers. He has a PhD in theoretical physics and never uses it, so that was a good use of four years.

Patrick now lives in Wales, U.K. with his wife, the awesome writer Stephanie Burgis, their two sons, and their cat, Pebbles. Right now, in Wales, it is almost certainly raining.

He has published almost twenty short stories and novellas in magazines and anthologies, including *Realms of Fantasy*, *Interzone*, *Strange Horizons*, and *The Year's Best*

Fantasy, as well as two novels for children, SECRETS OF THE DRAGON TOMB and THE EMPEROR OF MARS.

LEGACY OF A HATED GOD is his fourth novel for adults. It is the sequel to SHADOW OF A DEAD GOD, NECTAR FOR THE GOD and STRANGE CARGO.

facebook.com/patricksamphireauthor

x.com/patricksamphire

instagram.com/patricksamphire

ACKNOWLEDGMENTS

The Mennik Thorn series, complete now at four books, is the longest series I have ever done. Over the years of working on it, I've been helped enormously by the many readers, bloggers, and reviewers who have been kind enough to give me encouragement and feedback. Thanks to all of you. I don't know if I would have made it to the end without you.

I have also been lucky enough to have a large number of beta readers, critiquers, and editors provide advice, suggestions, and improvements. The books would be lesser without you.

For this book, I would particularly like to thank Stephanie Burgis, Shaun Paul Stevens, and Marcus Lee (all fantastic writers in their own rights; check out their books) for their detailed feedback on the manuscript of *Legacy of a Hated God*. Your help was invaluable. Thank you, too, to Martin Owton and Robert Bull for finding and correcting typos in the book.

I would also like to thank my cover artist, Ömer Burak Önal, for his wonderful art that makes these books look so great.

I've been writing for a long time, even before the Mennik

Thorn series, and I've been lucky enough to get feedback from so many fantastic editors, agents, and writers over the years. It would be impossible to list all of you here, but please know that I recognise how much you've all done to help me on this journey.

Finally, I would like to thank my high school English teacher, Mrs. Mapes, for her encouragement quite a few decades ago that made me believe I could do this, even though I was a terrible writer at the time. It's teachers like Mrs. Mapes who make a difference.

www.ingramcontent.com/pod-product-compliance
Lightning Source LLC
Chambersburg PA
CBHW020307030826
48979CB00029B/2291/J

* 9 7 8 1 7 3 9 1 1 7 6 6 5 *